T0072566

Around the World
with
Auntie Mame

ALSO BY PATRICK DENNIS

Auntie Mame

Little Me

Around the World with Auntie Mame

By Patrick Dennis

BROADWAY BOOKS NEW YORK

AROUND THE WORLD WITH AUNTIE MAME was originally published by Harcourt Brace and Company in 1958.

AROUND THE WORLD WITH AUNTIE MAME. Copyright © 1958 by Patrick Dennis, renewed in 1983 by the Tanner family. "Auntie Mame and Mother Russia" copyright © 1990 by the Tanner Family. All rights reserved. Printed in the United States of America. No part of this book may be reproduced or transmitted in any form or by any means, electronic or mechanical, including photocopying, recording, or by any information storage and retrieval system, without written permission from the publisher. For information, address Broadway Books, a division of Random House, Inc., 1745 Broadway, New York, NY 10019.

This book is a work of fiction. Names, characters, businesses, organizations, places, events, and incidents either are the product of the author's imagination or are used fictitiously. Any resemblance to actual persons, living or dead, events or locales is entirely coincidental.

BROADWAY BOOKS and its logo, a letter B bisected on the diagonal, are trademarks of Broadway Books, a division of Random House, Inc.

Visit our Web site at www.broadwaybooks.com

Library of Congress Cataloging-in-Publication Data
Dennis, Patrick, 1921–1976.
    Around the world with Auntie Mame / by Patrick Dennis.—1st Broadway Books trade pbk. ed.
      p. cm.
    1. Travelers—Fiction. 2. Aunts—Fiction. I. Title.

PS3554.E537A76   2003
813'.54—dc21   2003041793

First Broadway Books trade paperback edition published 2003

Designed by Ralph L. Fowler
Illustration on title page copyright © 2003 by Edwin Fotheringham

ISBN-13: 978-0-7679-1585-4
ISBN 0-7679-1585-2

To the one and only

ROSALIND RUSSELL

CONTENTS

Auntie Mame and Posterity   1

Auntie Mame and the City of Light   9

Auntie Mame in Court Circles   45

Auntie Mame and the Fortune Hunter   83

Auntie Mame and a Family Affair   111

Auntie Mame in Her Mountain Retreat   151

Auntie Mame and Mother Russia   195

Auntie Mame and the Middle Eastern Powder Keg   233

Auntie Mame and the Long Voyage Home   279

Auntie Mame and Home-coming   317

Around the World
with
Auntie Mame

Auntie Mame and Posterity

CHRISTMAS IS NEARLY HERE AND I LOOK FORWARD to it more and more with loathing. All the shops that didn't have their holiday decorations up by Michaelmas made up for it with sheer ostentation by Halloween. Canned carols bleat from every corner. The clerks at Saks are surlier, the ones at Lord & Taylor lordlier, the ones at Bergdorf's bitchier than at any other season.

All about me I see children being led by the hand to wheedle toy department Santa Clauses out of the most ruinous remembrances. On the commuters' train each night I see fathers, burdened with bulky packages, discussing not taxes, not politics, not the market, but the complexities of assembling electric trains and English bicycles.

I hate to go to my office each day because all that awaits me is nothing—a message from that pompous young ass in the State Department saying that no reliable information has been uncovered as yet, but every effort is being made; a cable from the Countess of Upshot (the former Vera Charles) saying that she just missed making contact at the Aga Khan's funeral in July, but *thought* she saw them at the Copenhagen airport in September; a rambling letter from my London operative, Percy ("Peek-a-boo") Pankhurst, announcing that his detective agency is still hot on the trail and asking for yet another hundred pounds.

Even more, I hate to go home at night. Home is a Georgian-type house in Verdant Greens, a community of two hundred houses in four styles just over an hour from New York, if the train is on time. My wife and I hate the house. We also hate Verdant Greens. We only moved there when our son was born so that he could have grass beneath his feet, fresh air, and rather mediocre schooling under the collective gimlet eye of a meddlesome group of Verdant Greens mothers who have a smattering of psychiatric jargon. And now my wife and I have even come to hate each other. Our overpriced, ill-built little house—seven rooms, two-and-a-half baths, expansion attic—has become an empty echoing shell, the prison of two lonely, silent, frustrated people. The son, for whose well-being the house was bought, is no longer here. He was kidnapped in 1954.

When I say kidnapped I don't mean to imply anything like ransom notes and a ladder against the wall. He went away just after his seventh birthday with our kisses and our blessings. We even waved him off at Idlewild as the big Pan-American plane carried him off to India. But we have never seen him—and rarely heard of him—since. That was June of 1954. He was supposed to be back by Labor Day in time for school. Two and a half years have passed, and now we face another melancholy Christmas without Michael in the house. And all because Auntie Mame fancied the child and wanted to take him off on a little outing!

MY AUNTIE MAME IS A MOST UNUSUAL WOMAN. SHE raised me from the time I was orphaned at ten. Not because anyone wanted her to—far from it—or because she herself had any desire to take on a lonely only child during her heyday in 1929. It was simply that she was my only living relative. We were stuck with each other and we had to make the best of it.

But raise me she did in her own helter-skelter fashion, to the horror of my trustee, Mr. Dwight Babcock of the Knickerbocker Trust Company, to the horror of the masters at St. Boniface Academy in Apathy, Massachusetts (where Mr. Babcock finally put me after Auntie Mame's forays into progressive education), and sometimes even to the horror of me.

We lived in many places together, Auntie Mame and I. We lived in a duplex in Beekman Place during the twenties when Auntie Mame was still Miss Dennis, still rich, and still in her Japanese phase. We lived in a carriage house in Murray Hill during the Depression before Auntie Mame found love and marriage and even more riches as Mrs. Beauregard Jackson Pickett Burnside. For a while we lived on a plantation in Georgia with Uncle Beau. Then, when Auntie Mame became the ninth-richest widow in New York, we lived in a big town house in Washington Square. We also lived in various other places around the world until I grew up and got married. After that, Auntie Mame's address—whenever she stayed still long enough to have one—was the St. Regis Hotel. Today I don't know where Auntie Mame is living. I wish I did, because that's where my son Michael is living, too. Assuming, of course, that the boy is still alive.

But as unorthodox and eccentric—her detractors have even used such adjectives as depraved and lunatic—as Auntie Mame's methods of child care may have been, I don't think that any of the unusual things she did ever hurt me.

This, however, is not the opinion of my wife, Pegeen. When I got home to Verdant Greens last night, Pegeen was waiting at the door.

"Chilly out, dear," I said, kissing her. "Anything in the mail? I mean like especially terrible Christmas cards."

Pegeen knew perfectly well what I meant and went on to say so. "I know perfectly well what you mean. You mean is there some word from our child or from that madwoman who carried him off. And the answer is No. Just as it's been every day for the last four months. No! No! No! My God, Patrick, I can't eat, I can't sleep, I can't even think, worrying about my baby in the hands of that old maniac. For all we know, poor little Michael may be dead and buried."

"Oh, I scarcely think so. We'd have heard, surely."

"Heard? What have we heard? Six cables, a few miserable scribbled post cards—the Taj Mahal, a bathhouse in Tokyo, a lamasery in Tibet, an apartment house in Tel Aviv that looked like a dresser with all the drawers open, the Istanbul Hilton, the Mozart Festival, *Animation sur la Plage* from Cap d'Antibes; those and about a dozen more and not one more word about our child in two and a half years!"

"That's not quite true, Pegeen. Both Michael and Auntie Mame have been very good about remembering our birthdays, our anniversary, Christmas—and very handsomely, too. I still wear that mandarin . . ."

"Christmas. How can you *say* the word? This will be our third Christmas without a child in the house. Don't you think everyone in Verdant Greens is talking?"

"I'm certain they're talking but it's rarely interesting enough to . . ."

"That boy's almost ten years old. I haven't seen him since he was seven. He'll never be a cub scout and *I'll* never be a den mother."

"Not if *I* have anything to say about it you won't."

"Well, I grant that it sounds dismal. But think of the other things our baby is missing. Proper schooling. The companionship of children his own age. Sports. Sunday school. Christmas."

"Nonsense," I said, trying to be as bland and offhand as possible because I was just as worried about Auntie Mame and Michael as Pegeen, only I didn't want her to know it. "As

Auntie Mame . . .

Auntie Mame always said, I could learn more in ten minutes in her drawing room than I could in ten years at school. She was right, too. I saw more of children my own age than I wanted to. As for Christmas, she gave me some damned nice things."

"Such as what?"

All I could remember, offhand, was a list of items that would hardly have comforted a worried mother—a live alligator, a samurai sword, a chimpanzee that promptly died, and a lifetime course at Arthur Murray's. "Oh, nothing. Just some very nice things."

"But don't you realize that she's simply stolen our child away from us? If he were to march into this room right now he wouldn't recognize his own parents. Oh, I know her game. I'm a woman, too. She plans to take over our child entirely, to twist him around her finger, to teach him life on *her* terms—life as Mame Dennis Burnside sees it—so that he'll end up just as scatterbrained and eccentric as she is."

"If you please," I said. "She raised me from the time I was ten until I escaped—that is, until I met you. Do you find me so odd? Don't I manage to shower every day, hold down a decent job with a reputable firm? Do I keep a collection of boots and whips in the cellar? Don't I pay my taxes and come home every night on the six-oh-three? Sometimes I even wish I were a little more colorful—a little less dull."

"So do I. But that's beside the point. The point is that your aunt took our child away two and a half years ago. She promised that he'd be home by Labor Day, and here it is 1957 and . . ."

"Do be fair, Pegeen. Auntie Mame didn't say *which* Labor Day."

"Don't interrupt! Bit by bit she's taken over. First a cable begging to let him stay until Christmas. I never should have consented, but I did. Then a long letter telling me how good he was at skiing and how wonderful the snow was at Chamonix and what an aptitude Michael had for French. It was the French that did it. She *knew* what a pushover I was for Racine."

"I've always found him rather tiresome."

"The next thing, we heard Lady Bountiful had our little boy in an Aqualung down with sharks and barracuda and I-don't-know-what."

"Well, you were complaining about his having no sports."

"And then that wonderful opportunity to get into the Forbidden City, play with the Dalai Lama. Next it was a papal audience. Then the Red Dean of . . ."

"And you were complaining about religion."

"I'm complaining about *everything*. It was bad enough when we knew where they were. But for the last four months there hasn't been one word—not a letter, not a cable, not so much as a line scrawled on a post card. That mad aunt of yours has probably got that innocent child smoking, drinking, taking dope. . . ."

"Now don't be ridiculous! He was sneaking cigarettes by the time he was six. You've always let him sniff away at that stuff you use to remove nail enamel. And that old father of yours had him swilling beer in his bassinet. Auntie Mame may be unorthodox, but she's not unreliable. I'm not in the least concerned myself," I lied.

"You see! She's reared you to be an unnatural father. Well, I'm plenty worried. Sick with worry! *He's* too young and *she's* too old."

"She'd scratch your eyes out if she heard you say it. Besides, she makes a most colorful traveling companion. I can attest to that. She took me around the world, and where am I now? Verdant Greens. Gaining weight, losing hair, married, settled, and middle aged."

Auntie Mame . . .

"When did she take you around the world?"

"Oh, a long time ago. Before the war."

"Why didn't you ever tell me?"

"Didn't I? Well, if I didn't it was probably because there wasn't much to tell. You know, Pegeen, just tourist stuff."

"Well, we have all night. You can start telling me now. Just when was this grand tour?"

"Oh, a long time back. Ten, fifteen, twenty years ago. It was in 1937, right after I was kicked—right after I finished at St. Boniface Academy; before I went to college."

"How long were *you* gone?" Pegeen asked.

"Well, it was for an indefinite stay. Almost all of Auntie Mame's visits are indefinite and she's rarely any place on time. That may account for Michael's being so late in getting home."

"Two and a half *years*?"

"Why don't we have a drink, dear?"

"Sit right there and start talking. I can hear you while I mix them. Now commence."

"Well, there's nothing to tell, really. Michael went to India and started from there. We went the other way."

"What other way?"

"Well, we set out in May of 1937 on the old *Normandie*. What a ship that was!"

"I've seen it," Pegeen said, handing me a drink. "Go on."

"Well, we weren't going to take Ito. . . ."

"You mean that inane, giggling, Japanese houseman of hers?"

"Ito has always been a very good friend," I said with dignity. "Both to Auntie Mame and to me. He did join us later, but we set off alone—in the Deauville Suite of the *Normandie*, the Captain's table, and all the pomp and circumstance in the world. Well, that's about all."

"Go on," Pegeen said in an I-mean-business tone of voice.

"Well, if memory serves, the *Normandie* used to land in France."

"And so?"

"And so we went to Paris . . ."

Auntie Mame ...

Auntie Mame and the City of Light

"YOU'RE BEING RIDICULOUS TO WORRY THIS WAY," I told Pegeen, trying hard to conceal the concern I felt. "How could the boy get into any trouble traveling around the world with his great aunt? An elderly woman, actually, and hardly likely to debauch a ten-year-old child."

"She certainly tried hard enough with you," Pegeen said.

"Why, that's outrageous," I sputtered. "She did no such thing. Take Paris, for example. Now what do most people bring back from Paris?"

"A social disease?"

"Certainly not! They bring back memories—the Eiffel Tower, the Louvre, Versailles—you know, things like that."

"And what did you do when she took you to Paris?"

"Why, nothing much. I mean we went to the usual places—Notre Dame, the Bon Marché, Maxim's. We did all the museums and galleries and churches and . . ."

"And?"

"Oh, yes, once we even attended the French National Theatre."

"So?"

"So that was all."

That wasn't all, but I'd rather be hung by my thumbs than tell poor Pegeen about Auntie Mame in Paris.

. . .

A H, PATRICK, my little love," Auntie Mame said, squeezing my hand, "don't you feel the magic of Paris? *Paris mon coeur! La ville lumière!*" The taxicab swung off the Rue St. Honoré with a suddenness that threw Auntie Mame to the floor. "*Merde!*" she said.

I said yes, I did feel the magic of Paris and didn't Auntie Mame think *she'd* feel a whole lot better if she just sat back and relaxed until we got to the hotel. She was still adjusting her rakish off-the-face hat as the taxi, somewhat more sedately, circled the Place Vendôme and pulled up at the Ritz.

Paris was to Auntie Mame more a Macy's than a metropolis, and the Ritz was within spitting distance of Schiaparelli and Chanel and Elizabeth Arden and Cartier and most of the other departments that Auntie Mame liked to patronize. And she was enchanted to see a huge bouquet from César Ritz himself waiting in her sitting room.

"Ah, dear old M. Ritz," she said wistfully. "He never forgets me."

"Few do," I said, casing the Louis Seize splendor of the suite.

Auntie Mame drew off her gloves, overtipped the men with the luggage, and gazed dreamily out of the window in the general direction of Schiaparelli's.

"Ah, Patrick, my little love," she said once again. "*Paris mon coeur!* To see this fabulous, civilized city again through your young, blue eyes. Heaven! Now be a lamb and order me a nice sidecar—and something for yourself, of course—while I get organized and call Vera. She's staying here, too."

Auntie Mame ...

The Ritz telephone operator was just recovering from the impact of my St. Boniface Academy irregular French verbs when Auntie Mame swept back into the sitting room and took over the telephone. After a couple of severe electric shocks and a lot of static Auntie Mame was connected with Vera Charles and there was a very brief burst of mellifluous French. "*Vera, chérie!*" Auntie Mame cried. "*C'est moi! Je suis ici*. . . . I said, Vera," Auntie Mame translated impatiently, "it's Mame. I'm here in the Ritz. So's Patrick. Come right down. *A bientôt!* . . . No, silly, that means I'll see you in a moment."

Auntie Mame rang off and spread her arms dramatically. "Ah, my little love, isn't it divine! Here I have you and all of Europe to show you before you go off to college—an aware, attractive young escort with whom I can share the more gracious culture of an older and wiser civilization. You and Europe and Vera, too. Oh, Patrick, I simply feel it in my bones—this is going to be the most wonderful summer of my whole life! Now where in hell is the waiter with my drink and what's keeping Vera?"

There was a tap at the door and both Vera and the waiter entered, although Vera had managed to sweep Auntie Mame's sidecar off the tray and had half finished it.

"Darling!" Auntie Mame said.

"Dulling!" Vera said.

Vera Charles needs no introduction to anyone who ever went to the theater between the Civil and Korean wars. She was a fabulous clothes horse, an absolute star, and is said to have killed off more producers than alcohol, heart disease, and suicide put together. She was also my Auntie Mame's best friend most of the time. Today she was looking very Parisian in a Molyneux suit, pearls, fox furs, a hennaed upsweep, and a face that was at least ten years younger than the one I'd seen her wearing two years earlier.

"Mame, dulling," Vera said dramatically, "what a pity you

missed my conquest of London, but now yoah heah in Peddiss to see me wow these frogs." Vera was born and brought up in Pittsburgh, but she spoke with such a determined Mayfair elegance that not even the English could understand much of what she was saying. This may or may not have accounted for her enormous success on the London stage. The ladies embraced once more and rubbed their cheeks together and then Vera got down to cases.

By cases I mean that Vera talked exclusively about Vera for the next half hour. She told us how she had been a sensation in London and the darling of Palace circles; how they had begged her to come to Paris as a special feature of the Exposition Summer, presumably to add a little luster to such unknown performers as Noël Coward, Yvonne Printemps, Sacha Guitry, Maurice Chevalier, and Josephine Baker, who were all playing in Paris that season. The waiter reappeared with a tray covered with sidecars and as the ladies drank, Vera grew more and more expansive.

"Yais, dulling," Vera said, "it's one thing to have ull of Ameddica at one's feet; one thing to be the toast of London; but what an ecktress of may *statuah* ecktually needs is a trayumph on the Continent. And heah you ah, may uldest and diddest chum, on hand to share this victory with me!" Vera simpered elegantly and reached out for another sidecar.

Auntie Mame was very interested in the theater. As a matter of fact, she and Vera had first met in a road company of *Chu Chin Chow* during the first World War where they had kicked away happily in the second row of the chorus until my grandfather found out about it and sent Auntie Mame back to school. But even so she was still sort of a theater buff and claimed to have grease paint in her veins.

"How divine, Vera," Aunt Mame cooed. "Patrick and I will be right there on opening night clapping our hands off. But, tell me, darling, um, what language are you going to . . ."

Auntie Mame . . .

"Frrrench. *Net*-turally," Vera said with great hauteur.

That struck us both as very odd. Vera could barely speak English.

"But, Vera," Auntie Mame said, "what's the play?"

"Well, it isn't ecktually a drawma, de-ah," Vera said uneasily. "It's the Folies-Bergère."

"*Vera!*" Auntie Mame said. "You're *not* going back to burlesque after all these years?"

If there was one thing Vera did not like to be reminded of it was her humble beginnings in a traveling burly—not that it wasn't more wholesome in those days, but it just didn't seem suitable to the First Lady of the American Stage. "Certainly *not*, Mame," Vera said coldly. "It just so happens that the Folies happens to be the *commedia dell' arte* of Frahnce. They don't even have a runway—just a sort of ill-yewminated promenade around the awkestra pit. *I* have accepted a sidious role— that of Catherine the Great. It's a dremetic paht. And, what is more"—and here Vera's voice lost its staginess and lapsed back into the pure Pittsburgh accent Vera used when angry or discussing money—"they're paying me two thousand clams—dollars, not frances—a week for fifteen minutes' work each night and *no* matinees."

Auntie Mame was still very dubious about Vera's undertaking any venture so *declassé* as a music-hall appearance, even if the Folies-Bergère was, so to speak, the Palace of Europe. So, goaded at last to expenditure, Vera strode elegantly to the telephone and instructed the hall porter to get three Bergère seats for that very night and to charge them to her, Vera Charles.

WE GOT INTO OUR SEATS JUST BEFORE THE ORCHESTRA started its erratic tuning up and just after I'd learned that in France one tips the ushers—an unsettling and expensive experience if you don't happen to have any small change on you. Then the lights went out, the curtain went up, and the Folies-Bergère began with a bang in all its tawdry splendor. Actually, the Folies was then, as it is now, a kind of Radio City Music Hall with bosoms—only much more elaborate and not nearly so professional. In fact, it was even more elaborate in those pre-war days; probably because the costumes and scenery were all a lot newer then and the girls a lot younger.

But it was more or less the same old endless show it still is, for the French musical stage prides itself on quantity rather than quality. There were the customary English chorus girls and Hungarian show girls (hardly anybody in French musicals is French), who shrieked "Allo, 'oney!" from time to time in a mélange of fake French accents for the benefit of the English-speaking members of the audience. There were the usual high-wire acts and low-comedy acts; the cyclists, the acrobats, the sopranos, the female impersonators, the contortionists. Then there were the *tableaux vivants* involving water effects, fountain effects, fire effects, mirror effects, and, of course, girls.

Girls were lowered from the roof and catapulted up from the cellar. Girls were suspended precariously from wires or atop swaying columns. Girls trooped up the duty aisles or meandered down long stairways. Girls traipsed about in tarnished sequins, dirty wigs, molting plumes, and balding furs, dragging grimy trains behind them.

Toward the end of the first act Auntie Mame began to doze and Vera jabbed her viciously.

Still the girls came on. Girls listlessly waggled hips and maracas in the Latin American Number. Girls staggered beneath huge panniers in the Versailles Number. Girls sweltered beneath their furs in the Winter Number. Girls shivered in mermaid tails and goose flesh in the Underseas Number. Girls sagged under the weight of fake ivory masks in the Chinese Number and came back gamely in hoop skirts and sausage curls in the Ole Plantation Number, for which a medley of Negro spirituals had been considerately translated into French. Well, as I said, the Folies-Bergère gave the customers an awful lot for their money.

"Vera," Auntie Mame said, stifling a yawn during the Birds of Paradise Number, "surely you're not serious about lending your talents to a dreary charade like this."

"Be still," Vera hissed. "The big dramatic number comes on next."

Sure enough, it did.

In those days the management of the Folies-Bergère always treated its customers to at least one dramatic episode, usually involving a Tragic Queen, always featuring a Great Star, at least half a dozen changes of costume and scenery, quite a lot of girls, and a boy or two. It is a practice mostly abandoned since the postwar tourist boom. The Tragic Queen for that edition of the Folies was Mary Queen of Scots. It was tragic, all right, but at least she kept her clothes on. Auntie Mame was terribly relieved to see that all her friend Vera had to do was stomp around the stage bellowing of love and sorrow and do a series of quick changes from one elaborate gown to another.

"All right," Auntie Mame said. "Now I've seen it. Let's get out of here."

As we left, the girls—blowzily got up in soiled lace and tricornes—came bobbing out in the most unseaworthy gondolas for the big Venetian Number.

"Tacky" was Auntie Mame's word for the Folies-Bergère. But she realized that Vera's sole motivation was greed, and two thousand dollars a week was an unheard-of amount of money in Paris of 1937. And, as a matter of record, Vera would have sold her own mother to the devil for two dollars cash.

... and the City of Light

AFTER THAT FIRST EVENING OUR LIFE IN PARIS SETtled down to a sort of routine. In the mornings I'd go off on little sight-seeing excursions of my own while Auntie Mame and Vera ordered lots of new clothes with daring fifteen-inch hem lines from Vionnet and Alix and Maggy Rouf and Lucien Lelong. They would both appear at lunch in new outfits which they described as having "a whole lot of pizazz." Don't laugh. Women looked much better in 1937 than they do this year.

In the afternoons Vera would excuse herself to rehearse for her dramatic debut as Catherine of Russia at the Folies-Bergère and Auntie Mame would take me along on some mission of her own. She knew quite a lot of famous French people and was usually more than welcome to drop in on Colette or André Gide or Christian Bérard or somebody arty like that. Auntie Mame kept something of a *salon* herself in New York and she liked to see how the foreign competition was making out. If no one she knew was holding a *jour* on any particular afternoon, we'd set off to see something interesting or go to the Paris Exposition. The Exposition stretched along the Seine from the Place de la Concorde to above the Trocadéro, and after we'd sopped up enough culture there we'd end up at Mme. Lanvin's Club des Oiseaux on top of the Pavillon d'Elégance, where Auntie Mame could rest her feet, have a stiff drink, and look at some more new clothes.

Every night Auntie Mame and Vera would put on new evening dresses with a whole lot of pizazz, get me into my dinner jacket, and we'd go off to some place spiffy like Maxim's or Les Ambassadeurs, where Auntie Mame and Albert, the headwaiter, would go about ordering dinner as though they were planning the Creation of Man. Then we'd go to the theater—something of Auntie Mame's choosing like the

Comédie-Française or a good gloomy French tragedy or a light, airy thing like *Three Waltzes*.

Then we'd do a night club like Bricktop's or Suzy Solidor's or Le Boeuf sur le Toit. And finally back to the hotel, where Auntie Mame would open all the windows, take me out to the balcony for a good-night cigarette, and tell me all sorts of interesting things about the history of France—like the time she was inadvertently caught in a bordello, the wise thinking behind the installation of bidets, and how the Maginot Line had made France forever impregnable. Every day was a full one.

HOWEVER, OUR PARISIAN IDYLL CAME ABRUPTLY TO an end in the Gardens of Versailles when we ran face to face into my trustee, Dwight D. Babcock of the Knickerbocker Trust Company, armed with guidebook, camera, and shooting stick, and reinforced by his wife, Eunice, and his son, Dwight Junior.

I was orphaned at the age of ten, and Auntie Mame was my guardian. But, by the exotic terms of my late father's will, Mr. Babcock, as trustee, had complete control over my upbringing and education and he had a free hand to exercise his authority whenever he felt that Auntie Mame was doing something too eccentric. For the past seven years that authority had been exercised like a race horse. Mr. Babcock was in banking. He lived in Scarsdale. He wore rimless glasses and Herbert Hoover collars. His opinions were formed by the *Literary Digest, Dun and Bradstreet Reports*, and the *Wall Street Journal*.

Auntie Mame was the first to regain her speech. "Why, *Mis*ter Babcock! *What* a pleasant surprise. And how nice to see you again, Alice."

"Eunice," Mrs. Babcock said, correcting her primly.

"Of course, Eunice. And Junior!"

"Hi," Junior said flatly.

Junior Babcock and I had shared the same room at St. Boniface and the less said about him the better. He was just like his father—only with acne.

"W-well, hrumph, this, um, certainly *is* a surprise," Mr. Babcock said, implying that he had rather expected us to be found tossing fitfully in an opium den on the Rue Mouffetard. "I *understood* that you and Patrick had run off to Europe—*without* my permission, needless to say—but I didn't . . . um, ah . . ."

Auntie Mame could charm birds off trees when she chose to. Even Mr. Babcock was not entirely immune to her magnetism, although she'd given him good reason to be damned suspicious of it. "Dear Mr. Babcock," she said, dimpling prettily, "why would I bother a busy executive like you over a trifling little thing like taking my nephew off on a cultural tour of Europe before he starts college this fall? I can imagine how you financial wizards must feel—sitting down there in Wall Street plotting a big stock-market coup and then having some hysterical old widow derail your whole train of thought by calling with silly questions about the grocer's bill. It must be *maddening.*"

"Well," Mr. Babcock conceded with a constipated smile, "um, yes, um, sometimes that sort of thing is annoying."

I could see that Auntie Mame's charm was beginning to work, and I was awfully thankful because I still had a few months to go before I became eighteen and would be set free of Mr. Babcock's insidious power.

"Well, I'm sure you *need* a good vacation, Mr. Babcock," Auntie Mame said. "And don't you *adore* France? Your first trip?"

"Indeed not," Mr. Babcock said dryly. "I was over here with

Auntie Mame . . .

the A.E.F. in seventeen. Had I known then what I know now about these decadent, arrogant, dishonest French, I would have gone to jail before raising a finger to help them. Of all the corrupt, indolent, swindling . . ."

I could see Auntie Mame getting that old Joan of Arc look and this was no time for her to get into an argument with Mr. Babcock over ethnic groups or over anything else, for that matter. "Where are you staying, Mr. Babcock?" I asked too loud and too fast for Auntie Mame to start in on one of her bigger speeches.

Mrs. Babcock answered me. "We're staying with some cousins of mine, Patrick. Dr. and Mrs. Gilbreath. They were missionaries in Saigon for many years and they now have a hostel out near Neuilly for young divinity students en route to Indochina."

Auntie Mame shuddered.

"Isn't that nice!" I said quickly.

"*Nice?*" Mr. Babcock snarled. "If you were to see what passes for plumbing in that house, you wouldn't . . ."

"Yes, it's nice, Patrick," Mrs. Babcock said dubiously. "They lead a very simple life. Serve good, plain American food—we brought over a whole case of Beechnut peanut butter; that seems to be one thing the students really crave. And they show the most interesting lantern slides of their travels every night after dinner."

"Isn't that nice," I said again, but without much conviction.

"Ye-ess," Mrs. Babcock said a little wistfully, "it *is* nice, but somehow I'd always thought of Paris as—well—sort of *gay* and . . . oh, I don't know. Out-of-door cafés and pretty clothes and . . . Well, it *is* restful and my cousins the Gilbreaths are a perfect peach of a couple . . . but . . ."

It didn't take any great insight to sense that Mrs. Babcock's first trip abroad was being something of a washout. Even

Auntie Mame took pity on her, because she suddenly said, "*I* know what let's do, Eunice. There's a marvelous little restaurant right here in Versailles with a terrace and a garden and a superb cellar and . . ."

"Are you going to eat in the basement?" Mr. Babcock asked darkly.

"They don't ink-dray," I said to Auntie Mame under my breath.

"Well, it's a divine little place," Auntie Mame went on rapidly, "and I wish you'd all come as my guests. It's so hot here and . . ."

Mrs. Babcock looked wanly hopeful, and Auntie Mame cinched the deal before Mr. Babcock could open his mouth to say no. "Here I am, a poor, silly widow just like the ones you have to deal with, Mr. Babcock, and I really *need* a good, sound financial head around to help me count out the francs and pay the bill and tip the waiter. And, oh, you know. . . ."

It was a direct appeal to Mr. Babcock's patriotism, and I felt that he would have gone to hell if only to save a fellow American from the rapaciousness of the French. Under a sort of armed truce we were off to the little restaurant of Auntie Mame's choosing.

IT *WAS* A GOOD RESTAURANT—ALMOST A GREAT RES-taurant—and since the staff remembered Auntie Mame from previous trips, they fell all over themselves making us comfortable. Auntie Mame was being very much the Gracious Hostess and there were only two or three bad moments.

The first occurred when the captain said, "Does Madame wish a cocktail, wine?"

"Why, I think . . ." Auntie Mame began.

"No!" Mr. Babcock said, taking over completely.

Auntie Mame looked as though she'd been stabbed, but

Auntie Mame . . .

she recovered quickly. With a sly grimace she said, "Nothing alcoholic, please. Just bring a nice cool bottle of Veuve Cliquot. A magnum, I think."

"What's that?" Mr. Babcock asked.

"It's a kind of carbonated grape juice, Mr. Babcock. Catawba grape juice. I think you'll enjoy it. So cooling on these warm days."

"How nice," Mrs. Babcock said.

The champagne was poured and nobody seemed to mind it at all.

When Mr. Babcock asked what we'd been seeing in Paris I was eager to tell him all about the interesting people and restaurants and night clubs and plays Auntie Mame had taken me to see, but Auntie Mame was too quick for me. "Oh, you know, Mr. Babcock," she said. "The sort of thing boys of Patrick's and Junior's age should visit—museums, cathedrals, things like that."

"*Catholic* cathedrals?" Mr. Babcock asked loudly. He was a sort of Inquisition in reverse.

"Well, I don't think there *are* very many Protestant ones, Mr. Babcock. And I just hustle him through. Here, do let me fill up your glass."

Lunch was delicious and the champagne was beginning to have its tranquilizing effect. Over the salad Mrs. Babcock, who had become quite rosy, turned vivaciously and said, "Tell me, Mame dear, how is your dear friend Vera Charles?" It was the first time she had ever called Auntie Mame anything other than Mrs. Burnside or—in Auntie Mame's unmarried days— Miss Dennis. Auntie Mame was so pleased with the champagne's effect that she beckoned to the waiter and, with a broad wink, called for another bottle of that good Yankee Catawba grape juice.

"Why, as a matter of fact, Eunice, Vera's right here in Paris at the Ritz. She's opening in a new play tonight."

... and the City of Light

"Oh, *what*?" Mrs. Babcock trilled. "You know I've seen every one of her plays twice. So refined. Such a great, great lady. I can't wait to tell all the girls in Scarsdale that I've seen Vera Charles in *Paris*."

"Why, Mrs. Babcock," I began, "Vera's working at the Fo . . . Ouch!"

Auntie Mame fetched me a kick under the table that nearly broke my ankle. Then she took over. "Isn't that dreadful, Eunice. Here Vera's my dearest friend and I can't for the life of me remember the name of the play or the theater or anything. Hahahaha! Can *you*, Patrick?" she asked ominously.

"No," I said. "Isn't that funny? My mind's gone completely blank."

Other than that, the lunch went splendidly. So well, in fact, that Eunice and Junior were nodding into the Grand Marnier soufflé and Mr. Babcock was decidedly tipsy. "No joy dee veever," he kept saying of them.

The luncheon party broke up with Eunice and Junior being sent *chez* Gilbreath in a taxi and Mr. Babcock unsteadily joining us in Auntie Mame's car bound for Paris. He *said* it was to pick up some mail at the American Express. It was around four when Auntie Mame finally waved him out of the car with the tenderest of good-byes and drove back to the hotel.

"What I need now is a real, honest-injun snort," Auntie Mame said, tossing her hat across the sitting room. "All that sweetness and light has undone me. Now, my little love, be a pet and pour poor Auntie Mame about twelve fingers of cognac and I'll cheer up poor Vera. You know how these actresses get on opening nights."

There was a faint rapping at the door. I opened it and there stood Vera. She was dressed in black with a wide straw hat hung with heavy black veiling.

"Who died?" I asked.

"Vera Charles did," Vera said, stepping into the suite and

Auntie Mame . . .

leaning dramatically against the door jamb. "Lock the door and then *look* at me." Vera lifted her veil, and her face was a sight. It looked okay from the left side, but the right side was black and blue and swollen out almost to her shoulder. "*Look* at me!" Vera said again, wresting the brandy glass from Auntie Mame.

"Vera!" Auntie Mame cried. "What in the world . . ."

"That man!" Vera said. "That beast! He's mauled the beje-sus out of me."

"But Vera. How could you allow any man to . . ."

"I couldn't *help* it. I was in such agony."

"But, Vera. I didn't even know you had a lover. You never told me a word about . . ."

"Lover, my eye!" Vera spat. "It's that God-damned dentist. 'Ook," she said, thrusting her finger back into her mouth. " 'Isdom toof. Imfacted. Damned near killed me getting it out. I'll never be able to go on tonight." She downed the brandy and made for the telephone. "There goes two grand a week." She picked up the telephone and got on to the man-agement of the Folies-Bergère.

It was quite a conversation. Vera didn't know much French and Auntie Mame was often called to pick up the telephone and fill in for her. It lasted the better part of an hour. When it was over both ladies were so spent that I filled up their glasses to the brim.

"Thank you, Patrick," Auntie Mame said absently. Then she said, "Well, they were fairly definite about it, weren't they?"

Vera moaned, sipped, moaned again.

"Of course I'm not entirely *certain* about the French verb meaning 'to sue,' but I got the general idea that the Folies management had some sort of stringent legal action in mind."

"You're God-damned right they have," Vera moaned. "I

should never have left the Shuberts in the first place. Now I suppose I'll spend my declining years in the old actors' home."

"Couldn't you complain to Actor's Equity?" I asked.

"They don't cut any ice over here," Vera said.

"Ice!" I suggested. "With enough cold compresses your face might . . ."

"No good," Vera sighed. "I've had my jaw embedded in ice like a shrimp cocktail all day. Only makes it swell more. I look like the Swedish Angel and still those bastards insist that I sign in tonight and go on or . . ." Vera paused, sipped again at her brandy, and gave Auntie Mame a long, searching look.

"Wh-what is it, Vera?" Auntie Mame said, gulping at her drink.

"I . . . *think* . . . I . . . might . . . *just* . . . have . . . an . . . *idea*. . . ."

"Oh no you don't, Vera Charles!" Auntie Mame said, polishing off the drink and thrusting the empty glass at me.

"Why couldn't *I* go to the theater tonight, with you as my maid . . ."

"No, Vera! No! Not in a million years. Not for a million dollars. Not . . ."

"*I* could wear this hat and the veil and sign the book, Mame, and *you* could . . ."

"Out of the question!" Auntie Mame said, snatching the newly refilled glass from me. "We don't look at *all* alike. I couldn't possibly . . ."

"You've always wanted to be on the stage, Mame," Vera said hypnotically.

"N-not any more, I don't, Vera. It's absolutely out of the . . ."

"And as for looking like me, Mame de-ah, that isn't important. We're the same size and you play the whole thing in powdered wig and a mask. . . ."

Auntie Mame . . .

"Not this chicken, Vera. Not on your tintype. I wouldn't dream of . . ."

"You see, dulling, the Empress Catherine is at a masked ball in the Winter Palace and she meets this young officer (actually some French faggot who couldn't act his way out of a paper bag) who falls in love with her, not knowing that she's the Empress of all the Russians. . . ."

"The Russians can have it, Vera Charles. I've said no. No. No. *No!*"

"And the young officer has this huge affair with her. . . ."

"Right on the *stage*? Vera, I'd never consider such a . . ."

"Certainly not, Mame. That is *implied*. And the costumes are divine. You get to wear this magnificent sable coat that cost . . ."

"I *have* a sable coat, thank you," Auntie Mame said. "It's in storage. No, Vera, I'm sorry, but I . . ."

"Fix your aunt another drink, Patrick," Vera said. "Haven't you any family feeling? And speaking of feeling, Mame, I should think that after you and I have been through thick and thin together for twenty years you would at least have the loyalty and consideration to come to the aid of your oldest, truest chum when she faces ruin—yais, rrrrrru-een—a ghastly lawsuit, a penniless old age, and a stretch in the Bastille. . . ."

"Oh, Vera . . ."

"I always said, 'Loyalty is Mame's middle name,' but I can see now how wrong I was."

"Vera," Auntie Mame said reasonably, "don't you understand that the whole thing is impossible? I'd do anything to help you, but I don't even know the lines. I've never seen the script. I . . ."

"Lines? Faugh!" Vera said. "Your French is *much* better than mine."

That was true. Auntie Mame could just get through a dinner menu, whereas Vera could barely order lunch. "Besides there *aren't* any lines. All you have to say is '*Oh, mon amour!*' from time to time. This French fag does all the rest of the talking. You don't even go on until eleven o'clock. That gives us five—almost six—hours to rehearse. Why, I could teach . . ."

"N-no, Vera," Auntie Mame whimpered.

"*Now,*" Vera said, "the thing opens at a gala masquerade in the Winter Palace. The courtiers are all dancing this gay minuet when Catherine the Great comes down the stairs, heavily disguised. Now pretend that's the staircase, over there by the door."

"Oh, Ve-ra," Auntie Mame moaned.

THE DOORKEEPER AT THE FOLIES-BERGÈRE ALL BUT genuflected when Vera swept in, swathed in her veiling, and imperiously signed the artistes' register. A star was, after all, a star. But the backstage space in the theater was so cramped what with its mountains of scenery, its stagehands, its dressers, its dancing girls and dancing boys, its mannequins, its featured performers, its stars and its stars' retinues that visitors were discouraged from adding to the general mob scene.

Auntie Mame was stopped and the doorkeeper gave Vera a questioning look.

"*Ma femme,*" Vera said, indicating the hastily got-up maid's uniform Auntie Mame was wearing.

The doorman raised his eyebrows but a star was, after all, a star and the theater staff was accustomed to the odd little quirks of personality that sometimes accompany celebrity. Then the doorkeeper nabbed me and shot another questioning glance.

"*Mon amour,*" Auntie Mame said, almost to herself. The doorman scratched his head, shrugged Gallically, and let us pass.

Backstage all was pandemonium. I could hear the orchestra blaring out front and a shrill Greek tenor singing something about loving Paree both *midi* and *minuit* something-something *avec* his *chérie* something-something *c'est la vie*. Some Balkan tumblers wearing nothing but gold paint, gold jock straps, and gold teeth were having a big discussion in a tongue I took to be Croatian. A flamenco dancer was laying out her partner in a brand of Spanish that was never heard in Castille. And a statuesque woman, somewhat sketchily dressed in three rhinestone stars, was rocking a baby and crooning to it in German.

"My dressing room is this way," Vera said, elbowing her way through a throng of chorus boys got up as Princess of the Church for what I supposed would be a big Religious Number. They were mad for singing "Ave Maria" at the Folies-Bergère. Vera tripped over a performing seal, gave it a vicious kick, and dragged Auntie Mame up the stairs. You had to be a mountain goat to get to and from the dressing rooms, and the stairway made me think of the subway at rush hour except that practically everyone was naked. However, nobody paid much attention except me.

"It's this one," Vera panted, pushing Auntie Mame toward a door.

Auntie Mame opened the door and was immediately knocked flat by six enormous Russian wolfhounds that kept barking and wagging their tails and licking her face until I could get them off and help her.

"Vera," Auntie Mame gasped, "what *is* this? An *animal* act?"

"No, Mame," Vera said apologetically, "they're part of your props. You go on with them in the big love scene."

"Vera! That's *sodomy*! I won't . . ."

"Oh, nothing like that, de-ah. See, they *like* you."

"Well, *I* don't like *them*."

"Never mind, de-ah, Patrick will look after them. Won't

you, Patrick? That's Sascha, that's Jascha, there's Vanya, that's Pavel, and Boris and Morris."

"*Morris?*" I said.

"Well, I can't remember," Vera said nervously. "They all sound like Santa Claus's reindeer. Now sit down, Mame, and I'll make you up to look just as much like me as possible."

"But, Vera, if I'm going to wear a mask all during this—this ordeal . . ."

"Don't ask a lot of questions, de-ah. Just sit still."

HALF AN HOUR LATER WE EMERGED. AUNTIE MAME led the way, looking lovely in an eighteenth-century ball gown encrusted with so many rhinestones that it weighed more than she did, and a diamond mask. But the fenders of her skirt were so wide and the white wig so tall that she had to undress again to get through the door.

"Nevah mind, de-ah," Vera said, looking rather incongruous in the maid's uniform. "All your othah changes will be made in the wings."

Auntie Mame minced unsteadily down the dressing room stairs. Vera followed, carrying Auntie Mame's train, her fan, her gloves, her cloak, and her muff. I came last with the Russian wolfhounds. They yelped with pleasure at being released from the tiny dressing room and lifted their legs ecstatically at every corner.

Down below, a path was reverently cleared for the Great Star. "*Allez! Allez!*" the stagehands yelled. "Mees Sharl."

One of the chorus boys thrust an autograph book and a pen into Auntie Mame's face. She hastily wrote "Anna Q. Nillson" and trudged on.

"*Ah, Signorina Charles,*" he said, "*grazie!*"

"*Prego,*" Auntie Mame said.

Auntie Mame . . .

"You see, Mame," Vera said, her face discreetly lowered, "even the rest of the performers think you're me."

"B-but, Vera," Auntie Mame said, "what about the man I have to act with. *He'll* know."

"Nonsense, Mame. He'll be so busy counting the house he wouldn't know if he were playing with Sybil Thorndike. Now, up these stairs and ready for your entrance. You're on next. Come, Patrick, and bring the dogs."

Out front a falsetto Polish tenor was singing something about Paree and a girl named Marie being something-something *et jolie*. Auntie Mame struggled up to the summit of a rickety wooden platform and just avoided being decapitated by a painted drop of the Winter Palace at Petrograd that was being lowered.

"Vera, I'm sorry but I just *can't*," she panted.

"Oh yes you can," Vera said. "Remember, all you have to say is '*Oh, mon amour!*' Do it just the way I taught you and ham it up good and proper. You know that flamboyant French school of acting. Overplay everything. Aim for somewhere between Gertie Lawrence and Walter Hampden. They'll love it. The French worship stars and . . ."

The strains of a minuet drifted up to us. At the foot of a long white staircase I could see the boys and girls of the chorus all done up in powder and patches cavorting about the palace ballroom. The romantic young officer entered looking just like Octavian in *Der Rosenkavalier*. There was a fanfaronade of trumpets and the stairway was ablaze with light.

"Vera," Auntie Mame quavered, "I . . ."

"You're on, kid," Vera said, giving her a shove. And, indeed, Auntie Mame was on.

I could see Auntie Mame gliding down the stairs, the white wig nodding dreamily on her head. The audience burst into applause.

. . . and the City of Light

"You see how the audiences adore me, Patrick," Vera said. Then she hissed, "Pssssst, Mame! Toss 'em a kiss."

Auntie Mame threw a kiss and the audience went wild. Somewhere from down front a raucous voice shouted, "Take it off!"

The Empress and the romantic young officer met. They began to dance. He jabbered away quite a lot and then Auntie Mame bellowed, "*Oh, mon amour.*" The applause was tremendous. The same voice yelled, "Take it off!" and the curtain came down. Auntie Mame swayed to the wings, where Vera snatched off everything but Auntie Mame's girdle and brassière.

"H-how was I?" Auntie Mame said.

"Magnificent," Vera said. "You were almost as good as I would have been. Now here. Get into *this* wig and the sable cloak—put the hood up, de-ah—*and* the muff. Now get into the sleigh. This is the wild elopement to your hunting lodge for one night of perfect . . ."

"But, Vera, what about a skirt? My legs are . . ." One of the dogs—Morris, I think—licked Auntie Mame's bare knee.

"You don't need a skirt," Vera said, throwing Auntie Mame into the sleigh and pulling an ermine robe over her lap. "This is where he makes violent love to you and . . ."

"Vera, that man's been eating . . . Eeeeeeee!" The sleigh with the Empress and her lover was hoisted off the floor and tilted at a crazy angle in mid-air. There were the sounds of muffled hoofs and sleigh bells and then rapturous applause. Two dispirited stagehands tossed a few handfuls of artificial snow down onto the sleigh from a light bridge. The romantic officer burrowed his face into Auntie Mame's throat and, in a position of wild abandon, Auntie Mame croaked, "*Oh, mon amour!*"

"The French are wild about the aerial effects," Vera said to me as the curtain fell.

Auntie Mame . . .

Once again on terra firma, Auntie Mame limped toward us, wild-eyed with fear. "V-vera, wh-why didn't you tell me I was going on for the Flying Concellos? My God, I nearly fell out of that . . ."

"We haven't time to talk now," Vera said, snatching off the cloak, the wig, and a good deal of Auntie Mame's own hair. "And who the hell's that rube out front who doesn't know a great artiste when he sees one?"

"I—I don't know, Vera. It's so dark and the spotlights are so bright I can't . . ."

The rest of Auntie Mame's message was muffled in the pelts of a tentlike white fox cape that hung from her shoulders and dragged nine feet behind her.

"This is the scene on the battlements of your hunting lodge—just outside the imperial boudoir. He makes violent love to you and then . . . Here, stick your hand through that slit for your fan and . . . Ooops, you're on!"

The setting was as Vera said. Beyond the ramparts you could see a lighted village and onion towers. Stars twinkled. A full moon shone. Clouds drifted by. Buckets of snow fell. A massed chorus sang "The Russian Lullaby"—in French. The audience was orgasmic at this devastating bit of stage legerdemain. Then Auntie Mame drifted in through the snow languidly fanning herself—don't ask me why—with a huge frond of scarlet *coq* feathers. "*Oh, mon amour,*" she groaned, and collapsed into the frail arms of her lover, who then led her toward the imperial boudoir. The applause nearly rocked the theater, but through it all I could hear someone shouting, "Take it off!"

"Superb, dulling!" Vera kept saying as she got Auntie Mame into yet another wig and a negligee made of lamé and pink ostrich. "Now, be sure the mask is on securely because in this scene he tries to discover your identity just before he gets into the hay with . . ."

"Vera! You didn't tell me about . . ."

"Oh, don't worry, de-ah, the curtain comes down in plenty of time."

"But, Vera, what do I say?"

"You say '*Oh, mon amour,*' naturally. Can't you remember your lines?" Vera gave Auntie Mame a shove onto the stage and there she was in the Russian imperial bedchamber, which looked exactly like the Palace of Versailles the week before. Needless to say, the audience found the scene terrific and the one lone cry of "Take it off" came even louder and oftener. The romantic young officer made some pretty eloquent love to the Empress at the very edge of the imperial Beautyrest, but just as things began to look kind of sticky for Auntie Mame the guards burst in and dragged him away while she sobbed, "*Oh, mon amour!*" in a hoarse tremolo that would have put Sarah Bernhardt to shame, and collapsed on the bed. The curtain fell and not a moment too soon, because the bed collapsed right after that. The audience howled its appreciation.

"Mahvellous, dulling, simply soo-*pub*," Vera said as she was getting Auntie Mame into her final costume—a court dress of solid seed pearls and chinchilla, a wig that towered four feet above Auntie Mame's head, and a picture hat with nodding plumes that towered four feet above the wig. "Now," Vera said, "this is where you go down to the dungeon and condemn your lover to death."

"What for?" Auntie Mame asked.

"Why, for taking liberties with the Empress, silly."

"Well, he really hasn't done anything so terrible except to eat garlic sausage for the past forty-eight hours."

"Don't ask a lot of foolish questions, Mame. This is almost over. You use the dogs in this scene. Come! Come Yascha, Sascha, Pavel, Vanya, Boris, Morris!" The six wolfhounds bayed joyously and bounded over to yet another flight of steps

Auntie Mame . . .

leading to a high platform. Auntie Mame followed unsteadily but at the bottom step she stopped dead.

"What's the matter?" Vera whispered. "The curtain's going up."

"I—I can't make it."

"Can't make what?"

"Vera, this Empress drag is so heavy I can't manage the stairs."

"Oh, that's easy," Vera said. She gave one of the dogs a whack across the rump and all six of them bounded to the top, hauling Auntie Mame up with them.

This setting—a dungeon far beneath the icy waters of the Neva—was one of the Folies-Bergère's more sordid attempts at grim realism. Folies-Bergère muscle men in breechclouts were avidly torturing Folies-Bergère chorus boys, also in breech-clouts, on wheels and racks. The boys squealed like stuck pigs, and tormented shadows were projected onto the sweating walls. The audience loved it. The romantic young officer was led in, stripped to the waist. I felt that this was something of a mistake since he was pitifully thin and had forgotten to put any of his robust brown make-up on his chest and arms. Then there was another fanfaronade of trumpets and Auntie Mame appeared at the top of the stairs in a mass of yelping wolfhounds. And let me tell you that the audience wasn't exactly sitting on its hands when *that* happened.

"*L'Imperatrice!*" two flunkies bawled.

Then Auntie Mame began descending the stairs and, aided by all those Russian wolfhounds, she got down a lot faster than she had got up, her hat and wig rocking violently. She managed to keep her footing—*just*—and the house roared with admiration.

"*Oh, mon amour,*" she sobbed.

"Take it off, Queenie!" that voice called up from the audience.

"This is where she condemns him to death," Vera whispered to me.

I was feeling so relieved to think that this was almost over that I began to take a little more interest in the *mise en scène*. "I don't quite follow the plot, Vera," I said. "It's a little like *Elizabeth and Essex* except that . . ."

"The French don't care about *plots*, de-ah," Vera said, "as long as they've got enough costumes and scenery and biggish effects."

Well, they certainly had plenty.

Some way—don't ask me how—the Empress indicated that she wanted her innocent admirer broken on the rack, then flayed alive, then drawn and quartered by shouting, "*Oh, mon amour.*" A trap door opened, flames licked out of it, and the hapless young man was thrown in with a hideous scream and a chillingly realistic thud. Then the massed offstage chorus sang the *old* Russian anthem (in French), Auntie Mame shrieked, "*Oh, mon amour!*" and slumped to the floor as the curtain fell.

The house was in an uproar with cries of "*Brava*" and "*Bis! Bis!*"

Fortunately, the Folies-Bergère never grants encores, but the curtain was raised and lowered four times and still Auntie Mame stayed on the floor, struggling weakly to rise while the dogs wagged their tails feverishly and sniffed at her wig.

"Vera! Patrick!" she called piteously. "I can't get up. This damned dress has me weighed down." The orchestra was playing hell-for-leather as Vera and I with two stagehands got Auntie Mame out of the pearl dress and disentangled from the wolfhounds, but even over the sound of the music and the rumble of the shifting scenery I could hear the audience cheering and calling the name of Vera Charles. I could also hear the voice shouting "Take it off!"

There wasn't a dry eye backstage. As I led Auntie Mame to

Auntie Mame . . .

her dressing room, performers and stagehands alike stopped whatever they were doing to cheer for Vera Charles. "*Oh, mes amours!*" Auntie Mame cried, quite carried away with her triumph, and the company cheered again.

UP IN THE DRESSING ROOM AUNTIE MAME AND VERA collapsed into each other's arms while the dogs fell to scratching and licking themselves. "Mame," Vera cried emotionally, "you were magnificent. Only *I* could have done it any better. What I need now is a drink."

"What *I* need," Auntie Mame said, "is a general anesthetic. Come on. Let's get out of here."

"Oh, but Mame de-ah," Vera said, "you've forgotten the grand finale."

"What grand finale?" Auntie Mame asked blankly.

"Why, there's *always* a grand finale, Mame."

"I didn't see one last week," Auntie Mame said.

"That's because you didn't stay until the end, de-ah. Now, your costume for that is . . ."

"Vera Charles, you didn't say one mumbling word about any grand finale. I've gone through hell for you and now I . . ."

"Perhaps it did slip my mind, Mame dulling," Vera said. "But you'd better make your change right away. It comes on right after the Arabian Nights number."

"Now see here, Vera," Auntie Mame said crossly, lighting a cigarette, "if I have to wear another one of those public monuments that I can hardly breathe in . . ."

"Not at all, dulling," Vera said, lifting the wig off Auntie Mame's head and substituting a towering headdress of jet beads and black monkey fur, "this outfit is coolness itself."

"That's good," Auntie Mame said. "Now just what do I have to do?"

"First of all," Vera said absently, "take off that brassière and put this one on. Same with your pants. Well, you simply wait until you hear the master of ceremonies call Vera Charles and . . ."

"I don't need fresh underwear, Vera," Auntie Mame began, "I put this on just before we . . ."

"Do stop chattering, Mame, and hurry," Vera said, unhooking Auntie Mame's brassière. "Turn your back, Patrick. Then you and the wolfhounds come down this long flight of stairs. . . . Now the pants, de-ah. Put these on. That's right. . . . Oh, there's also a page boy—this very nice unemployed juggler from Lyons—to carry your train. There! You look divine. Now for the train. Then you simply walk along the promenade that encircles the orchestra pit, go back onto the stage, smile, bow, and that's that."

Vera knelt down behind Auntie Mame and snapped a long train made of black monkey fur to the seat of her pants, if indeed that garment could be dignified by the term pants. It was flesh-colored net with a scattering of jet beads where jets were needed most. The brassière followed along the same general lines.

"And," Vera said, getting up, "*you* get to wear the *longest* train of anybody in the company. Not even the mannequins or the *danseuse nue* have anything that comes within two yards of yours."

There was a tap at the door.

"*Entrez*," Vera called.

The door opened and a morose young man came in. He was wearing gold pantaloons and a big gold turban trimmed with monkey fur. "Ah good," Vera said. "Here's your page boy. Good luck, dulling."

"But where's the rest of my costume?" Auntie Mame looked down at the considerable expanse of herself relieved only by the scattering of jet beads.

"Oh, I'm so glad you reminded me," Vera said. "Here are

Auntie Mame . . .

your gloves and here's your fan." Vera handed Auntie Mame a pair of long black gloves and a big fan made of monkey fur.

"*And?*" Auntie Mame said.

"And *what*, dulling?"

"Do you mean to stand there and tell me that this is *all* you expect me to wear? Well, Vera Charles, if you think I'm going out there in . . ."

"But, Mame," Vera said, "it's the most expensive costume in the whole finale. Real jets and genuine monkey fur. It's . . ."

"I don't care if it's made of the Missing Link. I'm not going out there practically naked with a totally strange unemployed juggler holding up my . . ."

"Oh," Vera said airily, "if *that's* all you're worried about, Patrick can do the train bit for you. Here you," she said to the page boy, "dis-robez. Strip. Shuck. Peel."

"Hey, listen," I began. But Vera had my shirt off and was plucking at my belt and the callboy was rapping at the door.

I CAN'T TO THIS DAY RECALL EXACTLY HOW EVERY-thing happened, but the next thing I knew, the six wolfhounds were pulling Auntie Mame, cursing and protest-ing, down the dressing-room stairs. I followed blindly behind in gold pantaloons, clutching at Auntie Mame's monkey-fur train with one hand and trying to get the gold turban out of my eyes with the other hand. The dogs dragged us up to the top of another flight of stairs. I heard Auntie Mame cry, "I won't go on. I'm damned if I . . ." A Romanian tenor was squealing something about Paree, *les belles de nuit*, something-something *cher ami*.

I got the turban out of my eyes just as the master of cere-monies called, "Mees Verah Sharl." The orchestra struck up "My Miss American Beauty." The dogs leaped forward. So did Auntie Mame. So did I.

... and the City of Light

As I say, the exact details elude me. I was blinded by the light and deafened by the applause. It was said that not since Josephine Baker appeared there ten years before had such an ovation been accorded any American star. But I wasn't thinking about ovations. I was thinking about sucking in my bare stomach and thrusting out my bare chest and not falling ass over elbow down those steps. They seemed longer than the stairs from the top of the Eiffel Tower but eventually my feet touched ground. The lesser stars had taken their bows and there was nothing now but for the counterfeit Vera Charles to make her circuit of the orchestra and call it a night.

The six wolfhounds—seasoned troupers, it seems—capered off across the footlights in smart single file and blazed a trail along the yard-wide runway that surrounded the orchestra pit. Auntie Mame followed, clutching their six leashes in one hand while with the other she flapped her big monkey-fur fan, trying ineffectually to cover as much of her torso as possible. I followed in the caboose, so to speak, the monkey-fur train leaving a gap of some fifteen feet between us.

The crowd rose to its feet, stamping and cheering and roaring its adoration. The air was thick with cries of "*Brava*" and "Vera." And from the first row I heard a voice shout, "Yo, Queenie! Take it off!"

And just then I saw a shooting stick thrust out onto the runway in front of Auntie Mame. "Look out, Auntie Mame!" I called.

It was too late.

The shooting stick caught Auntie Mame around the ankle. She paused. She faltered. She swayed. And then she plummeted down into the first row, dragging the wolfhounds with her, snarling and yelping at the ends of their leashes as her mask flew into the air. I followed, having been too stunned by the whole thing to let go of her train. In a second we were all struggling and thrashing there in the first row, Auntie Mame,

Auntie Mame . . .

Sascha, Jascha, Vanya, Pavel, Boris, Morris, and I in a hopeless tangle of dog hair and monkey fur. I heard Auntie Mame cry, "My God! It's *Dwight Babcock*!" Then she fainted.

That seemed like a splendid idea, so I pretended to faint, too. The crowd did the rest, for the French are fiercely loyal to their stars. With cries of "*Cochon*!" "*Brigand*!" "*Voleur*!" they fell upon Mr. Babcock and dragged him bodily from the theater. Opening one eye, I saw him being buffeted and pummeled all the way up the aisle. I hated Mr. Babcock like poison, but I didn't like to think of his being lynched.

BACK AT THE HOTEL VERA POLISHED OFF A TUMbler of cognac, yawned, and said she thought she'd turn in. It had, Vera allowed, been one hell of a day.

"Just a moment, Vera," Auntie Mame said, rubbing her bruised thigh, "there is a little favor I would like to have you do for me."

"Well, not tonight, de-ah," Vera said. "Openings take so much out of a star."

"Sit down, Vera," Auntie Mame said. "Before any of us goes to bed we are going to find out just which jail Mr. Babcock is in and then you and I are going to see him."

"Are you out of your mind, dulling?" Vera asked haughtily. "Just give me one good reason why I, a Great Star, should go to see some old masher who is, after all, your problem and not mine."

"I can give you an excellent reason, Vera," Auntie Mame said. "It is this: Mr. Babcock may or may not know that it was *I* who went on for *you* tonight. He can still take Patrick from me. I want you to go to him and assure him that it was you he pulled down into his nasty lap this evening."

"And if I refuse?" Vera asked haughtily, but not with her old confidence.

"If you refuse, Vera," Auntie Mame said calmly, "then Mr. Babcock will not be the *only* one to know just who was the Great Star tonight. I'll talk, Vera. I'll talk plenty. I'll talk to *Time, Life, Paris Soir,* Reuters, A.P., U.P., I.N.S.—I'll talk to anyone who'll listen and *you'll* be not only out of work, but also the laughingstock of . . ."

"That's *blackmail*!"

"I prefer to call it *quid pro quo*—a Latin term meaning that I did a big favor for you and now you're coming around to the lockup with me, Vera. *Or else!*"

HOUSED IN A SETTING NOT UNLIKE THE DUNGEON portrayed in the Folies-Bergère, Mr. Babcock was a piteous sight. He had been badly beaten up, his clothes all but torn off his back. He hurried eagerly to the wicket, but he recoiled when he found that his visitor was Auntie Mame, demure in black organdy without any pizazz whatever.

"Oh, it's you, you Jezebel," Mr. Babcock moaned.

"Jezebel indeed, Mr. Babcock," Auntie Mame said. "I have come on a mission of mercy after prevailing upon my dear friend Vera Charles to forgive you for your shocking lapse of this evening. And speaking of Miss Charles, Mr. Babcock," she added cattily, "I'd always understood that it was *Mrs.* Babcock who had the great crush on Vera. Not you."

"You know damned well that it was you up there on that stage tonight cavorting around without enough on to . . . You and that delinquent orphan brat of yours." He seemed a bit uncertain. Woozy, you might say.

"He's drunk," Vera snapped, "obviously drunk. Just who else do you think could replace *me*, you dirty old man?"

"Ohhhh," Mr. Babcock groaned. "If I was . . . if I was not myself this evening, it's because *you*, Mame Dennis Burnside, put something in my grape juice."

"Nonsense," Vera said harshly. "He was stinking. I smelled his breath myself when he dragged me off . . ."

"Drugged," Mr. Babcock said weakly, any conviction he may ever have had deserting him.

"La, Mr. Babcock," Auntie Mame said, waggling a coquettish finger through the wicket, "the days of the Borgias are long since dead. But, alas, the days of rapine, lust, and bestiality, I fear, are still with us—and in some very surprising circles. Can you think that I, a poor, lone widow, would have taken an innocent youth to a carnal display such as the one you attended—and all too conspicuously—this evening?"

"Gee, Mr. Babcock," I piped up, "Auntie Mame and I were even thinking of driving out to Neuilly for some real home-style peanut butter and those keen lantern slides."

"Indeed we were," Auntie Mame added, "and I have been heartsick at the prospect of having to tell poor Eunice of the disgrace brought upon her and her son—yes, and that peach of a couple, the Gilbreaths—by your conduct . . ."

Mr. Babcock's hysterical gibbering drowned out the rest of her message. Auntie Mame waited sadistically for his sobs to be stilled before she went on.

"But if you are not grateful, Mr. Babcock, for my willingness to stand staunchly behind your poor, deluded wife, you should at least thank me for begging Miss Charles to forgive you. And also, *not to press charges*."

"B-but . . ." Mr. Babcock stammered.

"Happily," Auntie Mame charged on, "Vera Charles is a true trouper with a heart of pure gold. What other woman would forgive you for mauling her, for disgracing her in public and for doing *this*"—dramatically Auntie Mame ripped the veil from Vera's hat and pointed to her swollen, discolored jaw. Mr. Babcock choked. "For doing *this*, Mr. Babcock, to a face that has been dear to drama lovers for the last half-century."

Vera bridled, but there wasn't much she could do.

"I—I left you at the American Express this afternoon," he said brokenly, "and I had this—this odd feeling. I stopped off in a—in some low saloon and ordered a drink of liquor and then—then . . . Well, everything went black. I . . ."

"That is indeed a sad story, Mr. Babcock," Auntie Mame said, holding up a pious hand, "but a squalid tale and one which I should not like you to relate before my innocent young ward. It is bad enough that a man of your Jekyll and Hyde character completely controls this poor orphan's inheritance, probably squandering his pitiable income on voices too vile to contemplate. So I will thank you to bear in mind that Patrick's *spiritual* welfare remains in *my* hands and I should not like his young mind polluted by any accounting of your disgusting fall from . . ."

"Please, please," Mr. Babcock said, a broken man. "I'll do anything you say."

"Ah, but there you are wrong, Mr. Babcock," Auntie Mame said. "It is not *you* who are here to help *me*, but *I* who have come to this sinkhole of drunks and criminals to help *you*. Now tell me," she said with honeyed venom, "wouldn't you like me to telephone Mrs. Babcock? Eunice must be wondering what can have hap . . ."

"Oh, no! *Please* no!"

"Very well then," Auntie Mame said. "Vera is not only willing to forgive you, but also to pay your fine. *Aren't* you, Vera?"

Vera looked as though she'd been struck by lightning at the very suggestion of parting with so much as a centime, but she said, "Yais," with icy grandeur.

"You will be released almost immediately, with no police record to blight your holiday among your friends the French. I have arranged for a limousine to take you out to the American Hospital at Neuilly. In an hour's time I shall call poor Eunice and tell her that you met with a motor accident while

Auntie Mame . . .

borrowing my car and that you can be found in the hospital. That will account for your deplorable physical appearance. Patrick and I are leaving Paris tomorrow and no one need ever be the wiser."

"I—I can never th-thank you," Mr. Babcock blubbered. I snickered. The sight of that self-righteous old bantam cock groveling before Auntie Mame was too much for me.

"Please don't be too affected by this simple show of loving kindness, Patrick," Auntie Mame said, patting my shoulder and giving me a sharp jab in the nape of the neck. "Life teaches us many lessons. *Many!* Ah, here comes the turnkey now to give you back your ill-earned freedom. Come, Mr. Babcock!"

THE CROWD AT THE FOLIES-BERGÈRE HAD BEEN A good deal rougher on Mr. Babcock than I had suspected. His shoes and socks and a bit of underwear remained to him, but not much else. He made a ludicrous spectacle out on the street. The night had turned cool and he shivered helplessly.

"You may see me to my car, Mr. Babcock," Auntie Mame said grandly. "Remember, this is the automobile you allegedly cracked up. A silver Panhard sedan. That's how the car was traced to me and how I was the first to be notified. Get in, Vera, Patrick. And would you just hand me that lap robe, my little love? Thank you."

She turned to Mr. Babcock and hung the robe around him. "Here, Mr. Babcock," she said, "this will help you cover your, um, *shame*. Your hired limousine is just behind." She got into the car and started the motor. Mr. Babcock looked like a very small Sitting Bull draped as he was in Auntie Mame's motor rug. I snickered again.

"Then Mr. Babcock," Auntie Mame said, "all is forgiven. Forgiven ... and ... *forgotten?*"

... and the City of Light

"Oh, y-yes," Mr. Babcock said, his teeth chattering. "But just one thing . . ."

"Yes, Mr. Babcock?" Auntie Mame said sweetly.

"Wh-what shall I do with your lap robe when I get to the hospital?"

"*Take it off!*" Auntie Mame shouted. With a roar the car raced up the silent street.

Auntie Mame in Court Circles

"SO AFTER ALL THOSE MUSEUMS AND GALLERIES and the French National Theatre what did the old maniac do with you?" Pegeen asked.

"Well," I said glibly, "Auntie Mame felt that Paris was getting too hot for her. I mean even in the early spring there are some real scorchers there. Not so much the heat, it's the . . ."

"Go on," Pegeen said.

"Well, so we went to London."

"What for?"

"To visit the Queen. Quite literally. Only it was a King and Queen then."

"Cut the comedy."

"I mean it. What trouble could anyone possibly get into in a staid old town like London. Besides," I added, "Auntie Mame has always moved in Court circles."

Unable to face the distraught mother, I went out to the pantry to step up my drink. The drink needed bolstering and so did I.

. . .

L ON D O N was *just* getting over Mrs. Simpson and the Coronation when Mrs. Burnside and the entourage checked into a suite at Claridge's. The entourage, by that time, consisted of Auntie Mame's best friend, Vera Charles, First Lady of the American Theater, who had collected so much money from the Folies-Bergère for indignities suffered there that it was easier not to work at all that summer—and, of course, me.

Auntie Mame had been to London many times before and knew quite a lot of people left over from the twenties. At that early age in history they had been called the Bright Young Things. But after a couple of Auntie Mame's Little Afternoons and Big Evenings—and a stern rebuke from the management—she had to confess that her companions of the past had not kept pace with the times. They were just middle-aged delinquents.

"Oh, my little love," Auntie Mame moaned from beneath her ice cap the day after her third Big Evening, "I'm afraid that I'm in the Wrong Set. My old friends are neither bright nor young any longer."

"Well, they were certainly trying," I said.

"*Trying?* Darling, they were *impossible*! Too Evelyn Waugh for words. No, Patrick, I have reached an age when there should be beauty and dignity in my life. I am no longer Madcap Mame, but Mrs. Beauregard Jackson Pickett Burnside, a widow—still young and attractive, perhaps—with a certain amount of wealth and position. I also have the crushing

Auntie Mame . . .

responsibility of guiding a young nephew through life and . . ."

"Don't worry about me, Auntie Mame," I said. "I'll be in college this fall and then you can go right on doing . . ."

"Don't interrupt!" Auntie Mame snapped, setting her ice cap down with a clatter. "As I was saying, these elderly Bright Young Things are wrong for me now. Wrong, wrong, wrong! Oh, we were all mad and gay ten years ago, but today—in the grim cold light of 1937—all those immature, hard-drinking, pleasure-crazed playmates of yesteryear seem too shoddy for words. Look at the way they've left this lovely room! Cigarette burns! Glasses overturned! That chandelier hanging by a thread! No, Patrick, my little love, England means to me beauty, dignity, serenity, a sense of the past. . . ."

Vera, who had been asleep on the sofa for some time, got up and lurched off toward her bedroom, last night's evening dress trailing raggedly behind her. Vera said a short but unprintable word and slammed the door.

"That," Auntie Mame said, "is exactly the sort of thing I'm talking about. It is not the sort of London society I wish to present to an impressionable young man such as you, darling. I wish *you* to know a more gracious England—a sovereign nation of rich tradition, of pomp and ceremony. And for that reason, my little love . . ." Auntie Mame paused dramatically and clapped the ice bag back on her head.

"Yes, Auntie Mame?"

"And for that reason, Patrick, *I* am going to be presented at Court."

WHENEVER AUNTIE MAME MADE UP HER MIND TO do something, she got it done in a hurry, and so she didn't waste any time at getting into Court circles. The first thing she did was to cable New York to have her Rolls-Royce and Ito, her Japanese houseman, shipped over on the *Queen Mary*. It seemed sort of like carrying coals to Newcastle to have a Rolls sent from America to England, and Ito drove so badly that I was a little worried about him in London traffic. But Auntie Mame said that the Rolls and Ito were a Family Tradition and that since Ito had always driven on the left-hand side of the street anyhow, he might find London his Spiritual Home.

The next thing Auntie Mame did was to get in touch with Lady Gravell-Pitt and then she *really* started moving.

Just where Auntie Mame ever found Hermione Gravell-Pitt I don't know—don't even like to contemplate. All I can tell you is that the day after Auntie Mame's great declaration I came back from a tour of the Abbey to find Auntie Mame and Lady Gravell-Pitt being arch and ladylike over tea, and I knew that Auntie Mame had entered a New Phase.

"Jewels," Auntie Mame was saying, "will be no problem, Lady Gravell-Pitt." She flashed her large uncut emerald ring and there was a discreet twinkle of rather good diamonds at her ears.

"Of cawss," Lady Gravell-Pitt said, her beady eyes taking in the considerable glory of Auntie Mame's rocks. Then she smiled broadly, and I was stunned by the saffron splendor of her teeth. There must have been sixty of them. Very long, very false, they were the color of old ivory set into gleaming titian gums, and for some time I could think only of the double keyboard of an antique harpsichord. "And since we're going to be such grand chums, my dear, you must call me Hermione—or even Hermie."

"Why, certainly, Hermione," Auntie Mame said, "and *you* must call *me* Mame."

"Of cawss, Mame," Hermione said with another ocher smile. "But have you a tiara?"

"Two," Auntie Mame said.

Auntie Mame ...

"A pity," Hermione said with a wistful little smile. "I have such a lovely one. Heirloom, of cawss, but I'd have let *you* have it for a song. Howsomever," she continued, touching her brassy gold-dyed long bob, "we must do something about your living quarters. I mean, as your social sponsor, I really couldn't permit you to live in an hotel." She gazed around Auntie Mame's suite at Claridge's as though it were the county workhouse. "Luckly, I *do* know a little jewel of a house right here in Mayfair which we can lease for the season and . . ."

"*We?*" Auntie Mame asked.

"Yais," Hermione said with a lackluster flash of dentures. "You, Miss Charles, your neview and *I*—all of us. Now, Lady Styllbourne is a chum of mine and so I *think* I could coax her to let you have it for a thousand guineas the mouth. Plus, of *cawss*, the servants' wages."

I tiptoed quietly off to my room as I heard Lady Gravell-Pitt saying, "Now if you will simply give me your check"—or cheque.

GRAND, I BELIEVE, IS THE TERM FOR THE LITTLE jewel of a house Auntie Mame had rented through Lady Gravell-Pitt. It was a vast marble mansion in Grosvenor Square, close enough to the American Embassy so that Auntie Mame could annoy her countrymen whenever she felt it necessary, yet far enough across the square so that they couldn't keep too careful an eye on her. Auntie Mame pronounced the house "divine" and the location "ideal."

Lady Gravell-Pitt, very much the chatelaine, met us at the door surrounded by a platoon of footmen. "Welcome, welcome, dear Mame! Patrick, dear! *Miss* Charles." Lady Gravell-Pitt did not care for Vera. "Now let me show you through our lovely, lovely new home. Your, um, *setting* as it were." She smiled her horrible crockery smile and said, "The perfect setting for a lovely Ameddican jewel."

Vera gagged.

Hermione led us between the ranks of flunkies and then guided us through a series of marble halls hung with Waterford chandeliers and dusty French tapestries and portraits of dead people. It was quite a place. Adam rooms opened into Chippendale rooms and Chippendale rooms opened into Heppelwhite rooms and Grinling Gibbons rooms and Regency rooms and Louis Quinze rooms and so on.

It wasn't very cozy, or even very clean, but Auntie Mame loved it. Eventually Hermione wound up her conducted tour in what she called "the sheerest Directoire conceit of a garden room" for tea. It was the cheeriest room in the house, which doesn't say much for it, and it did look out over a sooty little patch of greenery, in the center of which a marble Apollo displayed with undue pride a pitiful array of amputated parts.

"Now, Mame dear," Lady Gravell-Pitt said finally, with a vivacious clatter of dentures, "about your presentation of cawss, anyone with *my* connections could have you presented immeejitly...."

"Then why don't you?" Vera said.

"*But*"—Lady Gravell-Pitt held up an imperious hand—"the best way is the gradual approach. First a little series of cocktail parties, luncheons, dinners. That way you can become intimate with the cream of Court circles. Then I shall arrange to have you invited to a Royal Garden Party. And lastly, a full presentation at St. James's."

"How long do you think it will be?" Auntie Mame asked.

"And how *much*?" Vera said.

AUNTIE MAME'S SEASON BEGAN AT LUNCH THE NEXT day when a gaggle of dowdy gentry showed up at twelve sharp,

Auntie Mame ...

descended on the table like a flock of cormorants, and departed sharply at three. An hour and a half later, six more showed up to devour three large cakes, five platters of sandwiches, and I don't know how much tea. At eight o'clock a dozen more appeared in slightly soiled dinner clothes and tucked into an enormous dinner as though they hadn't seen food since the Diamond Jubilee. The rest of the week followed just about the same pattern, except that twice Auntie Mame was permitted to take Hermione's friends out to the theater, with dancing afterward at a supper club in which, I later discovered, Hermione had a slight financial interest.

I must say that none of Auntie Mame's myriad guests struck me as very attractive. They were mostly provincial English or superannuated White Russians with, as I now know, either minor or dubious titles. None of them was a minute under sixty and they were all related to Lady Gravell-Pitt. The women were given to whiskers and the men to rheumatism. They all dressed like something out of a rummage sale, and if *they* were the cream of Court circles, I felt awfully sorry for King George and Queen Elizabeth—"Bertie and Bessie," as Lady Gravell-Pitt called them in Auntie Mame's presence.

Nor did it seem to me that any of them was in much of a hurry to repay Auntie Mame's lavish hospitality with so much as a cup of tea. Vera noticed it, too. But Auntie Mame was so busy being the gracious hostess, while Hermione hovered around her, teeth clattering like castanets, that I guess she didn't have time to think about it. During the mornings, Hermione kept Auntie Mame occupied with learning the Court curtsy, which she demonstrated with a fearful wobbling and a crackling of joints that reminded me of someone eating peanut brittle. After the first lesson Auntie Mame could curtsy like a prima ballerina, so there wasn't much else for Lady Gravell-Pitt to do but invite her relatives to feed on out-of-season delicacies at Auntie Mame's table and to try to sell things to Auntie Mame. These included an elderly Daimler; a rather dented Queen Anne tea service; almost new liveries for the footmen; a crisp old ermine cloak, which she said—and there was no reason to doubt her—once belonged to Queen Charlotte; a dinner service for thirty-six in chipped Limoges; an emerald stomacher, size forty-two; a sorrel riding horse; a ruined abbey in Wales; and a Saint Bernard puppy.

After a week of living under the same roof with Lady Gravell-Pitt Vera began to crack, almost visibly. "Come in here," she said in pure Pittsburghese and with none of the unintelligible Mayfair accent she used on the stage.

I went into her bedroom and she closed the door.

It hadn't taken any crystal ball to see that Lady Gravell-Pitt rather looked down on Vera, although Vera was a Great Star and, even in London, more or less in a league with Gertrude Lawrence. "Theatah people, of cawss," Hermione always said, dismissing Vera with a brisk click of her uppers, as though Vera had been sentenced for importuning in Park Lane. And she displayed her scorn in such little ways as excluding Vera entirely from conversation, neglecting to introduce her to the cream of Court circles, seating her far below the salt, and placing her in the smallest, dingiest bedroom in the house while far nicer ones remained unoccupied.

"Well?" Vera asked pregnantly, helping herself to one of my cigarettes.

"Well, what, Vera?" I said.

"You know what, Patrick. This auction gallery she's living in. The toothless wonder. All those tatty old frauds who show up at mealtimes."

"Oh, you know Auntie Mame and her phases, Vera," I said. "She'll get over it in time. She just wants to be presented at Court. After that she'll be sick of all this and move on to something else."

Auntie Mame . . .

"Well, for Christ's sake," Vera said, "if she only wants to stick three feathers in her scalp and do a full curtsy, she could manage it easier than this. After all, Mame's a damned attractive woman, and a prominent one; *and a rich* one. The American ambassador's wife could have her presented in a *minute*." Vera fixed me with a cold green gaze. "I suppose you think that Lady Hormone doesn't *know* that Mame's the ninth-richest widow in New York. Why, she's taking poor Mame for such a ride that . . ."

"Oh, Auntie Mame's enjoying herself," I said. "She'd be going in for yoga or the Oxford Movement or the modern dance if she weren't so hipped on getting into Court circles."

"Court circles, my ass!" Vera said eloquently. "I've been playing royalty on the stage for the last fifteen years and if those old frumps are anything but down-and-out deadbeats, I'm Queen Mother Mary. Anyway, it isn't the principle of the thing, Patrick, it's the money. That bitch is going to bleed poor Mame for every penny she can get and then some. Why, Mame could rent Windsor Castle for what she's paying for this mausoleum, not to mention all those servants and all the free groceries she's passing out to Gravell-Pitt's poor relations."

"She's very generous," I said. "Extravagant, too."

"And yet," Vera said, "a couple of days ago when I, Vera Charles, her oldest and dearest friend, asked her if she wouldn't like to invest a few thousand pounds in this new play I'm considering for Cochran—and a beautiful, beautiful play, Patrick, you should *see* the clothes—Mame said she didn't think she could *afford* it. Fancy that, if you will. Never lost a nickel on one of my shows in her life and now she . . ."

"She must have been joking."

"She was not. Hermione's got the screws into her good and proper. Here *I* can work my ass off doing eight performances a week while that slob Hermione—a total stranger, if you please—wallows around in Mame's Rolls, orders the servants around, invites her dreary chums here, shuts *me* up in this maid's room. I tell you, Patrick, that woman is sinister."

I was so accustomed to Vera's outbursts against other women that, at first, I put her dislike of Lady Gravell-Pitt down to jealousy and didn't think much about it. But only a day or so later I began to see at firsthand that when it came to a quick deal, Hermione was next to none.

It all arose over the state of my clothes, which I had always considered neat if not flashy. "Of cawss, Mame dear," Hermione said, gazing at me as though I were a ragpicker, "I don't see how you expect Patrick to attend the bigger dinner parties and balls inadequately clad as he is."

I looked down to see if anything was undone, but my clothing was intact.

"Whatever do you mean, Hermie?" Auntie Mame asked absently.

"Ektualleh, Mame, a dinner coat is one thing, but for the really *gala* functions a tail coat, white tie, silk hat, opera cloak are *de rigueur*."

"An opera cloak?" Auntie Mame laughed. "That's too silly, my dear; Patrick's only seventeen."

"And, of cawss, for the Royal Garden Party, gray striped trousers, a cutaway, a gray topper . . ."

"Mmmmm. That *is* true," Auntie Mame said.

"Well, I suppose that if I really get invited to any of these things," I said, " I can just rent the outfits from Moss Brothers. What would I ever need with a gray . . ." The words died on my lips. If I'd suggested going naked, Lady Gravell-Pitt couldn't have looked more horrified.

"Moss Brothers!" she spat, "Really, Mame, it's quite difficult enough for me to bring Ameddicans out in the best London society. But even to consider *hired* clothing . . ."

"Oh, all right," Auntie Mame said reasonably. "He can

Auntie Mame . . .

always wear the evening clothes at college dances, and as for that Garden Party drag, I suppose he'll be an usher at someone's wedding someday. You might just run down to Dover Street, darling. I know a lot of beautifully turned-out men who have their clothes made at Kilgour, French and . . ."

"However," Lady Gravell-Pitt said, eying me, "I know a young duke—my cousin ektualleh—who is just Patrick's size. His suits would fit perfectly and I *think* I could get him to part with the lot for, um, for a hundred guineas." That seemed to take care of that.

Lady Gravell-Pitt was the sort of woman you dislike at first, but after you get to know her a little better you detest her. I got to know Hermione like a book, although I never overcame a sense of wonderment at her long, rawboned frame, the synthetic glory of her yellow hair and teeth. Somewhere between fifty and death, Hermie seemed to have been unduly influenced both by photographs of Lady Sylvia Ashley and some self-help article urging readers simply to emphasize their worst points. The final effect was pure Douglas Byng.

I could have forgiven Lady Gravell-Pitt her hideous physical appearance if only there had been somewhere in her makeup one kindly or generous instinct. But there was none. Hermione was one of those horrible women who make a true profession out of being a Lady. If she did not stoop to posing for face powders and cleansing creams it was because no cosmetic firm was insane enough to ask her. But I never once saw Hermione when she wasn't up to her eyeballs in a dozen little deals vaguely connected with being titled. For a fee she would get rich Canadian or Australian or American women presented at Court. At a slight consideration she could find you a dear little service flat in the West End or a duck of a house by the sea or a castle in Scotland. Hermie dealt in secondhand jewelry and silver, in used furs, in hastily cleaned ball gowns, in antiques and decorations, in household servants and social secretaries, in world cruises and sight-seeing tours of stately homes. She was delighted to lend—or rent—her name to new night clubs and restaurants, dress shops and art galleries; to anyone or anything willing to pay for the temporary use of her title. I don't *think* that she trafficked in narcotics or white slaves, but I'll bet that if I'd asked for a sniff of cocaine and a half-caste concubine, Hermione would have been on the telephone in a trice. *Service* was Hermie's byword, and, in her slightly soiled silks and satins, her frumpy furs and dirty diamonds, she looked as though she'd seen a great deal of it.

I couldn't understand just what Auntie Mame ever saw in Hermione, but on the other hand I was never too surprised by any of the fads or people my aunt picked up. Auntie Mame—who could be astonishingly astute about some people and equally gullible about others—almost reached the breaking point during Ascot Week when she learned that she hadn't been invited—nor apparently had Hermione—into the Royal Enclosure. Nor was Auntie Mame any too pleased when Vera, wearing more fox furs than the Queen herself, went sashaying off to Ascot on the arm of a naughty old duke.

"Of cawss, Mame, *nobody* nice goes to Ascot," Hermione tried to explain weakly.

"Oh, of course not!" Auntie Mame growled. "Just the King and the Queen and Queen Mary and the Duke and Duchess of Kent—trash like that!"

"And besides, Mame," Hermione said cloyingly, "you're entertaining the cream of Court circles at luncheon today."

"If they're in Court circles," Auntie Mame said, "why aren't they out at the Royal Enclosure with the *Court*? Why aren't Patrick and I? And, for that matter, why aren't *you*?" Auntie Mame said, and stamped off to her room.

After that I heard Lady Gravell-Pitt making several surreptitious and desperate-sounding telephone calls. In fact, all through the day, while Auntie Mame spread charm and caviar among the same old free loaders, Hermione was constantly excusing herself to make yet another urgent call.

Nor were the household tensions eased when Vera came back that evening with her duke, her winnings, and her impressive roster of great names with whom she had lunched alfresco or had tea or just gossiped. Vera was laying it on thick and said "Of cawss, I'm only an actress" three or four times. And when Hermione came into the room, after what must have been her hundredth urgent trip to the telephone, Vera pushed her duke forward and said, "But certainly you two must be aold, aold friends, so there's no need to introduce you."

The duke looked absolutely blank and Hermione looked as though she could have crawled under the rug.

The duke said, "Er, I—I don't believe . . ."

Hermione said, "Of cawss," with a dismal clack of her upper plate and excused herself once more in favor of the telephone.

The duke's title was very recent, Hermione explained later. He was no one, really.

But that night Lady Gravell-Pitt somehow managed to wangle invitations for Auntie Mame and me to the next Garden Party. She crowed with relief and pride as she raced in, flapping the envelopes aloft. Auntie Mame was delighted to think that at last she was getting somewhere in Court circles.

"There are only three, of cawss," Hermione said horridly. "I was so soddy not to have got one for Miss Charles."

"Thet's quate all raight," Vera said in her stage accent, "I've had mine for days."

THE DAY OF THE ROYAL GARDEN PARTY DAWNED unusually hot and humid. The household was in a furor. Maids scuttled up and down the corridors trailing freshly pressed dresses in their wake. Out in front, Ito polished first his buttons and then the Rolls, then the buttons again and once more the Rolls. There was even a little excitement in it for me with the arrival of my slightly used ducal clothes.

It was only when I tried to put the outfit on that I began to entertain serious doubts as to this particular tailor's superiority over Rogers Peet. The trousers were much too large and much too short. Held up with braces, as they had to be, they cleared my ankles by a good inch. If I let them down to reach the tops of my shoes, then a dazzling array of shirt front appeared between the trousers and my gray waistcoat, which happened to be so tight that all the buttons strained every time I breathed. The coat was short in the sleeves and narrow through the shoulders, but so large across the stomach that I was almost able to get it around me twice. The tie, however, was perfectly fine. I was still trying to discover a way to stand so that my new finery wouldn't look quite so grotesque when Auntie Mame called up to me from the garden.

"Patrick, my little love, do come down. We're just having a snack here before we go. It wouldn't do to be late."

"I—I'll be down soon, Auntie Mame," I said. "I just can't seem to get this suit right."

"Never mind, darling," she called, "come down and Vera and I will help you."

Auntie Mame and Vera and Lady Gravel-Pitt were preening themselves in the hot sunlight. Auntie Mame looked very Gainsborough in her pearls, a sweeping gown of ivory with parasol to match, and on her head a platter of nodding plumes in all the colors of sweetpea. Vera, too, looked dazzling, in a stagey sort of way, in mauve lace and, to be as one again with the Queen of England, several dozen fox pelts dripping from various parts of her. Lady Gravell-Pitt's costume had quite a lot of wrinkles and some indelible spots insufficiently covered with cameos.

Auntie Mame . . .

"Well," I said, stepping out bravely, "you're certainly all looking . . ." I couldn't go on. I stood there frozen beneath the awe-stricken stares of Auntie Mame and Vera.

Vera was the first to speak. "Jesus," she said, simply and succinctly.

"Patrick," Auntie Mame gasped, "what *are* you got up as? If you think this is a joke, you're . . ."

"It's my new suit," I said. "For the Garden Party. It just arrived."

"*New?*" Vera said. "*I* should live so long. Why, it's positively green with . . ."

"Really, Hermione," Auntie Mame said, "I *do* happen to know something about clothes, and this ridiculous getup is simply . . ."

"It's what all the best-dressed men in London are wearing," Hermione began, but even she wasn't able to bluff it through. One look from Auntie Mame and Hermione's statement trailed off and stopped with a dismal little click of her teeth.

"It's surely just some sort of mistake," Auntie Mame said. "Undoubtedly there's been some mix-up and Patrick has received the wrong package. This bedraggled old rag is certainly not the sort of thing that anyone would pay a hundred guineas for."

"A hundred guineas!" Vera said and whistled.

Lady Gravell-Pitt looked so crestfallen at being caught out in her shabby trick that I almost felt sorry for her. But she rallied and said, "Of cawss. It can all be straightened out tomorrow. But now we'd best be off. It wouldn't do to keep Bertie and Bessie waiting."

"Very well," Auntie Mame said. "Patrick, my little love, you'll just have to make do, somehow. Perhaps no one will notice."

"Maybe," I said dubiously. I put on my gray topper. It sank down to the bridge of my nose.

The traffic in London has always been bad, but on that particular Garden Party day it was so heavy that it took the better part of an hour to travel the last two blocks to the gates of Buckingham Palace. Nor were matters improved when Ito nicked a very old Daimler limousine and crumpled the fender of the Peruvian Ambassador's Packard. By the time we got there the temperature in the car was about ninety and the humidity was unbearable.

Never having been to a Royal Garden Party before or since, I have no similar function with which to compare this. But the only difference I could see between the Royal Garden Party and a giant rally at Yankee Stadium is that Yankee Stadium has rest rooms and it's easier to get refreshments. We got into the receiving line behind several hundred thousand overdressed people and began inching forward in a long serpentine queue toward the marquee where the Royal family received. An hour went by and we were still standing. Vera was the first to crack. "To hell with it," she said, and went off to join some people she knew. In fact, it seemed to me that Vera knew a lot more people in Court circles than Lady Gravell-Pitt did. Every two or three minutes someone with a most impressive title would spot Vera standing on line and barge up to greet her, whereupon Vera would introduce us all around.

Lady Gravell-Pitt, on the other hand, would just caw, "Oh, there's the Marquess of Something or the Duchess of Somethingelse," and wave frenetically, only to receive the blankest of stares. But Auntie Mame was too pleased to be there, and too happy chatting with Vera's gay friends to notice.

Another hour went by and we were not much closer to our goal. However, the sun had disappeared behind a cloud and there was quite a breeze. "Thank God for a little relief from this heat," Auntie Mame said. I agreed with her whole-

Auntie Mame . . .

heartedly, but I noticed that quite a few people began casting nervous glances toward the heavens.

Still the line moved on. But now the breeze became a wind. The long filmy skirts of the women's dresses fluttered nervously, and more than one picture hat was sent skimming across the lawn.

"Oh, dear," Lady Gravell-Pitt began, "I do hope that it's not going to . . ." Her words were drowned out by a terrible clap of thunder. The wind mounted to gale velocity and I could feel the tails of my coat flapping out behind me. Lady Gravell-Pitt's dowdy flowered georgette skirts were caught in a gust that sent them flying up to her waist, thus affording all of smart London a grisly view of the largest feet and the thinnest shanks in the whole British Empire.

Then the rains came. Gently at first, in big, splattering drops, and then more wildly, whipped into a foam by the wind. Several men who had had the foresight to bring umbrellas chivalrously put them up to protect their ladies, but those that didn't turn inside out instantly were wrenched free of their owners' hands to go bouncing and bumping across the grass. The marquee above their Britannic Majesties flapped wildly and there was a definite feeling of exodus among the guests.

A procession of shrill debutantes ran shrieking past us, hair plastered to their skulls, their white lawn dresses clinging to them like winding sheets. The lawn was now a morass of hats and umbrellas with people dashing every which way, stumbling, slipping, falling, and bumping into one another. I let go of my own hat just long enough to have a minor monsoon sweep it into the air. It landed just under the foot of a bishop who was hell-bent on getting to shelter.

Then it happened. There was a long, low rumble, a flash, a crash, and a blinding something that hit the earth nearby with the force of a blockbuster. I heard somebody shout, "Oh, my God, it got Sir Hubert!" And then the crowd dispersed in real earnest. No British reserve about it. It was every man for himself and devil take the hindmost.

Hermione bolted like a steer. I called out, "Auntie Mame!" and reached forward to take her arm, but I was knocked flat by the Dowager Marchioness Somebody. I was joined on the ground by a woman in blue who assured me that this sort of thing never happened in Capetown. We wallowed helplessly in the muddy grass for a moment, and by the time we were back on our feet there was no sign of Auntie Mame. It was raining so hard that it was almost impossible to see anybody.

Auntie Mame's rakish Rolls-Royce town car usually stood out in any crowd, with its sleek black paint job, its polished rivets and silver wire wheels, the jaunty angles of its squared-away corners. But at a Royal Garden Party it was just one among hundreds of big black cars. The chauffeurs weren't having any too easy a time of it, either. Engines, thoroughly inundated from the cloudburst, refused to start; sodden *grandes dames* in soggy finery screamed like fishwives for their cars, but to little avail. The few cars that were operating sloshed and skidded on the pavement, sending up huge sprays of water. The collapse of the Axis was only narrowly averted when the German embassy's big Mercedes-Benz locked bumpers with the Italian embassy's Isotta-Frascini.

It simply was not Ito's element. In fact, Ito was nowhere to be seen. Lightning struck again, somewhere on the Palace grounds, and the panic reached a fever pitch. At that point I decided to trust to luck and public transportation. I raced out into the road and jumped onto the first bus that came along. It had gone several miles before I realized that it was headed straight for Putney.

SOME TWO HOURS LATER I ARRIVED AT AUNTIE Mame's house via bus, tube, and taxicab. Although the rain had finally stopped, Grosvenor Square was under a foot of water. A sporty open car was parked in front of Auntie Mame's door.

I let myself into the house and slogged across the porphyry floor, my shoes squishing with every step. The vast marble rotunda was dark and empty, with none of Auntie Mame's rented footmen doing their usual sentry duty. Feeling that I was the only one who hadn't gone down with the Royal family, I called out, "Anybody home?" but without much hope.

Then I heard Auntie Mame, sounding unusually chipper. "Is that you, my little love? I'm in the garden room."

I sloshed back to the garden room and, through the gloom, made out Auntie Mame's silhouette. She was curled up on the floor in front of the fireplace with a drink in her hand.

"Some picnic," I said.

"Wasn't it just, darling?" she said. "I can't remember *when* I've had more fun."

"*Fun?*" I said.

"Oh, and darling, I'd like you to meet Captain Fitz-Hugh. Basil, this is Patrick Dennis, my nephew, my ward, my life. Patrick, this is Captain Fitz-Hugh."

"Is there somebody else in here?" I asked. "The place is as black as . . ."

"Oh, of course, my little love. I hadn't even noticed. Do turn on a light."

I switched on a lamp and there, looming above me, was about seven feet of Coldstream Guardsman. "Hahjudu?" he said, grasping my hand firmly.

As I said, Captain Fitz-Hugh was very tall. He had red-brown skin, red-brown hair, red-brown eyes, and a red-brown mustache. That he was extremely well built was abundantly evident, for he was wearing only my old blue dressing gown, with "St. Boniface Academy, Apathy, Mass." embroidered over the heart. The robe was too small even for me, and from it several yards of Captain Fitz-Hugh's well-turned legs, splendid forearms, and muscular chest were shown off to almost too much advantage. Except for his English accent and the mustache, Captain Fitz-Hugh reminded me of Auntie Mame's late husband, Beauregard Burnside, and in a rare flash of intuition, I sensed Something was Afoot.

"Captain Fitz-Hugh valiantly rescued me from the Garden Party this afternoon. I couldn't find you or Vera or Hermione or Ito or the car. Indeed," she said, with a silvery little laugh, "if it hadn't been for the captain and his adorable little car, I should probably still be treading water at Buckingham Palace." She gathered her skirts demurely around her and for the first time I noticed that she was wearing a very special velvet negligee Molyneux had designed for her. Auntie Mame had always said that it had more pizazz than *anything* she owned.

Auntie Mame got to her feet and executed a little whirl to show off even better her trim ankles and the glory of Captain Molyneux. Captain Fitz-Hugh was most appreciative. "Now, my little love, you must run upstairs and get into some dry things. You'll find Captain Fitz-Hugh's clothes drying in front of the fire in your bedroom. I knew you wouldn't mind. Oh, and would you just stick your head in the kitchen and ask for some more boiling water. Captain Fitz-Hugh and I are warding off pneumonia with hot toddies and I suggest you do the same. Don't be long, dear." As I made for the service hall, I could hear Auntie Mame's tinkling laugh and Captain Fitz-Hugh's genial chuckle and I received the distinct impression that Auntie Mame's Season was beginning to look a lot brighter.

Auntie Mame . . .

WHEN I WENT BACK DOWN TO THE GARDEN ROOM I
found Auntie Mame curled up on the sofa, a full glass in her
hand, regaling the captain with carefully chosen anecdotes
from her colorful past, while the captain chuckled intimately
from close, but discreet, range. Captain Fitz-Hugh had been
to America, which he described as "ripping," knew some of
the people Auntie Mame knew, whom he called "smashing,"
and admired her negligee by labeling it a "bit of all right." It
looked like one of those situations where three can be a crowd
and I was about to tiptoe out when the crowd was increased
by the entrance of Lady Gravell-Pitt.

If Hermione had looked awful before the Garden Party, she
was beyond adjectives now. Her dress was soaked, the colors
running hideously into one another. It was also torn and
splattered with mud and had shrunk so that the hem line
barely covered her bony knees. Her fusty ostrich boa hung like
wet seaweed. Her hat was missing entirely and the tarnished
gold of her dyed hair dangled in long, soggy ropes to her
shoulders.

"*Well!*" Hermione roared, charging in, her teeth in a chat-
ter. "I see that *you* managed to get home safe and . . ."

"Hermie!" Auntie Mame said genially. "I do hope that you
were able to find Ito and the car. Lady Gravell-Pitt, Captain
Fitz-Hugh."

The captain bowed to Hermione although she barely nodded in his direction. Then, looking down at his bare legs, he
said he'd chance getting back into his clothes if I'd show him
the way to my room.

When I returned, Lady Gravell-Pitt was haranguing Auntie
Mame for all she was worth.

". . . bad enough," Hermione was shouting, "to desert me at
an important Royal function. But to come back with a totally
strange man . . ."

"Isn't he divine looking, Hermione?" Auntie Mame said. "And that heavenly voice."

"He's probably some little nobody from some Colonial regiment," Hermione stormed.

"No, he's with the Coldstream Guards," Auntie Mame said dreamily. "But he's been released or set free or on a sabbatical or whatever they call it. And marvelous shoulders."

That stopped Hermione for a moment, but she took a deep breath and started in again. "Well, do get rid of him before any of *my* people come to dinner. In Court circles it does not pay to . . ."

"Oh, Hermie, I'm so sorry. But I've called off the dinner party, owing to the bad weather. In fact, Captain Fitz-Hugh has asked me to dine with *him*—just the two of us."

"Mame! Do you mean to say that you're leaving us for some nobody who . . ."

Hermione's speech was cut short by the reappearance of Captain Fitz-Hugh, looking very much like Somebody. And she was further put to flight when Vera came in with yet another duke, who fell upon Captain Fitz-Hugh as though they were long-lost brothers. It was simply not Lady Gravell-Pitt's day.

Auntie Mame was out awfully late with Captain Fitz-Hugh. I know, because I heard a terrible crash out in the street at half past three that morning and looked out to see that Ito had run into the captain's water-logged sports car as he brought Auntie Mame home. But I heard her say, "That's all right, Ito," and watched her bidding a long farewell to the captain.

The next morning there was almost a scene in the big marble rotunda. It was about eleven o'clock and I was up in my room sending post cards of the Houses of Parliament and the Changing of the Guard back to America when I heard the doorbell ring. Looking down from my window I saw Captain Fitz-Hugh, done up to the nines in his Guards uniform and carrying what must have been twelve dozen white roses. Since Auntie Mame was still asleep, naturally, I started down the stairs to make the captain feel at home, if such a thing were possible in that tomb of a house. But Lady Gravell-Pitt got there first.

I hadn't even rounded the bend in the stairway when I heard her nastiest tone of voice echoing in the rotunda. "Gud mawning, Leff-tenant," she said horridly. "I'm so soddy to say that Mrs. Burnside is *not* at home."

"Oh?" Captain Fitz-Hugh said dismally. "She said that I might call . . ."

"Of cawss," Lady Gravell-Pitt said. I peered down the stair well and saw her standing there, flanked with footmen so that she looked like the Notre Dame backfield. "Mrs. Burnside was called away, to Colchester in fact. And I'm teddibly afraid that she won't be back until late this . . ."

I knew that Auntie Mame saw something very special in the captain and I was just about to go down and say that Lady Gravell-Pitt was lying in her teeth. Happily, Ito did it for me.

"Oh, no, major," Ito said, "you come in. You sit. Missy Burnside back already. I drive velly fast."

"Capital!" the captain said.

I didn't hang around to see or hear any more of Hermione. Instead, I raced into Auntie Mame's room and snatched the sleep mask from her eyes.

"Wake up, Auntie Mame," I said. "Wake up. He's here."

"Wh-who's here?" she said, blinking owlishly in the morning sunlight."

"He," I said. "Hhhhhhhim!"

"You make it sound like the second coming," she snapped. "And what's more, I don't care if it is. How *dare* you come pounding into my room in the middle of the night, waking me out of a sound . . ."

"But it's Captain Fitz-Hugh!"

"For God's sake, why didn't you *tell* me, child?" she said, bounding out of bed. "Now go down and keep him company while I get dressed."

Sitting in the gloomiest of the Chippendale rooms under the beady eye of Lady Gravell-Pitt, the captain seemed almost overjoyed to see me.

"Mrs. Burnside will be right down," I said in my best manner. "Cigarette, sir?" I added, showing him how worldly I was.

Captain Fitz-Hugh and I then had a conversation suitable to a growing boy. We discussed boarding schools (he had gone to Eton) and colleges (Oxford). Hermione didn't seem very pleased to hear any of this. Then Auntie Mame, who could change her clothes faster than a fireman when pressed for time, swept into the room in a cumulus cloud of chiffon. "Basil, my dear," she said, "how good of you to come for elevenses. Patrick, be a love and ring for Ito."

"I do hope you'll be able to have lunch with me," the captain said.

"Oh, but I'd adore . . ."

"What a pity, Mame dear," Hermione said, "but of cawss you're having luncheon here today for . . ."

"Oh, no," Ito said, appearing in the doorway. "I telephone everybody and say no lunch party today. Missy Burnside have to go to Colchester. Also no tea party, no cocktail party, no dinner party. Velly far, Colchester."

Hermione said something that sounded like "Awk!" and marched out of the room. Soon afterward, Auntie Mame did another quick change and went off to lunch, and later in the day still another change before the captain showed up in spectacular evening attire to take her out for a night on the town. And as Auntie Mame flew down the stairway, dazzling in diamonds, I knew that she had that Old Feeling again.

I was dressing for dinner, as was the custom of the house, when Vera burst into my room.

"Why, Patrick, what pretty legs," she said, handing me a glass of brandy.

"Is it your habit to burst into men's rooms?" I asked, stepping into my trousers.

"Frankly, yes," Vera said. "And besides, this is about the only place in the house where we can talk without old horse face snooping around. Here's how."

"Cheers," I said.

"Well, isn't it divine?"

"Isn't what divine, Vera?"

"*It*, stupid. Mame and Basil. I tell you, Patrick, I've done twenty-four hours' intensive research on him and the news *couldn't* be better. Rich as the Bank of England—richer, really. Forty-one. Single. *Not* queer. Knows everyone. Related to half of Debrett. And he's an Hon., hon!"

"He's a *what*?"

"He's an *Honourable*, honey. His family have been the earls of Upshot ever since Ethelred or somebody like that. And Basil's the only son. That means *he'll* have the title when his father cools—and there won't be too long to wait since the old fool's nearly ninety and can't live forever—so that Mame will be a lady! Our Mame and a belted earl!"

"Not so fast, Vera," I said. "He hasn't asked her yet."

"Oh, but he will. They're already making book on it at his club. And as for Mame, I haven't seen her this way since poor Beauregard was alive."

RATHER THAN SIT AROUND AND TALK TO LADY Gravell-Pitt, I turned in early that night with a copy of *Gone With the Wind* and I got so fascinated with it that Atlanta was being burned to the ground before I realized that it was almost four o'clock. I turned off the lights and was raising the window when I saw a car coming up the wrong side of South Audley Street and I knew it could only be Ito. Sure enough. The car stopped at our door and Auntie Mame and Captain Fitz-Hugh stepped out. They were both laughing and then he kissed her for a long, long time before she ran gaily into the house.

It seemed to me that as long as I was awake anyhow, we might have one of our Little Morning Chats and I could tell Auntie Mame all the interesting things Vera had found out about the captain. I opened my door just in time to hear Hermione's voice vaulting up the rotunda. "I want a word with you," she said.

"Oh, Hermione, it's so late," Auntie Mame sang. "Won't it keep?"

"No, it won't," Lady Gravell-Pitt said peevishly. "Come into the library where we won't be disturbed."

"At this hour, who'd want to disturb . . ." But the door shut on what Auntie Mame was saying.

I put on my robe and waited. Then I got tired of just waiting and picked up *Gone With the Wind* again. Hermione must have had quite a lot of words for Auntie Mame because Scarlett was saying she'd never be hungry again when I heard Auntie Mame finally coming up the stairs.

I opened my door and stepped out into the corridor. Auntie Mame was coming up the stairs all right, but it wasn't the same woman who had flitted down them earlier that evening. Auntie Mame looked tired and haggard and old and I felt that she was fighting back the tears.

"Auntie Mame . . ." I began.

"What are you doing up at this hour?" she snapped. "I won't have you prowling around all night, do you hear?

Now go to bed this instant!" Her bedroom door slammed behind her.

THE NEXT DAY HERMIONE GRAVELL-PITT WAS BACK in the saddle. People—Hermione's people—were expected for luncheon and tea and dinner, and Hermione twittered grimly about the house all morning bullying the servants over all the arrangements.

Auntie Mame didn't come down until it was almost time for luncheon. She looked pale and sad and as though she'd slept very little. Almost as if it had been prearranged, Hermione summoned all the servants and lined them up in the rotunda. And then Auntie Mame addressed them. "This is to tell you," she said, "that if a Captain Basil Fitz-Hugh calls, either in person or on the telephone, and asks to speak to me, he is to be told that I am out."

"*And . . .*" Hermione prompted.

"And," Auntie Mame said miserably, "any of you who gives him any information will—will be dismissed forthwith."

Just then the doorbell rang and Auntie Mame's hand flew to her heart. Three footmen started for the door, but the butler did it. "Mrs. Burnside is out," I heard him say and the door closed with an imposing thump. Auntie Mame started for the window, but Lady Gravell-Pitt said imperiously, "That is all. You may go." And then she said, "Come, Mame. We'll wait for our guests in the Adam room."

All that day and the next and the next Auntie Mame moved like an automaton among the same old deadbeats Hermione kept inviting in. She seemed neither to see nor hear them, which was, in a way, to be envied.

Poor Captain Fitz-Hugh never gave up coming around to the house and he telephoned nine or ten times a day. Knowing that Auntie Mame couldn't very well fire me, I always tried to get to the door or to one of the extension telephones and was always beaten to it by one of the servants. So Auntie Mame moped. Vera moped. I moped. Ito moped. Only Lady Gravell-Pitt seemed to be enjoying herself.

On the fourth day I discovered Auntie Mame alone in the garden and so I tackled her. "Auntie Mame," I said, "why can't Captain Fitz-Hugh come here any more?"

"Ah, my little love," she sighed, "that's a long story."

"I've got lots of time."

"Ah, but you wouldn't understand."

"I might. At least I could try."

"Very well. It's simply this. It seems that I've picked a bounder—an utter rotter. Isn't that enough for you?"

"But, Auntie Mame," I said, "some of your best friends have been bounders—utter rotters. Besides, I don't believe it for a minute. Who told you this, anyhow?"

"H-Hermione. She—she said that if people in Court circles ever found out that I was—was going about with him, then I'd—I'd never be presented. She said I'd have to choose between my—my presentation and B-Basil."

"But, Auntie Mame," I said, "what do you care about the silly old presentation? Besides, it seems to me that the captain is a lot more aristocratic than old Lady Gr . . ."

"You wretched little ingrate," Auntie Mame said, her eyes blazing behind the brimming tears. "Here I'm sacrificing everything for you and that's the way you talk. Don't ever speak to me again!" With that she flounced off into the house.

I was so stunned by Auntie Mame's performance that I thought I'd better get out of that madhouse. I took off through the mews out in back of the house. When I reached the street, the first person I saw was Captain the Honourable Basil Fitz-Hugh, armed with white roses and looking as

Auntie Mame . . .

though he were about to shoot himself. It was an embarrassing social encounter.

"G-good morning, Captain Fitz-Hugh," I said.

He dropped the roses and grabbed both my arms as though he were drowning. "Patrick," he said brokenly, "I've got to know. Why? Why won't your aunt see me? What have I done? I haven't been able to eat, to sleep."

A minute later he had propelled me into a taxicab and we were on our way to his club for a man-to-man luncheon. It was a very elegant club, but kind of a lousy meal.

Lulled, however, by a great deal of gin and lime, and feeling very sorry for the captain as he sobbed into his whisky, I became less and less evasive in my answers to his questions and finally broke down and told him all.

"She does like you, Captain Fitz-Hugh," I said. "She likes you a lot. But you see, Auntie Mame wants very much to come out."

"To come out?" he said.

"Well not exactly come out. She did that way back in . . . well, several years ago. But she's really doing it for me. She thinks I should see London society at play."

"What a ghastly sight," the captain said.

"It certainly is," I agreed. "But Lady Gravell-Pitt says . . ."

"Who *is* this old dragon, Lady Gravell-Pitt?"

"Well, nobody seems to know. It's just that Auntie Mame wants to be presented at the Court of St. James's and . . ."

"But, my dear boy," the captain said, "nothing could be simpler. My old aunt could do it. Or my sister. Or the American ambassador's wife. Or any of a dozen . . ."

"Yes, I know," I said. And for once I actually felt embarrassed for Auntie Mame. "But it seems that Lady Gravell-Pitt has been, um, *engaged* to present Auntie Mame at the next . . ."

"But that's impossible!"

"Wh-why?" I said. "Auntie Mame's very well bred, most of

the time, and she's never been divorced and not in very *many* scandals. Actually, she's considered rather social back home."

"But I mean she's not even on the list."

"The list?"

"Well, you see," Captain Fitz-Hugh said, "I happen to be one of the King's equerries—albeit junior . . ."

"Equerry?" I said. "Junior?"

"Quite," he said. "It's rather a foolish post, but we do know everything that's going on at the Palace. In fact, I'm rather helping to run off the next herd of old cows—if you'll forgive me—right after we get the debs presented. The list is all drawn up." He reached into his breast pocket and hauled out an alphabetical list of names, all very official looking.

I scanned the list quickly. It read something like "Aponyi, Countess László; Argenta, Señora Juan Carlos María-Jesus; Atterbury, Mrs. Edward; Bechstein, Mrs. Julio; Bliss, Mrs. Erskine; Capehart, Mrs. Farnsworth . . ." There was no mention of Mrs. Burnside, nor, in the list of ladies who were serving as sponsors, of Lady Gravell-Pitt.

"Gee," I said, "Auntie Mame will be brokenhearted. Once she starts something she . . ." Then a brilliant idea struck me. "I'll bet *you* could arrange it, couldn't you?" I said.

"It would be most highly irregular," the captain said primly.

"But I'll bet you could, couldn't you? Especially if you wanted to see Auntie Mame again?"

"Well, I hardly . . ."

"And there's that aunt you were talking about—or your sister . . ."

FIFTEEN MINUTES LATER WE WERE SITTING IN THE drawing room of a mammoth house in Belgrave Square and

Auntie Mame . . .

the Hon. Basil's aunt, Griselda, Lady Spavin, was saying "Gravell-Pitt, Gravell-Pitt? I do seem to remember some most unwholesome tale about her but . . ."

"My aunt has a fantastic memory for these things," the captain said to me.

"Well, I shan't have, Basil, if you don't stop interrupting my stream of thought," Lady Spavin said. She'd already gone through Burke's without finding the name. Not that it really mattered, for the captain was obviously the apple of her eye and she'd agreed to take Auntie Mame under her wing sight unseen. It was just that she was so old I was afraid she wouldn't last long enough to get Auntie Mame through her curtsy, and Court was in session, so to speak, that night.

Griselda, Lady Spavin, had kicked up quite a fuss telling the captain how irregular it was to slip in an extra name on the list, but while she was fussing and fuming and saying that this never would have been countenanced in dear Queen Victoria's reign, Captain Fitz-Hugh had already telephoned the Palace to announce that a ghastly error had been made in overlooking a Burnside, Mrs. Beauregard Jackson Pickett, of New York City and her sponsor The Lady Griselda Spavin. Since his aunt seemed to cut quite a lot of ice in posh circles the list had been amended without a murmur.

"Gravell-Pitt," Lady Spavin said, jabbing a needle into her embroidery rack. "It seems to me that some sort of sordid case came up in Jubilee Year. . . . No, not Jubilee Year, for that was the year poor Spavin took sick and died at Heaves."

"Her husband, my Uncle Alister," the captain said to me in a whispered aside. "Very draughty, Heaves."

"Or was it the year when the Queen—by that I mean Queen Mary—began her *gros-point* carpet? Ah, yes, it all comes back to me now. I'd come into town from Heaves to match some wool, for I was just finishing the needlework seats for the chairs in the dining room at Heaves. Basil, do take this young man down to the dining room and show him the chair seats. It's so damp in the house at Heaves that I've had them moved in."

"Please, Aunt Griselda," the captain said, "do try to remember."

"But, of course, I remember perfectly, Basil. Don't be such a goose. There were thirty-six William and Mary chairs and I'd got to the last seat cover—birds of paradise on an off-white ground—when to my vast annoyance I found that I hadn't got any more blue left. Nor could I find the correct shade at the little draper's in Heaves Priory. A sweet shop. Pure Cotswold but woefully understocked. So, since I found that I'd got to come into London, I'd decided to take the nine o'clock train from Heaves Priory, which gets into Charing Cross Road at . . ."

"Aunt Griselda, *please*. Lady Gravell-Pitt. *Hermione Gravell-Pitt!*"

"Basil, dear boy, if you would only stop interrupting. So I'd got this blue wool from a little shop in Oxford Street, which has far nicer wool and much cheaper than . . ."

"*Grrrravell-Pitt!*" Captain Fitz-Hugh said.

"Exactly, Basil. But when I came out of the little shop in Oxford Street it had started to rain and, whilst I had my umbrella, I was afraid that the rain would soak through the paper sack and spoil the wool, for blue, as you know, has a dreadful tendency to fade . . ."

"Aunt Griselda, please . . ."

"And so," she continued holding up an imperious hand, "I bought the first newspaper I could find—oh, one of those dreadful tabloids—to wrap up my wool. And then, as luck would have it, a taxi put a man down right in front of me. So I got into the taxicab and came back here. But I couldn't help noticing this frightful scandal all over the front page of the paper."

"About Gravell-Pitt?"

Auntie Mame . . .

"But, of course, dear boy. In any event, I was to lunch with Maude Brockway-Teal at Gunter's, so I put the blue wool, paper and all, away. Then we talked for so long that I was afraid I'd miss my train and went directly to the station, leaving the wool here, only to find when I'd got back to Heaves that I'd really got *plenty* of blue wool, which I'd mislaid in the morning room. (The morning room at Heaves faces north and is consequently very dark.) So I needn't have come to London at all."

"But what did the story *say*?" Basil said, his face working dramatically.

"How should I know, dear boy? I don't interest myself in such tittle-tattle. However, the newspaper *and* the blue wool are right there in my sewing table."

"D'you mean you *have* the paper?"

"But, of course, dear boy. 'Willful waste means woeful . . .' Basil! Do be careful with my sewing table. You'll mix up all the colors!"

Basil snatched out an old London tabloid that was as yellow as Lady Gravell-Pitt's teeth, and with it some blue wool, which, as Lady Spavin said, *had* faded. Right there on the front page was a photograph of Hermione, teeth grinning eerily from beneath a cloche hat, and a headlined feature article reading:

PARK LANE 'PEERESS'
CALLED CONFIDENCE WOMAN

'Lady' Hermione Gravell-Pitt, of 25 Park Lane, née Beryl Green, was formally charged with operating a confidence game today . . .

The story went on to say that a certain Mrs. Schwarz of Durban, South Africa, had been bilked out of £25,000 by Lady Gravell-Pitt with the promise of being presented at Court. It went on to say (continued on page 6) that Lady Gravell-Pitt had a most unsavory record, describing some of her shadier deals both in the business and social worlds, and it added that she wasn't a Lady at all, having been divorced by Mr. Nigel Gravell-Pitt some years before he had been knighted for conspicuous archaeological work in the ruins of Kush. (So that explained where Hermione had found her teeth.)

"If I may borrow this newspaper and your list," I said to Captain Fitz-Hugh, "I think you can see Auntie Mame very soon. In about an hour, in fact."

I RACED INTO THE HOUSE IN GROSVENOR SQUARE just as the last of Hermione's rag, tag, and bobtail were leaving, replete with chocolate éclairs and tea sandwiches.

"Where's Auntie Mame?" I asked Hermione.

"She's resting in her room and does not wish to be disturbed," Hermione said, giving me a big insincere ocher-colored smile. "Where have you been all day?"

"In Court circles, Beryl," I said, bounding up the stairs.

"I thought I told you not to speak to me," Auntie Mame said tearfully from her big canopied bed.

"Come off it," I said. "Get out your white evening gown and your feathers—you're being presented tonight."

"Did Hermione finally arrange it?" Auntie Mame said, sitting bolt upright.

"Hermione didn't have a damned thing to do with it," I said. "Now, dry your eyes and take a look at this. Then give me Beryl's—I mean Hermione's—dinner list for tonight and I'll call off the wolves."

HALF AN HOUR LATER AUNTIE MAME DESCENDED looking stately and serene in her white brocade Court gown,

Auntie Mame ...

her diamonds flashing. As she reached the bottom step, the doorbell rang.

"That will be Basil," I said, looking at my watch.

One of the footmen stepped forward, but Auntie Mame said, "I will answer the door myself, thank you." She did, and Captain the Honourable Basil Fitz-Hugh stepped in, wearing his decorations. He didn't say anything. He just took Auntie Mame in his arms. It was that way that Lady Gravell-Pitt found them.

"Well, I must say that this is a pretty picture," Hermione said.

"One of the most beautiful in the world," Auntie Mame said coldly.

"But your dinner guests. What about the party?"

"The party's over, Beryl. I'm being presented tonight."

"What?"

"I said I am being presented at the Court of St. James's. Tonight."

"B-but, Mame," she spluttered, her dentures dancing, "I haven't had a chance to make any arrangements. These things take . . ."

"I feel certain that you have not made any arrangements, Beryl. And what is more, you are not going to have a chance to do any further arranging. Here is your copy of the Court Circular," she said, handing Lady Gravell-Pitt the yellowed tabloid. "I believe that the only court you've ever really known is the Old Bailey."

"That's a hot one, Auntie Mame!" I said. Basil chuckled with a certain self-conscious embarrassment.

"B-but, Mame, I can . . ."

"You can go upstairs, get a few things together, and leave this house tonight," Auntie Mame said. "I'll have your baggage sent to you tomorrow. All I want you to do now is get out of my sight."

There was nothing else for Lady Gravell-Pitt to do.

Auntie Mame put an arm around each of us and swept us into the garden room, where she poured heroic drinks.

"Thank you, my darling," Basil said, "and drink up. You'll need all the strength you can get for the ordeal of tonight."

"Oh, Basil," Auntie Mame said, caressing him with her eyes, "you must think I'm such a vain, silly, empty-headed, foolish . . ."

"I certainly do, my beloved," he said, "and you are to be repaid for your asininity tonight. First by sitting for hours in the car, whilst the traffic is at a standstill; then by waiting about for even more hours in rooms that are either too hot or too cold with a lot of gabbling females in white and diamonds, and finally by trooping out like a horse in the circus to make your curtsy. But when that is done, then you can come back down to earth and be with me."

"Oh, Basil," Auntie Mame said.

"And now we'd better think about leaving. You know what the traffic will be."

"So early, darling? We haven't even eaten."

"Nor will you be likely to for hours and hours and hours. My Aunt Griselda always takes the precaution of tucking a few sandwiches into a special pocket she has built into her train for these Court functions. She may take pity on you and share one. Now, my fond and foolish angel, we must go."

"Patrick, my little love," Auntie Mame said, "would you mind running up and fetching my wrap? And if you'll look in the cupboard in your room, darling, you'll find a surprise—a present I bought for you to make up for those dreadful old duds Hermione tried to sell you."

"What is it?" I asked, heading for the stairs.

"A lovely new opera cape, darling. And a black top hat."

"Just what I've always wanted," I lied.

Auntie Mame . . .

INDEED THERE THEY WERE. AND THEY BOTH fitted. I thought the effect was rather dashing, even if I did look a little like an unemployed magician.

Auntie Mame's room was dark but I managed to find her ermine wrap. However, I tripped and fell over something in the middle of the floor. Turning on the lights, I saw that it was her jewel case—quite empty. Auntie Mame was wearing a lot of rocks, I knew, but there were plenty more where they came from. I grabbed her wrap and hurried to tell her that her jewelry had been stolen. But just as I got to the corridor, I saw Lady Gravell-Pitt sneaking quietly down the stairs.

"Hey!" I shouted. "Auntie Mame's jewelry has been . . ."

Lady Gravell-Pitt turned and gave me one terrible look, then she stumbled on the stairs and went headlong down their entire length, landing with a splat at Auntie Mame's feet. But that isn't all that landed. Rings and necklaces and bracelets and brooches and Auntie Mame's second-best tiara spewed out of Hermione's hands like water.

I raced down the stairs and swept up the loot in my new opera cape.

"All right, Hermione," Auntie Mame said. "Now get out. Get out this instant, before I call the police."

Lady Gravell-Pitt scrambled to her feet and bolted, and that was the last we ever saw of her.

SITTING IN THE CAR, IN THE TRAFFIC, ON OUR WAY to call for Basil's aunt, Auntie Mame again vilified herself for being such a fool.

"It's all right, darling," Basil said, kissing her gently so as not to spoil her paint job.

"And Lady Gravell-Pitt didn't really get away with anything,

Auntie Mame," I said. "See. I have all your other jewelry right here in my opera cape. Look."

I produced my opera cape, which made a commodious bag, and emptied it into Auntie Mame's lap. Rings and bracelets and necklaces tumbled out onto the white brocade. And there in the center, grinning up from among the sapphires and rubies and emeralds and pearls, were Lady Gravell-Pitt's teeth.

Auntie Mame and the Fortune Hunter

RETURNING TO THE LIVING ROOM, I FOUND PEGEEN waiting patiently. She's the first person I've ever met who seemed *genuinely* interested in anyone's trip abroad.

"Well, I think it's criminal to take a growing boy off for a vacation and then not let him get one breath of fresh air or sunshine. I mean just keeping him in hotels and houses and . . ."

"Nothing could be further from the truth, dear," I said. "Auntie Mame was always vitally concerned with my well-being. We had a lovely sunny holiday while we were gone—swimming, sailing, all that sort of thing."

"Where? In the Trafalgar Square fountain?"

"Not a bit of it. In Biarritz—or very near there. Auntie Mame took a lovely villa and she invited Vera Charles and Lady Spavin and—well quite a lot of her pals—for a simple, pastoral outing. She was also more than selfless in her contributions to the Spanish Civil War."

I looked at Pegeen sitting tearfully on the sofa and then I looked at my stepped-up drink and put it down. There are times when alcohol does more harm than good. *In vino veritas* and *veritas* was not for us that night.

. . .

I SUPPOSE THAT AUNTIE MAME could have gone right on being the toast of London as Captain the Honourable Basil Fitz-Hugh's special lady friend and as the protégée of Griselda, Lady Spavin. But once Auntie Mame conquered anything she generally wearied of it. And after a few weeks of constant social life in Court circles Auntie Mame decided that sunnier climes were calling, and besides, she said, English cooking gave her the pip. The next thing I knew, she'd rented a villa near Biarritz.

A division of labor was then decided upon: I was left behind to deal with temporarily closing the house in London, while Auntie Mame and Vera went on to open the villa temporarily in Biarritz.

Okaying invent'ry lists and so forth took over a week—a cold, damp week—and so I was delighted to see the sunshine of Biarritz. Auntie Mame met me at the station, brown as an Indian and looking very jaunty in rose-colored slacks and *espadrilles*. She kissed me many times, threw my luggage in the boot of Captain the Honourable Basil Fitz-Hugh's two-seater, and took over the wheel.

"Ah, my little love," she said, patting my hand, as she careened past the casino, "welcome to the Pyrénées. You'll love it. Rather brassy, perhaps, but quaint in a feral way. Delicious bathing and the natives all so sweet and friendly—neither French nor Spanish but Basque, the best of both cultures." She very nearly crashed into a sight-seeing bus, and the driver shouted after her, shaking his fist. "See what I mean, darling? Real Basque camaraderie. Basil and I just love it."

"How is Basil?" I asked.

"Oh, darling, we're so happy."

"Are you engaged?"

"Well, dear, no. I mean being engaged is so silly for people of our age. Basil wants to marry me and I want to marry him and we'll be doing it sometime in the fall. It's all rather vague and not a bit official. Basil and I simply have an Understanding."

"That's nice," I said. "And how's Vera?"

"Oh," Auntie Mame said, with a sweeping gesture that almost sent the Hon Basil's car over a cliff and into the Atlantic Ocean. "poor, poor Vera. She's taken leave of her senses completely. She's gone mad, mad, mad. *And* over a man."

"No kidding," I said. Vera Charles had had a succession of gentlemen companions during her many years as a star, but they had all been Just Awfully Good Friends and—leaving some simple token of friendship such as a diamond bracelet or a mink coat—they usually went back to their wives after discovering that Vera was really too selfish to share very much of herself with anyone.

"*If* you can call him a man," Auntie Mame sputtered. "He's more like something from the reptile world to me. Basil thinks so, too."

"Well, if Vera cares so much about him, he must be very rich."

"*Rich?* Hoooo! That's a hot one! Amadeo hasn't anything besides the clothes on his back and what he can mooch from Vera—*and* from me. His name is Amadeo Armadillo. He's a shifty little spick from some silly South American country that nobody ever heard of until Amadeo married so many rich women that he put the place on the map. He seems to be the principal export and they're lucky to be rid of him."

"But how did Vera manage to meet him?" I asked.

"Oh, it was just one of those silly moth-and-flame encounters one reads about in magazine stories. Vera went down to the casino one night for a go at the roulette and came home with ten thousand more francs *and* Amadeo. He's been with us ever since. To hear *her* tell it, she looked across the table into Amadeo's nasty little snake eyes and it was love, love, love at first sight. My own version is that Amadeo looked at all of Vera's bracelets and that big stack of chips in front of her and decided that poor Vera was the target for tonight."

"That doesn't sound like Vera," I said. "It usually works the other way."

"True, my little love," Auntie Mame said, "but you must remember that Vera's getting on. She's a good deal older than I am and she's finally reached the Dangerous Age. Although why she couldn't reach it with a nice old banker or one of her dukes is beyond me. At any rate, Amadeo has moved right into my villa—*my* villa, if you please. He orders my servants about, arrives late for meals, borrows money, flirts outrageously with every woman except, possibly, Griselda Spavin, has no visible means of support, and Vera thinks he's sheer heaven. *What* she sees in him is beyond me."

"Looks?" I ventured.

"*Looks*? Wait till you see him! He's ugly. He's stupid. He's rude. And he's a bore. He's lived entirely off women—don't ask me how. But Vera's not *that* rich, even if she does have the first nickel she ever made. Oh, Patrick, my little love, I've *got* to make Vera see the light. And *you've* got to help me!"

Auntie Mame swung the car viciously to the right and we lurched through some fancy wrought-iron gates, jounced along a rutted driveway, and stopped in front of a huge watermelon-pink house of the Spanish persuasion.

"Here we are at Villa Dolorosa, my little love. Isn't it divine?"

It was terrible. It had been built during the twenties by an

Auntie Mame . . .

old silent-screen star who had managed to combine the worst of Granada, Bauhaus, and Hollywood and set it all incongruously down on a beautiful, natural promontory between Biarritz and St. Jean de Luz. The uncompromising pink of its stucco was set off by a red tile roof, by grilles and balconies, by twisted columns and bottle-bottom windows. Inside, if anything, it was even worse. There were archways and pillars and niches and grottoes. There were gates where doors should have been and doors where windows should have been. Everything that was supposed to be marble was really painted wood, and everything that was supposed to be wood was really painted plaster, and everything that was supposed to be plaster was really painted papier-mâché. It was furnished vaguely in the period of the Spanish Inquisition with a few touches of leopard and chromium. Happily, Auntie Mame had taken a very short lease.

"I'm putting you in the Velázquez Room, darling, right next to Vera. Get into your bathing things and come right down. Everyone's on the beach."

When I was unpacked and ready, Auntie Mame was waiting in the patio in a sleek swimming suit; she insisted that I tuck into a Continental breakfast. "Eat, darling," she said. "It isn't wise to see Amadeo on an empty stomach."

We wandered through some rather garish gardens and down a long flight of stone steps to the beach where Auntie Mame's guests were gathered. Save for Vera's inamorato, I had met them all before.

The Hon. Basil Fitz-Hugh came capering up, looking very English-gentleman-on-holiday in bathing trunks and something he called a "boskbeddy," which I came to realize later was British for Basque beret. He said I was looking jolly well and that it would be ripping to have some young blood around the place.

Vera, beneath the spell of Amadeo Armadillo, had gone all

girlish and soft. She greeted me with a certain regrettable ingénue charm and even kissed me.

Next came Basil's old aunt, Griselda, Lady Spavin. She was sitting under a straw hat, under a veil, under a sunshade, under a Deauville umbrella, doing a bit of needlework. I gathered that her function was to chaperone the middle-aged lovers.

Last came Vera's South American fortune hunter, Amadeo Armadillo. I could see Auntie Mame's point instantly. He looked like a gigolo and talked like a dialect comedian. He wasn't as tall as Vera, even in his Cuban heels. He was partial to suitings in powder blue, maize yellow, and rose beige, with the shoulders padded out so far that he had to go through doorways crabwise. And I *think* he corseted. He favored navy-blue silk shirts with pale satin neckties, and all of his shoes that weren't suède were lizard—or both.

Amadeo's hair was glistening black and a good deal too long. It swept back from a low forehead in tarry, sculptured waves, arriving at its final destination in a long deep V low on the nape of his neck. His eyebrows met in the middle and seemed to creep down his narrow nose—except on Thursdays, when he plucked them. He did have very fine, dark eyes, except that they were a bit too close together and had the merest tendency to protrude. I guess he was born without facial muscles, since his only expression was one of sultry petulance. "Rotten sort" was the Hon. Basil's summary of Amadeo—mine, too.

"Señor Armadillo," Auntie Mame said in her Gracious Hostess voice, "this is my nephew Patrick."

Amadeo extended a furry hand with glossy nails and a big glassy-looking diamond ring and grunted. I guess he didn't like other males very much. They didn't like him, either.

Life at Villa Dolorosa was fairly relaxed. During the days we mostly swam and lazed on the beach. There would be excur-

Auntie Mame . . .

sions into Biarritz or St. Jean de Luz, or even right down to the Spanish border so that Auntie Mame could hear the freshest gossip about how the Spanish Civil War was faring. From time to time she'd invite a few people in to dine informally, and on rare occasions Auntie Mame and the Hon. Basil would get dressed up for dinner at Biarritz and a quiet evening at the casino.

She didn't talk very much about her Understanding with the Hon. Basil, but they were almost never apart and Auntie Mame seemed happy and relaxed and in love. I liked Basil a lot and I was glad that Auntie Mame had found a nice new husband to settle down with.

All of Vera's plans were centered around the repugnant Amadeo Armadillo, and he, knowing where his bread was buttered, fell in with those plans with a sullen Latin shrug. That left me paired off with Lady Spavin.

There was considerably more than half a century between us, but I found Lady Spavin a stimulating-enough companion. Besides her needlework, Lady Spavin had plenty of other outside interests. She was a voracious reader and an inveterate card player. She kept up a voluminous correspondence with half the British peerage and, in her maundering way, was able to tell me about quite a lot of hot scandals that occurred during the reign of Edward and Alexandra. She had a passionate interest in the Spanish Civil War and said that she'd have sent the Hon. Basil into the skirmish if he'd only been ten years younger and didn't have an Understanding with Auntie Mame. Lady Spavin seemed to like Auntie Mame an awful lot and told me, more than once, how pleased she was that her nephew Basil was marrying a lively American widow instead of some horsy girl from the counties. She must have really meant it, since she borrowed Ito and the Rolls one day to buy out all the wool shops in Biarritz. That very afternoon she started work on a big petit-point bedspread which featured

Basil's family's arms, and Auntie Mame's and Basil's initials intertwined on a field of white strewn with roses.

Technically, Lady Spavin was chaperoning Auntie Mame's household, and while Auntie Mame and the Hon. Basil behaved themselves with a certain casual decorum, there was a good deal going on in Villa Dolorosa that Lady Spavin did not see.

What Lady Spavin did not see, *I did*.

I knew, for example, that Amadeo Armadillo stole into Vera's room every night, because the walls were so thin that I couldn't help hearing them. I knew, too, that whenever Vera went in to Biarritz to get her hair hennaed, Amadeo was popping corn with one of the maids—an affair that ended noisily when he tried to put the squeeze on her for five hundred francs. I also discovered that he was down to his last I.O.U. on the morning a paper fluttered out of Amadeo's window and landed at my feet in the patio. It was a letter from the Excelsior Hotel in Rome threatening to bring suit if Amadeo didn't settle a slight bill of four thousand dollars which he'd run up some years ago.

If I live to be a thousand, I will never be able to explain what *any* woman, let alone Vera, saw in Amadeo Armadillo. As Auntie Mame had told me, he was totally without looks, charm, manners, intelligence, or wit. Griselda, Lady Spavin, being among the grandest of *grandes dames*, was civil to him, if nothing more. Auntie Mame, although trying hard, barely managed even that. The Hon. Basil was most clipped with Amadeo and frostily polite, although when he was alone with Auntie Mame and me he let himself go so far as to speak of Señor Armadillo as a cad and a bounder and one who would never be tolerated in any decent officers' mess. Although the Hon. Basil had eyes only for Auntie Mame, he also shared the English gentleman's rather awe-stricken attitude toward ladies of the theater, and he found Vera a ripping good sort.

Auntie Mame ...

Amadeo, who was hardly cordial to the adults, treated me like something the Department of Health had just discovered lurking behind a garbage pail. I didn't really care. I thought he was a big schlemiel and the less I saw of him, the better.

Vera, however, was perfectly hopeless. She doted upon Amadeo, sighing over the sight of his padded shoulders and nipped-in waists as though he were Michelangelo's David. Auntie Mame once commented that if Vera ever saw Amadeo in a bathing suit—a view to which none of us had ever been treated—she'd come right back to her senses and throw him out. From the noises I'd heard through the walls every night, I felt pretty certain that Vera had experienced Amadeo in a good deal less, but I knew that Auntie Mame would be hurt and disturbed if she heard about it, so I kept my mouth shut. As happy as Auntie Mame was in Villa Dolorosa, her concern over Vera and Amadeo Armadillo marred her whole stay on the Basque coast.

After a little research, Auntie Mame told Basil and me that Amadeo had been the son of a major in a minor South American republic. His first step up the matrimonial ladder had occurred with his marriage to the local dictator's daughter. But the dictator got shot in the leftist junta—wherever *that* was—and so Amadeo divorced his bride and moved on to greener fields. In Europe, Amadeo married Amelie Amoreux, the famous French movie star. After they were divorced, he married Gloria Glockenspiel, the cigar heiress. After *they* were divorced, Amadeo figured as corespondent in three divorce cases of international notoriety. Then, after he'd been chasing a beautiful Romanian movie queen, he settled down, briefly, with Babs Bourbon, the chain-store heiress. That, too, ended in the divorce courts, and now, Auntie Mame said balefully, it was Vera's turn.

The blow finally fell one afternoon when Lady Spavin and I returned to the Villa Dolorosa from a heavy tea at the Palais

Hotel. Auntie Mame was alone in the patio, pacing up and down like a caged leopard. "I'm so glad you've finally come back," she said. "My whole day has been unsettled."

"What's the trouble, Auntie Mame?"

"It's Vera. She came mincing idiotically into my room, like some Barrie character, and said that she was going to marry that snake. *Nothing* I've been able to say can shake her. She's out ordering her trousseau now—and *he's* out ordering *his*."

"What a ghastly shame," Lady Spavin said. "It so puts one in mind of poor Mollie Petherbridge-Bouverie and that dreadful tango dancer. I remember it was in the summer of eleven—no, twelve, because that was the year we installed electricity in the house at Heaves. I was working on a petit-point waistcoat for . . ."

"Wouldn't you think," Auntie Mame said, cutting short Lady Spavin's recollections of nobility and needlework, "that a woman as smart as Vera—and as *old*—would be able to see through that slick little fortune hunter? I've talked to her until I'm blue in the face and all Vera can say is that she wants *me* to be her matron of honor. If I could only find some way to . . ."

"What you ektualleh mean, Mame," Lady Spavin said, "is that if you could only find some other woman with more *money* than Vera has, Señor Armadillo would transfer his rather, um, fleeting affections to her. Isn't that about the size of it?"

"You know perfectly well it is, Griselda," Auntie Mame snorted. "All he's interested in is some sap of a woman with a fat bank account who'll pay him off when she's fed up with him."

"It shouldn't be too difficult to find one, Mame dear," Lady Spavin said. "Biarritz is filled with them at this time of year. Why, only this afternoon Patrick and I saw this vulgar Hungarian woman wearing trousers and diamond bracelets up to

Auntie Mame . . .

each elbow. It so reminds me of Coronation Year—George's and Mary's, of course—when this . . ."

"Yes, yes, yes," Auntie Mame said impatiently, "but I'd have to pry him loose from Vera long enough to get him into Biarritz, and that's not easy, what with her planning white satin and orange blossoms. If there were only some rich woman right under his nose who could lure him away just long enough for Vera to come to her senses. . . ." She paused, an unearthly light coming into her eyes. "But of course! There's *me*!"

"Auntie Mame!"

"But what could be simpler? I'm much better fixed than Vera. All I'd have to do is dress up. Flirt with Amadeo. Pretend to be mad about him. Just show Vera what a fool she's been. It's a terrible sacrifice to make, but for dear Vera I'd be willing . . ."

"And what of Basil?" Lady Spavin asked dryly.

"Why, Basil would understand," Auntie Mame said with complete assurance.

"If he did, he'd be the only man in history who ever had," Lady Spavin said. "No, Mame, Basil's a dear, sweet boy, but he's not a saint. This can lead to nothing but . . ."

"This can lead to nothing but Vera's ultimate happiness," Auntie Mame said.

As she gushed on with her plans for Vera's ultimate happiness, I tiptoed silently away.

Auntie Mame was a caution in the role of a siren. She wasn't really cut out to be a vampire, but she played it with the fervor of a little-theater *Madame X*. She appeared at the beach the next afternoon in an alarmingly brief black satin bathing suit. She had on a lot of green eye shadow and a diamond bracelet around her ankle. I was so stunned when I saw her that I nearly drowned. Lady Spavin raised her eyes toward heaven, closed them for a moment, and then went back to her needlework. Vera snickered uneasily and said, "You look like a comic valentine, darling." But she stopped snickering when she saw the expression on Amadeo's face.

Auntie Mame was just as handsome as she was rich, and although she looked like a Park Avenue housewife gone to the dogs, the total effect wasn't entirely unpleasant. She undulated over to Amadeo and said, "Darling, rub my suntan oil on me—there's a love." While he did it, she wriggled like an eel. I was so embarrassed I had to look away—but not Vera.

That night Auntie Mame was entertaining an antique countess at dinner, and she was awfully late coming down. When she swept into the room I knew why. Having confined her wardrobe to slacks and blouses, this time she wore a black lace dress so tight she couldn't eat and diamond bracelets to the armpits. She'd put on artificial eyelashes and a rakish court plaster. There was an audible moment of silent admiration, and Vera's green eyes were about as cheery as a February sky as Auntie Mame glided across the room like a nautch dancer. I was speechless with admiration, and so was Amadeo. He was placed at Auntie Mame's right during dinner and couldn't have been more attentive, although he appeared to be more interested in her diamonds than her wit.

After dinner when Vera urged Amadeo out to "sniff the lemon trees," he hesitated at the door and gazed tenderly back at Auntie Mame and her diamonds. They weren't gone long and when they came back Vera looked bitter and cross.

"Oh, that awful, *awful*, man!" Auntie Mame exploded as I helped her unload the ice back into her jewel box. "He's a boor and a bore and a . . . Shhhhh." There was a rustling noise outside in the hall and then an envelope slid silently under her bedroom door. Auntie Mame swept it off the floor and ripped it open. "Phew! Get a whiff of that cheap perfume!" Then she started reading: " '*Señora deliciosa . . .*' "

Auntie Mame . . .

THE STILL OF THE MORNING WAS RENT BY A SERIES of explosions from the driveway. I hurried to the window just in time to see the Rolls lurch out of the gates. Through the rear window, I could see the backs of two heads: one black, which was Amadeo's; one in a huge leghorn hat, swathed in mauve veiling, which fluttered out of the side window. I knew it could only be Auntie Mame as The Menace and as the veil whipped out in the breeze, I tried not to think of Isadora Duncan's hideous fate.

I turned back to bed and saw a note on my desk in Auntie Mame's stylish scrawl:

> *Darling boy—*
>
> *The repulsive one has asked me out on a picnic—just us and the hard-boiled eggs. Ugh! Don't think I've gone mad. This is all for Vera's sake. Just make sure that she's conscious of our absence every moment. I'm planning on motor trouble, so we'll be back late. Don't let on that you know where we've gone.*
>
> > *Love, love, love,*
> > *Auntie Mame*

By the time I got downstairs, Vera seemed conscious of their absence and of nothing else. When I said good morning, she nearly snapped my head off. The Hon. Basil was down at the beach, glumly staring at the water. Lady Spavin looked up from her needlework and sighed Delphically.

Luncheon was a funereal affair. Vera didn't touch her food, and Basil seemed off his feed, as well. I ate heartily and tried to keep up a bubbling conversation filled with speculations as to Auntie Mame's whereabouts, but without much success. During the afternoon Lady Spavin got up a game of bridge,

... and the Fortune Hunter

Vera and the Hon. Basil were partners and played so dispirit-edly that I was able to make a little slam in hearts with the ace and queen out against me, whereupon Vera burst into tears and fled.

By dinnertime Vera was fit to be tied. She kept clattering up and down the drive in her heels, searching for the holiday-makers, but there was no sign of them. The meal was post-poned and repostponed until almost ten. By then it wasn't even edible. I only addressed one remark to Vera, and she screamed, "For God's sake, shut *up*!" We finished in silence.

Afterward, Vera and Basil got to work on the brandy bottle while Lady Spavin taught me six-pack bezique. About mid-night the Rolls lumbered in.

"Darlings! Did you think we'd *died*?" Auntie Mame trilled.

"How *dare* you?" Vera said, facing Auntie Mame furiously.

"What's that, Vera dear?"

"I said *how dare you*! How *dare* you run off with never as much as a word to anyone? Where have you *been*?"

"But, Vera," Auntie Mame said ingenuously, "*darling*, what do you mean where have we been? You knew that Amadeo was planning this little picnic. He told me *you* didn't want to go, didn't you, Amadeo?" Auntie Mame turned with a helpless gesture, but Amadeo was nowhere to be seen. "Oh, Vera, you *should* have come. I didn't want to go without you, but Amadeo practically kidnapped me. It was the most fun! We drove out into the country and had this divine picnic in the hills, and picked flowers and did all sorts of things. . . ."

"Um-hmmmm?" Vera injected menacingly.

"Of course we should have been home *hours* ago, but Ito had some motor trouble and when he finally set it to rights it was so late—and we were hungry as *bears*—that we stopped off in this quaint little native chili parlor. Really, so primitive they hadn't even a telephone. So what could we do except . . ."

"*Oh!*" Vera shouted, and stamped out of the room.

Auntie Mame . . .

The Hon. Basil gave Auntie Mame a shattered look and followed.

"B-Basil . . ."

"Mark my words, Mame," Lady Spavin said, "this insane charade will bring nothing but trouble." Then she went back to the bezique hand.

I WENT UP TO AUNTIE MAME'S ROOM AND HELPED her out of her war paint. She was rather the worse for wear. Her eye shadow was badly smeared, the mauve veil hung in shreds, and the court plaster dangled by a limp corner. "Most gruesome day I've ever spent, my little love. He was just revolting. I feel like having a bath and a shampoo and an enema and everything else whenever I'm near that man. But it did work. Vera *was* jealous."

For the rest of the week Auntie Mame had her guns trained on Amadeo. She managed to get him locked into her bedroom the next night and made such a racket hammering on the door that the whole house was aroused. Vera listened coldly to Auntie Mame's limp excuse about borrowing a book. Auntie Mame looked deliciously disheveled in a black nightie. I thought I heard something like a sob issue from the Hon. Basil, but I couldn't be certain.

The next day Auntie Mame arranged to get becalmed in a sailboat with Amadeo, and the moon was up before they returned. The day after that they drove to the hairdresser's in Biarritz to call for Vera, but Vera came home alone in a taxi three hours later, seething. Instead of picking up his inamorata, Amadeo had allowed himself to be lured off to the Miramar, where he and Auntie Mame danced until two in the morning. When Auntie Mame got home Vera had been confined to bed and the Hon. Basil wasn't speaking to anybody.

Spurred on by her triumph, Auntie Mame decided to hold

. . . and the Fortune Hunter

The Vamp over for a second week. She switched and twitched around the house in chiffons and satins, sparkling with sequins, flapping with feathers, dazzling with diamonds. But if she and Amadeo enjoyed the performance, they were the only ones who did. Vera was almost suicidal and the Hon. Basil was red-eyed and morose. The two of them would sit silently in the library for hours on end or strike out on long, gloomy hikes.

But I thought the act had gone too far when Auntie Mame gave Amadeo a set of canary diamond studs and links so big that they looked like fog lights. That was enough for me. Boiling mad, I went right to Auntie Mame's room and confronted her with it.

"Listen, Auntie Mame," I said, "it's one thing to act like a tramp around that louse Latin for Vera's sake . . ."

"Vera! Faugh! What a fool! And I'll thank you to watch your language. Remember, I'm still . . ."

"But when it comes to giving him a present like that— something that must have cost thousands—when there's a depression on and people are . . ."

"Oh, so now the boy economist is telling *me* how *I* shall spend *my* money! Well, listen to me. Keeping Amadeo happy means a great deal to me. . . ."

"What about Basil and your so-called Understanding? About the only thing that remains to understand is how you can keep out of a home for fallen women."

"Ah, poor child," she said mysteriously, "what can you know of love?" Then she tittuped to the corridor and cooed, "Amadeo, *chéri*! Come and help me go over my financial statements."

Amadeo wasn't very intellectual, but when it came to figures he made I.B.M. unnecessary. Having won him with her face, figure, clothes, and jewels, Auntie Mame now laid her cards on the table and gave him a fair picture of just how much dough Beau had left her. Amadeo lit up like a pinball machine and they spent all afternoon in the library poring over Auntie Mame's nest egg. He was the only man I ever saw who could figure oil in millions on top of a desk and grope for a woman's knee underneath it. I was so disgusted I left the room.

I found myself alone with Amadeo before dinner that night and he was unaccustomedly cordial to me—uncomfortably so. He put an arm around my shoulder and called me "Son" twice.

Dinner was horrible. No one spoke, except Auntie Mame and Amadeo, and every so often she'd squeal "Oh, let *go*!" and "No! *Naughty!*" Vera was the first to crack. She threw down her napkin—during salad—and slammed out of the room. The Hon. Basil followed, and then Lady Spavin took to her heels. I was about to leave them alone, too, when Auntie Mame looked earnestly down the table and said: "Please wait for me in my room, my little love. I have something important to say to you."

Mystified, I went up to her room and waited. After a long time she came in. Pausing dramatically at the open door she said, "Amadeo wants to marry me!"

"Auntie Mame!" I whispered. "You're joking!"

"Joking?" she said, walking into the room. "Why should I joke? He's found me extremely attractive—surely you could see *that*. He asked me in the library this afternoon and I . . ."

"But, Vera . . ." I began.

"Vera will just have to . . ."

"Vera will just have to *what*?" a voice asked. We both looked up and there was Vera standing in the doorway. She was white and tense and she looked ghastly. "*Vera will just have to what?*" she repeated. She moved ominously toward Auntie Mame.

"W-why, Vera, it's just that Amadeo and I have . . ."

"Lisssen," Vera hissed. The elegant staginess had left her

voice. "Amadeo is mine. I found him and I brought him here. He . . ."

"Vera," Auntie Mame said, "can't you see by now that he doesn't give a rap for you? He . . ."

"He's been dazzled by you and your dirty low-down tricks. He's been swept off his feet by your diamonds and your money. You've *bought* him, but he doesn't really love you. He loves . . ."

"Vera! How can you buy a man with . . ."

"Shut up!" Vera snarled. "You've broken poor Basil's heart and you've tried to break mine. But you haven't succeeded. Amadeo is mine. I'm going to marry him first thing in the morning. And what's more, I'm going to get back at you for this if it's the last thing I ever do." She turned on her heel, went down the hall to her own room, slammed the door, and locked it.

"Vera!" Auntie Mame cried, running after her. Then she turned, came back into her own room and shut the door. "She's *not* going to marry Amadeo, not if I have to kill myself." She turned to me. "Wait here and don't let Vera out of her room. Use force, if necessary. I've got to get to Amadeo first." She snatched up her bag and her coat and ran downstairs to the library.

"Hey!" I called. But she was out of earshot. A few minutes later I heard the front door slam, a small explosion, and the roar of a car streaming down the driveway. Then there was silence. I watched Vera's door until midnight. There wasn't a thing stirring in the house, so I went to bed.

The next morning I was awakened by what I briefly took to be the end of the world. There was a lot of screaming and shrieking from the lower part of the house and then I heard Vera's heels clattering on the tile floor of the halls. She burst into my room and started vilifying me at the top of her lungs.

She was so hysterical that I couldn't make much of what she said except the word "gone," which she repeated twenty or thirty times. She kept waving a sheet of paper in my face and shouting invective until Lady Spavin marched into the room and called for order. She took the paper away from Vera and read it. "Well," she said briskly, "they've done what I was afraid they'd do. They've run off together."

"Wh-*who*?" I asked. Then I realized it was a silly question.

"*Who?*" Vera screamed. "Who, but that dirty, double-crossing . . ."

"Leave the room, Vera," Lady Spavin said, pushing her out. "I'm afraid, child, that your mad aunt and Amadeo Armadillo have gone to Gretna Green."

"Greta who?" I said, rubbing the sleep from my eyes.

"It's just an expression, child. Now get up and get dressed."

DOWNSTAIRS THE PLACE WAS LIKE A WAILING WALL. Vera had more or less composed herself and wept steadily into a lace handkerchief. The Hon. Basil paced up and down working his jaw and cracking his knuckles. Lady Spavin was playing patience. There was no question about it, Auntie Mame and Amadeo had fled in the night, leaving only an incoherent note written by Amadeo—I always suspected he was illiterate—and no forwarding address.

I was so sick and depressed to think that Auntie Mame had fallen into her own trap that I went upstairs and packed. I was also nearly broke and there didn't seem much of anyplace to go except to Auntie Mame's big, empty house in London. By hocking my wrist watch I had just enough to pay for third-class tickets back to England. The compartment on the train was stifling and I was jammed in between two Spanish refugee women—each with a baby. I had no money for food and I was feeling a little giddy when I changed trains at Paris. A glimpse at the headlines of the English-language papers made me feel even worse. The *Continental Daily Mail* had:

FORTUNE HUNTER FLEES

WITH WEALTHY WIDOW

Somewhat less staid, the Paris *Herald* wrote:

MADCAP (MILLIONS) MAME MISSING

KIDNAP PLOT FEARED

After that I went to the lavatory to be good and sick and I remained sick all the way across the Channel.

It was early morning when I got to Grosvenor Square. The house looked dark and empty and there were a lot of reporters milling around in front. So I went around to the mews and cut through the garden. The house had been officially closed and the servants were all gone, the chandeliers hung in big baize bags, and there were ghostly looking dust sheets over all the furniture. I hadn't eaten for two days and I hoped—without much conviction—that there might just be something down in the kitchen to keep me from starving to death.

I felt my way down to the big basement kitchen and groped for a light switch. A tremulous voice said, "P-put your hands up or I'll fire."

"Auntie Mame," I said, "it's Patrick."

"Oh, thank God you've come, my little love," she said. The lights went on and I saw her huddled at the big kitchen table. She was wearing a woolen robe and, for some reason, a chinchilla cape. "Have a cup of coffee," she said bleakly. "It's awfully stale and not very good. I made it myself. I have to do everything myself. The servants are all gone and all those

Auntie Mame . . .

reporters out in front keep ringing the bell and calling on the telephone. Oh!" A tear trickled down her cheek.

"Can't your husband send the reporters away?" I asked.

"My what?"

"Your husband!" I said, speaking louder than necessary, as though she were simple.

"Beauregard has been dead for years," she said coldly. "Have you taken leave of your senses, child?"

"But aren't you married to Amadeo Armadillo?"

"Certainly not!" she snapped.

"Well, are you, um, living in, ah, *sin*?" I asked.

"Really! I'll thank you to keep a civil tongue in your head. If you think—"

"But where *is* Amadeo?" I asked desperately.

"I'm sure I couldn't tell you," she said haughtily, "but if my calculations are anywhere near right he should be on his second day of basic training with the fighting forces of Republican Spain."

"Where did you leave him, Auntie Mame?"

"When last seen, Amadeo was locked in the toilet of a chartered plane." Then she looked at her wrist watch. "I expect that by now he's doing about-faces and all that sort of thing. His feet must hurt dreadfully if he's still wearing those patent-leather pumps."

"But who locked Amadeo in a toilet? What are you . . ."

"I did," she said with simple eloquence.

"But why did Amadeo want to join the Spanish army?" I said.

"Amadeo! Amadeo! Amadeo! Can't you ever talk about anybody but *him*? Don't you care what happened to *me*? The rigors I've endured?"

"Well, sure, but . . ."

"But what?"

... and the Fortune Hunter

"But I thought you and Amadeo ran off together."

"As indeed we did. Didn't you read his note?"

"But I thought the two of you were getting married."

"*I* marry a greaseball like Amadeo when I have a man of Basil's stature on his way to me at this very moment? Don't be ridiculous!"

"Auntie Mame, I just don't understand."

"Well, if you'd only stop interrupting, I'd tell you. Oh, how little you know of the pioneer woman's trials and tribulations, you crossing the Continent in a de luxe railway carriage."

"So begin," I said.

"Well," Auntie Mame said, "I just knew that it was no good showing up Amadeo as the louse he is when he was always on hand to lure poor Vera back into his web. So I decided that the only thing to do was to elope with him and get him a good long distance from Biarritz. I didn't want to do it, but when Vera threatened to fling herself at his feet, I realized it had to be done. And a pretty penny it cost, too."

"Including those canary diamond studs and cuff links," I said hotly.

"Oh, those! They were just some yellow glass things that I ripped off an old tennis dress and threw into a Cartier box. He won't find that out until he tries to hock them, which should be about now."

"Go on," I said.

"I'm trying to. So, when Vera said that she was going to marry Amadeo the very next morning, I dashed downstairs to Pinchbottom—oh, Patrick, darling, that Amadeo's a pincher, too; a real menace. And I said, 'Fly with me!' And then I gave him a check for a hundred thousand dollars. . . ."

"A hundred thou . . ."

"To be signed when we said, 'I do.' Then I got Ito to drive us out to the airport and all the time I kept plying Amadeo with

Auntie Mame . . .

brandy. Oh, Patrick, that man can drink as well as pinch. I pumped enough brandy into him to fill a swimming pool and of course his nasty hands were all over me. Well, the only plane that was around was a private one that belonged to this darling Danish flier, and so I chartered it. I said to the pilot, 'What's the most godforsaken place you know?' and he said, 'Brönderslev, Denmark, madam. Where I come from.' So then I said, 'Wouldn't you like to go home for a little visit?' and *he* said, 'Not on your life, madam.' But I gave him a lot more money and he was very charming after that."

"I'll bet he was," I said.

"Of course Amadeo thought I was taking him to Paris, and he was pretty drunk by then, anyhow. Well, it was a terrible flight. The weather was simply unbelievable and I was almost beside myself, what with being tossed around from cloud to cloud and that repugnant Amadeo pawing me. Well, I'd planned to get off at Paris and just let Amadeo keep on going north. But that awful man simply would *not* pass out. You can imagine how I felt when I heard we were over Germany—and here Amadeo was still conscious. To make matters even worse, he'd finished all the brandy and was howling for more."

"So what did you do, Auntie Mame?"

"Well, happily I had a bottle of *Nuit de Noël* in my purse—thirty bucks an ounce, if you please—so I just emptied it into a paper cup and gave it to Amadeo."

"Did he *drink* it?"

"Like a fish. And the perfume seemed to turn the trick. He grew deathly pale and just made it to the rest room."

"What then?"

"Then I locked him in."

"But how did you . . ."

"Stop interrupting. Well, I went up to the pilot's little sort of driver's seat and said that Amadeo was sick and did the pilot think he could do any tricks that would make him sicker. You know, sort of arouse Amadeo's gastric juices. Well, that adorable Dane did things with a plane that I didn't know were possible. First he wrote my name and then he wrote his own. His name, by the way, was Jørgen Årup Hansen and he even flew back to put in all those diagonals and accent marks that Danes *will* use. Then he gave me a liverwurst sandwich."

"What about Amadeo?"

"Oh, by that time he was long lost to song and flight. But then the *awful* thing happened."

"What was that?"

"Well, we heard over the radio that the weather was so bad up north that we'd have to turn back. We were just about over Munich by then and the fog was so dense that landing was impossible. So Jørgen said, 'How about going back to Paris?' Because he'd always wanted to see Paris with a beautiful woman, he said. Wasn't that sweet? Oh, don't worry, darling, it means nothing. He was years younger than I am, albeit most attractive. Well, I was sorely tempted, but I knew that if Amadeo was in a big, convenient place like Paris with lots of planes and trains and telephones, he could get back to poor Vera in no time at all. So I said no. Then Jørgen said that I'd have to make up my mind pretty soon because the only reason he'd come to Biarritz was that he was going to enlist in the Spanish Republican Army, plane and all, even if he couldn't speak a word of Spanish."

"Auntie Mame," I said, "you didn't . . ."

"I did," she said. "I said to Jørgen, 'Isn't that a coincidence, my dear. I just happen to have a gentleman locked in the toilet who speaks fluent Spanish and I see no reason why you shouldn't be buddies through the whole civil war. You can do the flying and Amadeo will do the talking,' I said."

"You mean that you had Amadeo shanghaied into the Spanish Republican Army?"

"In a word, yes. Jørgen said he had just enough fuel left to

Auntie Mame . . .

get to Barcelona. And I said could he assure me that Amadeo would be in the thick of things down there. Jørgen said he could guarantee it. So I said that was divine and I'd send Jørgen a food package every week. And then I said, 'But what about me?' and Jørgen said I could either go to Barcelona or jump."

"So what did you do?"

"I jumped."

"You jumped with a *parachute*, Auntie Mame?"

"I would hardly have jumped without one," she said coldly. "Jørgen strapped me into this rig and told me how to count to ten and then to pull the string. And that is just what I did."

"Gee. Where did you land?"

"On my rear end, I'm sorry to say."

"No, I mean what country?"

"Oh, in Germany, just south of Munich, although I swore that I'd never go there as long as that Hitler is . . ."

"Gosh, after that I'll bet it was easy," I said admiringly.

"*Easy?* I was dragged halfway to Austria before I could get that damned parachute off my back. Since then I've traveled by oxcart, hayrack, motorcycle, car, truck, milk wagon, train, plane, and bus. And every inch of the way in a georgette dinner dress—most inappropriate for travel. But you must admit that I got rid of Amadeo Armadillo. I wonder if the army will make a man of him? I don't suppose so, do you?"

"Where's Ito?"

"He's driving the car back. I told him to follow the Atlantic Ocean until he got to Calais. He'll be along any day now, if only he didn't get it headed the wrong way and end up in Spain, too."

"Well, Auntie Mame," I said, "now all your problems are solved."

"All save one," she said. "Basil. Tell me, darling, how was poor Basil?"

"Well, he seemed a little out of sorts to me," I said, not wanting Auntie Mame to know how terribly hurt he had been.

"Ah, but my little love, he's coming to me. I know he is. I've called Villa Dolorosa a dozen times trying to reach him. He's not there. Everyone's left. But he'll find me. I've left a trail."

"I'll bet you have," I said.

"Yes, I've sent telegrams to all his clubs, to Birdcage Walk, to the Palace. Never fear, he'll find me."

"But do you still think he'll *want* to? I mean, he thinks you've eloped with Amadeo Armadillo and . . ."

"Basil and I have an Understanding," Auntie Mame said. "And as for poor Vera, I'll bet she's thanking me right now for what I've done for her."

We moved to the drawing room, and I started pulling the dust sheets off the furniture.

Peering through the draperies she said, "Thank God those reporters are thinning out." They were, too. The house looked so empty from the front that I guess they gave up hope of catching Auntie Mame.

The telephone rang and Auntie Mame raced to answer it. "Hello!" she said in her brightest voice. "No, this is not the lady who washes . . . Oh, go to hell!" She hung up and came back snarling about practical jokers. "I did so hope it would be Basil," she sighed. She sat down and lighted a cigarette, but I could see that her hand was trembling. The telephone rang again. "It's been like this ever since I got back," she said, "and it's never dear Basil." She got up and answered. "No," she roared, "I *don't* want to make a statement to the London *Daily Worker*!" She stomped back in and threw herself on the sofa. "Communists!" she muttered.

Then the doorbell rang.

"Don't answer it!" Auntie Mame warned. "Peep out first and see if it's a reporter. If it is . . ."

"My God!" I said, letting the curtain fall.

Auntie Mame . . .

"Is it Basil?"

"Yes, Auntie Mame," I said. "It's Basil—*and Vera*."

"Oh, the darling!" She flew to the door and flung it open. "Darling, darling, Basil!" Auntie Mame cried. "I *knew* you'd come!"

"Mame!" Vera shouted. "Darling!" She threw her arms around Auntie Mame and kissed her.

I had the feeling that Auntie Mame would much rather be in the Hon. Basil's arms, but she still felt guilty about her friend Vera.

"Oh, Vera! *Have* you found it in your heart to forgive me?"

"Yais, Mame, yais. Oh, Amadeo was so wrong for me. And it took you to make me see what was right. Now I do and I'm eternally grateful."

"Good, Vera," Auntie Mame said heartily. "I hoped you'd see the light."

"Oh, I have," Vera said, beaming up at Basil. "And, Mame, darling, I do want you two to be happy."

"I'm sure we will be," Auntie Mame said, also smiling at Basil.

Basil blushed brick red.

"Ah, Mame," Vera said with a sweeping gesture, "do kiss Basil—to please *me*." Auntie Mame obliged with great ardor and the Hon. Basil blushed even more. "My dear," Vera gushed on, "when Basil and I found that note, I thought my heart would break. And his, too. But Basil understood."

"Naturally," Auntie Mame said.

"And you know the old saying, darling, 'Two lonely hearts beating as one. . . .' So Basil and I simply slipped off to Paris and we were joined in a sweet little civil ceremony at the Georges Cinq. Auntie Griselda was my only attendant."

Auntie Mame's jaw fell.

"But," Vera continued, "when all those telegrams started arriving, we knew that you must want us to come and dance at your wedding. And here we are, just an old married couple, Captain and Mrs. Basil Fitz-Hugh."

"Well, don't start dancing just yet," Auntie Mame said slowly.

"We were going to Bad Gastein for our honeymoon," Vera said, "but *you* came *first*, my oldest and dearest friend. Besides, I wanted to give you an opportunity to be one of the original investors in this divine play I'm going to do for Freddie Lonsdale next fall. So I said to Basil . . . Mame, you look so pale. Can I get you something? Where's Amadeo?"

"Amadeo is in Spain," I said.

"In Spain?" Vera cried. "But Mame, darling, when will the wedding take place?"

"The wedding will take place," Auntie Mame said, "as soon as Amadeo finds another chump of a rich woman—a woman with too many dollars, not enough sense, and no best friend to save her."

Auntie Mame and a Family Affair

"SO AFTER YOU SWAM AND SUNNED ON THE BASQUE Coast what did you do?" Pegeen asked, eying me suspiciously.

"Why, nothing much. We went on to Italy."

"Where in Italy?"

"Venice mostly."

"I'll bet Venice! I can just see that old phony now, the life and soul of every down-and-out old countess and duke in the International Set."

"Pegeen, how can you talk that way? We did no such thing at all. Auntie Mame took a house in Venice and we led a very quiet, cultural life—just the family."

"Family?"

"Yes. Family. Just a sweet old cousin from down South who dropped in for a visit. In fact, my dear, he was so tiresome I won't even bother telling you about it."

. . .

ISAPPOINTED IN LOVE, Auntie Mame developed a certain soft, sweet piety. She spoke a good deal of God and the Hereafter and even went round to Berkeley Square for a brief fling with the Oxford Movement. The Oxford Group loved Auntie Mame, but Auntie Mame didn't love it. She found the proceedings "much too modern and intellectual" and "totally lacking in the mystery and pageantry of the older sects." So she decided to quit England and go straight to the source—Italy—reeking of *l'Ame Perdu* and armed with her Book of Common Prayer, although she regretted as we passed through Rome that it wasn't available in a Douay version.

Venice had a certain ecclesiastical splendor that appealed mightily to Auntie Mame, and it took her no time at all to establish herself as *the* Pearl of the Adriatic. She leased a pink Palladian *palazzo* right on the Grand Canal—all very nice if you didn't mind the terrible dampness or the faint odor of garbage that wafted up from the lapping waters. The house featured some imitation Veronese frescoes, a genuine Bronzino portrait, some so-so Canalettos, and quite a lot of rococo furniture.

Auntie Mame also hired a private gondola and four strapping Venetians to make it go, but she was sick with disappointment when she learned that all the gondolas in Venice had to be black. She made up for it by designing the gondoliers' costumes—I use the word advisedly—herself. They were black and pink with long, fluttering pink streamers on the hats, and they caused a distressing number of low, lewd whistles when Auntie Mame's men rowed past the other gondoliers. In fact, they got into so many fist fights proving their masculinity to less spectacularly dressed oarsmen that Auntie Mame's gondola often looked more like the emergency ward at Bellevue than the regal barge it was supposed to be. However, Auntie Mame cheerfully applied liniment to bruised jaws and beefsteak to black eyes, doubled their salaries, and threw in a sort of homemade workmen's compensation policy to keep her boat afloat.

The proper background created, Auntie Mame then set about finding suitable society to keep her amused during her indefinite stay in Venice. Find it she did one humid afternoon when her gondoliers, rakish in pink and studded with Band-Aids, were skimming homeward along the surface of a narrow back alleyway. I wasn't paying much attention to anything besides the old crates and orange rinds bobbing on the murky water when I was interrupted from my daydreaming by loud cries of *"Stae!"* and *"Po'pe!"*

"Would you look at that big ostentatious gondola right out in the middle of . . ." Auntie Mame cried, rising to her feet.

I was just able to see a gigantic regatta-sized craft with *six* gondoliers in bright blue bearing down on us. Then there was a loud impact that sent Auntie Mame over backward into my lap. When we scrambled to our feet, fists were flying and a large blonde—in the same shade of blue as her six gondoliers—was shrieking something in Italian that sounded like "Give 'em hell!"

Auntie Mame got to her feet again and cried, "Boys! Now, boys, you stop that this minute!" No one paid the slightest attention to her. Auntie Mame shook her fist at the woman in blue and yelled, "If you'd just tell your reckless gondoliers to stay on the right side of the . . . Why, *Bella*!"

"*Mame*!" the woman cried. In a flutter of blue skirts she was in our boat and in Auntie Mame's arms. They embraced warmly and then the blonde screamed something in Italian so electrifying that all the gondoliers stopped fighting and crossed themselves.

"Patrick, my little love," Auntie Mame said, "this is one of my oldest friends in all the world—one of my playmates from Buffalo, Bella Shuttleworth!"

Fifteen minutes later we were having cocktails in Bella's *palazzo*, just a bit upstream from Auntie Mame's, while the pink gondoliers and the blue gondoliers, parked, so to speak, out in front, jabbered amicably about the vagaries of American employers.

Bella Shuttleworth was one of those old Buffalo girls—I had heard Auntie Mame mention her often while recalling her childhood on Delaware Avenue—who felt that she had more to give Buffalo than Buffalo was able to absorb. So, like Auntie Mame, she had cleared out as early as possible to come to more pleasant terms with life in places like New York City and Paris and Cannes and Venice. Bella had married an Italian marquis whose title was almost as attractive to her as her fortune was to him. Alas, he was not able to keep pace with Bella and he died before so much as a platinum cigarette case had changed hands, leaving Bella a *marchesa*, the chatelaine of his leaking *palazzo*, and even richer than she'd been when she left Buffalo. By now Bella Shuttleworth was more Venetian than the doges. She spoke both Italian *and* Venetian with a lusty fluency that would have horrified the headmistress of Miss Rushaway's School. Rather plain and pudgy to begin with, she had turned into a perfect dumpling of a middle-aged woman, her hair the color and consistency of spun sugar, and everything she wore dyed a blue that was midway between a robin's egg and a baby's bonnet. While at first glance—and even second—Bella may have looked like someone's cook got up for a Hibernian Outing, she was witty and jolly and created quite a stir in Venetian society. Auntie Mame

Auntie Mame...

could hardly have found a better patroness to guide her through the dark waterways of Venice.

And so Auntie Mame settled happily into the faintly foolish social whirl that Bella dominated. Every morning the pink gondoliers and the Bella-blue gondoliers set out in a vivid armada in search of new dresses at Capellini's or lunch at the Taverna La Fenice or even out to the Lido, where Bella displayed her rotund little figure, shamelessly contained in a frilly blue bathing suit plus a lot of pearls and diamonds. Within a week Auntie Mame was the heart and soul of a sort of international set made up of titles, artists, writers, and rich dilettantes, who liked nothing better than to be entertained in Auntie Mame's damp dining room and to banquet her and Bella in their equally moist houses and apartments.

And, best of all, Auntie Mame found not one, but two, most eligible beaux. Both were tall, handsome, single, and rich. Auntie Mame was naturally nervous about having another fortune hunter crawl out of the woodwork, but Bella, who knew to the last lira every income in Venice, was perfectly able to reassure her as to both suitors. One was a dashing, dark Italian princeling named Marcantonio della Cetera. The other contender for our girl's hand was a blond Swedish viking named Alex Falk. Between the two of them, Auntie Mame rarely had a free moment—not that she had ever wanted many free moments. I could tell that Auntie Mame's broken heart was well on the mend. In fact, Auntie Mame was so far out of the dumps that she was hell-bent on giving a big party, which was geared to come at the height of the season.

Auntie Mame and Bella decided to give the party together, and they settled down to solve such knotty problems as: 1) what sort of party it was to be; 2) which five hundred lucky people were to be invited; and 3) in whose house it was to be held.

The final plans were being drawn up on Bella's balcony one

sweltering afternoon when people with better sense were all napping behind closed blinds. I stretched sweatily out in a deck chair and tried to read *Death in Venice* while Auntie Mame and her old school chum haggled over the final details and swilled down a good deal more gin than seemed wise. What with the intense heat beating down on my skull and the genial bickerings of the ladies bleating into my ears, I didn't absorb very much of the book. What I did get, aside from a mild heat stroke, was that it was to be a period ball and that the period was to be, after a lot of discussion, Renaissance. The costumes were to be neither Auntie Mame's pink nor Bella blue, but black and white. Bella said this would be easier on the *Life* photographers, because surely *Life* would want to come to the party. There were to be fireworks in both pink *and* blue, and they tossed a coin to see in which house it would be given. Auntie Mame won.

The guest list presented a serious problem. Auntie Mame said, "No fascists, darling, absolutely none." Then Bella said, "For Christ's sake, ducky, it's a fascist *country*!" Then Auntie Mame said that if Bella was going to ask a lot of fascists, *she* was going to invite some Ethiopians. Bella said, "That was *last* year, ducky, but go ahead and ask all the Ethiopians you know." Auntie Mame didn't know any. After that the list was made up in a spirit of friendly compromise. Auntie Mame said that she could not invite Count and Countess Ciano because of political reasons. However, she decided that it was all right to ask the antique redhead who was the mistress of the deposed Kaiser Wilhelm, because the kaiser was practically dead—as was the mistress—and was no immediate international threat. You can see why I didn't get much reading done.

The sun had sunk in a big red ball and the gin had sunk to a pitiful little drop in the bottom of the bottle before the girls had threshed out their problems. By the time I helped Bella to

Auntie Mame ...

her bedroom and steered Auntie Mame down to her gondola, it was almost dusk.

But plenty more was to happen that day. The bobbing gondola had barely scraped the mossy steps of our house when an excited servant rushed out and cried, "Signora Burnside. Come quickly, Signor Burnside is here!"

Auntie Mame's hand flew to her heart and she said, "M-mister Burnside?" Then she got control of herself and said, "Impossible." But she looked pale and stricken and had to be helped out of the gondola.

Auntie Mame's husband, Beauregard Jackson Pickett Burnside, had been dead for three years, and since I had Viewed the Remains—if that's the correct term—and had watched Uncle Beau's outsized casket lowered into the red earth of Peckerwood, his plantation in Georgia, there was little doubt in my mind that he was as dead as an old light bulb. Once inside, though, even *I* wasn't too sure.

When we got into the house the loggia was dim and empty. "Well, where is he?" Auntie Mame said. Then a voice—exactly Uncle Beau's voice—said, "Mame? Mame, honey, here Ah am."

I looked upward among the artificial Veronese frescoes, depicting a lot of trompe l'oeil people leaning over both genuine and painted balustrades and there was a real-life, moving Uncle Beau. Auntie Mame looked up, too. "B-Beau?" she said. Her knees sagged and she turned the color of alabaster.

"Course it ain't Beau, Mame honey," the Uncle Beau-man said. "Beau's daid. It's Cousin Elmore."

"Oh," Auntie Mame said, regaining her strength somewhat. "P-please come down."

We went into one of the rooms off the loggia and Auntie Mame poured herself a tremendous drink. She'd downed half of it by the time Elmore Burnside made his entrance. The similarities between Elmore Jefferson Davis Burnside and Beauregard Jackson Pickett Burnside were amazing, but only at a distance. For the differences were equally amazing, and I often felt that, uncanny as the resemblance could be, Cousin Elmore was only a cheap imitation of Uncle Beau, hastily put out to please a less discriminating market.

Uncle Beau had been the best of the Burnsides. I know that isn't saying much, considering the rest of his awful family, who had all been horrid to Auntie Mame when Uncle Beau married her. But now, with Uncle Beau dead and buried, they were all beholden to Auntie Mame for every nickel they got. A person less generous and forgiving—the word "saintly" comes to mind, but I reject it—might easily have let the whole lot of them languish in the county almshouse, which was too good for most of the Burnsides. But not Auntie Mame. As Uncle Beau's sole heir she doled out generous allowances to all the hangers-on in the family and even kept her flatulent old termagant of a mother-in-law wallowing in laxatives and luxury at Peckerwood. By tacit agreement, Auntie Mame and her in-laws kept to their own sides of the Mason-Dixon Line, corresponding only at Christmas, when each of them sent her a tacky greeting card and when she mailed each of them a fat check. But Cousin Elmore was one Burnside we had never met before and he also occupied a unique position in that distinguished old family in that he was the only one of a hundred and some close relatives who worked for a living and wasn't on the family payroll.

I knew that Auntie Mame had never really got over Uncle Beau, for all of her flirtations since widowhood, but I also knew that if the superficial similarities between Beauregard Burnside and Elmore Burnside had stunned me, they must have done even more to Auntie Mame, who, even cold sober, was slightly nearsighted and too vain to wear glasses except when there was something she *had* to see.

But after the initial surprise had worn off, the dissimilarities grew ever more obvious, to me at least. Cousin Elmore

Auntie Mame . . .

was almost as tall as Uncle Beau, but where Beau had been what I believe is called a Big Man, Elmore was gross; blubber replacing muscle. Beauregard had had a Southern accent—naturally—but it was more or less under control. Cousin Elmore sounded just like an End Man. While Uncle Beau had had an absolute genius for making money, he never mentioned it or business. Cousin Elmore rarely talked of anything else, except sex. The first thing he said, after soundly kissing Auntie Mame, was "Ah travel in ladies' undahway-ah," an unsettling statement that instantly had my gaze fastened on his open sport shirt to see if I could catch sight of a lacy camisole peeping out among the pineapples, hula girls, and hair.

And that brings up the subject of clothing. Uncle Beau always looked like a million dollars, not because he had millions in the bank, but because he had billions in taste. He was the kind of man who could have appeared in a fig leaf and still been faultlessly dressed. Not so Cousin Elmore. Elmore Burnside was wrinkle-prone, a pattern pushover, and color-crazed to the point of dementia. He reveled in green gabardine, in bright blue tweed, in chocolate browns, damson plums, and pearl grays. His shirts all had very virile brand names like Cowboy Casual, Rogue, Buccaneer, He-Man Haberdashery, and Sir Sportsman, but they all ran to the pansiest of colors—the more the merrier—in frightfully gay prints, and he wore them all hanging outside his trousers as though he might be just the tiniest bit pregnant.

Some nights when I have trouble sleeping, I find myself looking back upon Cousin Elmore's considerable wardrobe and trying to pick out just which items impressed me—or depressed me—the most. There were, for example, his shoes. He had dozens of pairs, for Cousin Elmore often confessed—without even being pressed—to foot trouble. The shoes, too, often had manly names such as Lothario Loafer, Bronco

Brogue, Robin Hood, Kadet Kasual, and Mr. Metatarsal, but when you came right down to them, they all squeaked like *castrati*. Elmore favored two—or even three—tones of gray calf; woven straw and fabric mesh; boxed or pointed toes, and more eyelets and perforations per square inch than seemed possible. His socks, however, were always white.

Or could it have been Elmore's jewelry? He loved big studs and links of simulated—Elmore wittily called them "stimulated"—rubies and sapphires; great gobs of garbage gold, intricately machine-stamped; beaten silver and wondrously wrought glass. His fingers and lapels always glittered with an impressive array of lodge rings and emblems, worn interchangeably because Elmore was quite a joiner and hadn't nearly enough digits to display the spoils of his good fellowship. Nor were any of Elmore's neckties complete without a golf club, an eight ball, a skull with crossed bones, or a scotty—brutally hanged from a silver link chain—to hold them in place. *Naturally* he had all the latest fads in key chains, lighters, souvenir cigarette cases, fountain pens, and automatic pencils.

At other times I think it must have been Elmore's hats. He was the kind of person who is incapable of invading strange territory without instantly adopting its native head-gear. For that reason he had—*and wore*—a ten-gallon Stetson, a blue beret, a sola topee, a cricket cap, a gondolier's hat, a green Tyrolean with brush, a huge Panama, said to be woven under water (where it certainly should have remained), and quite a collection of less remarkable hats in velours to match—or contrast with—his vivid suitings.

Well, I don't know exactly what one *could* say about Cousin Elmore's clothes that would do them full justice. To sum it all up in a nutshell, you could sell him *any* garment simply by telling him that no other man in town owned anything like it.

But Cousin Elmore, while admitting to sartorial splendor,

Auntie Mame . . .

fancied himself not so much Beau Brummel as Samuel Johnson. It was his sense of humor that was the most agonizing thing about him. I don't mean that he actually *had* a sense of humor. He was totally without one, although he thought he was killing and would have fought to the death anyone who so much as ventured the opinion that he was not. What Cousin Elmore really had was total recall of every joke he had ever heard from Joe Penner's radio program, from lodge stag parties, from smoking compartments, and from World War I. What he did not bank on was that everyone else remembered them, too, when reminded, and that few of them had been funny to begin with.

The pun was Cousin Elmore's bluntest instrument of torture, and he never let any opportunity for injecting a sodden riposte elude him. During his seemingly endless stay in Venice, he was introduced three times to girls named Virginia and each time he said, "Virgin foah short, but not foah long! Ha*hahahahaha*!" When he finally and mercifully left you, he always said, "Abyssinia! Ha*hahahahaha*!" At parties he invariably said, "Let's all make merry" (with a wink toward any woman named Mary) "and feel rosy" (same for women named Rose). "Ha*hahahahaha*!" He was perfectly terrible, if you see what I mean.

Unfortunately, with the sun and the gin and the shock, Auntie Mame wasn't seeing much of anything that evening.

"I-I simply can't get over it," she said, unwisely belting down the rest of her drink and blinking owlishly through the gloom at Cousin Elmore. "It's almost as if Beauregard himself had come into the room."

"Are you out of your mind?" I muttered.

"Ah was always motty fond of Cousin Boragod, Mamie," Elmore said.

"Oh, but you must think I'm so rude," Auntie Mame said. "Do let me offer you something to drink. And I might just have another myself. Patrick, be a lamb and do the honors." With that she toppled down onto a little sofa, whether from drink or emotion I don't to this day know.

"What'll it be, sir," I asked, "whisky or gin?"

"D'yawl have inny sow-ah may-ush bubbun, bub?"

"I'm afraid we can't get bourbon in Italy," I said. "But we do have Scotch."

"Oh," Cousin Elmore said, gazing at the Scotch bottle, "Vat 69. Ah always thought that was the pope's tellyphone numbah. Ha*hahahahaha*!"

I had first heard that joke in 1933 on the day Prohibition was repealed, but I made a manful attempt at a chortle. Auntie Mame tittered inanely. "Scotch then?" I asked.

"That's right, sonny, Scotch and bray-unch wattah. But not too much wattah. Rusts the pipes. Ha*hahahahaha*!"

I mixed a strong drink for Cousin Elmore, hoping to shut him up; a *very* weak one for Auntie Mame; and a fair-sized scoop for myself. I needed it. But I put it down after one sip when I heard Auntie Mame say, "But of course, Beau—I mean Cousin Elmore—of course you'll stay to dinner with us."

"Why, Cousin Mamie, that'd be motty nice."

It was not without a certain horror that I saw Auntie Mame, empty glass in hand, sway unsteadily across the floor. "I may just have another. And I'll mix *this* one *myself*," she said ominously. Then she turned to Elmore Burnside. "And do let me step yours up, dar . . . uh, Cousin Elmore."

"That's right, Mamie. Duck cain't fly on one wing. Ha*hahahahaha*!"

They were together at the liquor table pouring out what looked like cough syrup when Auntie Mame first got a close-up of Elmore's hula-girl sport shirt. "What a divine blouse. Hawaii?"

"Ah'm fine, Mamie. How ah *yew*? Ha*hahahahaha*!" With

Auntie Mame . . .

that he whacked Auntie Mame across the back with a force that almost sent her sprawling.

"How too funny! Oh, Elmore, you're killing me!"

"As the actress said to the bishop! Ha*hahahahaha*!"

Auntie Mame was in paroxysms of laughter. I excused myself, thinking I might be sick. When I came back downstairs they were back at the liquor table again and Cousin Elmore was saying, "Centipede cain't walk on two laigs. Ha*hahahahaha*!" From the looks of Auntie Mame, I didn't think she could make it to the dining room on all fours, but she was flushed and radiant and said, "Oh, Elmore, I haven't laughed so much in years!"

DINNER WAS FINALLY ANNOUNCED.

Auntie Mame and Cousin Elmore, arm in arm, led the way lurchingly into dinner. En route they passed the genuine Bronzino portrait, a crooked reflector lighting the young man's pale face.

"Who's that purty Eyetalian gal?" Cousin Elmore said.

"That happens to be a pretty Italian *boy*," I said nastily.

"Well, he's settin' on the on'y place where yew could tell the diffrunce. Ha*hahahahaha*!"

"Oh, Elmore, you *are* dreadful!"

"*Dreadful?*" I murmured.

"It's a portrait by Bronzino. It's an Old Master," Auntie Mame giggled.

"Well, yew kin keep youah old mastuhs. Jess give me a *young mistress*. Ha*hahahahaha*!"

The two of them could hardly stand up, *that* remark was so funny.

Dinner was a nightmare. Auntie Mame, glassy-eyed by now, sat between us, and Elmore told one of his favorite stories—a joke we were to hear *many* times in the future—ending up "Ah, vi-ola! Lucky Pee-ayuh, always in zee middle! Hahahahahaha!" He spoke of the cold kidney bean hors d'oeuvre as "sheet music"—a sally that was lost on Auntie Mame but which had been a standard thigh-slapper at boarding schools since 1888. Out of grim politesse, I had tried at first to muster up a counterfeit chuckle after each of Cousin Elmore's sallies. By the time we got to dinner, I hadn't the strength. Nor, I discovered, was it even necessary to smile. Cousin Elmore was his own best audience; he went into such gales of laughter that he didn't even notice whether anyone else was amused or not.

Auntie Mame was so far gone by then that she simply giggled all the time and, between snickers, kept herself and Cousin Elmore refueled by ordering two additional kinds of wine. I suppose anesthesia of any sort helped.

That Elmore! What a card! When the fish came in he said, "This is motty good, Cupcake. What is it?"

"It's uh, it's, uh—what the hell, darling, it's Baccala Mario." Mario was the cook who came along with the house. He named all the dishes for himself.

"Shoot mah shoes, what's tha-yut?"

"It's fish balls," I hissed.

"Best part of the fish! Hahahahahaha!" I'd heard that witticism every Friday at school for seven years, and Auntie Mame had probably heard it seventeen years before that. Even so, she was helpless with laughter and choked on her wine.

"Oh, Elmore, darling. You're too killing! *So* like dear Beau. Tell me," she said, eyes glistening even if they weren't exactly focusing, "where are you staying?"

"Some wop dump, Tidbit, honey. Heah, Ah got it written down."

"Well, you're not going to stay there any longer. You're moving right in with us. . . . Ouch!" I'd fetched her a kick under the table that hobbled her for three days.

I should have kicked her in the head and harder because she went right on talking about how Cousin Elmore must move in with us for the whole summer. Then, with a fluency that she could never have managed had she been sober, she gave instructions to have Mr. Burnside's belongings picked up in the gondola and brought to the *palazzo precipitevolisimevolmente*. (That is the longest word in Italian. It means quickly.)

At that point the greens came on, and Cousin Elmore, flushed with triumph, said, "What *Ah* lak best is Honeymoon Salad. Yew know what that is, Dollfeather? *Lettuce alone, without dressing!* Ha*h*a*h*a*h*a*h*a!"

Auntie Mame rolled helplessly in her chair, sobbing with laughter. "Oh, Beau," she wailed, "darling!"

I thought grimly, Just one more course to go and then I can get away from Joe Miller and his straight man. How wrong I was.

We had fresh figs for dessert. Cousin Elmore then displayed the only word in Italian he ever bothered to learn. "*Fighi, fighi!* Ha*h*a*h*a*h*a*h*a!" Auntie Mame didn't get it. She just giggled out of habit. But it wasn't lost on the elderly servant. He dropped a platter and bolted for the kitchen, *precipitevolisimevolmente*.

"D'you wish coffee?" Auntie Mame said, simpering sweetly.

"Jewish coffee? Hell no, Cupcake, I don't want no Jewish coffee. Give me *gentile* coffee! Ha*h*a*h*a*h*a*h*a!"

Auntie Mame rose and said, with a distressing slur, "Patrick, do shee that Beauregard—*Elmore*—has an itty-bitty ship of brandy. I'm going slap into—I mean schlitz into something comfy." With that she lurched out, leaving me alone with that great humorist and traveler in ladies' underwear, Elmore Burnside.

"What would you like, sir?" I asked as politely as possible.

"Whaddaya sujjest, kiddo?"

"A little straight curare?" I said, with a hospitable smile.

"Naw, none of them fancy dago drinks. Jus' some brandy. Then siddown. Ah got some stories to tell yew. Real man stuff. Wouldn't be suitable in mixed company."

I poured out two brandies—one for Elmore and one in self-defense.

Cousin Elmore's boy-type jokes were, if possible, older than his coeducational ones and even less funny. "Stop me if yew've heard this one," he said, "but it seems that this fellah with a twitch in his eye gets in a taxi an' sez . . ."

"Stop," I said.

Cousin Elmore went right on and finished the joke.

"Now stop me if yew've heard this one, kiddo, but it seems that this constipated Scotchman goes inta the drugstore an' sez, 'Hoot may-un . . .' "

"Stop!" I said. Undaunted, he rambled on until his own orgasm of joy all but shattered the glasses on the dining table. I wouldn't have minded hearing all these old, old favorites yet again if only Elmore had told them well. He didn't. He was always leaving out things, always having to regress, always interrupting himself to say, "Oh, Ah should of tole yew that it was a *mulllatta* whoor. Innyways . . ."

My head was reeling by the time Auntie Mame called, "Come in, boys, I'm lonely," and rescued me from the old bore's exclusive attentions.

Auntie Mame was stretched out on a sofa drinking champagne, although she was so boiled she could hardly hold her glass. She looked comfortable all right in a whisper of white chiffon trimmed with *coq* feathers, which kept getting into her drink, her eyes, her nose, and her mouth.

"Come sit by me," she said, patting the sofa seductively.

I almost broke a leg getting there before Elmore did.

"Hi-yah, Dollfeather!" Cousin Elmore boomed. He was

Auntie Mame . . .

drunk as an owl, but he was certainly holding it better than Auntie Mame, although she *had* had a head start.

"Patrick, darling," Auntie Mame said, handing a glass of champagne to Cousin Elmore, "you must be exhausted. Why don't you run up to bed?"

"Who, *me*?" I said, all wide-eyed vivacity. "Nonsense. It's scarcely two-thirty. I'm having a wow of a time. It's a riot." I wouldn't have left Auntie Mame alone with that old goat—in her condition—for a million dollars cash.

"Now donchew worry about Tidbit an' I, bub," Elmore said. "With us things is strickly *platonic—play* foah *me* an' *tonic* foah *her*! Ha*haha*hahaha!"

That set off a two-hour recitative of hoary old saws which Elmore described as "slightly riss-kay"—jollifications so ancient that Auntie Mame wouldn't admit to having heard them if she'd been put to the rack. Instead, she smiled sweetly, made pretty little *mouses* and finally dozed off, sighing, "Beauregard. Beau, darling."

Around five o'clock I gave her a jab with my elbow and she awoke with a snort. "Heavens, how late it's become! I've had your things put in the room across the hall from me, Cousin Elmore. Just ring when you want your breakfast. What do you usually like?"

"Me? Why, Cupcake, Ah lak a *French* Breakfast. Yew know what that is, Dollfeather? It's a *roll* in *bed* with *honey*! Ha*haha*-*ha*haha!"

I could stand it no more. "I'll take you upstairs now, Auntie Mame," I said. Then I added pointedly, "Remember, you've got to get up *early* in the morning."

"Ah, yes," Auntie Mame sighed, rising limply to her feet. "Up with the birds."

"That's what *Ah* always say, Mamie, 'Up with the birds; to bed with innything.' Ha*haha*haha*ha*!"

I snatched Auntie Mame out of the room and practically kicked her upstairs. I pushed her into her bedroom and locked the door from the outside. Then I went to my own room and gobbled down half a dozen aspirins. As I was going to sleep I heard Cousin Elmore in the adjoining bedroom humming "Roll Me Over in the Clover."

KNOWING EXACTLY HOW AUNTIE MAME WOULD BE feeling the following morning, I had sadistically planned a surprise raid on her bedroom at ten sharp and had set my clock accordingly. But before the alarm ever went off I was awakened by Auntie Mame's frantic pounding on her door and faint cries of "Patrick! Patrick!"

"What's the matter now," I said, opening her door, "delirium tremens?"

"Oh, Patrick, thank God you've come! The most horrible thing. Of course it's silly of me to be so upset—I know it's only a nightmare—but this ghastly man, got up as I—don't—know—what in the maddest outfit was out on my balcony calling me Horsefeathers, or something like that. . . ."

"Do you mean *Doll*feather?"

"Exactly, darling. How did you know? Well, it was simply too ghastly. I mean, there he was as clear as day talking about Tidbits and Cupcakes in that awful Georgia Cracker accent. Almost like one of the Burnsides."

"It *was* one of the Burnsides," I said levelly.

A terrible look of partial recollection came over her face. "P-Patrick," she began, bluffing it out, "you know when we came home from Bella's I had the strangest feeling . . ."

"I'm sure you did," I said.

"Well I don't know what got into me. . . ."

"*I* do. *Gin.* Gin and Vat 69—the pope's telephone number;

hahahahahaha! And then three kinds of wine at dinner and then . . ."

"Patrick, it was the hot sunshine at . . ."

"Hot sunshine, hell. It was cold moonshine. Cold moonshine and Cousin Elmore. Don't you remember, Uncle Beau's cousin—*Elmore Burnside*."

"Oh, Patrick. I do hope that one of Beau's relatives didn't come here and get the wrong impression and . . ."

"I think he may have."

"Well, I mean I hope he didn't go away thinking that . . ."

"Right you are. He didn't go away at all. He's moved in right across the hall—to *stay*. You asked him for the whole summer. He . . ."

The bedroom door burst open and there stood Cousin Elmore, dressed like nothing human in a loose-weave lavender mesh sport shirt through which I could see "Mother" tattooed on the right arm, "K K K" on the left. "Hey, Sig-norina Doll-feather! Heah's yoah ole cousin, Machiavelli—Machiavelli good chop suey! Hahahahahaha! How's about a gon-*do*-la ride, Mamie?"

"Is—is *that* Cousin Elmore?" Auntie Mame whispered hoarsely.

"It is," I said.

"Patrick," Auntie Mame croaked, "*call Bella!*"

AUNTIE MAME'S FRIEND BELLA THRIVED ON CRISIS. I had just managed to propel Cousin Elmore, punning every moment of the time, into Auntie Mame's gondola with instructions in halting Italian to take him for a long, long ride when Bella's blue boatmen came churning down the canal, the marchesa herself looking like Gorgeous George as Lohengrin in a full-speed-ahead-and-damn-the-torpedoes stance.

. . . and a Family Affair

Auntie Mame was waiting, stretched out across her unmade bed, a cold towel pressed to her brow.

"Now, ducky," Bella said in a businesslike manner, "start from the beginning and tell me all. Tell it straight. No play-acting."

"Well, Bella, darling," Auntie Mame whimpered, "the trouble is that I *can't.* A slight touch of the sun . . ."

"*I can,*" I said.

"All right, kid," Bella said, "*you* tell. And tell *all.*"

"A pleasure," I said. Then I began. "Well, it seems that this Cousin Elmore looks quite a lot like Uncle Beau. At least Auntie Mame seemed to think . . ."

"You should have your mouth washed out with soap, you little liar!" Auntie Mame said, rising to a sitting position. "He doesn't look in the least like . . ."

"Shut up, ducky," Bella said. "Patrick knows what happened. *You* don't. Go on, kid."

Granted the floor, I gave it everything I had, tucking in—here and there—some rather devastating impersonations of Auntie Mame and Cousin Elmore. I must have done it pretty well because my monologue was interrupted now and then by baleful moans from Auntie Mame and by Bella's malign chuckling. "And so," I came reluctantly to a close, "*at Auntie Mame's gracious invitation*, Cousin Elmore is here with us—two trunks and three satchels—*for the whole summer.* Summer lucky, summer not. Ha*hahahahaha!*"

"Ohhh," Auntie Mame gasped, "it was the sun. A touch of the sun."

"It was not," I said firmly. "You were boiled by the time you left Bella's."

"That's it," Auntie Mame said, sitting up again. "It's that gin you serve, Bella Shuttleworth. That poisonous cheap gin!"

"You're a God-damned liar, Mame Dennis," Bella shouted. In moments of emotion the girls always lapsed back into

Auntie Mame . . .

maiden names. "That was the best English gin—straight from London. And if it's good enough for Neville Chamberlain, it's good enough for you, ducky. But that isn't the point. The problem at hand now is how to get rid of this slob."

"Exactly, darling, it's up to you to save me," Auntie Mame said, and fell back on the bed.

The rest of the morning was given over to changing Auntie Mame's compresses, to sporadic plans for the forthcoming Renaissance ball, and to thinking of ways to get rid of Cousin Elmore.

By noon Auntie Mame was just able to dress for luncheon—and a rather important luncheon, at that, since both contenders for her hand were coming. They arrived punctually at one, and Auntie Mame, looking pale and interesting, urged them and Bella to have cocktails while she stuck to Fernet-Branca and murmured something about a slight indisposition. To round out the party, Auntie Mame had also invited a distinguished German rabbi, a French cardinal, and a Greek poetess said to be the biggest thing since Sappho. Lunch was served in the *cortile* and almost everything was pink—linen, *prosciutto*, and wine. Auntie Mame was white, and only toyed with her food, but she turned the color of ashes when, in the midst of a brilliant discussion of Jean Cocteau, she looked up and saw Cousin Elmore making his way noisily across the pavement in his lavender mesh sport shirt and a pair of oxblood Jesus sandals that squealed with every step.

"Looks good enough to eat," he said, pulling up a chair right next to Auntie Mame. "Ha*hahahahaha*!" The discussion of Cocteau came to an instant halt.

However, Elmore Burnside felt right at home in *any* society and was never at a loss for something witty to say. Within five minutes he had managed indirectly to insult everyone at the table. He polished off Auntie Mame's two serious suitors, Axel and Marcantonio, with a long dialect story about an Italian and a Swede improvidentially caught in a Turkish bath on ladies' night. Of Elmore's fifty thousand old jokes, at least forty-nine thousand depended entirely on the most unlikely circumstances. As an encore he told me about Izzy and Paddy Paddy—a *very* long story involving mackerel, ham, circumcision, and rosary beads—and that just about took care of the cardinal and the rabbi. I was a little relieved to discover that, owing to their and Elmore's unfamiliarity with English, they didn't understand it. I shouldn't have been. Elmore retraced his steps and painstakingly explained the whole sordid joke with lots of "*Oi wehs*" and "Faith and bejazuses." Auntie Mame went from white to a delicate green.

Another feature of Cousin Elmore's great sense of humor was his love of gimmicks. He wouldn't have been caught dead without some witty appurtenance such as his false nose, his itching powder, his badge that read "Chicken Inspector," or his electric cane. He doted upon boutonnieres that squirted water, fake roaches that could be slipped into coffee cups, and rubber dog turds. However, one of his favorites was a murky glass bubble which he would insert into one nostril while pretending to blow his nose. When the handkerchief was taken away, the sight was one that made strong men weak.

"Guess Ah caught mahself a li'l ole cold," Cousin Elmore said, elaborately whipping out his handkerchief. Then he blew his nose and left the glass bubble protruding horribly from his right nostril. My stomach was already churning, but Auntie Mame saved the day. She rose weakly from the table and fainted dead away. Luncheon could not be said to have been a great success.

A WEEK LATER AUNTIE MAME WAS AT HER WIT'S END. She had lost ten pounds and twenty friends and still Cousin Elmore stuck to her like glue. Every ruse she and Bella worked

Auntie Mame . . .

out failed dismally; even the trumped-up cable from the Belle Poitrine ("Come Fill the Cup") Brassière Company of Buffalo—Bella owned the controlling interest—offering Cousin Elmore the sales-managership at fifty thousand a year left him curiously unmoved and unmoving.

Auntie Mame didn't like Cousin Elmore in the least, but she made the mistake of dismissing him as merely a big, good-natured oaf, who also happened to be the bore of creation. Bore he was, and oaf, too, but no one who really knew Elmore could possibly call him good-natured. Behind his appallingly hearty façade, behind his endless protestations of being just a country boy, Elmore was deceitful, stingy, bigoted, pig-ignorant, and very, very cruel. During the all-too-many times when I was alone with him and he felt free to cast aside the dubious delicacy which he affected in the presence of women, he regaled me with such jolly reminiscences as a lynching party he once organized in South Carolina; how he had dipped a cat in kerosene and set fire to it; how he had once foisted a shipment of faulty girdles on a Jewish merchant and then reported him to the Chamber of Commerce for selling shoddy goods. When I didn't laugh he accused me of being dolefully short on humor.

"WELL, I GIVE UP!" AUNTIE MAME SAID TO BELLA and me on one of the rare occasions when Cousin Elmore wasn't around. "That braying jackass follows me like a shadow. I can hardly take a bath without having that bloody bore swim up the drain. I've tried every way to get rid of him short of suicide."

"There's always murder," Bella suggested.

"Don't think I haven't considered it. Here I have my choice between two of the most attractive men in Europe and what happens? Every time Axel or Marcantonio invites me out,

Cousin Elmore tags along, telling his dreadful old jokes and . . ."

"Well, I'm glad that *you* realize it, ducky," Bella growled, "because now it won't come as such a surprise when I tell you that socially you're going to be the deadest duck in Venice if you can't get rid of that cousin."

As though to prove Bella's baleful prophecy, the telephone rang. It was Axel Falk begging off from the afternoon at the Lido that he and Auntie Mame had planned. Without knowing exactly what, I realized that Something Must Be Done.

Auntie Mame decided to spend the afternoon at Capellini's being fitted for her ball costume under the watchful eye of Antonietta. Since Cousin Elmore had once almost caused a riot at Capellini's by putting on one of Auntie Mame's hats and wandering in and out of the dressing rooms doing what he considered a riotous imitation of a woman, I took him in hand and dragged him off to the Piazza San Marco for a few beers. He was in his usual grim form, calling Giuseppe the waiter, "Juicy-Soupy," and saying killing things about leading a dog's life in the Doge's Palace. I sat with a stiff, set smile wishing I were dead when suddenly, with his third beer, Elmore became serious. If there was anything worse than a jocular Elmore, it was a serious one. It wasn't so much how he said things, it was what he had to say.

"Ah wonder if Dollfeather's finished orderin' her dress foah that party she's givin'?"

"Oh, no, Cousin Elmore," I said. "She'll be there all afternoon—*at least*. That period ball means a lot to her."

"An' it means a lot to me, too, kiddo. Ah've kinda set it as mah deadline."

"To leave Italy?" I asked hopefully. "That's a very good idea. You know the monsoon season starts in Venice just about then—big tidal waves and . . ."

"No, kiddo, it's mah deadline with Tidbit—with yoah Auntie Mame. Ah'm already fixin' mah costume."

"You're not planning to *come* to the party?"

"Yes, and Ah'm goin' as a gesture."

"A *gesture*?"

"That's right, son. A court gesture. Lak Ah am in real life. You know, always cheerin' people up, makin' 'em laugh, helpin' 'em forget their troubles."

"I—I don't think you'd enjoy it very much," I said hastily. "You know, it's a lot of trouble wearing costumes and . . . besides, I'm not sure that they *had* court jesters in the Renaissance."

"That don't mattah. Besides, Ah got somethin' motty important to take up with yoah aunt that night. Ah want to save her."

"*Save* her? Who, Auntie Mame?" Cousin Elmore in an evangelical role seemed odd, to say the least.

"That's right, kiddo. Now tell me the truth, how'dja lak a new uncle?"

"A new uncle? Why, it really wouldn't mean much to me one way or another. I'm practically grown up—going to college this year. I suppose Auntie Mame will want to marry again and it doesn't much matter to me whether she picks Axel or Marcantonio. They're both . . ."

"Theah both a couple of dirty foreigners, that's what they are!" Elmore said with some feeling. "One's a slick Swede and the other's a dirty dago. That's what Ah'm tryin' to save her *from*. What Ah'm tryin' to tell yew is that *Ah* plan to carry yoah auntie off mahself."

"You *what*?"

"Yew hudd me. We're Amurricuns and, what's more, we're *Burnsides*. Ah mean to marry Mamie mahself an' save her from that sneakin' Swede and that stinkin' wop!"

I was too stunned to speak, but not too stunned to notice a rather evil-looking man in a black uniform eying Elmore from the next table. He wrote something in a notebook. In a flash I began to see a way to get Cousin Elmore out of Venice and out of Auntie Mame's hair. A band was playing somewhere and I pretended that I hadn't heard.

"I'm sorry, Cousin Elmore, but with all that racket I didn't quite hear what you said about Marcantonio. Would you mind repeating it—just a bit louder."

"Ah said he was a stinkin' wop—just like the rest of these stinkin' wops, and by Christ Ah hate 'em all."

"Thank you, Cousin Elmore," I said, averting my face just as the man at the next table took a candid camera shot. At that moment the square was filled with sound and color. First came a brass band playing the "Giovinezza," a sprightly marching air of the Fascisti and then the *carabinieri* trooped in. In their slightly silly operetta uniforms, their feathered Napoleonic hats, they made for a picturesque though rather inefficient police force.

"Gawd damn if that don't look lak one of mah lodge uniforms," Cousin Elmore said.

I'll grant that the *carabinieri* did look a little like Knights Templar gone gaudy. "What lodge is that, Cousin Elmore?"

"The Stalwart Sons of the Secession—Lodge Numbah One-one-five. Even sounds lak one of ouah marchin' songs. It goes lak this:

> "*Stalwart Sons of the Secession*
> *Evah marchin' to the fo-ah*
> *Fightin' Yankees' crool aggression*
> *Fo' the States' Rights we adoah*

The tune ain't *exackly* the same, but it's *close*. We Sons have a big convention every year. Why, last year at Chattanooga, Ah

Auntie Mame . . .

raised more hell than innybody in the whole lodge. They all call me the Big Cutup."

"What did you do, Cousin Elmore?"

"Well, ha*hahahahaha*! Ah had mah ee-lectric cane—the same one I got with me heah—an' Ah'd come up behind these people an' . . ."

"You know what I'll bet, Cousin Elmore," I said, "I'll bet these are the southern Italian branch of the Stalwart Sons of the Secession. See that big one there with the sword and the mustache? Why don't you take your electric cane and . . ."

The words weren't out of my mouth before Cousin Elmore and his electric cane were halfway across the Piazza San Marco. I turned to the man in black at the next table and said dramatically, "*Anarchisto!* Anti-Mussolini!" pointing in the general direction of Cousin Elmore. Then all hell broke loose and I had just time to get under a table.

IF AUNTIE MAME HAD BEEN, SOCIALLY SPEAKING, A dead duck that afternoon, she was a bird of paradise that evening. With Cousin Elmore carted off to God knew where, she was perfectly free to get up an impromptu gathering with no fear of Elmore's lousing it up.

Although I didn't tell her what had happened, I assured her that Elmore wouldn't be around for at least twenty-four hours. I didn't like to think of Elmore undergoing heroic doses of castor oil or mustard enemas or any of the other anal forms of torment so popular with the fascists. But, as Elmore had so often proclaimed, he was an Amurricun citizen, and so he would get off with little more than a fine and sharp reprimand. "Go ahead, Auntie Mame," I said, "ask anyone you like for this evening. The coast is clear. I fixed everything."

"Oh, Patrick darling, you're an absolute genius," she said, kissing me on her way to the telephone.

The company that evening was made up of the few Serious Thinkers in Bella's and Auntie Mame's Venetian circle. Aside from Bella and Marcantonio della Cetera, there were the former Chinese ambassador and his wife, a famous Lutheran anti-Nazi, a wounded Spanish Republican aviator, a left-wing Yugoslav lady lawyer, and a Liberian Whig leader.

Finished with eating, the Serious Thinkers had settled down to Good Talk, which was mostly about the wars raging in Spain and in China and the sorry state of the world. Auntie Mame had a well-furnished mind when she chose to display it and that evening she was being very much the liberal intellectual leader.

Correct me if I'm wrong, Dr. Chung," she was saying, "but I had always thought that in the last Chinese election . . ."

"Yah know when the Chinks have their best elections, Dollfeather?" a voice called out. "Just before bleakfast! Hahahahahaha!"

Auntie Mame's jaw dropped. So did mine. There stood Cousin Elmore, dirty and disheveled. "W-why, C-Cousin Elmore," she said, giving me a look that should have stunted my growth forever, "I—that is Patrick—I mean I didn't think you'd be home tonight."

"Better late than never, Cupcake. Hahahahahaha!"

"Who says so?" Bella growled, gathering up her bag.

Auntie Mame hurriedly rushed into a flurry of introductions beginning with the Yugoslav woman and adding, "Of course you know Marcantonio."

"Ah sure do. Yugo your way and dago theirs. Hahahahahaha!"

He called the Liberian "Snowball" once and "Uncle" twice. He greeted the Loyalist aviator with a hot one involving Spanish fly, and said to the Chinese ambassador, "Lissen One-Hung-Low, is it true what they say about Chinese women?" Within fifteen minutes all the guests had left.

Auntie Mame . . .

Auntie Mame was so furious that she slammed her bedroom door in my face and wouldn't give me a chance to explain. But when I turned out my bedroom lights and opened the window I did notice the man in black lurking in the shadows of Auntie Mame's house. This rather unsettling sight gave me hope for the morrow.

THE NEXT MORNING AUNTIE MAME WAS UP AND OUT before I even got down to breakfast. I figured that she was either hopping mad or else getting a final fitting for her ball costume, or—more likely—both. It wasn't long before Cousin Elmore joined me, dressed for the day in a Confederate cap and a scarlet slack suit. Two cameras and a light meter dangled around his neck. "Rooty-tooty, tutti-frutti!" Elmore said, helping himself to oranges and grapes.

"Would you like an egg?" I asked.

"*Egg*-zactly! Then Ah wanna tell yew my programmy foah today. First Ah wanna go out an' git some things foah mah costume to wear at the party tomorrah. Then Ah thought Ah'd take some photos. An' then Ah'm gonna hire me a boat."

"What do you want with a boat?"

"Why for when Ah take mah little Cupcake off, right after the big party."

"Listen, Cousin Elmore," I said, "have you, um, *discussed* this at all with Auntie Mame? I mean I'm not at all sure that she'll be receptive to such . . ."

"Now lissin, kiddo, Ah'm a man of the wuld an' Ah kin tell when a little lady kinda takes a hankerin' for me. Why, yew saw how she acted the very first time we met."

"Auntie Mame, um, wasn't herself that night," I said.

"Besides, I bin motty lonely jes travelin' in lonjeray. Motty lonely. An' Tidbit's been lonely, too. Ah'd lak to settle down, quit sellin' an' jes sorta keep an eye on that little lady's affairs." I gazed at him quizzically. Cousin Elmore flushed and once again I could almost see the meanness and craftiness of his nasty little soul bubbling up through his veneer of good-fellowship. "Now lookee here, kiddo," he said almost angrily and almost as though he were trying to convince himself as well, "Ah'm older'n yew an' Ah know a *lot* about the ladies. Ah know it's me she wants. That's why she's tryin' to make me jealous with all them foreign gigolos. That's why..." Elmore went on and on. Like most men who are supremely unattractive to women, Cousin Elmore was somehow able to find invitation in every insult, a caress in every blow, come-hither in every go-yonder and a yes in every no. "Besides," he said, "Ah got a way with the gals. Ah happen to of read that famous book *How to Keep a Woman Happy*. It's by *Ryder Haggard*! Ha*h*a*h*a*h*a*h*a!"

Elmore was still going on about his sexual conquests as he parked his big rump in a hired gondola. As I got aboard, I noticed that *two* men in black were putt-putt-putting slowly behind us in a small motor launch.

"I'll wait for you here at the landing," I said to Cousin Elmore as he made his way toward a dim shop that sold souvenirs and novelties.

"Okay, kiddo. Ah'd prefer yew not to come. Ah want mah costume to be a big surprise. 'Specially to Dollfeather."

"I'm sure it will be," I said. Then I saw one of the men in black trailing Cousin Elmore. As I reached into my pocket for a cigarette, the other—the man I'd seen the day before—sidled up to me.

"Who is he?" the man asked in heavily accented English.

"*Buon giorno*," I said. "Who's who?"

"Him," he said, darting his head toward Elmore. "The man in the red shirt."

Looking at the man's black shirt and then at Cousin

Auntie Mame...

Elmore's red one gave me an inspiration. "Don't tell any-body," I muttered, "but he's the leader of the Red Shirts. Sinister." Then I added what I hoped was an Italian translation. "*Sinistro.*"

"*Sinistro?*" the man said, giving me a piercing look.

"*Si. Molto sinistro.*"

"American?" the man said, writing furiously in his note-book.

"*South* American," I said. "And the leader of the Stalwart Sons of the Secession. They're very active in keeping the Civil War going. They call him *Il Big Cutup.*"

"*Cutup?*"

"*Si, si,*" I said, reveling in my pidgin Italian. "Cutup. You know—knife. *Grosso coltello.*" That was enough to send him hotfooting to the nearest telephone.

I settled down in the gondola to wait for Cousin Elmore. He wasn't long in coming, this time loaded down with ominous-looking packages and followed by *three* men in black.

"My, you must have bought quite a lot," I said as Elmore got into the gondola. Out of the corner of my eye I saw that we were now leading a grim little convoy of three boats.

"Ah sure did," Cousin Elmore said smugly. "Theah all stunts Ah got planned foah the party tomorrah. Look, Ah'll show yew one—but *jest* this one." Reaching into a bag he brought out the deadliest-looking .45 automatic I've ever seen.

"Hey, be careful," I said.

"Don't be scared, kiddo. It's on'y a squirt gun. But now let me take some photos an' then we'll have lunch. Know what Ah'd like? A lotta *gnocchi* an' some coffee-oh-*lay.* Ha*hahaha-hah*a! Now, where'll we go so's I kin git some good shots, kiddo? You know this town."

Flushed with my earlier triumphs and seeing the boats still behind us, I pushed my luck hard. "How about getting some pictures of the Casermette?"

"The what?"

"The Casermette. That's Italian for you know what kind of house, Cousin Elmore. Plenty of hot stuff. All the big guns go there. Ha*hahaha*ha*ha*!" Oh, let me tell you, I was really killing myself.

"Yeah?" Elmore said with a hot gleam in his little pig eyes.

"Sure. You can tell all your lodge about it. Get some really great pictures. Let's go. The Casermette," I called to the gondolier.

With Elmore brandishing his new gun, we made a half-circle of the island and, the three motorboats still following, pulled up to the big, bleak barracks near the Fondamenta Nuove. "Don't look like much," Elmore said, getting out his camera and light meter, and standing up in the gondola.

"Oh, but wait till you see the inside," I said.

"Ah cain't seem to git it in focus," Elmore said. Then the three boats began to swoop down on us. "What the hell?" Elmore asked, rocking the gondola fearfully.

"Oh, oh," I said. "It's the Italian Communists. A regular maffia. Better swim for it, Elmore." I gave him a slight push. There was a fearful splash. "Home," I said to the gondolier.

Back at the house the servants were on the verge of hysterics and every drawer in every room had been ransacked. From what I could understand, the Gerarchi, the Balilla, the Avangardisti, the Giovani Italiana, the Figlia della Lupa—every fascist save Mussolini himself—had been through the place during the last hour and had finally left empty-handed. Elmore's room had suffered the most thorough going over. However, the place was put to rights before Auntie Mame returned, still seething.

Auntie Mame...

"Well," she said, "what are *you* looking so pleased about, Judas Iscariot? I suppose you're going to tell me that you pushed Cousin Elmore into the canal and we'll never see him again. Is that it, Suet Pudding?" she asked caustically.

"How right you are, Alum Cake. We won't see Elmore until the Armageddon. And that reminds me, Armageddon kind of sick of your stinking attitude. Ha*hahahahaha*! *I* didn't ask him here, *you* did and . . ."

"Oh, shut up! I know it isn't your fault, but if I don't get him *out* of here, I think I'll . . ."

"But this time, it's been done, Auntie Mame." Then I told her what had happened.

Auntie Mame laughed until the tears came. She hugged me and kissed me and hustled to the telephone to call Bella. "Tomorrow," she said, "is going to be an evening that all Venice will remember. At last Elmore's gone and my darling Patrick did it all. Get out your glad rags, Bella, tonight I'm going to give a party in Patrick's honor. He's saved me, saved me, *saved* me!"

Auntie Mame gave a dinner party for me at the Casino with *both* Axel and Marcantonio dancing attendance. I got kissed by a pretty girl named Marina who said that I was cuter than Mickey Rooney, and when we got back to Auntie Mame's house at three in the morning there was still no sign of Cousin Elmore. "He's gone, my little love," Auntie Mame sighed happily, "and tomorrow night at the party I'm going to give you a divine new uncle. Both Axel and Marcantonio asked for my hand tonight. So now I've got two to choose from."

I was just about to tell her that she really had a choice of *three*, if she'd like to consider Cousin Elmore. But she looked up at the clock and said, "Heavens! Look at the time! I'll be a sight tomorrow if I don't get my beauty sleep. Good night, my little love. Auntie will never forget what you've done for her."

I AWOKE LATE THE FOLLOWING MORNING WITH THE household in an uproar. There were men on the roof setting up fireworks, men in the *cortile* laying a dance floor, men putting up a band shell, floodlights, and Renaissance garlands. In the kitchen the caterers were quarreling with the servants and there was already talk of mutiny because the waiters had seen the Renaissance costumes which Auntie Mame and Bella had planned for them—black tights with white appliquéd codpieces, black-and-white harlequin tunics. Auntie Mame was off at the hairdresser's being pummeled and pounded, crimped and enameled for the big evening. There was still no sign of Cousin Elmore—not even so much as a request for bail—and I happily wrote him off as lost in action. Then I rolled over again and went back to sleep.

By the time I'd finally got up, bathed, and shaved, the orchestra—also Renaissance—was down below practicing such pseudo-Italian favorites as "The Isle of Capri" and "The Piccolino." At dusk all the lights went on amid loud cheers. Then they went off, accompanied by loud cursing. Finally they went on again and stayed on. Looking out of the window, I saw Bella's gondola charging downstream toward Auntie Mame's door, so I got into my costume—a matter of seconds. Since I don't go much for costume parties, I had chosen comfort over style. I went as a monk in a long white terry-cloth beach robe with a hood. Tied with a black rope and with sandals it looked reasonably authentic, and worn, as it was, over nothing, it was a lot cooler than the velvet doublet-and-hose outfits that prevailed that night.

I got down in time to greet Bella, who marched in looking like a tub of spoiled ricotta cheese, enveloped in white damask and ermine tails. "My God," she said as she saw me, "Fra Lippo Lipschitz!" I was too tactful to reply. But then Auntie Mame swept down the stairs, delectable in black velvet sewn with pearls. The orchestra struck up a rousing Renaissance rhumba and the party was officially on.

Three hours later it was even more on. There were better than five hundred guests, not counting the *Life* photographers and gate crashers. Everybody who was anybody in Venice had dug up some sort of black-and-white Renaissance rig to come to the party in. Auntie Mame was whirled off her feet, what with Marcantonio, dashing and very Italianate in striped hose and white linen, dancing with her whenever Axel, looking like a blond Hamlet in slashed black wool, wasn't. It was almost midnight before I got to dance with her myself.

"Having fun?" I asked.

"Oh, darling, more than I've ever had at any party before. And I have only you to thank."

"Made up your mind about my new uncle yet?"

"Oh, Patrick, that's the awful part of it. *I can't.* They're both so divine. So divine, in fact, that I've decided to ditch them entirely. I'm still too young for any permanent entanglements. Heavens! It's almost time for the fireworks. I must ask Bella if she . . ."

"Mame!" Bella's raucous voice called out. "Mame!" I could see a mountain of white with bobbing ermine tails forcing her way through the dancers. "Ducky!" Bella cried when she got to us. "Do you see what *I* see?"

Our gaze followed her trembling forefinger, and there, coming down the stairs, was Cousin Elmore, got up like nothing human. His costume—I can never forget it—was an old union suit, one leg ineptly dyed yellow, the other green. His middle was wound in a plaid muffler, his stomach bulging below it, while above he sported a billowing magenta rayon cowboy shirt with bells insecurely attached to its lavish fringes. A ruff of toilet paper encircled his neck and on his head he wore an orange balaclava helmet, streaming with dowdy ribbons.

"Patrick Dennis," Auntie Mame said through white lips, "*you told me* that . . ."

"And it was true, Auntie Mame," I said, still not quite believing what I had seen. "I swear to God it was. Wait, I'll get rid of him." In ten paces I was across the floor and propelling Cousin Elmore into a cloakroom. "Cousin Elmore," I said, "what in hell are you doing here?"

"Ah came on wings of love. Ah escaped from the jail. An' Ah knew that if Ah came here when Mamie was holdin' this masquerade party, nobody'd evah notice me."

"Nobody'd *notice* you?" I said, eying his costume. "You've got to get out of here. It isn't safe. You're wanted by the police."

"Ah know it. Ah'm goin' an' Ah'm takin' Dollfeather with me. Yuh know what they thought when they arrested me theah in the wateh?"

"I haven't the faintest notion," I said, averting my eyes.

"Well, Ah'll tell yew. They thought *Ah* was a *Red*! An' yew know *why*? It's because of all that foreign riffraff that's always hangin' around Mamie. That Marcantonio, he's a wop, ain't he?"

"He's an Italian," I said icily.

"Well, he ain't even in favor of Mussolini. What kind of Eyetalian is that?"

"An intelligent one, you damned fool. Nobody in his right mind would be for Mussolini."

"An' that Axel. He's a *Socialist*. Prob'ly got a bomb on him right now. Jest imajun, a *Socialist*!"

"So's the whole Swedish cabinet, you bloody nincompoop. It happens to be a Social-Democratic country."

"That's just what Ah mean. Reds an' Bolsheviks, the whole lot of 'em. Why, when Ah told 'em down at the jail about all these radicals and revolutionaries and spies hangin' around Mamie they carried on somethin' terrible. Course Ah couldn't

Auntie Mame . . .

understand their lingo. So Ah got a boat outside—to save yoah auntie."

"Everybody in Venice has got a boat outside this house tonight, you loudmouthed slob!"

"P-Patrick," Auntie Mame said, floating toward us. "The man at the door says that there's some sort of official . . ."

"Dollfeather," Elmore blubbered, "Ah come on wings of love to save yew. Ah know yew cay-uh foah me an' Ah . . ."

"Old Jabberjaws here has shot off his big mouth to the Fascisti and God only knows what stupid lies he's told that pack of Black Shirts. But you can be sure that he . . ."

"Cupcake, Ah on'y told 'em that . . ."

I'll never know exactly what Cousin Elmore did tell them. At that moment armed Black Shirts burst in at every door. There was a blast of a whistle and then all the lights went off.

"Mamie," Elmore called, "come with me!" He reached out and grabbed my arm, tugging at it. With my free arm I swung out, connecting, I guess, with Elmore's potbelly. Free at last, I caught Auntie Mame by the hand. "Come on," I said, "we can get out the side way. There's a window right over the water."

"Oh, Patrick! My party . . ."

"The party's over. Come on!"

We jumped into the first boat we could find, a trig motor launch.

"This'll do," I said. "We can always send it back in the morning."

"Do you know anything about running one of these, Patrick?" Auntie Mame whimpered.

"More or less." I started the motor with a resounding roar. The boat backed up and crashed into the foundations of Auntie Mame's house. There was a lot of shouting and yelling. I poked something and the boat shot forward, throwing both Auntie Mame and me to the floor boards. Struggling there in our voluminous costumes, I heard a lot of yelling and cursing and faint but definite splintering of wood. Then I was back at the wheel and we were free of the mass of boats around the pink *palazzo* and headed straight for Isola di San Giorgio, just as the pink and blue fireworks began exploding off Auntie Mame's roof.

"Should we try to make it all the way to Yugoslavia?" I asked dubiously.

"I th-think not, darling. *Mal de mer*, you know. Why don't you just try to get to the station. We'll think of something there."

"I'd better keep off the Grand Canal and go by back ways. That is, if I can."

"I do hope you can, my little love. I'm rather weary of Venice. So—so damp," she added, as a wave splashed over the side of the boat. "This is such a *peppy* craft, so much faster than a gondola. I wonder who owns it?"

"There's something painted on the side," I said. "See if you can make it out while I slow down and get my bearings."

When the next barrage of pink and blue rockets lit up the skies, Auntie Mame leaned precariously out of the boat to read its inscription. "Oh, Patrick," she said, "it says that it's the property of the Venetian Police Department."

"Oh my God!" I gasped, giving the throttle a jab that fairly lifted the fast boat out of the water. We roared forward into the night, churning up a wide, white wake behind us. I saw Auntie Mame's hair blow wildly in the cool wind. I looked again and saw that she was smiling. Then she began to laugh.

"Don't think this is any big comedy, Dollfeather," I bellowed over the roar of the motor.

"It's a riot—in every sense of the word—Cupcake," she yelled back. "I think we'll catch the next train for Austria—Vienna, I guess. After all, Vienna lot of trouble. Ha*hahaha-*ha*ha*!"

"You're damned right we are and don't forget that this is a

police state, we're driving stolen property, and *you're* the hottest thing in Italy. We'll probably get a gallon of castor oil apiece when they catch us."

"Nonsense, my little love." Auntie Mame laughed. "In Italy what could be better—a police boat with a monk at the helm. Why, I couldn't be safer with Il Duce himself. Now, off to the station. *Precipitevolisimevolmente!*"

Auntie Mame in Her Mountain Retreat

"AND OF COURSE WE WENT TO AUSTRIA," I SAID. "Auntie Mame was violently anti-Nazi and refused to go near Germany. However, you never used to run into that sort of thing in Austria—at least not in 1937."

"Austria seems an odd place for a woman like your aunt to visit. What was she up to?"

"My aunt is a jewel of many facets," I said pompously. "Actually she was interested in a real-estate venture and made quite a pretty penny during her Austrian visit. It was also very healthy for both of us, as we spent most of our time high in the Tyrolean alps. In fact, I think I have some snapshots upstairs. I'll show them to you. Excuse me, dear."

I went upstairs and counted to a thousand. At 956 I was saved. The telephone rang. When Pegeen finally finished talking, she'd more or less forgotten about the whole thing. Feeling safer, I took a cautious sip of my drink.

. . .

ACH, MY LITTLE LOVE," Auntie Mame said, pushing back from our table at Am Franziskaner-platz, "*such* a good dinner—*Rindsuppe mit Nudeln, Butterteig-pastetchen mit Geflügelragout, Rahmschnitzel mit Hausgemachten Nudeln, Essiggurken*, and *Nussrollade mit Schokoladeüberzug*. Too *gemütlich!*"

"Kind of fattening, also," I said.

"Nonsense, darling. Now be a dear and give me a light. Are you *sure* you wouldn't like one of these?"

"No thanks," I said. "Lucky Strikes are good enough for me."

"*Ach*, no spirit of adventure." Auntie Mame poked a cigar at least a foot long into one corner of her mouth, inhaled deeply, and had a frightful coughing fit.

"Do you really *like* smoking those stogies?" I asked, knowing that she didn't.

"*Ja wohl, Liebchen!*" she lied. "It's so utterly Viennese." She blew a big smoke ring up over my head, said, "*Rechnung, bitte*," to the waiter and, the cigar still clenched between her teeth, began to draw on her long, black gloves.

In less than a week Auntie Mame had grown more Viennese than the Danube itself. She began each morning in her big tufted bedroom in the Hotel Sacher with an early snack of coffee and rolls, then *Gabelfrühstück*—which usually included a couple of big sausages, a schooner of beer, coffee, and maybe a side order of goulash—at eleven. That usually held her until she was able to make it to lunch. Around four in the afternoon there was her *kleine Jause*, which featured coffee, lots of whipped cream, and several dozen pastries. We dined at seven or eight. She spent her days strolling the Ring, saying "*ja*" and "*bitte*" for no reason at all, and going to Farnhamer on the Kärntnerstrasse for a lot of new costumes which were straight out of *The Merry Widow*. I mean her getups were so very Viennese that even the Viennese stared at her. But as though the picture hats, the plumes, the boas, the muffs, and the ten pounds she had already gained weren't enough, the big cigars were the newest fillip to transform Auntie Mame into the true *Alt Wien gnädige Frau*. It was just too much.

"Now, my little love," she said, inexpertly flicking an ash, "off to the Volksoper for *eine kleine Nachtmusik*."

"Oh God, what's for tonight? *The Student Prince? The White Horse Inn? Der Zigeunerbaron?*"

"No, *Liebchen*, it's *Die Pillangóprinzessin. Auf Wiedersehn*," she said to the waiter and tripped out to a waiting taxi in an aura of plumes and cigar smoke.

Auntie Mame puffed furiously away at her cigar all the long distance to the Volksoper and said, "*Alt Wien!*" several times. I was quite dizzy from the cigar smoke, and it seemed to me that Auntie Mame was looking a trifle peaked. Nonetheless, she descended from the cab with a twitch of her boa, tossed her cigar butt into the gutter, and minced into the theater, all satin and feathers and saucy light-operatic tosses of her head.

Die Pillangóprinzessin had already begun, but since I'd been dragged to an operetta every night since we'd arrived in Vienna, I knew just about what to expect. It was the usual Austro-Hungarian strudel about a lovely Graustarkian princess who, in order to avoid marrying the unknown princeling her mean uncle, the regent, is trying to foist off on her, runs off to a quaint alpine village disguised as a goose girl, where she falls in love with a dashing young lieutenant of the guards, little wotting that he is a Graustarkian prince who, in order to avoid marrying the unknown princess his mean uncle, the regent, is trying to foist off on him, runs off to a quaint alpine village disguised as a lieutenant of the guards, where . . . Well, you get the idea.

The first act drew to a thundering finale with a sweet duet between the two stars—whose combined age was just over a hundred and whose combined weight was just under five hundred—that established their love pretty firmly. Although considering their years, sizes, and corseting, I couldn't imagine how they'd ever be able to consummate it. The Viennese adored it. Auntie Mame pretended to. I didn't even try.

"Well, off to the lobby for a good cigar," Auntie Mame said without too much conviction. She looked awfully pale, but she was still full of the old Viennese spirit. "Isn't *Die Pillangóprinzessin* tuneful, darling, and have you ever seen anything so lovely as that sweet butterfly ballet?"

"Not since the Hippodrome closed," I said.

"*Pillangó* means butterfly in Hungarian," she said, ostentatiously flourishing her petit-point cigar case.

"Do tell," I said. "Are you sure you're feeling all right?"

"Nonsense, *Gansel*, I never felt better," she said, lighting up her cigar to the horror of all the dumpy *Hausfraus* standing nearby. She took a couple of drags and got even paler.

"What's the matter, Auntie Mame?" I asked, watching her go from white to yellow to green to gray.

"N-nothing, Patrick, it's just that it's so . . . so very close in here," she stammered, puffing weakly again at the cigar.

"I think maybe those cigars are bigger than you are," I ventured. "Or *almost* as big."

"D-don't be silly, darling. All the smart Viennese women smoke them. Besides, I love the bouquet of a good . . ." Her eyes rolled heavenward and then Auntie Mame swooned, with a flutter of feathers, into the thick of the crowd. There was quite a lot of commotion and people shouting things I couldn't understand in German. Then I saw Auntie Mame being carried out to the street in the arms of a tall, handsome young man.

Pushing my way through the crowd, I got to the pavement just in time to see Auntie Mame being deposited in a taxi. "*Achtung*!" I called. "*Halte*!" thus exhausting my German. "*Attendez!* Hey, wait a second!"

Auntie Mame's savior turned and gave me a charming smile. "You need not worry, sir," he said, "I speak English."

"Oh, that's nice," I said. "Well, thank you very much."

"At your service," he said, clicking his heels smartly. I tried to do the same and knocked my ankle bones together most painfully.

"Well, thanks again," I said. He didn't look like the sort of person one would tip, dressed as he was in a faultlesaly tailored English suit. "I'll just take my aunt back to the hotel."

"Please," he said. "I insist. I shall accompany you. What gentleman could do less?"

"That's very nice of you, but I can manage," I said crowding into the cab beside Auntie Mame's supine body. "Besides, the operetta isn't over yet."

"Nonsense," the man said forcefully, getting in behind me. "I am, after all, a Hodenlohern."

"W-we're Americans," I said.

"Your address?" he asked, cutting off any further protests.

BY THE TIME WE GOT BACK TO SACHER'S IN THE Philharmonikerstrasse, Auntie Mame was moaning softly, her eyelids aflutter. I tried to pay off the driver, but Auntie Mame's knight in armor, flaunting an alligator billfold and a torrent of colloquial German was there ahead of me. "Well, thank you very much again," I said decisively. "We really can't ruin your whole evening. I can get my aunt upstairs alone. Thank you very much."

"Shut up!" Auntie Mame said out of the corner of her mouth. She gave me a vicious jab with her elbow, then her arm fell limply, and she sighed, "*Ach, Gott!*" She stepped weakly down from the taxi and then managed another neat faint, right into the arms of her good-looking swain. That just about took care of that. He picked her up and carried her to our suite, where she reposed—all pale languor—in her tufted bonbon box of a sitting room. The picture of limpid frailty was somewhat diminished the three times Auntie Mame scooted off to the bathroom to be sick and when the physician I had summoned told her that the only thing the matter with her was gluttony and cigars. But she managed to keep her cavalier around long enough to change into a filmy peignoir and to send down for a bottle of champagne. Neither of them paid much attention when I excused myself and turned in.

I awakened the next morning to find Auntie Mame already up. She was doing a pretty hesitation waltz all by herself in the sitting room, humming "*Ich War So Gern Einmal Verliebt*" (Kreisler), her nose buried in a huge bouquet. I watched and listened for three asinine bars before she saw me. Flustered, she said good morning and set to work arranging her floral tribute.

"Feeling better?" I asked.

"Oh, divine, my little love," she said, humming away. "And aren't these flowers lovely? The *Zimmermädchen* just brought them up."

A card fluttered out of the bouquet. I picked it up. It read simply: *Freiherr Werner von Hodenlohern.*

"Who's this?" I asked, flashing the card.

Auntie Mame . . .

"Why, dear, that's Baron von Hodenlohern, the charming gallant who rescued me at the Volksoper last night."

"My God, is he expecting you to die?"

"Certainly not! But isn't he nice? So handsome and so polished. Bursting with healthy youth and yet so *weltlich*."

"So *what*?"

"Worldly. I really haven't met a man who interested me so since . . . well, since . . ."

"Since last week?" I said.

"Oh, this is nothing like that. But last night's chance meeting with Putzi . . ."

"With what?"

"Putzi. That's Werner's . . . I mean the baron's nickname."

"I see. Go on."

"Oh, well, it's nothing really, Patrick. But I *do* find it so interesting to get to know people from other lands—I mean really well. That is, I mean to say . . ." The telephone interrupted her. "Oh!" she said into the mouthpiece. "Oh, *yes*! *Do* come up."

"Who was that? The doctor again?"

"No, Patrick, it's Putzi. I mean Baron von Hodenlohern. He's asked me to luncheon at the Kursalon. Keep him entertained while I make myself presentable." For a sick woman, she moved awfully fast toward her bedroom, and I could hear her singing just as there was a rapping on the door.

Putzi—I can think of him by no other name—clicked his heels smartly and marched in, a symphony in browns from his Homburg right down to his suède shoes. On a lesser man the outfit might have been considered foppish, but Baron von Hodenlohern was so natural, carried himself with such a relaxed military bearing that the total effect was very pleasant.

"My aunt will be ready in just a few minutes," I said. "Please sit down."

He seated himself elegantly on one of the little Maria Theresa chairs, smiled, and offered me a cigarette from an alligator case.

A little hard put for any common subject of conversation except Auntie Mame's cigar smoking, I said, "Do you go to the Volksoper often?"

"Oh, yes," Putzi said charmingly. "Whenever I'm in Vienna I try to go. I'm very fond of music." Well, after that there was no need to try to make conversation. Putzi told me all about his favorite operas at the Staatsoper, his favorite operettas at the Volksoper, his favorite Heurige singers at Grinzing, how he had organized a glee club as a young cadet in the Theresianum, how he and his brothers had always sung back home, and how he never missed the music at Christmas Eve mass in the Church of St. Maria am Gestade. That was the nice thing about him, you didn't have to work to keep a conversation going—just throw Putzi a line and he was on. I've probably made him sound like a windbag, but he wasn't. Everything he said was interesting and it was always said with great warmth and friendliness.

"You certainly speak English well," I said.

"Oh, thank you. But I should. When we were very little, my brothers and I had an English governess on our estate and, until the war broke out, I had a few years in an English boarding school. Of course I was very young then but . . ."

Auntie Mame's door opened and she sailed out in a clatter of violet taffeta, her middle tightly cinched. "*Gut' Morgen, mein Kavalier!*" she said with a coquettish wag of the finger that recalled all the operettas I'd seen that week.

"*Gnädige Frau,*" Putzi said, clicking his heels smartly and kissing her hand.

"*Aug Wiedersehen, Liebchen,*" she said to me with a maddening wave of her scented hankie. Then they were off.

Auntie Mame . . .

I spent the day combing Vienna for a cup of coffee that wasn't hidden under whipped cream. When I returned, defeated, there was no sign of Auntie Mame. It was after six when she rustled in.

"That must have been some lunch," I said. "What was it today, *Hühnerleber mit Speck und Reis* under *Schlagober*? I thought the doctor told . . ."

"Not now, my little love," Auntie Mame sang. "Putzi's asked me to dinner and the opera and I've simply got to *tear* into my clothes." With that she disappeared and I could hear her singing the great love duet from *Die Pillangóprinzessin*.

With a clicking of patent-leather heels, Putzi reappeared, this time in flawless evening clothes and so handsome and aristocratic looking that even I was a little startled. Instead of being the thick-necked, shaven-skulled, dueling-scarred, yellow-haired type I'd always associated with the Teutonic peoples, Putzi was tall, dark, and rather romantic looking. He had beautiful manners and an easy laugh. While he awaited Auntie Mame he told me about the boyhood he and his brothers had spent on the family estates in Mähren, which I gathered was Moravia, before it was turned into Czechoslovakia. Now, it seemed, they were on a much smaller estate in the Tirol. It was all very romantic—just as romantic as Putzi. He was beginning to recount his cadet days at the Theresianum when Auntie Mame sallied forth, looking just like a Winterhalter portrait. "*Auf Wiedersehen*, my little love," she said, kissing the top of my head. "Baron von Hodenlohern and I are off to dinner and the Staatsoper, but I've left our tickets for the Volksoper for *you*. I know you'll adore it. It's by Kalman or Lehar."

"Or Romberg or Friml or Straus or Strauss. It won't make any difference," I said.

She swept up a sweet nosegay of Parma violets, gave her girdle a surreptitious tug, and they were off. "That dear Patrick," she said to Putzi, "such a lover of gay, Viennese music." I took the tickets and flushed them down the toilet.

IT WAS FIVE-THIRTY BY THE LITTLE TRAVELING clock on my bedstand when I heard Auntie Mame let herself in.

"My God," I called, "did you sit through the complete works of Wagner?"

"Still awake, Patrick darling?" Auntie Mame said as she drifted into my room. She sat dreamily on the foot of my bed and gazed at her crushed violets as though she were a very hungry cow about to devour them. "Oh no, my little love, it was only *Der Rosenkavalier*. We left after the second act."

"Well, it took you a hell of a long time to get back across the street."

"Ah, my little love, Putzi hired a carriage and we went out through the Vienna Woods to a dear little outdoor café where the gypsies serenaded us and we had *Gespritzenes*. Too divine."

She looked as though she'd had a lot more than that, but I didn't say anything. She hummed a few bars of some dismal *tzigane* dirge and then she said, "How was the operetta, darling?"

"Oh, it was just *keen*," I said acidly. "It was about a lovely Balkan empress who disguises herself as a shepherdess and . . ."

"Isn't that nice," Auntie Mame said dreamily. "I wish I'd seen that. Go on, my little love." She hummed again and I knew she wasn't paying any attention at all. From there on I improvised.

"Well, it's called *Die Krankenhauskaiserin*. The sheep all come down with anthrax and die, so little Stigmata—that's her name—and the villain, Baron Charlus, change clothes with each other and run off to Vienna where she gets a job selling contraceptives at Walgreen's-im-Prater and falls in love with a homely corporal who's disguised as a Balkan archduke, and she, little realizing that the Moxie which the wicked sorceress, Dichotomy, gives her to drink has turned her into a hopeless Lesbian . . . damn it," I roared, fetching her a boot with my foot that sent her sprawling onto the floor, "you're not even *listening*!"

"Oh, I *was*, Patrick, really I was," she said, blushing prettily. "It's just that . . . well, I mean I . . . Patrick, pack your things. We're leaving Vienna just as soon as Ito gets here with the car."

"Leaving? For where? New York?"

"No, Patrick, for Stinkenbach-im-Tirol."

"For *where*?"

"We're going to Putzi's old family place—Schloss Stinkenbach—for a little visit."

TWO DAYS LATER WE ROLLED INTO THE VILLAGE OF Stinkenbach-im-Tirol. Stinkenbach was about three hours' drive from Salzburg, from Innsbruck, and from Bad Gastein, but proximity to more attractive places had not caused it to thrive. It was halfway up and halfway down an alp and situated just so that it was neither above nor below the clouds, but always *in* them. I mean it was humid.

The Rolls lurched into the church square just as mass was letting out, and all I could think of was the opening number of every operetta I'd seen since we hit Austria. The jolly peasantry—a thousand strong—were promenading the *Kirchenplatz* all dirndls and *Lederhosen* and apple cheeks. Bells were ringing in the hideous old gothic church and there was even a genial old lush with drooping mustaches hefting a seidel of beer in front of the local inn. I almost expected them to burst into song.

"*Ach*!" Auntie Mame cried, "so *gemütlich*. Just as Putzi said, fourteenth century—the whole village—and doesn't it have flavor!"

Indeed it had. From a glance and a sniff I realized that Stinkenbach-im-Tirol had no plumbing and no sewage system.

Then all the picturesque burghers parted and there, at the wheel of an antique Mercedes touring car, was Putzi. After an affectionate but restrained greeting, he loaded us into his automobile and started us out on the final lap of our journey to the fourteenth-century seat of the Von Hodenloherns.

"And now we start upward to Schloss Stinkenbach," Putzi said, throwing his old car into low gear.

"Heavens," Auntie Mame said, "is *all* this land yours?"

"My family's," Putzi said with proud modesty.

Well, it was quite a lot of land. The only thing wrong was that it was all perpendicular. Way, way up over us loomed the ruins of an old fortress. That was the original Schloss Stinkenbach. Somewhat below that stood a huge Frankenstein's castle kind of place, so grim that, at first sight, it had an imposing grandeur. Putzi's Mercedes whined up the mountain, with Ito following. Finally we came to a ramshackle stone hovel with a pair of decrepit gates permanently rusted ajar. An old gaffer in *Lederhosen* came hobbling out and actually *did* tug his forelock. What I took to be his wife bustled after him, shooing a lot of chickens off the roadway. "Here we are," Putzi said genially. We drove on past some rickety outbuildings and the car stopped before a hodgepodge of masonry, plaster, timber, arches, eaves, beams, buttresses, battlements, and turrets. It was Schloss Stinkenbach.

When the huge, iron-clad door swung open we were in a

Auntie Mame ...

lofty stone hall, sparsely furnished with ugly carved wooden pieces, black with age. The plaster walls, painted with mottoes and family arms, were bristling with antlers. A towering tile oven in one corner gave off a wistful warmth. Otherwise it was chillier than it was outside. Beneath the feeble, unflattering glow of an iron chandelier stood two men and a woman. They were Putzi's brothers and his sister-in-law.

"Ah," Putzi shouted merrily, "the reception committee! Mrs. Burnside, Mr. Dennis. Here is my family—all of it—the last of the Von Hodenloherns. My elder brother Maximilian, my younger brother Johannes, and Maximilian's wife, Frieda. Maxl, Hannes, Friedl."

I noticed that, as in everything at Schloss Stinkenbach, Friedl, the reigning baroness and hostess came in last. She was a weary, washed-out blonde whose Dresden prettiness had long since faded as she faced menopause and melancholia with a grim, unhappy resolve. Friedl seemed always to have a cold—not that I blamed her in that house. She wore a dingy white cardigan over her unbecoming peacock blue "best" dress as she stood hugging her elbows and shivering in the drafty hall. I did the Austrian bit, clicked my heels somewhat more successfully than usual, and kissed her cold, red hand.

"*Enchanté*," Friedl said between chattering teeth.

Maxl, the head of the family, was dark like Putzi, but far less attractive, being fifty pounds heavier and ten years older. He wore English-style country clothes that were much too tight and a hairnet. Hannes, the baby of the family, was only a few years older than I. He was one of those Teutonic-god types, lean and muscular with azure eyes and golden curls. He would have been the handsomest of the lot save for the total absence of any animation or warmth in his chiseled face and his frosty eyes. Taciturn to the point of muteness, his social repartee consisted mainly of jerky little bows and nods. Not that his manners left anything to be desired; it was simply that Hannes always made me feel that I was in the company of a very well-bred robot.

"Did you open the salon, Friedl, as I asked you to?" Putzi said.

"*Ja!* Yes, Putzi. Poldi did the *Kamin*—uh, the, er . . ." Friedl, whose English was not as good as that of the Von Hodenloh-ern brothers, groped for a word.

"Stove," Putzi translated. Then he turned to us with a winning grin. "As you probably know, central heating is not popular in Austria. All over we are heated by our beautiful old porcelain stoves."

"How charming," Auntie Mame said, beaming at the family.

"Now please to ring for Poldi, Friedl, and you can show our guests to their rooms."

Friedl tugged at a moth-eaten old bell cord, and a harried-looking peasant woman of unfathomable age scurried in, gathered up our bags, and labored up the stairs.

"Follow me, pleece," Friedl said.

It was some trip, up stairs, down stairs—no two rooms in the *Schloss* seemed to be on the same level—and along dank, echoing corridors. The house was an eccentric structure, to say the least, with rooms, wings, and ells added on at random over the centuries. There must have been more than a hundred rooms in Schloss Stinkenbach, although most of them were closed off, locked against everything but icy drafts. Auntie Mame's room, up on what seemed like the fifteenth floor, was a snug Biedermeier affair. Mine was down the hall, a perfectly circular stone affair in what had possibly once been a defense tower. There was even a sort of battlement running between our two bedrooms—Auntie Mame called it a terrace—providing more fresh air than seemed absolutely necessary and what Auntie Mame referred to as a "panoramic view of the valley."

Auntie Mame . . .

"Isn't this old storybook castle too incredible, darling?" Auntie Mame said, bursting into my room a few minutes later.

"It certainly is," I said. "It puts me in mind of those happy days at Count Dracula's old place." I surveyed my round bedroom again, its cold stone walls, the embrasures, the vaulted ceiling. The bed looked like a flamboyant gothic tomb. A sinister carved piece that appeared to be an iron maiden turned out to be a clothes cupboard. It was the sort of chamber where Jan Hus might have been terribly tortured by one of the earlier ecclesiastical Von Hodenloherns—of which there were many—before being put to the stake in Prague. A primitive fresco of some unidentified martyr undergoing a kind of surgery I dread even to think about heightened the effect. I couldn't help wondering where they'd put poor Ito. But Auntie Mame thought that everything was too perfect for words.

"Ah, my little love, the centuries of *Kultur* that have gone into creating this gracious family seat. I hope you realize, Patrick, that we have the honor of being entertained by one of the oldest families in Europe. The Von Hodenloherns are legitimately descended from the Hapsburgs, laterally descended from Barbarosa, and illegitimately descended from the Babenburgs."

"Poor bastards," I said.

"Why, darling, they're so blue blooded that the only people fit to associate with them are in the Kapuziner-gruft. You know, Patrick, that tomb in Vienna where all the Hapsburgs are buried."

"Well, I'll bet that tomb's a lot cozier than Schloss Stinkenbach. Nice for a visit, of course, but I wouldn't want to live here."

"Come dear, we'll try to find our way down to the salon. And mind your manners. Theirs are so very, very beautiful."

After a trip of half an hour or so we finally came to an

imposing pair of doors giving into the *salon*. It was a Maria Theresian folly of the eighteenth century that looked like the rooms in Shönbrunn Palace or the Hofburg, only not as well kept up. The walls were covered with a frayed brocade that hung in tatters in several places. At one end of the room a mildewed tapestry depicted a seventeenth-century Von Hodenlohern (Augustus-Christus, "The Muscular") single-handedly destroying the Ottoman Empire. The ceiling, except for some wet brown patches, was covered with an allegorical painting of one of the churchly Von Hodenloherns (Franz-Leopold, Prelate of Pilsen) climbing to heaven with the aid of six cherubs over the mangled corpses of some undressed Protestants whose hash he had presumably just settled. Elsewhere there were about seventy portraits of dead relatives in helmets and breastplates, in velvet and sable, in miters and copes, buckling within their tarnished gilt frames. Across a choppy lagoon of rococo chairs, rickety little tables, pungent oil lamps, and fly-blown vitrines, the brothers Von Hodenlohern and Friedl huddled around a baroque wedding cake of a porcelain stove. It was the color and texture of a very old teapot and gave off just about as much warmth.

The Von Hodenlohern men were talking. Sitting and talking. I make a point of this because it's all they *ever* did. Those three barons had worked sitting-and-talking down to an absolute science. Why they hadn't saddle sores and laryngitis is beyond me. Yet they seemed to thrive on it.

Life at Schloss Stinkenbach had settled into a rigid routine that was inactive but not quiet. After nine or ten hours' sleep they all sat down to a big breakfast to gain strength for the ardors of sitting all day. Then the men sat in separate parts of the house resting up from breakfast. At eleven the three brothers gathered in the *Herrenzimmer* and talked while Poldi raced in with sausages, beer, cheese, and coffee. That is to say that Maxl and Putzi talked. Hannes mostly sat silently in the window, displaying his better profile as he gazed moodily to the north and flexed his brown thighs in their old *Lederhosen*. Only when Maxl said something sufficiently explosive about the family's prewar life—which Hannes was much too young to have remembered—did Hannes come to life and give out with an impassioned telegram in his clipped, rather guttural English.

All the Von Hodenlohern boys spoke good English and they were so polite that they insisted upon using no other language in my presence. I'd as soon they hadn't because their conversation might better have been labeled "Remembrance of Things Past" than "Current Events." But that was mostly the fault of Maxl. As aristocratic as he may have been, he was a real slob—obese, verbose, indolent, and ignorant; a sort of Major Hoople overseas. His monologue was always about the Good Old Days before Woodrow Wilson shot Archduke Ferdinand at Sarajevo, thus getting the whole world to gang up on the Austro-Hungarian Empire so that the Von Hodenlohern alone had to suffer and watch their rich crown lands given away to that little upstart Jewish republic, Czechoslovakia. Hannes, who couldn't possibly have known, always agreed with him.

Putzi, however, seemed to have a little better grasp on reality. He politely pointed out inaccuracies and anachronisms, tactfully corrected Maxl's facts, and always tried to tip me a comforting wink whenever Maxl said something real outlandish, such as America's being a refuge for Austrian deserters and embezzlers, inferior in science, money mad, and a pawn of the Rothschilds. Familial as he was, I could understand why Putzi chose to spend as much time as possible away from the discomforts of Schloss Stinkenbach, the jarring verbosity of Maxl, the moody silence of Hannes.

Auntie Mame was usually awake by lunchtime. In her honor, Maxl always removed his hairnet, placed her on his right, and, with a captive audience, discussed such stimulating new subjects as how lovely everything had been before World War I, when the Von Hodenloherns had lost their town house in Vienna, their *Kronlands* in Moravia, and had been reduced to living in their old hunting box—Schloss Stinkenbach. Friedl sat at the head of the table, shivering and coughing, totally ignored except when Maxl thought of something for her to tell Poldi to do. It seems incredible, but I honestly believe that Poldi was the only servant in that vast house. At least she was the only person, except for Friedl, I ever saw doing a stroke of work.

After luncheon Friedl worked, Maxl napped, Hannes faced northward. But Putzi, always lively and charming and gay, generally took Auntie Mame off for a picturesque stroll. Quite often they invited me, too. It was a big day for the village of Stinkenbach-im-Tirol whenever *die Amerikanerin*, as they called Auntie Mame, appeared. Try as she would to go native in embroidered blouses and dainty dirndls, her make-up, her clattering bracelets, her sheer stockings, her uncut emerald ring, and Ito following in the Rolls to transport any purchases back uphill just didn't add up to the unspoiled peasant girl. If she'd appeared on a gem-studded litter borne by a dozen naked Nubians, Auntie Mame couldn't have created more of a stir. That's the kind of village it was.

Still, Putzi had a proprietary interest in the place and proudly pointed out some of the fourteenth-century examples. In fact, everything in Stinkenbach was an example—and some of the worst examples I've ever seen—from the ghastly gothic church to the *kitschig* houses, with their daubings of quainty-dainty Tyrolean hearts and flowers. "Sweet" was Auntie Mame's verdict, and she jumped just in time to avoid a pail of slops being poured from an upper window. It missed us, but it got the Rolls. I heard Ito squeal.

Well, the village was a horror, inbred and impoverished,

without electricity or radio or the telephone or any common-place modern convenience to bring in a breath of air from the world outside. I found the village, the villagers, and their unsettling subservience both depressing and embarrassing. But I was fond of Putzi and if he thought Stinkenbach-im-Tirol was okay, I was determined to like it, too. Auntie Mame, of course, was a pushover for *any* new experience.

We always got back to the *Schloss* in time for a kind of after-noon *Kaffeklatsch* in the dark, musty library. Here Maxl, refreshed by his nap, again held court, seated before a dispir-ited fire, telling Friedl where to place cushions under his big rump, how much whipped cream to ladle onto his coffee, and what was wrong with the pastry. Maxl, seconded by eager nods and grunts from Hannes, talked about *die gute alte Zeit* until it was time for him to preside over the dinner conversa-tion. In the evenings the *salon* was opened, lighted, and heated just up to the freezing point, and here, around the stove, the family gathered to sit down and discuss the doings of the day.

After a couple of days at Schloss Stinkenbach, I was more than ready to move on and amazed that Auntie Mame seemed so content in such a damp, dismal milieu. But on the fourth day I was awakened early by a lot of shouting from the drive-way down below and also by Auntie Mame's voice calling from the battlement outside my room.

"I said that we were going to the horse fair, Mame dear," Putzi shouted.

"I know you did, darling," Auntie Mame called. "And *I* said to wait just a second and I'd go along with you boys. I do adore these bucolic romps."

I opened the door and stepped out onto the battlement. Auntie Mame, wrapped in a dressing gown, was leaning over the parapet and shouting, "It won't take me a minute to slip into something appropriate."

Down below, the three Von Hodenlohern brothers were

seated in their ancient Mercedes while poor Poldi was trying to crank it.

"But, Mame," Putzi called up, "women aren't allowed."

"What are they showing, Putzi, horses or blue movies? After all, *I* might be interested in getting a few horses now that . . ."

"Sorry, darling. No women allowed. I'll be back in time to take you to the *Kirchtag.*"

"But, Putzi, that's perfectly ridiculous. I could just stay in the car and . . ." Whatever Auntie Mame could do was never heard. With a series of loud explosions, the old Mercedes started up. Poldi, spry for her years, leaped out of the way and handed the crank reverently in to Hannes. There were a lot more pops and bangs, and, above the roar of the motor, Auntie Mame might just as well not have bothered to try to make herself heard. The car lurched down the driveway, Maxl and Hannes staring straight ahead while Putzi turned to wave good-by.

"Well, I mean really!" Auntie Mame said waspishly. Then she turned and saw me standing out on the battlement. "Oh, good morning, darling. I suppose all that racket woke you up, too. It was enough to . . . Honestly, some of these old-world ideas are just too inane. The boys are going up north to a horse fair and they wouldn't take me. No women, if you please. Here I have this divine three-piece homespun suit and . . ."

"Maybe in Europe these horse things are stag affairs."

"Nonsense. You can't pick up a *Tatler* or a *Country Life* without seeing pages of the dreariest-looking women all got up like Vesta Tilly to look at a lot of old . . ."

"Well, this is Austria. What do you care about a lot of horses anyhow?"

"Oh, nothing actually, Patrick, but they're just a part of this divine life and as long as I'm . . . I'll tell you what, darling.

Auntie Mame . . .

Now that we're up at this ungodly hour, let's dress and tramp down to the village for breakfast in that quaint little *Gasthaus*. There are some letters I must post."

HALF AN HOUR LATER WE SET OUT, AUNTIE MAME looking like the natural child of William Tell out of Heidi. "Ah, my little love," Auntie Mame said, breathing deeply of the moist air. "Just look at that view. Miles and miles and miles and miles! Why, on a clear day you can see Germany *and* Italy."

"Well, let's not wait for a clear day. When are we going to pack up and get going?"

"Don't you like it here, darling? The peace? The quiet? The quaint foreign customs?"

"It's been different. But I've got to be thinking about college and . . ."

"I'm *so* glad you mentioned college, Patrick, because I've been meaning to speak to you about a European college. It's very chic to be schooled abroad. Who knows where I mightn't have sent you but for your Mr. Babcock."

"Who knows indeed?"

"And so I was thinking of the University of Vienna—fourteenth century, just like Stinkenbach. A brilliant school. Famous for Freud and Krafft-Ebing and . . ."

"And pogroms."

"Nonsense, darling. Schuschnigg settled all that Nazi business. Or there's Budapest or Switzerland. There are loads of good schools near here."

"It's out of the question. I wouldn't know the language. And who wants to be near here, anyhow?"

"Well, darling, I *told* you we were coming for an indefinite stay."

"Even so, I hardly think we'd be welcome to linger on through my four years of college. Besides I . . ."

"Well, Patrick my little love," she seemed slightly embarrassed, "you may think it odd of me, but I've found such serenity here in this little Austrian village tucked up in the hills that I've . . ."

"That you've what?"

"That I've bought Schloss Stinkenbach."

"You *what*?"

"I've bought Schloss Stinkenbach. Oh, Putzi had the longest time coaxing Maxl to part with it, but at last . . ."

"I'll bet he did—all of five or ten seconds. Are you out of your mind? You mean you'd do a mad thing like *buy* that crumbling old morgue nobody could give away? No heat, no light. One tin bathtub that leaves your bottom looking like a baboon's every time you . . ."

"Oh, but of course, darling, I plan to do the *Schloss* over entirely. Retain the ancient flavor, naturally, but it's going to be brought right up to the minute. Central heating. Ten or twenty nice pastel bathrooms—my own in black onyx, I thought—an electric kitchen. Who knows, I might turn it into a very profitable venture for a few select paying guests. I mean so many people are sick of chichi ski resorts like San Moritz and Bad Gastein and Kitzbühel that they might welcome a sweet unspoiled little village like . . ."

"Unspoiled? How can a town be dead for as long as Stinkenbach and not be rotten. You've gone . . ."

"Well naturally I wouldn't care to be living high on the hog and let the village continue to wallow in squalor. Without sacrificing any of its quaint charm I'd do that over, too. You know, darling, plumbing, electricity, telephones, medical aid, a decent school, perhaps a branch of Peck and Peck. Oh, I'd look out for my people."

"*Your* people? Who do you think you are, Mrs. God? I think you've lost your mind, and I'm getting out of this pest hole

Auntie Mame . . .

before I go just as mad as you have. Of all the soft-headed old middle-aged fools . . ."

"Shut your mouth, you bumptious little squirt. If you don't like it here you can get out. As for me . . ."

"That's just what I'm going to do. I'm going back to New York today and I don't care if I have to swim." With that I ran back to the house, now called, I suppose, Schloss Burnside, and raced up the stairs to my cold, stone cell of a room.

But if I'd counted on being alone, I was mistaken. I had banged open the door of my room with such force that it caught poor Friedl just as she was changing my bed. The impact had been enough to send her sprawling to the floor, where she lay coughing terribly.

"G-gee, I'm sorry, Baroness. I didn't know you were . . ." For a moment I was afraid I'd killed her. She was quite blue, and coughing like Violetta. Auntie Mame's motto—along with the Hennessy cognac people—has always been "Keep a little brandy handy." I snatched the big leather traveling flask from my suitcase, helped Friedl up to a chair, and tipped the bottle to her lips. It stopped the coughing. Then I poured quite a lot of brandy into a glass and offered it to her. "Here. Try some of this. Are you . . . are you all right?"

"Oh, thank you," Friedl gasped, choking slightly on the brandy. "Iss nothing. Chust a little coldt." She sipped again, this time more slowly. "*Ach!* Iss strong. But goodt. It makes me varm again." She held out the empty glass and I poured some more brandy into it. "How nice to be varm again." Her eyes looked glassy and I was still afraid that she might pass out on me. "Here iss alvace coldt—vinter, summer, alvace. Almost I candt remember how it iss to be varm. Not since Wien. You know Wien? Vienne?" She sipped again, rather elegantly.

"Vienna? Oh yes. Very pretty, Vienna."

"*Ja!* There was alvace varm. You know the Herrengasse?

The chentlemen's street? Iss there I lived in Pappa's house. Such a big house, andt varm. Alvace it vas varm." Her eyes began to shine, her cheeks grew pink. With another sip poor Friedl looked almost young again. "*Ach* dot house in the Herrengasse! Andt Mama's *jours*! You understand the *jour*? *Très Viennoise, le jour.*"

I understood that all Viennese with any faint pretense to fashion used a French word wherever it was possible or impossible to do so. "You mean a big tea party?" I said.

"*Ja! Exactement!* Chust so! Mama's *jours*. Every month the same day—second Saturday, Mama vas. *Ach!* The *Delikatesse!* Three kinds *Bäckerei* . . ." Her voice trailed off. She drained her glass and held it out again to be refilled. "Every month all Wien—Vienne—came to Mama's lovely party. Iss there I met Maxl, at Mama's *jour*. He vass young then and handsome. Not fat like now, but like Putzi—you know, *schlank*? How you say *élancé*?"

"You mean thin, slim, slender?" I said, refueling her tank.

"*Ja!* Chust so. *Schlank.* In the Vorld Var. Maxl vass *Kapitän*. Uniform . . . *so stilvoll . . . qui a du style . . . adel . . . aristocratique.* You understand?" I nodded, figuring that Maxl had once looked more like one of the family portraits and less like a tub of pure lard. And from a discreet glance at Friedl, I also wondered if there was a branch of A.A. at Stinkenbach-im-Tirol. The brandy had hit her hard and fast, but as she lost her inhibitions, she also was picking up what English she had learned, as well as the French affectations of her Viennese girlhood. "I vas so young. Pretty. My family . . . ve vere not *aristocratique*, but how you say *haute bourgeoise*. Pappa owned bank—*Privatbankgeschäft*. Private, you know? I had the biggest *Mitgift* in Wien. You know, *Mitgift*?" I didn't and it sounded faintly dirty, but from her delvings into other languages, I understood that it meant the dowry her father paid over as Friedl's price of admission into this noble family. The rest of the story, as I

Auntie Mame . . .

understood it, was pretty much history: the defeat of Austria, the collapse of the economy, the end of Pappa's family bank; and the dissolution of the Von Hodenlohern estates. Friedl was thus left—her dowry squandered on Maxl's debts and hairnets—old and cold, cheerless and childless as the mistress and servant of Schloss Stinkenbach, scorned as a commoner and despised as a pauper by her husband and his brothers. I wondered fleetingly how Auntie Mame would fare as mistress of this house if Bache and Company were ever to undergo such a sea change. But I was too annoyed with my eccentric relative to care. All I wanted to do was to get out, and the quickest way to do that was to get rid of Friedl. "Well," I said, briskly throwing some shirts into a suitcase, "I guess I'll be gone by the time the men get back from the horse fair. Please say good-by for . . ."

"Hah!" Friedl said, rising unsteadily and helping herself to more brandy. "Horses! The Von Hodenlohern chentlemen ride *two* horses—the Austrian horse and the Cherman horse in Berchtesgaden."

My mouth dropped open. "Berchtesgaden? You mean Hitler's place?"

"*Ja.* Berchtesgaden. Chust a few kilometers. So very nice for the fine Hodenlohern chentlemen. The great barons of Austria now vorking for a poor Austrian . . ." Her English broke down but her gesture clearly meant paper hanger.

"Do you mean to stand there and tell me that they're Nazis—all three of them?"

"No, not all three."

"Oh," I said, relieved. I knew that Putzi at least would have his feet on the ground.

"No, my Maxl iss fat, stupidt, lacy. Ven Hitler comes here Maxl vill not mind. If he doesn't come Maxl also will not mind. Maxl iss oldt, *dumm, dünkelhaft.* Hannes iss a baby yet—young and *albern.*" She tapped her head significantly. "He dreams only alvace of being the big *Schutzstaffel* officer for sports with boys. Those two are a big nothing."

"Well," I said, "I'm glad to hear that at least Putzi is . . ."

"Putzi!" she spat. "Putzi iss the vorst! He iss a how you say a *Landsknecht*! You understand?" I didn't. "Putzi for *years* vork for the Nazis. Every veek to meetings he goes. To Berchtesgaden, to Innsbruck. He hass no money, yet alvace he travels. To Paris and London and Rome he travels—alvace in beautiful clothes, alvace in lovely varm hotels. Andt *alvace* for the Nazis!"

I was too stunned to speak for a moment. Then I suddenly realized that Putzi and the whole pack of Von Hodenloherns would soon be moving on anyhow. "Well," I said heartily, "I guess that won't make any difference to you or me. I mean, I'm leaving here today. My aunt has bought the *Schloss*—I suppose you knew that—and so you'll be going, too. Then you won't be cold, and whatever Putzi does won't . . ."

"No," Friedl said flatly, "I am not going. Ve are staying—all of us."

"Oh, but you can't really. I mean after the place becomes my aunt's property you won't be staying on. Who'd want to any . . ."

"Ve vill be here. Ve vill stay on in dis coldt house until ve die or until ve are all killed. My money iss gone—all. The fine Von Hodenlohern barons need a new *Mitgift*—a new rich voman to be a new Friedl. Putzi will marry Frau Burnside. I promise you."

"Hey, listen. He's at least ten years younger than she is. He . . ."

Friedl clutched at my arm. "You! You lissen to *me*. Take her. Take her avay. She iss a good voman. She iss kind. Gay. Foolish. Like me. Take her avay now before like me she iss a prisoner in this terrible place."

"A prisoner? *Auntie Mame?*" Of course I knew she was

drunk, but a certain urgency in Friedl's manner kept me listening.

"*Ja!* A prisoner like me. A prisoner in this house, this terrible house. There are things in this terrible place you vould not belief. There are rooms that . . ."

"Friedl!" Maxl called. "Friedl!"

Friedl's face turned white, her eyes popped. "They are back. The men are back. I must go."

"Hey, wait," I began.

"No, I must go now. Pleece. Don't say nothing what I told you. Pleece." With that Friedl was gone—to trim Maxl's toenails I learned later. I began unpacking.

I WAS ABOUT TO GO STRAIGHT TO AUNTIE MAME AND tell her to clear out and clear out fast. Instead she came to me. "Oh," she said airily, "you still here? I expected you to be halfway to New York by now, burdened with tennis racquets, pennants, and No Parking signs for your college education. If it's money you need for transportation, I'll be happy to . . ."

"Listen, Auntie Mame," I said. "There's something I've got to talk to you about. It's vital that . . ."

"Thank you, no," she said with hammy grandeur. "You've said quite enough. Howsomever, as long as you're still enjoying *my* hospitality beneath *my* roof, there is something you can do for me. You can take me to the *Kirchtag*. I wish to learn the *Schuhplattler* and . . ."

"Take you to the *what?*"

"The *Kirchtag*. It's the village market day in the church square, and as long as I'm to be more or less the patroness of Stinkenbach, it's my duty to be with the people on these festive occasions. Believe me, I wouldn't be wasting your valuable time except that Putzi and his brothers have been called to some sort of landowners' meeting and . . ."

"But if they're not landowners any longer, why did . . ."

"Don't talk to me. Don't speak at all. Just try to look as pleasant as possible. Oh, and be sure to wear those cute *Lederhosen* I bought you."

Looking and feeling like a damned fool, I stomped down to the village while Auntie Mame, the new chatelaine of Schloss Stinkenbach, rode grandly in the Rolls. The village, a little less sleepy than usual, was decked out in some faded bunting. There were a few stalls set up with some incredible *Kitsch* on sale—bad carved figures, gaudy embroidered aprons, rustic barometers; junk like that. Beer, local wine, and crullers the size and weight of cannon balls were being listlessly hawked, and a four-piece band tooted away in front of the local saloon. There were a lot of village girls, looking like butter tubs in their tatty dirndls, some middle-aged village women, and a few old gaffers. None of the younger males seemed to be around.

"Not much of a stag line at these affairs is there?" I said.

"Never mind that," Auntie Mame said coldly. "They're undoubtedly waiting for me to open the festivities. If you'll simply help me to start things off with a gay *Schuhplatter*, I shall make no further demands on you."

"*Der Schuhplattler, bitte,*" she called to the band leader. "Come, Patrick."

The next thing I knew, I was out in the center of the square trying to follow Auntie Mame through the intricate inanities of a Tyrolean native dance. She was pretty good at it, and what she didn't know she could bluff her way through. I was not. "Listen, Auntie Mame. I don't care if you're mad or not, but . . ."

"Don't talk, child, concentrate. Now, clap your hands, slap your knees, and . . ."

"But I'm trying to tell you about Putzi. He's a dyed in the wool . . ." Before I could finish, Auntie Mame was out of sight.

Auntie Mame . . .

She turned up again behind me, bumping her rear end against mine in rhythm with the band. "Auntie Mame. Can you hear me?"

"I'm not listening. I'm dancing. Now kick." The crowd was almost wetting itself with merriment. "Clap your hands, slap your thigh. Kick again."

In my embarrassment and confusion I slipped and sprawled flat on the cobblestones. The villagers were in stitches. I'd struck my head pretty hard and all I was conscious of was a kind of aurora borealis going on in front of my eyes and the laughter of the local girls. Then the laughing stopped and there was utter silence for a couple of seconds, interrupted only by that phony, mellifluous voice so dear to the hearts of theatergoers everywhere. "Jesus," the voice rang out through the mountains, "do we have to be dragged all the way to Shangri-La for one lousy, God-damned gallon of gas?"

I looked up. Coming down the main drag of the village I saw a team of oxen dragging behind them a glittering English sports car. Sitting on the folded-back roof were Captain the Honourable Basil Fitz-Hugh and his wife, Vera Charles.

"*Vera!*" Auntie Mame squealed. "Basil! What on earth . . ."

"My God! *Mame!*" In a moment the two ladies were embracing in the middle of the church square. If the citizens of Stinkenbach-im-Tirol had found Auntie Mame foreign and exotic, they hadn't seen anything until they caught a glimpse of Vera Charles, her mahogany hair, her diamonds, the long lynx cape, the svelte suit, the pert Paris hat. "Mame, dahling," Vera shrilled theatrically, "Ah cahn't tell yew haow too uttahly divane it is to see a friendly face in the gudfawsaken countreh! Bezzle end Ay wuh maotorring beck from Bed Gastein when . . . And speaking of godforsaken," she said in her purest Americanese, "what in the hell are you doing in this hole got up like that?"

"*I*, Vera? I own it," Auntie Mame said. Then she babbled on.

"Oh, but it's too wonderful to have you and Basil here! You must come up and see my *Schloss*. And of course you'll stay the night. I won't hear otherwise. Ito! Do see to the Fitz-Hughs' baggage."

After that, any hope of getting a word in was madness. Auntie Mame and Vera, talking a mile a minute, swept Basil into the Rolls, and I was left to find gasoline for Basil's car and drive it back up to the *Schloss*. By the time I got back, Auntie Mame and her guests were nowhere to be seen—or even heard—in any of the main rooms. Depressed, I went upstairs to lie down and think things over. But no sooner had I hit the bed than the resonant voices of Auntie Mame and Vera came wafting in from the battlement outside my room. "Yes, Mame, yes," Vera was saying, "it's all very old-world and quaint but why the hell would you want to buy it? The place is older than God, bigger than the Waldorf, and as cold as Belasco's heart. Basil, ducky, fetch my cape."

"Righto, dearest."

"Oh, but Vera. The view! The view! Look at all that scenery and every bit of it mine!"

"So get a magic lantern. Besides, all these krauts give me the creeps. There's just something in the air around here that . . ."

Encouraged by what Vera was saying, I went out to join them on the battlement. There they were, passing the binoculars back and forth and looking out onto the valley. "No, Mame," Vera went on, handing the glasses to her, "you've bought a pup. You'll be miserable in this . . ."

"Be still, Vera, I'm trying to see. . . ."

"That's right, Vera," I said. "It's just what I've been telling her. She . . ."

The binoculars clattered from Auntie Mame's hands. "Patrick!" she said sharply, wheeling on me. "How many times must I tell you *not* to come eavesdropping. Now go back to your room and wait there until dinner."

"Hey, Auntie Mame, I only . . ."

"Do as I say this instant!" she snapped. "Now march!"

Hurt and angry, I started back to my room. I was just closing the French door behind me when I heard Auntie Mame say, "Vera. Take the glasses and look over there."

IF IT WEREN'T FOR WHAT FRIEDL HAD TOLD ME, I'D have packed up and left the *Schloss* then and there. But I swallowed my pride, got dressed, and went downstairs when Poldi sounded the dinner gong. Auntie Mame was obviously putting on the dog for Basil and Vera. Dinner was a black-tie affair and the food was better than usual. As always, Maxl presided over the table with Vera at his right, while poor Friedl, looking cold and puffy-eyed in lackluster lamé, sat opposite.

Maxl, who had an eye for handsome women—and rich ones—was putting himself out to charm Vera and he fairly bubbled over with new and interesting topics of conversation. "Yes, dear lady, before the Great War things were different for us. We had our great house in Vienna, convenient to the palace, and of course our *Kronlands* in Mähren. Our estate was huge and it was a latifundium—entailed, as you English say—passed down from father to son, not to be sold. Of course we never had to do anything about them. We noble families simply hired some smart Jew to run them at enormous profits."

"Re-ahlly?" Vera said. "Well, it's nice you don't have to do that here. Samuel Insull himself couldn't put this place in the black."

I sniggered into my soup, sending a fine spray of consommé into the centerpiece.

"Vera," Auntie Mame said and cleared her throat.

"Ay mean," Vera said, again in her elegant British English, "the terrain araound Stinkenbach is so glawdious that it would be crrrriminal to rrrruin it with anything that made mere moneh."

"Quite right," Basil said, looking uneasy.

At that point Putzi took over the conversation, all winning smiles and courtly nods, the very picture of the charming aristocratic worldling. Granted that he had once charmed me, too, I now saw him as nothing but a suave, slick, slimy con man who'd sell his name, his country, his own mother for a well-made suit of clothes, first-class accommodations, and the vague promise of being made a *Gauleiter* once his people had been properly betrayed. "Ah, yes, you're so right, Lady Fitz-Hugh." Vera wouldn't have a title until Basil's father died, but Putzi was laying it on thick. "As I told Mame when she bought this land, there is a fortune to be made here—especially in the winter when we have snow."

Friedl shuddered and hugged her thin blue arms.

"With this huge house as a hotel—a few minor improvements, naturally—Stinkenbach would be a great winter resort. Of course, no one in our family could go into trade, but with you Americans it's different. You know we Austrians have never been a very clever people when it comes to being opportunistic or being smart at business. But think what a joke it will be when skiers from all over Europe are coming to this very house to make Stinkenbach a rich village and Mame a richer woman. Naturally, I would remain to . . ."

"I don't quite see what you mean about Austrians not being very clever *or* very opportunistic, Putzi," I said, unable to stop myself. "Why, look at your little Austrian house painter, Adolf Schicklegruber. He started from nothing and now he's climbed over everybody's neck to the very top. And when it comes to being smart at business . . ."

"Patrick!" Auntie Mame snapped. She half rose from her chair and her eyes were blazing. "That's enough," she said more quietly. "Please don't interrupt when others are talking."

I noticed that Putzi's knuckles were white—white as Friedl's face—as he gripped his wineglass.

"Come now, old boy," Basil said blandly, "Hitler's done some jolly good things in Germany."

I was so shocked that I was just barely conscious of Poldi racing up the three flights of stairs that joined the dining room to the kitchen with a hot, puffy *Salzburger Nockerln*.

"Of course he has," Vera said. Hannes's handsome automaton's head bobbed wildly up and down.

"Ah, poor young American boy," Putzi said with a maddening smile, "you make a mistake so common to countries where there is a classless society. Of course Hitler is a hero, but only a peasants' hero. The aristocracy—even the upper classes—hardly consider him at all."

"It seems to me that there are quite a lot of so-called aristocrats around here who are only too happy to sell their souls to Hitler—for money, of course."

"*Patrick!*" Auntie Mame cried. She was standing now. "Leave the room immediately! I will *not* have my friends insulted by a rude, know-it-all schoolboy. Go to your room!"

"You're damned right I will," I bellowed. Throwing down my napkin I stalked out.

"Pleece . . ." Friedl murmured, but I heard no more.

For the third time that day I slammed into my room in a fury. I ripped off my clothes and got into bed. But it was still too early to sleep. I tossed and turned for who knows how long. Finally, just as I was beginning to doze off, I was awakened by the sound of talking out on the battlement. Listening a moment, I recognized the voices of Maxl and, of all people, Vera.

"Ah, the visssssta!" Vera was saying.

"Yes, gracious lady," Maxl purred, "below us the lights of Stinkenbach-im-Tirol."

"Yais," Vera said, "both of them." Then she giggled prettily and said, "Oh, Baron, *please!*"

"Oh, gracious lady," Maxl groaned, "if only I had a beautiful, understanding goddess like you to love me instead of stupid Friedl. Tell me—a friend of mine has a shooting lodge at Zell am Ziller. Could you come there with me?"

"Aoh, Bedden von Haodenlohern, Ay hoddly knaow what to say!"

"Say yes, gracious lady. Think, just you and me in the mountains."

"Ay'm tawn—teddibly tawn. May hot says yais—yais, yais, yaiss. But rrreason tells meh nay. Thiss grahnd ah-moo-ah we now knaow mate well tunn into a sssawdid beck-street ah-fay-ah."

"No, no, no," Maxl moaned.

"Yais, yais, yais! End be-sades, there is may husband. Ah, yew may think of him as the calmest of men—plessid and maild. But let meh tell yew, he is a beeeeessst! Yais, a beast! Aoh, yew dun't knaow haow Ah suffah! He gaoes med with jealouseh. He *beats* meh! And he has killed—yais, *slaughtered*—innocent young subalterns for even *looking* at meh. If he but knieuw that yew end Ay hed staolen away from the potty faw thiss brief maoment togethah, Ay kent eemejin *what* he mate do."

"Maxl! Maxl!" It was Putzi's voice.

"Gao naow, quickleh," Vera said, "Ay heah the othahs coming. Ay shall give yew may ahn-sah tomoddaow!"

"That's right," I bellowed, "get the hell off the back fence and give human beings a chance to sleep! And you on your honeymoon, Vera Charles!" With that I banged the French door shut so hard that one of the panes shattered. "My God,"

I said aloud, "the whole world's gone crazy." Only later did I realize that Vera was repeating word for word the big love scene from one of her greatest Broadway hits, *The Heart of Lalage de Trop.*

After a night of horrible dreams, I was awakened by the sound of something scraping on the floor of my room. I looked up just in time to see a note being slid under my door. Snatching it up, I opened it and read it. There, in Hannes's carefully drawn Germanic script, was an invitation, of sorts. It read:

> *Will you join my brother Maximilian and me on a walk in the mountains? We would be happy to show you the old Schloss Stinkenbach. We can be ready to go when it is convenient for you.*
>
> > *Faithfully,*
> > *Johannes von Hodenlohern*

Next to attending my own wake, I couldn't think of many things I'd rather do less, but as dreary as Maxl and Hannes were, at least they weren't actively in the pay of the Nazis. I opened the door and stepped out into the cold corridor just in time to see Hannes starting down the stairs. "Fine," I said. "Just swell. I'd love to come with you, just as soon as I get dressed."

"Fifteen minutes, then?" Hannes said with one of his rare smiles.

"Fifteen minutes."

THE THREE OF US MADE AN ODD PICTURE AS WE SET off. Hannes, all boots, *Lederhosen*, muscles, and sun tan, looked like a *Jugend* illustration for the Hitler youth movement. Even Maxl was dressed for the rugged life, his big rear end bifurcated by too-tight leather shorts. He also carried a great long rope, a revolver, and a first-aid kit. "Are we planning to scale Mount Everest or just take a hike in the hills?" I asked. I was less and less enthusiastic about this trip, but it did offer certain advantages in that I could get away from Auntie Mame and her Nazi boy friend long enough to make a few simple plans.

As we set off, I heard Auntie Mame calling, "Patrick! Patrick! Where are you going?"

I turned around. She was up on the battlement, leaning over the parapet. "Out," I said coldly.

"No, darling. No! We're going on a picnic—Basil and Vera and Putzi and Friedl. I-I'll need you to round out the party."

"Maybe you can get the Görings to join you—a charming couple. Where are you going, Berchtesgaden?" Maybe I shouldn't have said that, I thought, because Hannes and Maxl exchanged the fisheye with one another.

"Patrick. Wait! I forbid you to . . ."

I turned around and thumbed my nose at her. "Come on," I said.

THE OLD, ORIGINAL, RUINED SCHLOSS STINKENBACH didn't *look* terribly much higher up than the fourteenth-century version, but it was quite a hike and almost all of it straight up. It was some climb, and more than once I was grateful for Maxl's length of rope. Maxl was puffing like a grampus after the first hour, I was parched and winded, and even Hannes, our Strength through Joy boy, was panting a bit.

"Let's rest here, shall we?" Hannes said. Again he favored me with a frosty smile and tossed down his rucksack. "You are thirsty?" he asked, taking out two tall thin bottles of wine.

"A little," I said.

"Here." Hannes poured a tremendous amount into a cup

Auntie Mame . . .

and passed it to me. It looked like quite a lot of wine for so early in the day—especially since they had urged me not to wait for breakfast.

"Isn't—isn't there any water?" I said.

"Ah, water. Oh, yes, but not until we get up to the old fortress. Drink this now. We are nearly there."

I gulped the wine down, and before I could say no, Hannes had filled the cup again.

"D-don't you two want any?"

"Oh, no," Hannes said, thumping his chest. "I'll wait until we get to the water. Too much wine is bad for the body. Just look at my brother Maxl." Maxl was, indeed, a sight, lying there in the shade of some trees and panting like an old mastiff.

I finished the second cup of wine and wisely refused a third, although I was still very thirsty.

"Now come look at the view," Hannes said. "Over here."

I was a little weary of looking at views, which seemed to be the sole occupation of Stinkenbach, but I trudged dutifully after Hannes as he strolled athletically to the very lip of an abyss. "See," he said genially, "all Austria at our feet." He put his arm around my shoulder affectionately. I rather wished he hadn't. From time to time Hannes made me think of those rare types who are never happier than when chinning themselves and being manly—*except* when, behind locked doors, they find solace in a blonde wig and Mother's old evening wrap. Besides, there was a sheer drop of several hundred feet right at the tips of our shoes.

"Look," Hannes said, squeezing my shoulder slightly, "directly below you can see the *Schloss* and all the people there—like little insects." I looked down dizzily. What he said was true. There, indeed, was Schloss Stinkenbach, sprawling out in all directions. I could see Poldi putting out a wash behind the castle. Auntie Mame's Rolls and Basil's two-seater were standing in the driveway. I could also see fields and out-buildings I had never known existed. "Look," I said, pointing to two brightly colored specks, "there's Auntie Mame and there's Vera—Mrs. Fitz-Hugh, I mean—but what are they doing over there in that field so far from the . . ." I said no more. Hannes's grip on me tightened and I felt something cold and metallic at the back of my neck. It was sleepy old Maxl with his revolver.

"Now my fine young socialist friend," Hannes said, "prepare yourself for an accident while climbing in the mountains of your aunt's estate. The rope, Maxl. *Der Strick.*"

"Hey," I said, "what do you think you're . . ."

"I think I am binding you with this rope," Hannes said. "We shall wait until they leave for their picnic. Then will be the time for your fatal fall. The poor American drank too much wine, and . . ."

Realizing that I was dealing with a pair of lunatics, I tried to be reasonable. "But, Hannes, if they find me all tied up they'll know it wasn't an accident."

"You will be untied—at the bottom. When you are discovered you will look entirely naturalistic. Maxl . . ." Hannes began saying something in rapid, colloquial German as I felt the rope tightening around me. No need to struggle, however. One false step and I'd have been over the edge and dead—quite naturalistically enough.

"Hannes! Maxl! This is . . ." I said no more. A wide strip of adhesive tape from the first-aid kit was slapped over my mouth. Hannes and Maxl worked with calm efficiency, laughing and joking in German. For such feckless slobs, they were pretty good operators. I was bound and gagged to a fare-thee-well before I even had much time to consider that this was The Bitter End.

When I was nicely trussed up, Hannes smiled at me and

Auntie Mame . . .

said, "Ah, look down below. See. The cars are leaving." Then he slapped me calmly back and forth across the face. "This is for good-by. Maxl . . ." Just then there was an explosion that rocked the whole mountain. I mean the impact of it knocked all three of us down. Lying there with my head hanging over the edge of the cliff, I could see smoke and flames belching from one of the outbuildings down at Schloss Stinkenbach. There was another explosion that shook the whole mountainside, and yet another building on the estate went up.

"*Gott!*" Hannes screamed. "*Der Zeughaus!*"

Together the two Von Hodenlohern brothers started running down the hill, leaving me there halfway over the edge of the precipice. I struggled, but rather gingerly—considering my delicate position. The second explosion was followed by a third and then a fourth. Then I felt a hand on me, tugging me backward. I flipped over and looked up into the red-brown face of Captain Basil Fitz-Hugh. Well, I thought, it doesn't really matter *who* finishes me off—one Nazi is just as good as another.

"Patrick," Basil said, ripping the adhesive tape off my mouth. "We've been so worried."

"*You've* been worried? What about *me?*"

"Oh, no harm could have come to you," he said cutting the ropes. "I've been following you as close as seemed provident. And of course I was armed."

"Well, why didn't you shoot? I didn't feel so provident at the edge of that cliff."

"Don't stop to ask a lot of questions now, old boy. We haven't a moment to spare." He started at a dogtrot down the mountainside with me close behind—mystified, but happy to be still alive. Naturally we kept gathering momentum, so that scarcely ten minutes later we were down on the road leading out of Stinkenbach-im-Tirol. Auntie Mame's Rolls was pulled up at the side, waiting for us. Behind, I saw Basil's little sports car with Ito at the wheel. Beside him sat Friedl, huddled in Vera's lynx cape. She looked scared stiff, but at least she looked warm.

"Patrick, darling," Auntie Mame cried, bursting out of her car. She gathered me in her arms and held me. She was trembling terribly and her cheeks were streaked with tears. Then Vera, not to be upstaged, threw herself from the car and into Basil's arms, smothering him in marten furs, anointing him with smudgy mascara tears. "Basil! Oh Basil! My hero! I'm so glad you're safe. I aged a hundred years while you were up that mountain. Tell me, my darling, what did they . . ."

"Not now," Auntie Mame said, trying to light a cigarette. Her hands were trembling too violently. "Let's get out of this horrid place. We've no idea how many . . ."

"Right you are," Basil said. He got in behind the wheel and I, knowing the highways and byways of Stinkenbach, got in beside him. He threw the car into gear and we were off, with Ito following.

Except for having two eyes and two arms, the Hon. Basil looked just like Lord Nelson at the helm of the Rolls as we sped toward Salzburg. Totally mystified by everything that had happened that day, I prodded him for an explanation. "Well, you see, Patrick, your dear Aunt Mame discovered yesterday that Baron Von Hodenlohern—Putzi, that is—was a Nazi when she and Vera were looking out at the valley throught the field glasses."

"Well, I could have told her that, only she wouldn't listen."

"It was perhaps better for her to discover it for herself. And discover it she did when quite by chance she happened to see Putzi and his young brother Johannes out on a field drilling all the men and boys of the village. It was quite a shocker, according to Vera. The goose step, the Nazi salute—all that sort of rot. Well, needless to say, that was more than enough for your aunt. And you can just imagine how frightened she was for you when you said all of those unfortunate—but perfectly true—things at dinner last night."

"I guess I did shoot off my mouth a bit."

"And Mame had every reason in the world to be concerned. I discovered that for myself when I happened to be passing the *Herrenzimmer* and overheard Putzi instructing his brothers to do away with you on the mountain. If it hadn't been for those tiresome German lessons from that beastly old *Fräulein* of mine, I shouldn't have had the faintest idea what they were talking about. In fact, I couldn't believe my ears at the time."

"Well, you might have warned me."

"Patrick, Mame did. But you wouldn't listen to her. Instead, you went right along with Hannes and Maxl. However, that's not all the story by half. It seems that Friedl told your Auntie Mame everything last night and even showed her some of the things that are in the locked rooms of Schloss Stinkenbach. Guns. Dynamite. Cases and cases of munitions. And, for a house that doesn't even have electricity, one of the most elaborate radio stations I've ever seen. Those Jerries are damned clever at that sort of thing. You've got to hand it to them. Well, as I say, Friedl made everything pretty clear to Mame. She even told her about the ammunition in all the outbuildings. Well, you can jolly well see that Mame was beside herself with worry by then. It was a sticky situation and one that called for decisive action."

"Yes indeedy," I said, shuddering at the thought of what had almost happened to me.

"So when you set out innocently with those bounders this morning, I followed. Luckily, I know a bit about mountaineering—the World War, you know."

"But all those explosions?"

"Ah yes, jolly good show, what? Mame and Vera saw to that. They simply went round to the various arsenals with a tin of lighter fluid and started fires. It *is* Mame's property, after all."

"Gee, Basil, you must have been some army man to have thought of all that."

"Good God no, dear boy. It was Mame's idea. It seems that her husband's great-grandfather, General Lafayette Pulaski Pickett, created the same diversionary action at Second Manassas by blowing up an arsenal there. At least that's what Mame said. No indeed, she conceived the entire plan. Greatest military strategist since Joan of Arc."

"But did Putzi just stand by and . . ."

"Good God! Putzi! I'd forgotten all about him."

"Where is he?"

"In the boot."

"In the what?"

"The luggage compartment—whatever you Americans call it." He stopped the car and we all got out.

"Oh, Patrick, my little love," Auntie Mame said, wrapping her arms around me. "If anything had happened to you I'd have killed myself. You were so right about Stinkenbach—tatty, sinister little jerkwater town—and I was such a fool; it was almost too late."

"Mame," Basil said, "we've got to get rid of your Austrian baron."

"Oh, heavens, yes!"

"What's Putzi doing back there, Auntie Mame?" I asked.

"Well, Patrick, I hated to do it, but he simply would not leave Vera and me alone long enough to get our work done this morning. So I knocked him out."

"Knocked him out?"

"Yes, darling, with that ugly cloisonné vase in the *salon*. He was on his knees proposing to me and the opportunity seemed just too good to pass by. Then Vera and Friedl helped

Auntie Mame . . .

me carry him down and lock him up. I couldn't think of any place else to put him."

Basil opened the luggage compartment, and Putzi, incoherent with rage, unfolded himself and scrambled out. "Mame! If you think this is some sort of amusing joke . . ."

"Joke, Baron von Hodenlohern? I was never more serious in my life, you despicable little traitor!"

Putzi looked up toward Schloss Stinkenbach, his face contorted in horror. Great black clouds of smoke drifted up from the hardly visible roofs of the outbuildings. Then there was a horrible thundering roar and we saw the roof fly off the castle itself. Putzi sprang toward Auntie Mame with the speed of a panther. But I was even faster. I put out my foot and he fell with a splat into the road. "I'll have you in jail," he shrieked at Auntie Mame. "You've set fire to our house."

"Your house?" Auntie Mame said. "I have the bill of sale right here. And by the way, my answer to your proposal of this morning is no."

"But our munitions, our guns, our . . ."

"You sold it to me lock, stock, and barrel, Baron von Hodenlohern. I assume that the arsenal and the short-wave radio were included. Anyhow, I should think that your government might take a rather dim view of you and your subversive activities. Now get out of my sight!"

"Just wait," Putzi snarled. "You're the rich American who thinks she can buy a castle and burn it down. Money to burn, eh? But when we take over . . ."

"It isn't costing me a penny, Putzi. This fire's on the Allegemeine Bodenkredit Versicherungs and Handelsgesellschaft."

"What in the name of God is that, Mame?" Vera said.

"The Allegemeine Bodenkredit Versicherungs und Handelsgesellschaft? Why as any child could tell you, it's the biggest Nazi insurance company in Germany. I wanted to insure the place with Lloyds, but Putzi insisted on this firm. I mailed the premium yesterday. Now, Putzi, there's no need for you to tarry here any longer. Have a nice walk back to Stinkenbach."

"Oh, and would you mind taking a message to your brother Maxl?" Vera said. "Just tell him that he'll no longer be bothered with having a wife. I'm taking Friedl to England with us. And tell him that I won't be able to become his mistress. My grandfather, who is a rabbi in Schenectady, wouldn't like it a bit."

WE STOOD THERE IN THE ROAD FOR JUST A SECOND, Auntie Mame's arm around my shoulders, watching Schloss Stinkenbach go up in smoke.

Auntie Mame and Mother Russia

"SO AFTER THE TWO OF YOU YODELLED AROUND THE Tyrol, where did she take you?" Pegeen asked.

"To Russia."

"To *Russia?* How could you?"

"Very simply in those days. Before the war, tourists were more than welcome."

"I'll bet she wasn't."

"On the contrary, my aunt caused a minor sensation in the Soviet."

"I can believe that, but why would she want to go to a place like Russia anyhow?"

"Auntie Mame was a keen student of political science, always interested in learning more. Her Russian, um sojourn was, by and large, an experiment."

"What sort of an experiment?"

"An experiment in living."

. . .

A RE YOU COMFORTABLE, *dushka?*" Auntie Mame asked gaily. "That's Russian for darling, darling."

"As comfortable as can be expected," I said balefully surveying the plush and mahogany interior of our compartment aboard the *Krasnaye Strela*, or the Red Arrow Express, as it made its lumbering, jerking, halting, screeching way across the dismal Russian countryside.

"Ah, my little love, let those scoffers on Wall Street say what they will about the Socialist Republic, but we have nothing like the October Line in America."

"Nothing except, maybe, the Long Island Railroad," I said. The October Line was really the old Nicholas Line that ran, or limped, from Leningrad to Moscow on the most casual of schedules. The cars were European Wagons-Lits, antedating 1917. The trip took several days. The toilet didn't work and there was no dining car, although the train stopped every fifteen minutes or so for people to bring on tea and black bread. However, Auntie Mame was In a New Phase and would hear nothing against Russia.

"Are you comfortable, comrade?" Auntie Mame asked Ito.

"No, madam," Ito said and giggled.

"Ito! How many times have I told you to *stop* calling me *madam!* I have given you your freedom. I have released you from your bondage and set you free to find yourself in a world of men, after years of selfishly forcing you to the yoke of domestic servitude. I hope, Comrade Ito," she said more kindly, "that some day you will forgive me."

Auntie Mame ...

"You don't worry, Madam Comrade," Ito said, going off into peals of laughter.

"Besides," Auntie Mame said, "we should all feel very lucky to be riding in a first class compartment."

"First class?" I said, wondering what the masses were going through in the other cars. "But I thought that Russia had a classless society. How come, Auntie Mame?"

"Why, *dushka*, it's because, uh, it's because . . . Well, I mean to say that . . . Why don't *you* explain to Patrick, Dr. Whipple?"

"Why, um, certainly, um," Dr. Whipple began, stroking his straggly little gray goatee. "It's, ah, simply that, uh, ah, International, ah, guests and, ah, certain, um, Soviet intellectuals, um, are, ah, treated as guests of the, ah, government. Um. Yes, ah, that's it exactly. Just, ah, so."

I was accustomed by now to Dr. Whipple's making absolutely no sense and taking forever to do it. He was an old poop of about sixty. Just what he was a doctor *of* I never knew. Several things, probably, from the scrambled alphabet that appeared behind his name. Dr. Whipple was one of those people who are always going to other places to do whatever it is they can't do wherever they happen to be at the moment. He had spent most of his life taking courses in abstruse subjects in far-away universities and accumulating initials to put after the Euclid (that was his first name, no kidding) Alonzo Whipple, Junior. They looked very impressive on his grubby little visiting cards. Auntie Mame picked him up in Budapest after her flight from Austria. Dr. Whipple was studying *something* or other at good old Budapest U. and had come to her rescue with a neat Hungarian translation when Auntie Mame was having a little difficulty ordering a Sidecar in the Abazzia-Kaveha. The rest was history.

Auntie Mame had been living like an Eszterhazy at the Dunapalota for about ten cents a day when Dr. Whipple, having befriended her, and cadged a free meal in that pretty Danube cafe, took it upon himself to revamp her social conscience. Every day they drove out in the Rolls to the Angels' Field to see how the downtrodden Magyars lived under the Horthy regime, with Dr. Whipple as our guide. He was a great friend of the masses, although it occurred to me that the masses didn't think much of Dr. Whipple. And I also noticed that he came back in time to take his meals at the Dunapalota, apparently preferring the Ritz cuisine to the noodle-and-potato dishes of the Hungarian poor.

It wasn't romance with Auntie Mame, of that I'm certain, because only Dr. Whipple's mother could have loved him. But it was reaction, and Auntie Mame's reactions were just fine, thanks. Having run, sick with revulsion, from a Nazi culture in Austria, Auntie Mame ran just a little too far and ended up with Dr. Whipple. The next thing I knew, we were on a plane heading for Leningrad.

Russia was very interesting for a visit, don't think I'm trying to be blasé about it, but Auntie Mame was able to see it only through the eyes of Dr. Whipple.

Leningrad, which used to be Petrograd or St. Petersburg, was just about as baroque as Peter the Great could make it. We stayed at the Astoria Hotel which, in its threadbare way, reminded me a little of the Plaza, inexplicably taken over by the management of a Bowery flophouse. We went to performances at the Mariinsky Theatre, which used to be the old Imperial Opera House, and made reverent tours of the Winter Palace, out of Peterhof and the palace of Peter the Great, to Eyetskoye-Selo for Catherine the Great's place and quite a lot of other elaborate establishments that had once belonged to the rich and now were the property of just everybody.

Auntie Mame had been thrilled by the happy lot of the

Common People, not that she ever met any. "But simply *every-one* in Russia has a fur coat, my little love!" she cried. Since Auntie Mame was both nearsighted and In a New Phase, I hadn't bothered to point out to her that all the fur coats looked like ruptured tom cat. Besides, it would have spoiled her pleasure in buying all those beautiful sable skins at the Leningrad fur trading market. In addition, she found some down and out old White Russians who sold her a rather decorative, though splintered, antique triptych and some very elegant Fabergé Easter eggs. Thus fulfilled in Leningrad, we were on our way to G.H.Q., Moscow.

In 1937 Russia not only welcomed visitors from the West, the latch-string was a lassoo. I can see why. We put up at the Metropole Hotel, a hostelry that made the Astoria of Leningrad seem like Xanadu. There were no Louis-the-Whatever suites, just square, bleak rooms furnished in hard blue plush, a period I still think of as Stalin Standardized. Sagging balconies gave onto a bleak courtyard. There were private bathrooms, but in my own, I had to sit on the bathtub drain to keep the water from running out. There was no plug. But I knew it was pointless to mention this to Auntie Mame. She was In a New Phase, thanks to Dr. Whipple, and the Soviet could do no wrong, although, if any hotel in America had been just half as bad, she would have checked out before the bellboy had switched on the lights and opened the windows. I shared a room with Ito, her houseboy, who was terribly embarrassed and just couldn't get used to calling me Comrade.

But Auntie Mame loved it or said she did. With Dr. Whipple in command, she took Ito and me on endless tours of Moscow. Dr. Whipple had gotten out his soiled old Order of the Red Banner of Labor and, so honored, got us easily in to see such recherché sights as the new subway system; the taxidermy that was Lenin; a tractor factory; the Tretyakov Art Gallery; the Museum of the Revolution on Upper Gorky Street and the Sokolniki Park. It was all very interesting, but after a few views of public monuments, Ito and I were just as happy to go to the movies, where they showed double features, one film invariably a thrilling Soviet epic in which young Dmitri, head of the Konsomol, and his sweetheart, Sonia, go off happily into a red sunset on a new tractor; the other, and far more popular movie, was always something involving Shirley Temple.

Ito and I had had our fill of Moscow when Auntie Mame came bounding into our room. "We've done it, we've done it, we've done it!" she cried.

"Done what?" I asked, "got train tickets out of this place?"

"No, *dushka*, no. We're all going to Georgia!"

"But Auntie Mame," I said, "we've all *been* to Georgia and you hated it. Remember old Mrs. Burnside?"

"Not *that* Georgia, *dushka*! *The* Georgia! *Iberia!* You know, darling where the Mdivani boys come from . . ."

"Where I wish they'd go back to," I said.

"And that's just where *we're* going, my little love! Just outside Tiflis."

"Well, a few days of Tiflis, even syph'lis would look pretty good after . . ."

"A few *days?* Ah *dushka*, how light you can be, carefree youth, when the whole course of your life is being re-routed."

"What in the name of God are you talking about?"

"Hush, *dushka*, there isn't any God."

"Be that as it may, what *are* you talking about?"

"I'm talking about the most wonderful experiment ever conceived by mankind, the Mother Bloor Communal Farm (English speaking)."

"The *what?*" I cried.

Auntie Mame . . .

"Oh, Patrick, my little love. This is it. This is the goal, the target, the bull's eye of my whole empty life. All this wealth, this chi-chi, this dawdling about with wastrels who suck the blood of the workers in order to . . ."

"Who do *what*? What have you been drinking?"

"Only vodka with a beer chaser, like *any* good proletarian. Yes, my little love, Euclid, that's Dr. Whipple, *dushka*, has shown me the *way* and that is the Mother Bloor Communal Farm (English speaking)."

"Are you insane?" I asked.

"No, *dushka*, but I have been. All of my life. Yet now when we jolly comrades, English speaking, thank God, all get together down in Georgia; do everything together; live in complete independence of the Capitalistic world . . . Oh, my little love, I can't even *try* to describe what it's going to be . . ."

"I'll bet you can't," I said.

"Exactly, Patrick love! Oh, the hand at the plow; the community loom; the people of all cultures, colors, classes learning, living, loving together . . ."

"Hey!" I said.

"Oh *dushka*, if only you could have a good, long talk with Euclid, Dr. Whipple."

"I have had," I said. "But what about getting back to America and college?"

"College! Faugh! Why, Patrick, you'll learn more on the Mother Bloor Communal Farm (English speaking) in four *days* than you could in four *years* of some tatty shut-away ivory tower. Oh, my little love, this is *it*. I've been such a fool for these forty . . . for *ever* so long. But this is so right for me, right, right, *right!* Euclid says . . ."

"Did Dr. Whipple put you up to this?"

"Euclid is a great leader and it is he, he and I, with the help of this wonderful, wonderful government, who will prove to the Doubting Thomases of the Capitalistic world that Anglo-Saxons can live richly and productively in peace and harmony in a culture of *culture* and pacifism that ..."

"Okay," I said, knowing that this was just another storm to be weathered. "Just tell me what to do next."

"Oh, Patrick, *dushka*, I *knew* you'd be enthusiastic!" Auntie Mame hugged me and she smelled deliciously of *Nuit de Noel*. "Now you and Ito are simply to rush down to the Mother Bloor Communal Farm ..."

"English speaking," I added patiently.

"Exactly, my little love! And of course I know you won't mind taking a few of my things with you. Well, you're to get my rooms ready on this divine old Georgian farm and just give a hand to those who are already there. Dr. Whipple and I are to meet Stalin and Max ..."

"Who's Max?" I asked.

"Maxim Litvinov, naturally, *dushka*, and Micky Borodin, and I *may* just snoop around to see if Anna Louise Strong is in town ..."

"Do we drive there in the Rolls?" I asked.

"Oh how *like* you! That school! That trust fund! That Mr. Babcock! Trying to mould your life to the Scarsdale pattern! Whatever decadence have they all taught you? That you and poor Comrade Ito should be riding in a Rolls-Royce, manu-factured from the very *blood* of the British workers, while millions are hungry ..."

"What's the matter, Auntie Mame? Hasn't it got here *yet*?"

"Well, as a matter of fact, no. There's been a little labor trouble on the railroad. You and Ito are to go by boat, then by train, then by bus. You'll be met at Rostov and then ..."

"I see," I said. "And just how much luggage of yours do we have to carry with us?"

"Hardly anything, *dushka*. Just a trunk and two or three light hand pieces."

Auntie Mame ...

Ito and I set off with a pound of Halvah, Hugo's Simplified Russian Grammar and Auntie Mame's extra baggage. Ito spoke quite a lot of Japanese and some English. I spoke quite a lot of English, some French and four years of Latin (with pony). All told, we were a linguistic washout on our long, long trip South from Moscow to Georgia. Even so, we finally arrived at the Mother Bloor Communal Farm (English Speaking).

Georgia is a very funny section of Russia. It's way down south, as the name implies, and it's also called Iberia, Caucasia and Armenia, *as well as* Georgia. Part of it borders the Black Sea, part the Caspian Sea, part Iran and part Turkey, if *that's* any recommendation. It's one of the oldest existing civilizations, if it can be called that and many of the structures are said to be more than twenty-five hundred years old. I believed it when I saw the Mother Bloor Communal Farm. However, it's one of the prettiest, most clement sections of Russia, although very mountainous. It is also one of the most peaceful, or was in 1937, as both Stalin and his chum Beria were Georgians.

I digress. The Mother Bloor Communal Farm was ten miles from a hamlet called Psplat, which was forty miles from a town called Lyuksemburgi, which was no distance at all from Tbilisi, or Tiflis. In other words, it was isolated. It had once been the *datcha* of a local bigwig who had been liquidated with Zinoviev, Kamenev and fifty-some other Trotsky sympathizers a year earlier. Unlike most of the Georgian limestone buildings nearby, the Mother Bloor Communal Farm was built of wood in a kind of turn-of-the-century fashion that reminded me of the tragedies of Chekov. It was a big, ungainly structure bristling with towers and turrets, cupolas and curlicues. Grimy mullion windows, dirty dormers and dim stained glass embrasures stared blindly out at us. The lawn looked as though it hadn't been mowed since the Mongol Invasion. While the house was less than fifty, it seemed a lot older and creaked a lot more than some of the local buildings that were in their thousands. It had been discovered, naturally, by Dr. Whipple.

Ito and I got out of the oxcart that had carried us on the last lap of our journey and dragged Auntie Mame's baggage up the rutted, overgrown driveway toward the old house. The whole place had a haunted, funereal air, but there was a battered Fiat truck in the driveway. From inside the house I could hear hammering and a throaty voice singing "The Internationale." Wearily we hoisted the luggage and ourselves to the rickety verandah and collapsed on the steps.

The first person I saw was Natalie, a political science student from New York University, who called herself Natasha.

"Hello," I said, "Is my Aunt Mame here?"

"Hello, Comrade," Natalie-Natasha said heartily, "when did you turn up? Mame's coming with the Convoy. They should be here any day now. Well, don't just sit there. Come on, pitch in, lend a hand. We've all got to work together if the Experiment is going to amount to anything. Here, carry that stuff up to the third floor. It's pretty well cleaned up by now and I think we'll put you two up there. I suppose you've had lunch."

We hadn't. Nor, for that matter, breakfast.

I dragged my kit up the tortuous golden oak staircase and dumped it dispiritedly into a little round room up in top of a tower. It was awfully stuffy. All afternoon Ito and I swept and scrubbed and mopped the house's incredible accumulation of filth. It was a big, gloomy old barracks and stifling. Natasha picked up a lot of lumpy old cots from somewhere, as well as some crates, folding chairs and sawhorse tables. There was also some quainty-dainty quasi-French furniture, presumably the chattels of the last owner, that had been set up in the Meeting Room. It looked as forlorn in the old mansion as I

Auntie Mame . . .

felt. I got a big splinter in my hand during that first day and Natasha snapped at me and said not to be so babyish and to stop complaining. My revenge, however, came a little while later when Natasha inadvertently punctured a wasp's nest in the upstairs drawing room.

It was nearly dark when she announced that we'd knock off work and eat. Natasha said she was on a diet so we'd just have a salad and something to drink. The salad was a gritty head of warm lettuce, unwashed and unadorned by dressing, salt or pepper. I drank some rusty-tasting water out of the kitchen tap.

I didn't sleep very well that night. The bed was hard and I could have sworn there were bugs in it. The room was suffocating. None of the windows would open. There were also a lot of scurrying noises inside the walls.

The next day we had some stale bread for breakfast and then dug in again. By nightfall Ito and I had got most of the windows open and three of the toilets to flush. Then we scrubbed all of the parquet on the first floor and when we were finished, Natasha said that the place was just the kind of monument that a decadent, blood-sucking Trotskyite swine would build for himself.

Dinner that evening was a silent affair. We ate beans and the rest of the bread. The house was quiet that night and so cool that I shivered under the scratchy old blanket on my cot. About two o'clock a terrible rainstorm started and I got out of bed to close the windows. I needn't have bothered. Once open, none of them would budge. The roof sprang leaks in six different places and Ito and I spent the rest of the night emptying pots and pans of dirty rain water down the bathroom drains, which all proved to be hopelessly clogged.

At eleven the next morning, a dilapidated old London bus chugged up the drive and stopped dead. A limp sign on its side read, "Mother Bloor Communal Farm."

"Well, Comrades, *here* we are!" I heard the glorious voice of Auntie Mame carol. "And *isn't* it divine!"

Ito and I rushed out to the lawn to greet her. "*Dushka!* Oh, darling, I bet you've been having the most *heavenly* time!" She kissed me vivaciously. Dr. Whipple got down from the bus and jovially waved a clenched fist at Ito and me. "Greetings, ah comrades," he wheezed. "And, ah, here are your, ah, brothers!"

One by one, our brothers descended limply from the old double-decker bus. There were about thirty in all. The group was mostly American and English with a Danish couple, three Canadians. (Dr. Whipple, in fact, called Montreal his home on the rare occasions when he was in it). There was a deserter from the Australian Army and three English-speaking Russians thrown in for good measure. The English contingent was made up of a bright-eyed young man from Oxford; two Liverpool dock workers; the black sheep (female) of a titled county family; and an anarchist who advocated lining up the English Royal Family and shooting them down, just as the Romanovs had been liquidated. He was considered rather extreme in his views.

The United States had offered up an economics instructor from the Rand School; several unemployed garment workers; a brace of public school teachers; an assistant professor who had been asked to leave Williams; two girls from Bryn Mawr who talked like Katharine Hepburn; a recent Bennington graduate, who might have been quite pretty if she only hadn't dressed like Raymond Duncan; a pair of shipwrecked merchant mariners; an intense young renegade priest from Holy Cross; a woman with a crew cut who taught handicrafts to Indians; a young interior decorator named Ralph who'd worked for Ruby Ross Wood "until he saw the light" as Auntie Mame put it; and an uneasy black couple named Johnson, who'd brought along two shy kids of around my age.

The Russians were named Boris and Soso (which is the

Auntie Mame ...

Georgian diminutive of Joseph). They'd both lived in the United States for quite a while and they seemed kind of sinister to me. Soso had brought along a girl friend. She was named Masha and had once danced in the corps de ballet at the Bolshoi theatre. Masha was pretty and demure, except that her legs looked like totem poles.

In her red boots, full skirt and embroidered peasant blouse, there was a certain Muscovite *chicté* about Auntie Mame. In fact, she looked like a show girl from one of the Nikita Balief revues of the Twenties. Compared to her Slavic splendor, the rest of the followers of the Mother Bloor Communal Farm seemed seedy and ill-assorted, carsickness being their only common bond.

Auntie Mame stretched her lovely, long arms ecstatically and gulped in the mountain air. "Just *smell* it, Comrades! Isn't it *intoxicating?* Well, first a good hot tub and then to work!"

Natalie-Natasha snorted contemptuously.

"But, Auntie Mame," I said, "the drains don't work."

Auntie Mame looked as if she'd been slapped. "Nonsense, darling!" She smiled encouragingly. "Well, with all of us on the Project, we'll have the pipes working again in no time, *won't we! We're* not going to be dependent on the village artisans, are we?" The men looked a little dubious, but no one said anything. "It's a simple thing to do," Auntie Mame said, with a little less self-assurance than usual. "You just pour a little Drano down the pipe."

Boris, who never bathed anyhow, said it wasn't important. "What we must first do is assign the rooms and then hold a general meeting," he said. Some anonymous mutineer in the crowd said, "when do we eat?" There was a rustle of general unrest. Gradually, however, Boris got everyone organized and satchels and suitcases, duffle bags and boxes began to cascade from the top of the second-hand bus. It had been agreed that each person could bring one piece of luggage and the rain from the night before had not treated the travelers' possessions gently. One pasteboard suitcase burst soggily open and Soso's balalaika was badly warped. Auntie Mame, true to her word, had come with just one piece: a large custommade Gilmore trunk, snug in a canvas slipcover, rakishly adorned with labels from smart hotels all over the world. It took three men to get it down. Natasha sneered unpleasantly and slouched into the house.

There was a lot of confusion about rooms and, even in so big a house, there didn't seem to be enough of them. The main floor was to be used for the Mess, Meeting Room, Library and Executive offices. The next two floors were for sleeping. Auntie Mame had her heart set on the upstairs drawing room, which had a stunning view of the hills, but Boris earmarked that for himself. The old nursery, her second choice, was taken for a six man dormitory on the grounds that it was so large. I could tell that she wasn't pleased to draw one of the servants' rooms across the hall from me, but she preferred it to sharing the college girls' dormitory.

Auntie Mame, who was always strong for atmosphere, had packed a lot more into her trunk than peasant smocks.

She'd brought an elaborate ikon; a hand-tinted lithograph of Trotsky, framed in passe partout; her Fabergé Easter egg, studded with semi-precious jewels; a big samover and a gay Ukranian shawl.

Ralph, the decorator, was only too happy to lend her a hand at arranging the bleak liver-colored room and by the time the votive lamp was lighted under the ikon, he was shrill with delight. "But it's too divine, Mame, dear! It's perfect, pure Casino Russe!"

She and Ralph were still ebulliating over her decor when Natasha's sullen face appeared at the door. Eyeing the triptych and the ikon, Natasha grumbled. "The opiate of the Peo-

Auntie Mame . . .

ple!" But when she saw the picture of Trotsky, she gasped and went to tell Boris.

Lunch was the first square meal I'd eaten since I left Moscow. The placid Mrs. Johnson, still wearing her hat, had unpacked the kitchen utensils and enough of the supplies to lay on a glorious spread. No one had asked her to, she just did. There was a big cold ham, stuffed eggs, hot biscuits, two kinds of pickles, jam, a wonderful salad and fruit for dessert. At that moment communal living looked pretty good. I was embarrassed to go back for a third helping, but when I finally summoned up the courage, Mrs. Johnson's pretty face split into a big, wide smile. She said she loved to see boys eat and she was going to try to fatten me up on this here com-mu-nal farm.

Dr. Whipple said there'd be a general meeting at four and we could do as we liked before then. Auntie Mame grabbed my arm and said, "*dushka*, do let me show you around."

She put on a big straw hat, which she'd had copied from a photograph of Ukranian wheat threshers in the *National Geographic*, and off we went. Auntie Mame was a vivacious and fascinating talker, and as wearing and irritating as she can be, I've always been spellbound in her company. She showed me all over the place: the formal garden, which had long lost all traces of ever having been laid out in any pattern, and where a marble Pan lay pathetically on his side, as though he'd just been shot; the old kitchen gardens; the stables; the orchard. Her constant babble of commentary almost made the old place come to life again. After we'd walked and talked for a long while, she looked at her fragile diamond watch. "Goody," she trilled, "it's just two o'clock. We'll still have time for a walk in the woods." We headed into the forest and walked for a long way.

"You *do* like it here, don't you, *dushka?*" she asked anxiously.

"Y-yes," I said, avoiding her eyes, "it's very nice, now that you're here."

"I'm so glad you think so, my little love," she sighed. "Oh, Patrick, it's going to be *wonderful!* Dr. Whipple and I and all of these people, too, have worked so hard planning and figuring. It's cost me an awful lot of money. But it was worth it, darling, worth it! The farm is going to be an ideal Socialist community, all of us out here living together, building together, producing together! Everyone happy, everyone equal! Work together, play together, share together! There are going to be no rich people, no poor people, everyone just alike; rich in each other! *Dushka*, do you know that you're living a little bit of history at this very moment! This tiny experiment of ours, this little handful of people, will soon show America what it's been missing. Do you follow me, *dushka?*"

I wasn't sure, but I said, "yes, Auntie Mame."

"Child, someday you'll be sitting here in this very spot with your own children and you'll be able to say, 'why, in 1937 I helped Auntie Mame and Dr. Whipple start the Cooperative Farm that showed the world the way!' Oh, Patrick, I've always wanted to come to Russia to see how they were doing it, and *here* we are!"

Her face took on a look that I always associate with the visions of saints or with cataleptic seizures. "And, *dushka*, don't you think our community is made up of just about the *most* wonderful people? Don't you think it's a grand bunch?" Again her eyes sought out mine.

"They seem okay," I lied.

"You know, we've got all sorts of people here, some from well-to-do homes, others who are very poor; some extremely well educated, others with almost no learning; some who toil with their hands, others with their minds. Oh, the true blending of the worker and the intellectual, that's what makes a movement *go!*"

Auntie Mame . . .

We wandered idly through the woods for a long time.

"Well, *dushka*, Dr. Whipple set the meeting for four. I guess we'd better start back to be on time. If there's anything that can throw a cog into this wonderful experiment, it's . . ." Her face went ashen. "My God! This watch has *stopped*. It still says two o'clock."

We raced back to the house, but we needn't have bothered. By the time we got back, the first General Meeting was over.

Dr. Whipple was most upset that Auntie Mame had missed the meeting. "Dear, ah, Comrade Mame," he said, fidgeting with his goatee, "it had, ah, been, ah, my clear, ah understanding that I, ah, that is, ah, that *you* and I would be in, ah, complete, ah, authority. But now it seems, ah, that Comrade Markov . . ."

"You mean Boris?" Auntie Mame asked.

"Exactly. Well, ah, it seems that, ah, Comrade Markov, ah, also feels that, ah, *he*, ah, is in charge and, ah, well, really, ah, Mame, it's, ah, most embarrassing and I do wish you'd, ah, just have a word with him."

"Oh, certainly, Euclid, darling," Auntie Mame said, very much the Little Miss Fix-it. "Now don't you worry your dear gray head about a thing. I'll put Boris straight in a jiffy."

In the end it was Boris Markov who put Auntie Mame straight. He was most displeased that Auntie Mame had missed the meeting. He said that, in Russia, people who went about mooning over a rotten and dead past were exiled and instead of meandering around the countryside with some capitalist brat, (it gave me quite a start when I realized that he was talking about me), Auntie Mame should have had her shoulder to the wheel, with the rest of the Steering Committee. He also said that she had been unanimously voted *off* the Steering Committee because it was feared that a stream of decadence still flowed strongly in her. Dr. Whipple had also been voted out and the Steering Committee now consisted of

Boris and Soso, with Natalie-Natasha as head of the Ladies Auxiliary.

Auntie Mame found it difficult to disguise her disappointment. After all, the farm had been started on her money and it had been largely her idea, inspired by Dr. Whipple, so she felt that she should have some voice in the way things were run. But she was a good sport about it and said that, as long as we were all going to be equal, it didn't really matter. Dr. Whipple, for all his degrees, lacked Auntie Mame's philosophical air.

The Group had got a lot of things down on paper during that first meeting. One of the school teachers was chalking the Community Rules, there were no laws, in neat Palmer Method handwriting on a big blackboard in the Meeting Room. Boris was Supreme Commander; Soso in charge of the men; Natalie-Natasha in charge of the women. Mrs. Johnson had been appointed Mess Sergeant and Cook. Ito was head of K.P. Masha, the unemployed Russian ballerina was in charge of Recreation and Calisthenics. Sid, the English anarchist, was appointed head of the Ways and Means Committee. Desmond McLush, the defrocked priest, would see to trading our farm produce with outside merchants for things like light bulbs and salt that we couldn't create ourselves. As a sop, Auntie Mame was put in sole charge of the Community Loom, which wouldn't start till fall. Some of the garment workers were rather bitter about *that*, too.

Religion would play no part in the community, but everyone had to take one day off a week and, since the next day was Sunday, they decided that that would be the day of rest. "The habit pattern is so strongly entrenched in us, anyway," Desmond McLush said, with a pitying sneer.

Mrs. Johnson, singlehanded, got a sumptuous dinner on the table that night, which was marred only by having the electric system go off, but after a maximum of confusion, candles appeared everywhere and Natasha said it looked just

Auntie Mame . . .

like Ma Bloor's old cell. After dinner a lot of gin appeared as if from nowhere. Auntie Mame was famous for her homemade gin in the Twenties and her hand hadn't lost its touch. The entire colony sat on the verandah, watching the fireflies while Soso played his balalaika. Masha danced, and Auntie Mame regaled everyone with an account of her trip through a tractor factory.

At eleven, when I went off to bed, I noticed that Ito and Mr. and Mrs. Johnson and their kids were still in the kitchen washing up the dinner dishes. It seemed to me that if we were all to work together, maybe I'd better lend a hand, so we all spent a pleasant half hour drying and putting away.

The house was awfully noisy the first night and it struck me that the group was made up of the thirty most restless sleepers in history. All night long there were doors opening and closing; footsteps in the corridors and a lot of whispering and giggling.

At seven the next morning a wonderful smell of panckes drifted up to the third floor and I hurried downstairs. In the kitchen Mr. and Mrs. Johnson were alone, cooking griddle cakes on the big wood stove. They let me help and we had a lot of fun flipping flapjacks. All morning long, members of the community sauntered down for breakfast and the Johnson kids and I were kept busy making griddle cakes and frying bacon, while Mr. and Mrs. Johnson started putting up a huge picnic lunch.

At noon Auntie Mame awoke and Ito took her breakfast up to her.

The picnic was a great success. Mrs. Johnson had baked four big cakes and all the bread for the sandwiches and everything was delicious. We all lolled around on the fragrant meadow while Boris and Soso and Natasha made speeches about "Shoulder to the Wheel," "What's Mine is Yours," "All for One and One for All," and "Share and Share Alike." About three o'clock Auntie Mame was urged to go in and make some more gin, which she said wouldn't be a bit good if they all drank it right away; but nobody seemed to mind. At dinner-time they were still rolling around in the grass and Mr. and Mrs. Johnson took their kids and me into the kitchen and cooked supper. The house that night was even noisier and someone got very sick in the third floor bathroom.

The next morning almost everyone was ill. Boris was confined to his bed and Ralph had mysteriously acquired a black eye. But by lunchtime everyone appeared, including Auntie Mame, still in her Russian-cut pajamas.

Boris tapped his water glass and said that, owing to unforeseen circumstances, the Project had got off to a late start but everybody shoulder a hoe and off to the fields! There was a terrible moment when one of the garment workers asked what they were supposed to plant and where and a solemn girl from Bryn Mawr said that she was perfectly willing to do her level best, but there weren't any farm implements of any sort.

Everyone jabbered at once and another General Meeting was called while Mrs. Johnson cleaned up the luncheon dishes. Despite all the highflown ideals that went into founding the Mother Bloor Communal Farm, it was soon made painfully evident that nobody in the group had ever worked on a farm before, although Dr. Whipple had read a great deal about it. Mr. Johnson, however, had had some agricultural experience back in America with cotton, peanuts and tobacco; but he wasn't at all sure that such things would grow in Russia. Dr. Whipple, when pressed, was unable to remember just what ever *had* been grown in Georgia, if anything.

There was a lot of wrangling and some rather unpleasant name-calling, but around dusk Mr. Johnson had made up a list of essential farm implements and guessed as to their prices in rubles. It was unanimously voted that Auntie Mame be driven into the village of Psplat to cable her bank.

The next day, while Dr. Whipple led a discussion group on "The Collective Farm Movement in the Volyn Area," Mr. Johnson took his kids and me in the truck to Psplat and placed a staggering order with the Kolkhozni Ploshad or Collective Farm Plaza. Delivery on everything but a few rakes and hoes and pitchforks would take six weeks. The bill came to a terrifying total and it looked as though Auntie Mame or *somebody* would have to cable the National City Bank again. Then we went to a seed store and laid in a huge supply of future carrots, lettuces, radishes, cabbages and potatoes.

When we got back, everyone had finished lunch and was sunbathing while Mrs. Johnson and Ito scrubbed the kitchen floor. At an informal get-together that evening it was decided that the Johnson kids and I would manage the truck garden. "Every hand, no matter how little, doing a job!" Auntie Mame said, while the others would busy themselves in intellectual pursuits until the heavy equipment arrived.

Clearing the vegetable garden was backbreaking work. The soil was full of big rocks, the sun was blistering, and within a week I turned as dark as Carver and Aida Ward Johnson. Mr. Johnson stayed with us and did the really heavy work. Once Sid, the anarchist, came out and watched for a while. He said that it wasn't fair for us to be doing all the work and we ought to go on strike.

Meanwhile the two able-bodied seamen and the girl from Bennington discovered a springfed swimming hole with a real sand bottom and the adults mostly amused themselves with nude bathing, fashionable in Russia at the time, while we planted the truck garden. Otherwise the whole farm stood paralyzed waiting for the equipment.

Mrs. Johnson and Ito worked in the kitchen from six every

morning until midnight. Mr. Johnson and we kids lent a hand whenever we thought about it, but otherwise they worked alone. Her meals were always superb, but finally she reached the bottom of the larder.

"Mistah Mahkov," she said to Boris, (it was a general rule that first names were to be used, but somehow Mrs. Johnson and her family could never bring themselves to that intimacy), "they's no more eggs, no more flour, no more condensed milk, no more coffee and no more cans of nothin'. All the things Mrs. Burnside ordered from New York and London has been et."

A general meeting was called and there was a lot of talking and arguing and doctrine. Auntie Mame finally got the floor and said, "but it was my *distinct understanding* that we were to raise our own food and be independent of the outside world." Dr. Whipple took the pipe out of his mouth and backed her up.

"In all, ah, history it has been, ah, definitely proven that any cooperative, ah, movement that begins to, ah, weaken, that begins to spend money with outsiders is, ah, doomed." He bit his pipe dramatically. There was a lot of rowing and discussion and finally it was put to a vote. The Independent Spirit was high in those early days and the Group decided that, since there was no money anyway, it would be a bad idea to go out and buy food.

"Very well," Mrs. Johnson said calmly, "I jes' wanted to know."

Dinner that night was toasted stale bread; stale crackers; stale bridge cookies in the shape of spades, hearts, diamonds and clubs; a few slivers of canned tongue and some canned fruit salad. There was no breakfast the next morning and no lunch. Auntie Mame slept later than usual the next day and when she came downstairs in her Manchurian robe, she was confronted by thirty hungry colonists, more quarrelsome

Auntie Mame . . .

than usual. There was no dinner that night, although Mr. Johnson took us kids in to Psplat on the truck and bought us borscht.

The following day, after no breakfast, the Group held an impromptu meeting without Auntie Mame and there was an overwhelming majority decision to wake her up and get her to cable the bank again. Auntie Mame has always been famous for a sweet, if erratic disposition, but being roused in the morning is one thing that she never permitted. I know that she was seething all the way into Psplat on the truck, but at least the Group had lunch that day.

Having weakened to the extent of allowing Auntie Mame to spend some more of her money on the Outside, the Ways and Means Committee, under the leadership of Sid, decided that it would be economical to let her buy some practical, productive things like live chickens and cows to tide the farm over until the machinery arrived and we all started producing. So Auntie Mame cabled the bank again and the faithful Mr. Johnson drove the truck all over Georgia buying hens. A lot of chickens that Mr. Johnson *didn't* buy also turned up after the merchant mariners and some of the Young Intellectual Faction from the Eastern colleges went out for an evening stroll. Mrs. Johnson said that it was just plain stealin' and it was a sin, but Boris told her that conscience was a bourgeois affectation that must be replaced by reason, pure reason, for the sake of the Movement.

Then Auntie Mame and Dr. Whipple returned from a sylvan walk, leading the ricketiest looking cow I've ever seen. She said she'd bought it from a sweet old peasant and it only cost the equivalent of four hundred dollars. Pandemonium broke loose. Natasha said how dared she spend the money that way and Soso mentioned the frivolous excesses of a depraved aristocracy. There was a terrible scene and everybody screamed things about Mechanistic Thinking and the Individual versus the Party and High-Handed Monarchistic Gestures. Finally a meeting, and a rather noisy one, was held. There was a lot of bickering. Mr. Johnson, as the Agrarian Authority, mumbled that, in his opinion, the cow was mighty sick and not worth *four* dollars. Dr. Whipple kept repeating something about the Means and the End and what was right for the Party was right for them all. Auntie Mame wailed things about milk and dear little calves and dairy produce. A fist fight broke out during which I floored Desmond McLush. Auntie Mame was led to her room in tears.

The following day the cow died. Auntie Mame wept tenderly over its rawboned old corpse and Natasha, her face a mask of bitter triumph, accused Auntie Mame of bourgeois sentimentality. There was another big meeting and Auntie Mame was publicly reprimanded.

The Group divided itself into two factions and another big argument ensued. About four o'clock everyone decided to cool off with a dip at the swimming hole and we young people were sent back to work in the garden with Mr. Johnson while Mrs. Johnson cooked dinner.

The adults all seemed sort of restive sitting around with nothing to do. Dr. Whipple organized a series of Round Table discussions on subjects like "Resolved: Bloodless Revolution Is In Itself a Contradiction of Terms" but they only led to more passionate rows. Ralph and Auntie Mame tried to get up a bridge tournament but Natasha said that cards were the decadent pastime of a rotten monarchist regime, and wouldn't allow the women to play. Auntie Mame cried again.

That night there was a terrible fracas on the second floor and we all jumped out of bed to see what was the matter. One of the school teachers was screaming awful things at Sid and I noticed that a lot of the Group seemed to be coming out of the wrong rooms. I was curious, but Auntie Mame said that the whole mess wasn't anything I should hear and to go back

Auntie Mame . . .

to bed. Ralph flew up the stairs in a batik dressing gown, his face glistening with cold cream. He told Auntie Mame that I was upset and he'd be more than happy to spend the night with me. But Auntie Mame said firmly that Ralph's staying with me was the last thing she needed *that* night. Eventually the house settled back to sleep.

The next morning Auntie Mame remarked casually that the house was filthy, in fact that it never *had* been decently cleaned and it was a slothful crime. Natasha sprang to this bait like a tigress with a T-bone steak. She bit Mame.

At that point, Dr. Whipple and Masha and one or two other members of the Conservative Element decided that idleness was what was causing all the trouble and that something could be done about it until the farm equipment came. The garment workers got some money from Auntie Mame and made Mr. Johnson drive them all the way to Psplat to buy needles and patterns and yard-goods. That afternoon a sewing bee was inaugurated for all the women and the gentlemen garment workers. They all gathered in the Meeting Hall and stitched and cut amiably. Even Mrs. Johnson took time off from her cooking to come in and sew. Auntie Mame, who never knew one end of a needle from another, gave up after ruining a whole length of cloth and entertained the group by reading *Das Kapital* aloud. It seemed very peaceful and idealistic until Natasha stuck her finger and jumped up screaming, "I can't stand anymore of that God damned, cultured society bitch-voice yammering in my ear." Auntie Mame had a *crise de nerfs* and stayed in her room for a couple of days until Natasha commanded her to come out for calisthenics. Auntie Mame looked awfully sad and sort of disillusioned to me. But she got back something of her old fight when she discovered that Natasha had distributed all of her imported from France Russian peasant costumes to the other women under the share-and-share-alike clause.

The whole thing came to a boil when Auntie Mame had been lax about sweeping the third floor corridor and had neglected to make her bed. Natasha gave her such a terrible bawling out that Auntie Mame flounced out of the house, dragging me with her. "Come, *dushka*, darling, I mean, you're the only one in this whole God damned dump who understands Auntie," she whimpered.

We went to the woods and Auntie Mame had a good old-fashioned cry. "Oh, Patrick, sometimes I ask myself if I've done the right thing. I'd hoped for so much and this has all been such a bitter disappointment."

I really felt sorry for her, in what I confess was a patronizing sort of way; but it occurred to me that if I was ever to get out of Georgia and back home to college, this was the time to strike.

"Well," I said, "why don't you just face up to it and admit you're not cut out to be a Communist? You can make a big confession of it and they can all have a hell of a time reading you out of the Party. Then . . ."

"What do you mean, *Communist?*" Auntie Mame said, bristling. "Here I go and spend all this time and money with a noble experiment in socialized living and *you* go besmirching it with one of the filthy labels applied to the workers by a bunch of money-grubbing Wall Street despots!"

"Doesn't the money for this rat race come from Wall Street?"

"Oh! What's the use in even trying to *talk* to you, Patrick? What with that ghastly boarding school that's crowded all compassion for your brother man out of you and fed you nothing but dreams of capitalism, class against class and Republican snobbery . . ."

I'll admit that she had something of a point as far as St. Boniface Academy was concerned. The school had had a social science department, but about all we were ever taught

Auntie Mame . . .

was that Calvin Coolidge was a perfect peach and Herbert Hoover a living doll. Republicans, the history master had said, were all gentlemen. Democrats were common and had no breeding. When I asked about Franklin D. Roosevelt, I was told that he was a traitor to his class and then given ten demerits. But I had never gone along with the precepts of St. Boniface Academy any more than I did with those of the Mother Bloor Communal Farm (English Speaking).

"All right then," I said, "call it an experiment in socialized living, call it a free love colony, call it the Morris Plan, call it anything you like. But at least be honest enough to call it quits. It was a beautiful dream; but it was also a lousy idea. It isn't working. You hate those people and they hate you. Now cut your losses and get out."

"What do you *mean* it was a lousy idea, you little devil. It was my idea, mine and Dr. Whipple's, to start an ideal communal farm where people of all sorts and colors could work together in the soil to build a rich . . ."

"What in the hell do *you* know about working in the soil? You've never been on a farm in your life. You couldn't even grow snake weed in a window box. And as for Dr. Whipple . . ."

"Dr. Whipple is one of the greatest thinkers of our time. He has degrees from . . ."

"Dr. Whipple," I said, "is a platitudinous old windbag, one of the most fatuous old farts ever to come my way. He may have degrees from here to the Kremlin, but he hasn't got sense enough to pour piss out of a boot with the instructions on the heel."

"How dare you, you arrogant young . . ."

"And you know it, too. You've had to blow his nose and button his fly for him ever since you found him. He's a blathering old weakling and even if this fiasco is his idea, his and yours, he's nothing here. You two starry-eyed idealists have simply been taken over by a couple of real Moscow-trained

Commies like Boris and Soso and a hard-boiled little tramp like Natasha. They're running the show and you're paying for it."

"Oh, they are, are they?"

"Yes, they are. And as for the rest of this grand gang of comrades, what have you got, a few rabble rousers and jail birds, some half-assed college kids, a gay decorator and a pack of malcontents who are having a dandy vacation on you. The only people here who are worth the powder to blow them to hell are the Johnson family and they're working like slaves, along with your poor, silly Ito, in your wonderful classless society."

"Shut up, damn you!" Auntie Mame shouted, her eyes blinded by tears. "Shut up! Shut up! Shut up! This is my experiment and these people are my friends."

"They're your jailers," I said flatly.

"Oh, indeed? We'll see about that, young man. I'm absolutely free to do anything I like here. This is my farm as much as it's anybody's. I can come and go as I . . ."

"I'll bet you ten rubles you can't. Go on. Try. Just ask Boris to lend you your own truck, or the bus, for an evening in Tiflis. Go on. I dare you."

"Very well, you smart little so and so," she said, rising. "Just watch."

Auntie Mame marched down to the swimming hole, where Boris lay stretched out in the sun with Soso and Soso's girl friend, Masha. Boris was no oil painting, even fully dressed, but the sight of him naked, his back and arms covered with running sores, was enough to put anyone off his feed. Auntie Mame took one look, recoiled and then marshalled her strength.

"C-comrade," she said gaily, "I wonder if I c-could borrow either the truck or the bus to run into Tiflis for the . . ."

"Certainly not," Boris said calmly, scratching his rear end.

Auntie Mame . . .

"B-but I only . . ."

"Vy not, Boris?" Masha said. "Tiflis. The Rustaveli Theatre. The . . ."

"Shut up," Boris said coldly. "No, Comrade, you may not leave. Now go back to the house."

Auntie Mame trembled as we trudged over the meadow, whether from rage or fear I did not know. But all hell broke loose when we got to the house.

As we entered the front hall, Ralph was waiting there, whitefaced and trembling.

"Oh, Mame, darling, I've been looking everywhere for you," he blubbered. "The most *awful* thing!"

"What?" we chorused.

"Oh, Mame, you poor angel. That Natasha . . ."

"What about Natasha?" Auntie Mame trembled worse and her lips were white.

"She's . . . she's . . . oh, I can hardly *say* it," Ralph sobbed.

"Tell me, Ralph. Tell me quickly. What's happened?"

"Natasha took Boris up to your room and said that all of your lovely old Russian decorations were decadent and totemistic and were demoralizing the Experiment and that they were the relics of a dead and corrupt civilization. And then she . . . Oh, I *can't!*"

Auntie Mame clutched his arm. "Yes, you can. Go on. Then what?"

"Oh, Mame, darling, I *tried* to stop her. I told her those things were priceless and that your room was the only one in the whole house that had any real *friv*, but she . . . oh . . ."

"She what?" Auntie Mame asked evenly.

"She threw all your lovely things down the cesspool! And then . . ." Auntie Mame raced up the three flights of stairs. Sure enough, her room had been stripped, first her elegant peasant outfits, then her Russian decorations. All that remained was a cot and her empty trunks. Adding insult to injury, Natasha had also scrawled, "Dirty Trotskyite!" across the wall with Auntie Mame's lipstick.

"That bloody bitch!" Auntie Mame said in a manner that implied very little feeling of brotherhood. She looked around the barren room, then her face crumpled and she threw herself onto the hard bed and sobbed convulsively.

That night she didn't come down to dinner. Mrs. Johnson cooked a magnificent meal that night, but she looked haggard and miserable as she served it and even when I told her how good everything was, she didn't smile.

Masha had finally got around to observing that it was Mrs. Johnson and Ito who did all the cooking, serving and washing up. "But dot's not de right teeng, ees eet, Tashka?" she said to Natasha during dinner. "Mebbe ve should oll peetch een and help, eh, Comrade?"

"Listen, Comrade," Natasha said airily, "there are some who were just *born* to be slaves and no amount of education, no amount of revolutions can get 'em out of that class. Like they say, you can take a servant out of the kitchen, but 'you can't take the kitchen out of a servant.' Leave her alone, she probably likes it."

It made me sore to hear Natasha talk that way about Mrs. Johnson, who was one of the great women of any color I've ever met. But after dinner, when I tiptoed out to the kitchen to help her with the dishes, she was sprawled over the table, weeping noisily, her children standing silent and miserable in a dim corner.

"I thought maybe you'd like me to help you with the dishes," I said.

She only glared dully at me.

"But Mrs. Johnson," I said helplessly, "we always do the dishes together. Besides," I added, "I thought maybe there'd be something to take up to Auntie Mame. She's been crying in her room ever since Natasha threw all of her decorations down the cesspool."

"Okay," said Mrs. Johnson, balefully. "I'll just fix up a little mess of something an' then we go up and see your Auntie togethah."

Silently we climbed up the back stairs. No sound came from Auntie Mame's room and when I opened the door, she was sitting glumly on her bare cot staring into space. Mrs. Johnson closed the door and said, "Mrs. Burnside, the boy and I thought you better eat a little somethin'."

Auntie Mame seemed to brighten a little at the sight of Mrs. Johnson's famed corn bread.

"Mrs. Burnside, come to the party, this commu-nal farm just ain't workin' out. It ain't like I thought it was goin' to be. It all sounded so happy and grand when we first thought of comin' here. But it ain't like Dr. Whipple said. All these folks sit around and live off your money an' my cookin'. Booker hated bein' on the re-lief, but it was better than this place. These people gonna suck you dry, then turn you out. *You* know that. These people ain't like you. You may be excentric, Ms. Burnside, but you're different. You're a lady." She paused. "*And so am I.*"

Auntie Mame sat silent for a long dreadful moment and then she said quietly, "you're right, Mrs. Johnson. I see that now. You're absolutely right."

"Ms. Burnside," Mrs. Johnson said wildly, "we gotta get outta this place before it's too late. It's desperate. I heard what happened when you tried to get out *just for an evening*. We're trapped and I'm scared."

Auntie Mame's tear-swollen face began to recapture a little of its old brightness. "I *think* I have a plan, Mrs. Johnson, a plan that will work." She looked at me. "Patrick," she said in a businesslike voice. "Mrs. Johnson and I want to have a little talk. Why don't you just run off to bed, and remember, not a word to *anyone* about this evening."

The next morning Mrs. Johnson was bustling around the kitchen, singing at the top of her lungs. Breakfast was especially delicious and Auntie Mame was up before ten o'clock. She was avidly cordial to everyone, especially Natasha. Auntie Mame swept the corridor as it had never been swept before, then she dusted all the public rooms, humming *The Russian Lullaby* with determined cheer, and then she went out to help Mrs. Johnson with lunch. The meal that day was a triumph.

During dessert, Auntie Mame rose from her place and made an announcement in clear, bell-like tones. "Comrades, I have a little surprise for you. Today is *my birthday!*" There were cheers. "Yes, there comes a time when a woman doesn't like to be reminded that she's a year older, but out here with all you grand people, I don't care *who* knows it." I could have sworn that Auntie Mame was born in November, but I was intrigued. "And so," she said, incorporating one or two of the Stanislawski Method gestures, "I'm going to give a big birthday party for myself! Tonight we'll have cocktails and dinner and music and dancing and all the gin we can hold and all be jolly comrades together!" She sat down, beaming, among loud huzzahs.

Auntie Mame spent all afternoon in the pantry, making gallon jugs of gin. I'd seen her do it dozens of times. Her gin was famous; but it seemed that this time she was putting a lot more of her soul into it. There were tubs of it. Added to the local wine and the vodka, I could see it would enhance the festivities. I felt kind of lonely and useless and wandered out to the driveway where the Johnson kids were watching their father tinker with the old London bus. Its motor made an exhilarating roar and late in the afternoon, Mr. Johnson siphoned all the gas out of the truck and put it into the bus.

Auntie Mame . . .

The kids asked a lot of questions and so did I, but Mr. Johnson just smiled mysteriously.

At five Auntie Mame took a deep, hot bath and told me to take one too. While the others were swimming, she'd managed to retrieve all of her jewelry, except a rose quartz bracelet which Natasha had fancied, and also a great deal of her expensive clothing. I noticed that she smelled strongly of *Nuit de Noel* again.

The kitchen was even more fragrant. Mrs. Johnson appeared to have slaughtered dozens of hens and they were roasting to a delicate gold in big, black ovens. With a rattle of bracelets, Auntie Mame stirred up four gallons of the very special dry martinis she used to make. "Now remember," she whispered to Mrs. Johnson, "take *plenty* of time serving the dinner. Let everyone have all the cocktails he can drink and *don't* let Mr. Johnson near them. We'll need clear heads tonight."

At the call for cocktails, the Group came running from all directions. Auntie Mame was particularly expansive that evening and almost forced the drinks on her guests. "Have another glass, Natasha, do . . . Can I tempt you, Comrade? . . . Oh, don't you love the lavendar hour! I could just sit here and drink martinis forever." Oddly enough, though, she wasn't drinking anything. "Oh, come, now, Sid, just half and you, too, Ralph." The cocktail hour lasted from five until well after nine and Auntie Mame found it necessary to mix a fifth gallon of martinis.

By the time dinner was announced, the English girl and Dr. Whipple had to be helped to the table, but that only added to the general jollity. Dinner was magnificent. It started out with fresh fruit marinated in vodka and passed on to the chickens basted in wine. In fact, something alcoholic seemed to be added to everything except the rolls and butter. Enormous rams' horns of Ateni wine, which Auntie Mame had produced from some mysterious source, flowed throughout the meal. The climax was a great flaming bowl of fruit which looked delicious, but as I was about to give myself a generous helping, Mrs. Johnson grabbed my wrist and said darkly, "don't you touch none of that stuff, honey."

There was a sodden quality about the Group after the brandied coffee was served, but Auntie Mame supervised the revelry like a games mistress. "Come along now, Comrades, no fair slowing down, Matushka's birthday comes but once a year! On to the Meeting Hall for dancing and more drinks! Matushka means dear little mother, Patrick."

It was quite a bachannale. Auntie Mame's homemade whiskey proved to be the final touch for many of the guests. Desmond McLush collapsed while he was singing *Tiptoe Through the Tulips* with one of the school teachers. Masha passed out in mid-arabesque and Soso threw up into his balalaika. But those who were still conscious cheerfully put their less fortunate comrades to bed and capered back to join the fun.

Even Mrs. Johnson left the dirty dishes on the table and came in to watch. Ralph sang *Button Up Your Overcoat*, but of all the Group, Auntie Mame seemed to be the gayest and when I finally went upstairs to bed, she was being tossed up in a blanket by Sid and the two merchant mariners.

Because of the party downstairs it took me a long time to get to sleep. Whenever I drowsed, I'd be awakened by a shriek of hilarity and, every now and then, there'd be a dull thud from someplace in the house. At last I dozed off, but it didn't seem that I'd been asleep for a minute when I heard a cautious scratching noise outside my door. Auntie Mame whispered, "Patrick. Patrick, darling, wake up. Put on your clothes and don't make a sound."

"B-but, why?"

Auntie Mame . . .

"Don't bother Auntie with a lot of questions, now. We're going to take a little ride. Hurry and be still."

I scrambled into my shorts and shirt and wedged my feet into some shoes. Auntie Mame took my hand. "Now, come with me and don't make any noise," she whispered. "We don't want to disturb anyone, do we?" Good old Auntie Mame, I thought, always so considerate of others.

In the hall Mrs. Johnson's dark figure loomed solidly. She was wearing her hat and coat and carried a satchel. Her kids, Carver and Aida, were with her too.

"All ready, Mrs. Johnson?" Auntie Mame whispered. "Have you got your passports?"

"Yes."

"Very well, follow me. Watch out for the stairs and don't make a sound." We tiptoed behind her single file. The loose step just above the landing creaked eerily and a soft groan came from Boris's room. I jumped.

"Don't worry about *him* tonight," Auntie Mame said authoritatively. "Just follow me."

We reached the downstairs hall. A candle guttered in the Meeting Room and I could see a lot of bodies stretched out in abandoned positions. "Shhh," Auntie Mame warned. "Now, quickly, out to the bus." She hurried forward. Suddenly there was an awful noise that sounded like Ooof and Auntie Mame sprawled flat.

In the dim light, I could see Natasha lying supine with Auntie Mame next to her on the floor.

"Wha' th' hell, Comrade," Natasha said thickly, dazedly shaking her head.

"Oh, Natasha, Comrade," Auntie Mame breathed weakly, "it's *you!*" She laughed nervously. "Here, Comrade," Auntie Mame said, reaching for a half-filled glass. "I just wanted to give you another drink. Mustn't let the party die, you know," she added wildly.

... and Mother Russia

"Arishe ye prishners of shtarvation," Natasha croaked. She emptied the glass in one gulp and fell back again to the floor with a soft thump.

"Thank God," Auntie Mame breathed. Then that old look came over her face. "And this seems like a good time to recapture one of my barbaric symbols of a dead civilization." Deftly she removed the rose quartz bracelet from Natasha's limp wrist and popped it onto her own arm. "Now, follow me and quickly."

The Johnson kids and I hopped nimbly over Natasha's body, but I heard another sickening noise as Mrs. Johnson carefully planted her two hundred pounds on Natasha's stomach, waited there for an instant, stepped off and then followed me out of the house.

The motor of the second-hand bus was purring and we sat on the peeling old seats. "Is everyone ready?" Auntie Mame asked. Then she said, "oh, my God, my sables!"

"You don't worry," Ito said. It was the first time I'd known of his presence. "Baggage all packed and upstairs. Also very nice picnic lunch to eat. We have chicken on way to Turkey!" This sent him into perfect gales of giggling.

"Shhhh," Auntie Mame said. "Not a sound."

Just then the door flew open. "Mame! Mame Comrade! What are you, ah, doing? Where are you . . . Mame! Wait!"

"Oh, my God," she said. "It's Euclid Whipple!"

"To hell with him," I said.

"To hell with him is right," Auntie Mame said. "Step on it, Mr. Johnson."

"Mame! Stop!" Dr. Whipple shouted. "Our plan. Our farm. Our dream! Comrades! Boris! Stop her!"

A shot rang out.

"Oh, my God," Auntie Mame moaned. "Now they'll catch us and who knows *what* will . . ."

"Not gonna get *us* Mrs. Burnside," Mr. Johnson chuckled

Auntie Mame . . .

as he swung the bus into the road. "They's no gas in the truck. I syphoned it all out. If they wants any gas they'll have to walk ten miles into Psplat to git it. An' then they'll have to *pay* for it."

We drove all night along the treacherous mountain roads of Georgia, heading straight for the Turkish border. By the time we'd gone ten miles, Auntie Mame stopped trembling. By the time we'd driven ten more, she became quite chatty. "Oh, Comrades," she trilled, "don't you feel just like one of those old Romanov aristocrats fleeing the revolution? I keep thinking of those thrilling stories Count Orlofsky used to tell about escaping from St. Petersburg in a boxcar!"

A bus that's too old for Picadilly isn't necessarily the best vehicle for the Caucasus Mountains. The roads got worse and worse, steeper and steeper. Once we all had to get out and walk while Mr. Johnson coaxed the lumbering old double-decker up a steep incline.

Morning came and we were still far from Turkey. The gas was running low. We all stopped talking and simply concentrated on the road ahead, praying that we might make it. In the early afternoon, by dint of not only getting out and walking, but also by pushing, we got the bus to the summit of a huge hill. Directly below us lay the frontier. A wooden gate stretched across the road and some unfriendly looking members of the Red Army patrolled the customs house.

"Thank God we've made it!" Auntie Mame cried. "We're all American citizens and we have our passports. They can't stop us now. Climb aboard, everyone! Next stop Turkey."

How right she was. We all got back into the bus and Mr. Johnson released the brake. "Think of all those divine Bosphorus cigarettes we can get," Auntie Mame said as the bus began rolling down the hill. "Better than Melachrinos, really. Um, Mr. Johnson, must we go *quite* so fast? I mean we're almost..."

"Can't help it. The brakes gave out!"

"Oh, for Gawd's sake," Mrs. Johnson wailed.

Faster and faster we rolled downward upon the frontier. The Russian soldiers went through a smart little military routine right out in the road ahead of us. One of them gestured and shouted something that was probably, "halt or I'll shoot."

"Can't you stop this damned thing, Mr. Johnson? I mean it's only a formality. They simply . . . Eeeeee!"

With a crash and a splintering of rotten wood, we burst through the barricade. A shot was fired and there was a tinkle of glass from one of the rear windows. We were all of us on the floor, except for Mr. Johnson who was flattened over the steering wheel. A second shot rang out and still we kept on going.

I looked up just in time to see the gates of the Turkish frontier ahead of us. Some Turkish soldiers were running around hysterically. There was another crash and we were in Turkey. More shots rang out and finally the bus stopped.

With all the airs and graces of the Empress of Russia, Auntie Mame minced to the rear of the old London bus and descended. And she really managed to look more as though she were going to a court ball than to Fortnum and Mason's. "How do you do," she said to the furious looking Turkish officer who awaited her. "*I* am Mrs. Beauregard Jackson Pickett Burnside. *This* is my passport and *these* are my comrades. That is to say, my *friends*."

Auntie Mame . . .

Auntie Mame and the Middle Eastern Powder Keg

"I JUST DON'T UNDERSTAND IT," PEGEEN SAID. "How could a woman like your aunt go to a place so near Nazi Germany without getting into a lot of trouble?"

"Very simply," I said. "Finesse. Diplomacy. Tact. Call it what you like. Why, you should have seen her in the Middle East."

"In the Middle East?"

"Yes."

"What, pray, was that 'jewel of many facets' studying in the Middle East?"

"Racial relations."

"Well, having just heard more about that than I care to—that dismal Mrs. Rawlings down the street just called asking us to sign some new zoning petition—I'd rather not hear about your aunt and some Middle Eastern powder keg."

"Good," I said.

. . .

AUNTIE MAME HAD AN immediate affinity for the Middle East. Having lived like a pig in the Tyrol, she was delighted to see a section where you could live like potentates on only a modest outlay of cash.

She made her majestic way down the Danube, lingering in Budapest for refurbishing, cased the Dalmatian Coast, and then set sail for Egypt, touching upon the Isles of Greece.

The Rolls was waiting at Alexandria, and by the time the car was speeding down the long straight desert road joining Alexandria and Cairo, Auntie Mame was quite her old self again.

"Ah, my little love, Egypt," she said, patting my hand. "So modern and so chic, yet still seething with that indefinable mystery that has been here since the Ptolemys." She lighted a Fuad Premier Doré. They were terribly strong cigarettes and smelled of camel dung, but they were not without a certain glamour if your lungs were up to them. "And so cosmopolitan, darling! Where else could one see English, French, Greeks, Italians, Turks, Egyptians all gathered at the same dinner party?"

"Washington, D.C.," I suggested. "Mind if I put the window down a bit?"

"Of course, dear Alex—that's Alexandria, my little love—is fun in a strictly European sort of way, but now down to the big, beating heart of Egypt—Cairo! *Le Caire!* And don't worry, Patrick, I know all the ropes. Your Uncle Beau and I were here on our, honeymoon. And you and I are going to go native. There's going to be nothing touristy about *us*. We'll stay at

Shepheard's; I have guest cards to the Ghezira Sporting Club and the Turf Club. The food at Les Ambassadeurs is superb, *and*, thank God, they've got a branch of Elizabeth Arden. We're simply going to see how real Egyptians live. Not so fast, Ito," she called through the speaking tube.

AUNTIE MAME WENT NATIVE TO THE EXTENT OF wearing a lot of kohl around her eyes. She bought quite a lot of exotic jewelry—the most exotic of which was a wide gold bracelet which she shoved up above her elbow, where it stayed until it was sawed off at Tiffany's some years later. But except for trips to Elizabeth Arden and to restaurants and clubs that were just like any restaurants and clubs in any other big city, she stayed mostly on the veranda at Shepheard's drinking Suffering Bastards (a rude contraction of a lethal hangover mixture originally called Suffering Bar Steward), fanning herself, complaining of the heat, and moaning about what a fool she'd been at whichever party the night before.

But one day, after an extremely rough evening at an Anglo-American gathering out at Garden City, Auntie Mame decided that she'd had quite enough partying and that the time had come to go native. "We're off to the pyramids, my little love," she said, gulping down her third Suffering Bastard and signaling to the steward for a refill. "If we are to come to know this land we must know it from its very roots. All those years, all those dynasties ... *Merci*," she said to the barman, slipping her drink off the tray.

"Fine," I said. "I'll talk to the dragoman about getting us some sort of guide. What time do you ..."

"Guide?" Auntie Mame said, as though I'd used a word in Swahili. "We're *not* going tourist class. I've been here before and I'm perfectly capable of showing you the monuments of ancient Egypt without some hissing little wog snatching at my elbow. Just tell Ito to bring the car around while I go upstairs to change. *Addition, s'il vous plaît!*"

"Okay, lady," the barman said.

Half an hour later Auntie Mame emerged from Shepheard's in what I suppose was a smart desert costume. It consisted of a white linen bush jacket, a divided skirt, boots, and a pith helmet draped with about thirty yards of tangerine chiffon veiling. The effect was somewhere between Osa Johnson and Agnes Ayres, and it was devastating. "Come along, Patrick," she said, giving her boot a brisk thwack with her riding crop. She got into the Rolls, with a fluttering of veils, and we were off.

Business was far from brisk out at the pyramids, and we were besieged by guides and dragomen, one of whom offered me not only a tour of the tombs, but a Turkish carpet, a diamond ring, erotic photographs, hashish, his beautiful sister, and, finally, himself.

"*Yallah!*" Auntie Mame said, with a fine display of Arabic. "Shoo! All of you. We're going by ourselves." Then she picked out two camels—a white one named Fatima for herself and for me a kind of moth-eaten brindle old beast with horrible breath. It was named Badia.

"Hey," I said, struggling up to the summit of Badia, "have you ever ridden one of these things before?"

"Dozens of times, my little love," Auntie Mame said, perching elegantly on Fatima's saddled hump. "It may make you a little seasick at first, but it's quite easy and they're as gentle as lambs. Ito," she called, "follow us with the picnic things." She gave Fatima a smart crack with her crop and we started rocking and rolling down a sandy desert pathway with Ito giggling in the car behind us.

"Isn't this divine, darling!" Auntie Mame called over her shoulder. "I feel just like Cleopatra. No wonder they call these marvelous animals the ships of the desert."

Auntie Mame . . .

"No wonder," I said, feeling kind of squeamish from the oceanic undulations of my camel. "I wish I'd brought the Mother Sills seasick remedy."

"Nonsense, my little love. 'When in Rome . . .' "

"I wish we *were* in Rome," I said.

"Oh, don't be such a stick, Patrick. Isn't the desert beautiful?"

"Not particularly," I said, wondering if I were going to throw up.

"We'll ride on until we find some sort of lovely oasis and then stop for lunch. Is Ito still with us?"

I turned around and gave Ito a sick grin. He was giggling so hard he could barely steer the car. He waved to me, and then *it* happened: Ito's elbow struck the horn. It went off with a terrible blast. Both camels stopped dead and reared into the air. I was thrown flat onto my back, and Ito put on the brakes just short of flattening me. I picked myself up from the sand in time to see Auntie Mame and Fatima bounding over a hill. "Stop!" I heard Auntie Mame cry. Then she yelled, " *'Hom'd el Allah!*" which, I believe, means Son of Allah and is the Moslem equivalent of "Jesus!" It could only have offended Fatima, for she went still faster and disappeared entirely from sight.

"After her!" I shouted to Ito, jumping into the seat beside him. Terrified, Ito stepped on the gas. The big black car bounded off the road and into the sand. We went about fifty feet and then the Rolls got stuck. Inspired by Fatima's independent spirit, my camel bolted in the opposite direction.

And there we were, alone on the desert and up to the running boards in sand. By the time I scrambled up to the roof of the car to see if there was any sight of Auntie Mame and Fatima, the flapping orange veils were only a vivid, moving speck on the horizon.

For the next forty-eight hours a hundred dragomen, the camel patrol, and a small airplane searched for Auntie Mame and Fatima. She was found two days later and three-quarters of the way to Memphis, suffering from exposure. Fatima was never seen again.

Auntie Mame languished in the hospital for a week, hovering—as she described it—between life and death. Her physician, however, said that she was perfectly fine and had picked up a beautiful coat of tan. He said that all she really needed was a few weeks of rest in a pleasant climate, and even went so far as to lend her his own villa in the mountains of Lebanon.

Except that her nose was still peeling, Auntie Mame was the perfect picture of the fabulous invalid as the Rolls followed the Mediterranean coast up through Palestine toward Syria. In Tel Aviv, Auntie Mame was able to force down a couple of blintzes and a cold beer. Then she moaned softly—and belched once—all the way to Lebanon. At Tyre she peered wanly out of the window and sighed, " 'Lo, all our pomp of yesterday is one with Nineveh and Tyre' " (Kipling, I believe), and fell back onto the cushions. Tyre wasn't much to look at. Sidon was somewhat more prepossessing, and Auntie Mame allowed as how she'd just try a cigarette. In Beirut she asked for her make-up case and a few simple jewels.

By the time Ito had got lost three times in Beirut and finally headed for the foothills, Auntie Mame was feeling quite peppy again. "Ah, this mountain air," she said, taking a healthy swig from her brandy flask. "The cedars of Lebanon! What's the name of this place the doctor's sending me to, darling?"

"It's a town called Shufti. It's up in the mountains near Sofar."

"Ah, the simple life! Living in a little adobe house and sharing our bread and cheese with the Lebanese goatherds. Would you like a burnoose, darling?"

"I think it's a bit more elaborate than that, Auntie Mame.

The doctor said it was a resort town with a club and a big hotel."

Shufti was the next town up the mountain, and the villa the doctor had lent Auntie Mame was a simple little copy of the Petit Trianon just across the road from the club. It had a pretty walled garden behind it, adjoining the gardens of two neighboring villas. The one to the right was a great, sprawling, Moorish mass, while the one to the left was smaller, more in keeping with the Lebanese architecture, and just slightly going to seed. A gothic script sign in front of the Moorish house read "Villa Mont d'Or" while a brass plate on the other house proclaimed it as belonging to "Mr. and Mrs. Humphrey R. Cantwell." As I helped Auntie Mame out of the car, I noticed that eyes were peering at us through the blinds of both villas.

THE NEXT DAY, WITH AUNTIE MAME SETTLED DELI-cately onto a chaise longue and able, at last, to take a little nourishment in the way of a weak gin and lime, I set out to explore the village of Shufti. Its one main street was a fairly squalid Arab affair with a couple of cafés, a laundry or two, a variety store, and a Roxy theater where Dick Powell and Ruby Keeler were appearing in *Forty-second Street* along with Install-ment Nine of a Tarzan serial. But, ah, the *banlieues* of Shufti! A pretty mountain town within easy reach of both Beirut and Damascus, Shufti had attracted quite a crew of conspicuous spenders—Lebanese, Syrian, Egyptian, Turkish—plus some official French families and a smattering of rich Greeks, Americans, and English, whose summer houses all looked more or less like the Brighton Pavilion. Shufti, with its air of great opulence, its Arabian Nights villas, its unlimited supply of almost free servants, was the kind of place that looked—at first glance—as though you'd be happy to settle down there and vegetate forever. But after a couple of closer glimpses and a few afternoons at the European Union Club, you began to realize that you'd be bored to the point of suicide after a week of its petty, silly, provincial society.

The European Union Club was a perfect example of the lengths to which French and English colonials will go to create a little corner of home in a distant land and end up with a great big nothing. The club had once been the summer house of a rich Damascus merchant—an airy, lacy, cool pavilion set down in the most glorious section of the Lebanese mountains. But it hadn't taken the Europeans long to louse it up so that it had all the worst features of Liverpool and Toulouse. Parts of it looked like the Chivas Regal ads. Chintz held sway, embellished by antimacassars and horrid, florid French lamps. The smoking room was a vision in painted-on pine paneling and dusty heads of wild animals which had been destroyed by the more athletic members. France had been victorious in the dining room. The tables had been embellished with toothpick containers, trenchers of soiled salt, napkin rings, and grimy, set bouquets of bead flowers in a land where the most exotic blooms grew like weeds. The walls were upholstered in mustard cut velvet, and the grittiest curtains ever hung—brocade, over silk, over dirty lace, over net—resolutely shut out all light and any suggestion that a beautiful garden flourished just beyond. The food was English. Britannia ruled the billiard room with its electric log burning cheerlessly in a fake fireplace, its Tottenham Court Road Tudor reproductions, and its standardized sporting prints (although the French had cannily sabotaged *that* maneuver by hanging them too high). And in the bar even the good old U.S.A. had made its power felt by the installation of a hideous jukebox that both bubbled and changed colors and a cigarette machine.

Auntie Mame . . .

The entrance hall was pretty much unchanged, save for a green baize bulletin board bristling with announcements. Most of the notices to the membership in general were written in both English and French, but there were lots of private little appeals which showed, pretty well, how the club was divided. There were such things as:

> Will anyone finding a garnet brooch please return same to Lady Belcher. Great sentimental value.

> *Thé-dansant, le Samedi 19, 17 heures. Achmed Maloof et son Orchestre 'Swing' du le Kit-Kat Club (Beirut). 50 piastres.*

> Certain thoughtless junior members have been using the Card Room as a gathering place where, heedless of those *trying* to play bridge, they have talked in loud tones of voice, laughed, giggled, etc. This infringement shall cease immediately.
>
> Mrs. Humphrey Cantwell.

Some irreverent Francophile had penciled "*Merde*" at the bottom of this.

> Tambola Every Wednesday—20 hours.

> *Tambola Tous les Mercredis—20 heures.*

> Any Members interested in forming a group to present the plays of Noël Coward will please contact Mme. Mont d'Or—mornings *after* ten.
>
> Sari Mont d'Or.

The penmanship was so high-styled that I could barely read it.

> Any wishing to accompany Mr. Cantwell and
> myself to the ruins of Palmyra on Friday fortnight
> may do so in exchange for paying for the gasoline.
>
> Mrs. Humphrey Cantwell.

Another irreverent member had written "You look like the ruins of Herculaneum."

> Junior Tennis Tournament—Mixed Doubles.
> Seymour Mont d'Or, Captain Men's Team.
> Lucia Cantwell, Captain Ladies' Team.
> Sign below.

> Certain members and their guests have appeared
> at the swimming pool indecently garbed. It is to be
> remembered that the European Union Club is a
> *family* organization.
>
> Mrs. Humphrey Cantwell.

Whatever had been sketched under Mrs. Cantwell's signature this time had been thoroughly scratched out.

> Members interested in learning the *newest* Latin-
> American dances, please contact Mme. Mont
> d'Or—mornings *after* ten.
>
> Sari Mont d'Or.

Again, Mme. Mont d'Or's chichi, sway-backed handwriting—the I's dotted with huge circles, the T's crossed with sweeping diagonals. Her paper was pale green, each sheet stamped with a huge white coat of arms.

I was able to see from the bulletin board that Mesdames Cantwell and Mont d'Or just about ran the club.

———

Auntie Mame . . .

A SERVANT IN A RED FEZ USHERED ME TO THE MEN'S dressing room, where another servant helped me to undress and get into my bathing shorts. I could have done it myself, but the club seemed to have more servants than members. While I was wondering if my suit was ample enough to pass Mrs. Cantwell's inspection, a young man padded out of the showers singing "I Get a Kick out of You" in a melodious baritone. *Two* servants began toweling him dry. Then he noticed me and stretched out his hand. "Hello," he said, in a pure American accent. "My name's Seymour, but I'm usually called Sammy."

"How do you do?" I said. "My name is . . ."

"I already know. We're next-door neighbors. Don't worry. Whenever anybody new comes to Shufti the whole town knows about it."

He was dark and well built and only a few years older than I. About twenty, I guessed.

Chatting amiably about nothing in particular, we strolled out through the riotous garden to the big, circular mosaic pool. Except for two or three dozen servants in white nightgowns and red fezes, we were the only people there. Fifty empty cabanas flapped idly in the languid mountain breeze. The pool was spring fed, cold and clear. Sammy—or Seymour—dived in first and cut the surface of the water with long masterful strokes. But he got out even quicker when we were joined by a pretty blonde girl in a white Lastex bathing suit.

"This is Lucia Cantwell," he said, almost possessively, and his eyes caressed her tenderly during the introduction. Well, I didn't blame him. She was quite a dish. She was also an American and about eighteen.

"I'm awfully glad to meet you," Lucia said sweetly. "We live next door to you. Mother's been waiting hourly for you and your aunt to arrive. I expect she'll descend on you at any moment now. And of course she'll expect you both at her Tuesdays."

I was saying some fatuous social thing like How Nice, when I noticed that Lucia had placed her hand absently on Sammy's big chest. It was a funny innocent sort of gesture and one that held, for me at least, a world of meaning. He gave her a look that implied that he'd much rather be underwater with her than making idle chitchat with me. And then Lucia Cantwell came to, more or less, and said, "Last one in's a club president!"

The three of us disported ourselves in the water like dolphins for I don't know how long. From time to time I noticed that the population around the pool was increasing—not that anybody ever bothered to get wet; they just came and sat in front of their cabanas, occasionally clapping their hands for one of the club servants to bring lemonade or Shandy Punches. Sitting was almost a career in Shufti.

But just as Sammy was climbing the diving tower to demonstrate his jackknife, the dreariest of them all came marching down to the pool and called, "Lucia! Lee-ew-sha! Mother wants you, dear."

"Oh, oh!" Lucia said, coloring slightly. "Now we're in for it. I wish you'd come with me. Please."

From up on the diving board, Sammy was shouting, "Now here goes the famous . . ." But the words died on his lips as he saw Lucia marching toward the cabana marked Cantwell.

"Mother," Lucia said, pushing me forward into the clutches of the old dragon, "this is our new neighbor, Patrick Dennis."

"Howjudu?" Mrs. Cantwell said in her Madame Chairman voice. She had the smile of a shark. "I sent our cards around to your aunt this morning." Again the mechanical display of fangs. "She is one of the Georgia Burnsides, is she not? Very old stock."

Auntie Mame . . .

Mrs. Cantwell—her first name was Lucy, although one never thought of her as having anything so intimate as a first name—was a tall, rawboned, high-rumped American matron of uncertain age, proudly dowdy in a flowered summer dress that practically screamed Lane Bryant, a slightly battered Panama hat, and white nurse's oxfords.

"Dew sit down," she said. Again the man-eating smile. "Lucia, dear, dew run up to the lounge and fetch Mother's scarf." I felt that the scarf was going to be batik. "That's such a nice swimming suit," Mrs. Cantwell said to me. "Modest. Not like some of the costumes we see on Certain People," she added, looking pointedly at Sammy's somewhat briefer trunks. "I hope that you'll set some sort of Good Example with, um, Certain People who have not had, um, Our Advantages."

I didn't know quite what she was getting at, but I resolved to cut at least two inches off every bathing suit I owned. I was even contemplating a rhinestone in my naval when Mrs. Cantwell fixed me with a steely gaze and said, "Since you're new here at the club, I think it's only fair to warn you that there are, um, Certain People well worth avoiding. I mean I couldn't help noticing that you were mixing with, well, one of our more Undesirable Members. You look like a very intelligent, well-bred young man, and, well, 'A word to the wise . . .' "

I hadn't the faintest idea what the old biddy was talking about since the only people I'd met were her daughter and the boy named Sammy-Seymour.

"Of course my Lucia is Very Democratic. Our Position here, you know. But it isn't wise to get in with the Wrong Crowd. And when I saw you being such Good Friends with . . ." Again the oblique glance across the pool at Sammy.

"I'm sorry, but I don't even know his name," I said.

"I thought you didn't or you never would have allowed an

Intimacy such as . . ." Then she lowered her voice. "It's Seymour Mont d'Or."

"Oh yes," I said absently.

"You do speak French?"

"Enough."

"Then why don't you simply translate, young man?"

"Mont d'or; mountain of gold," I said, quite mystified.

"*Or?*" she said with a dramatic pause. "Goldberg." She simpered hideously.

My mouth dropped open.

"I knew you'd be horrified," she said with a vicious little V-shaped smirk. I was horrified, but for entirely different reasons. "Now we won't say anything more about it, shall we? Here comes Lucia with my scarf." It was batik.

Mrs. Cantwell settled down to getting things established. In her circuitous way, she found out where Auntie Mame lived, what her maiden name had been, where she came from, where I had gone to school, where I was going to college, the names of boys I knew in America and who *their* people had been. Looking back, I doubt that Mrs. Cantwell was either very clever or very subtle in her probing, but I had never before met anyone who operated that way. Midway through the interrogation, I realized what the woman was up to and I had a wild urge to do just what Auntie Mame would have done—to tell a pack of extravagant lies that would have upstaged Mrs. Cantwell forever: "Auntie Mame's maiden name was Bourbon and I'm the morganatic son of Franz Joseph and we live in the Taj Mahal and I'm only allowed to play with princes of the blood and my aunt's eunuch." Or else to put her to flight by saying that Auntie Mame ran a whorehouse in Paducah, that my father had been Al Capone's finger man, and that my grandfather before him was actually a receiver of stolen goods while pretending to keep a delicatessen in Jersey City. Alas, I was too honest and too late. I was regrettably established as both genteel and gentile.

Secure in the knowledge that Auntie Mame and I were All Right, Mrs. Cantwell then took over with an endless monologue which gave me an exhaustive glimpse of her *curriculum vitae*, her genealogy, her connections in America, and her friends all over the world. "I was a Lathrop of Lowell . . . my father, the bishop . . . when Mr. Cantwell was at Harvard . . . so difficult to be out here in the East and not Bring Lucia Out Properly . . . my cousins the Morris Redfields . . . my brother, Sturgis, who is known for his great love of animals . . . the Colonial Dames . . . the Mayflower Descendants . . . Mr. Cantwell's deep absorption in archaeology . . . one must be so careful about whom one meets out here . . . my debut dress from Worth . . . but Mr. Cantwell really *prefers* running his boys' school—not for the money, of course, it's more a hobby . . . my grandmother's lovely, lovely opals." Lucia looked embarrassed and occasionally glanced over to where Sammy Mont d'Or was splashing dispiritedly with a couple of frankly plain French girls. I was embarrassed for Lucia and furious with myself for being trapped by this old dragon.

It also struck me that Mrs. Cantwell was fiendishly possessive. She spoke of My Tuesdays, My View, My Mountain, My People, My Little Native Seamstress—so it *wasn't* Lane Bryant, after all—My Charity, My Drugstore, My Clever Little French Doctor. It seemed that quite commonplace things were elevated to the extraordinary by virtue of Mrs. Cantwell's ownership, patronage, or proximity. As she rambled on and on, punctuating each dismal sally with a series of smug, mechanistic smiles, simpers, smirks, and *moues*, I caught Lucia looking more and more longingly at young Seymour Mont d'Or. I wondered, absently, if they were sleeping together, then I decided that Mrs. Cantwell would never let the poor girl out of her sight long enough for more than a quick handshake.

"Of course Mr. Cantwell takes only a very few boys, and boys from the very best families out here." Mrs. Cantwell had launched into a description of her husband's dreary day school down in Beirut, which—to hear her tell it—put Eton and Harrow in a class with Father Flanagan's Boys' Town. "He takes some sons of French officials, but *no* Catholics and certainly no . . ."

There was a silent fanfaronade, every head at the pool turned, and there, bigger than life, was a woman I took to be the Queen of Sheba. She was thin and stately, standing almost seven feet tall in thick cork sandals and a towering turban of scarlet silk. She was wearing a silver damask bathing suit and she was hung with rubies which, distressingly enough, were all real. "Yoo hoo!" she called, waving at the pool in general, "*Ça va, chérie! Bon jour, mon Capitain!* Good afternoon, Lady Belcher! Seymour, *chéri*, bring *maman* a cushion, darling. There's a pet!"

"Who . . ." I began.

"*That*," Mrs. Cantwell said with a knowing glance, "is Mrs., um, Mont d'Or."

I watched Mrs. Mont d'Or seat herself on a cushion, clap her hands, order "*un petit café noir*" and grandly open a back issue of *Vogue*—Paris edition—while her diamonds and rubies glittered ominously in the sunshine.

"The Levantine invasion," Mrs. Cantwell said mincingly.

"Please, Mother . . ." Lucia began.

"Come, Lucia," Mrs. Cantwell said, rising haughtily, "I think we'll take this young man home for tea."

"I—I can't. Thank you very much," I said, desperate to get away from this dreadful old bore. "My aunt isn't well. I promised her that I'd be home. I'm really late now. Excuse me."

Auntie Mame . . .

WHEN I GOT HOME, AUNTIE MAME WAS JUST GETTING up from a nap. I saw a lot of visiting cards and two big, pale-green crested envelopes waiting on the tray in the hall. The cards read, "Mrs. Humphrey Cantwell," "Miss Lucia Cantwell," "Mr. Humphrey Cantwell," and, for little old me, I guess, another "Mr. Humphrey Cantwell."

"Here, Auntie Mame," I said, handing them to her. "You got some cards."

"Cards? My God, it's a royal flush. It's like Buffalo in the nineties. I'm surprised she didn't turn down corners or something. Who is this Cantwell woman, anyhow?"

I started to tell her, but she was opening a big green envelope that I knew was from Mrs. Mont d'Or. "Oh, dear," she said, reading aloud. "*Monsieur et Madame. H. Jules Mont d'Or vous prie d'assister à dîner ce soir à huit heures. Le smoking.*"

"*Le smoking?*" I said. "What are we going to do, sit around and puff on reefers?"

"No, my little love," Auntie Mame laughed, "it's just one of those French-English affections. It means wear a dinner jacket. But, oh dear, are we really going to have to gabble French platitudes all night. I'm not sure that I'm up to it, yet."

"I shouldn't think so. They're Americans. I met her son today. He's very nice."

"Well, I suppose we might as well go. I don't think a few cocktails and a square meal would tire me too much. Ito," she called, "I want you to run next door with a note. Let's see, 'Madame Burnside'—how the hell do you say 'accepts with pleasure'?"

I WAS ALL DRESSED AND WAITING SHARPLY AT EIGHT when Auntie Mame appeared in a cotton dinner dress and no jewelry except for her wedding ring and the bracelet that was wedged above her elbow. "Well, let's be off, my little love."

"Do you think you're quite—well, quite *elaborate* enough, Auntie Mame? I mean, didn't you want to put on any ice?"

"Nonsense, Patrick," Auntie Mame snapped. "You know nothing of *haute couture*. In a simple little mountain resort like this I don't want to look gauche. I'm sure these Mount Kiscos, or whatever they're called, are a nice, modest family who just want to share a little supper. . . ."

"Okay, okay, okay," I said. "Let's get going."

I'm not certain just what effect Mrs. Mont d'Or had striven for, but the inside of her Moresque house looked exactly like the lobby of Loew's Alhambra. We were admitted by two enormous Berber servants, whom I halfway expected to strip down to breechclouts and bang on a gong by way of announcing our arrival. Auntie Mame's eyes opened wide at the hideous grandeur of the reception hall, but they nearly popped out of her head when Mrs. Mont d'Or heaved into sight, covered in cloth of gold and diamonds. Automatically, Auntie Mame flashed her big uncut emerald ring, only to remember, too late, that it was at home in her jewel case.

With a maximum of *enchanté*-ing and *la-la*-ing and *après-vous*-ing we were ushered into the grand *salon*, which looked like some sultan's seraglio, except for an enormous Capehart in a Chippendale cabinet. There, among the orchids and the servants, were Sammy, H. Jules Mont d'Or, and one Mlle. de Chimay, a pretty but dim French girl who was, as Mrs. Mont d'Or confided to Auntie Mame, a likely prospect for a daughter-in-law—"*bien elévée*" and with a "*dot*."

I must say that H. Jules seemed an unlikely consort for Mme. de Mont d'Or. He was a sweet, sad, round little man with large moist eyes and a bald pink head. He seldom spoke, and when he did he never seemed sure that what he was saying might or might not displease his wife. He was wearing a

Auntie Mame . . .

cloth of gold mess jacket, to match his wife's dress, I suppose. Seymour-Sammy was in a baby-blue dinner jacket that set off his tan nicely, but seemed to give him a severe case of embarrassment. One felt that Mme. Mont d'Or had more to say about what her men wore than they did themselves.

There was champagne (French) and caviar (Russian) and then quite a long hike to the dining room, which was about the size of Madison Square Garden and fairly writhing with mosaic, twisted columns, and filigree work. A native servant stood behind every chair. The conversation at dinner was conducted in English, as Mlle. de Chimay spoke it fluently—fortunately for everyone concerned, especially Mrs. Mont d'Or, who talked endlessly about having her clothes flown direct from Paris, about her jewels, about the chef she had stolen from La Rue, about having her portrait painted by Marie Laurencin, about the white Citroën ("*pour le sport*") she was having built, about the redecoration of her winter house in Damascus—in short, about herself. In a flashier way I found her almost as tiresome as Mrs. Cantwell, but at last she took the ladies off to what she called "the *I'Imperatrice Salon*" and I was left, exhausted, with Seymour and H. Jules.

An impressive parade of servants brought in liqueurs and a bottle of Dr. Brown's Celery Tonic for H. Jules. For the first time that evening, H. Jules Mont d'Or spoke an entire sentence, and then another. "You boys forgive me if I don't drink liquor. I get this sent to me from New York."

"That's all right, Papa," Seymour said, "enjoy it."

"Cheers," I said, hoisting my brandy balloon in H. Jules's direction.

"New York," H. Jules said, fastening me with a dark, liquid gaze. "Tell me, what is New York like?"

"New York, sir? Well, that's quite a large order. Its population is . . ."

"No, no, young fellah. That I know. I was born in New York.

Almost I was born on Ellis Island. But ten years already I been away." With a sad, sweet smile, H. Jules looked deep into his celery tonic. "Yes, those were happy days—a little flat on Mosholu Parkway. Of course when the business did better Sadie wanted Central Park West. And even that was nice—lovely view, close to the subway, just around the corner from Columbia Grammar School for the boy . . . Yes, a wonderful country," Mr. Mont d'Or went on dreamily. "You know Pollack's Restaurant on Delancey Street? Every time I have a glass of celery tonic I think of the hot pastrami at Pollack's. Sometimes I dream of a big plate hot pastrami. And the Luxor Baths—every Friday night I'd take a Russian bath. Five buckets I could take! Yes, New York's a wonderful place. Where else could you arrive with nothing—of course Sadie comes from educated people, two brothers she's got, a doctor and a lawyer—and end up a rich man?"

"Gee, Mr. Mont d'Or," I said, "just how did you happen to end up in the, um, Arab League?"

"Silk," H. Jules said. "Back home I was in fancy dress goods. Then Sadie's brother—the lawyer—found this silk mill in Damascus, the finest quality silks, very cheap labor, no union. So, here we are. Sadie likes it. We go every year to Paris, to Milan, It'ly, all the places Sadie likes. We got no home. Now I do a little wool, essences, gold threads, fancy trimmings, a little bit oil. I can't complain, but when I think of New York and a big plate hot pastrami . . ."

"Zhuuuuul!" Mrs. Mont d'Or's strident voice called. "*J'attend!*"

"WELL, I NEVER!" AUNTIE MAME SAID AFTER WE GOT back home. "I didn't dream that anyone like Sari Mont d'Or existed."

"It just goes to show what a book of Berlitz tickets will do."

Auntie Mame . . .

"Oh, Patrick, I feel so sorry for that poor, sweet little husband. He made me think of my osteopath. And the son's a darling. But of all the shallow, pretentious, power-driven females I've ever seen . . ."

"Wait till tomorrow," I said.

"What happens tomorrow, darling?"

"Mrs. Cantwell's Tuesday."

CHEZ CANTWELL WAS, IF ANYTHING, WORSE THAN Villa Mont d'Or. While Mrs. Mont d'Or reveled in Oriental ostentation, Mrs. Cantwell had steadfastly ignored the Eastern architecture of her house and had tried to turn it into Lowell, Massachusetts. The twain did not meet. Horsehair love seats and American Chippendale chairs lurked among the tiles and arches, ruffled Priscilla curtains hung at the keyhole windows, and the walls were liberally salted with samplers and clipper ships and portraits of grim ancestors who looked as though they had terrible trouble with their bowels. Placed on a piecrust table, ever so casually but where no one could possibly miss it, was a copy of the Boston *Social Register*—many years out of date—which sprung open, as though by some complex mechanism, to the page where the Cantwells were listed. With a certain amount of amusement, I watched Auntie Mame calmly turn the book face down, only to have it instantly righted by Mrs. Cantwell.

Humiliated by having been dressed too simply at Mrs. Mont d'Or's the night before, Auntie Mame went to some pains to Look Right at Mrs. Cantwell's. She turned up in a black linen sheath, a huge black hat, long gloves, and all her pearls. Again she was Wrong. When she entered Mrs. Cantwell's frumpish circle it was as though Mata Hari had dropped in for tea with the Eastern Star. I could see that Mrs. Cantwell, in her pongee two-piece with "grandmother's lovely, lovely opals," rather disapproved, and the opals certainly suffered by comparison.

Mrs. Cantwell's set—and there was no question that she was the absolute *Führer* of it—was made up of lackluster Americans and English of middle age, middle income, and middle class. There were an addled old English vicar, an ancient archaeologist, a couple of American engineers with pregnant wives, a widow from the Isle of Wight, a reedy young Philadelphian who taught English at the American University in Beirut, a toothy spinster who was doing her damndest to lead the remaining Moslem population to Calvinism, a stuffy young New Yorker with a hot-potato accent and a name that was something like Chauncey Lawrence Whitney Brooks or Lawrence Chauncey Brooks Whitney or Whitney Brooks Chauncey Lawrence—well, it was one of those exhaustive collections of family names that nobody can ever remember in proper sequence, not that many would want to. He was something like a third-assistant-sub-undersecretary at the embassy in Damascus and gave Mrs. Cantwell her sole excuse for saying often that she traveled in "diplomatic circles." However, she practically thrust him at poor Lucia.

Well, people both undistinguished and undistinguishable kept coming and going all afternoon. Their only common bond seemed to be the English language and that they were insecure enough to endure Mrs. Cantwell's bullying for the sake of society and a cup of Lipton's. And what a despotic hostess! Mediocre as the assemblage was, Mrs. Cantwell endowed each guest with a spurious fascination, which embarrassed everyone. "I know you'll want to meet Mrs. Mayberry," she would bellow in stentorian tones, shoving a helpless stranger into an alien group, "she does such lovely dried arrangements. A real green thumb!" "Miss Trout comes from Shaker Heights and has a lovely soprano voice. Perhaps you

Auntie Mame . . .

can coax her to sing for us." "Mr. Hewlett's mother was a Hoare." With each unwelcome introduction, the brief biography, the thumbnail sketch, grew grander, for everything that Mrs. Cantwell possessed—and her guests were merely her chattels—had to be exceptional, if only by association.

And I had noticed before that, once removed from home soil to a place where a large house, a retinue of servants, and three square meals a day could be had for less than a hundred dollars a month, many of my countrymen gave themselves certain airs and graces they would never have dared to attempt back in Glendale or Forest Hills or Oak Park. Forgetting all too soon the tiny apartments and suburban bungalows whence they sprang, the expatriate civil servants and foreign representatives tended to become languid, lordly, and loquacious, patronizing of the native population, snappish at the vagaries of their cooks and nurses and gardeners—they who had never before had a charwoman to wait on them. Mrs. Cantwell spoke lengthily about her circle of friends being "terribly cosmopolitan." They weren't. They were hopelessly parochial, scared silly that someone might discover their true backgrounds, and they were living testimony to the fact that you can be just as big a hick in the Middle East as in the Middle West. None of the Mont d'Ors had been invited.

Knowing enough about Auntie Mame to be intrigued and not enough to be worried, Mrs. Cantwell obviously felt that she had a lioness on her hands. What she didn't realize was that she *also* had a tigress.

"Dear Mrs. Burnside," she gushed, flashing the shark smile, "dew let me introduce you to some of My People. You know My Tuesdays are famous both in Lebanon *and* Syria."

"*Famous*, my dear?" Auntie Mame said, with a smile that was pure barracuda. "They're notorious—even as far away as Transjordan."

"W-why, yes, I-I suppose they are," Mrs. Cantwell said. "Humphrey, do come and meet nice Mrs. Burnside. Lee-ew-sha! Lucia, dear! Mother wants you."

Mr. Humphrey Cantwell—or the Mr. Chipps of the Middle East—came forward with the booming false heartiness of a headmaster or a camp director. Mr. Cantwell's phony "Give-me-a-boy-and-I'll-give-you-a-man" approach reminded me of the masters at St. Boniface Academy. He was the kind of man who ran an obscure private school not through any love of youth or learning, but because he wasn't fitted for anything better than diluting his own inadequate education. Terms like "Good Stock," "Real Gentleman," and "True Aristocrat" were the cornerstones of his conversation. And I could almost see him in assembly hall, substituting his dusty social connections, his petty snobberies, his insignificant family tree as blatant counterfeits for quality, intelligence, and leadership, as he harangued a student body too far removed from better seats of learning to do more than suffer in silence. Humphrey Cantwell was a pompous old fraud. But compared to his wife he was Prince Charming. I couldn't help wondering just when, how, and why, a girl as lovely as Lucia had been born to them.

"NOW YOU MUST RUN OFF WITH MY YOUNG PEOPLE," Mrs. Cantwell said, as though she were directing traffic at the mouth of the Holland Tunnel. "But don't make Chauncey jealous. He's one of Lucia's most attentive beaux. (His mother was a Lawrence.) These young diplomats, you know."

Auntie Mame rolled her eyes dramatically and put down her teacup. She looked as though she'd commit arson for a drink.

Lucia seemed almost relieved that I was horning in on her tête-à-tête with Brooks Whitney Lawrence Chauncey, or whatever his name was. "Ackcherlly," he was saying in a New York voice that made me think he was having digestive difficulties, "I'm the only white man in the embassy. The rest of them are just a pack of New Dealahs. Oh, hel-laow," he said, looking at me as though I'd just crawled out of the plumbing, "I heah that you've beaten me out of taking Lucia to the club dance tonight."

"Wh-what?" I said blankly.

"Oh yes!" Lucia said with an imbecilic brightness and casting a desperate look at me. "Patrick asked me *ages* ago! *Didn't* you, Patrick?"

"I thought you told meh he only arrived yestahday," the G.O.P.'s gift to diplomacy said.

"I sent the invitation ahead via racing camel," I said.

"Well, I mean re-ally!" He moved petulantly off to inflict his favors on some other sweet young thing.

"Look, Lucia," I said, "it isn't that I wouldn't be glad to take you to the dance, but don't spring these things on me. I didn't even know there *was* a dance."

"You don't have to take me, if you'll just pretend you're taking me. I mean . . . Oh, please come out into the garden and I'll *try* to explain."

We went out into the garden which, despite Mrs. Cantwell's efforts to turn it into the pride of the Bay State Garden Club, doggedly retained its riotous Asiatic blooms.

"Now, what is all this?" I asked, once the door had been closed on the party beyond.

"Well, it's simply that I've been in love with Sammy Mont d'Or every summer—winters, too, except that we never see each other then—since I was twelve and I just don't want to go out with any boy except Sammy."

"Then why doesn't Sammy take you to the dance? I got the impression that he was pretty fond of you, too."

"Oh, he *is*, Patrick. He writes me beautiful poems and love letters. But his dreadful, chic mother won't let him ask me because we're not rich enough. And even if we were as rich and vulgar as she is, my mother wouldn't let me go because the Mont d'Ors are really Jews and Mother's a terrible snob."

"I—I guess both ladies are pretty grim," I said guardedly. People can say libelous things about their own families or homes or cities or countries, but they generally turn on you like vipers if you, as an outsider, have anything unflattering to add to their scathing appraisals.

"You don't have to be polite," Lucia said. "Mother's worse than grim. Sammy Mont d'Or—he's planning to change his name right back to Goldberg next week when he's twenty-one—is one of the sweetest, kindest, handsomest, smartest boys in the world, but Mother'd die if she knew I love him."

"Would that be so terrible?" I asked.

Not even hearing me, Lucia raged on. "Mother won't be happy until she gets me married off to some fathead like Chauncey who has a family tree she can bore people with at her stupid tea parties. Some boy just like Daddy—only richer. And I'd kill myself before I married anybody like . . ."

"Okay, okay," I said, growing almost frightened at her passion. "I said I'd be happy to take you to the dance. What else can I do?"

"You're sweet, Patrick. If you'd put on your evening clothes and call for me about nine and then . . ." She blushed becomingly. "And then let me meet Sammy in your garden, the way we always did when your Aunt's house was vacant . . ."

"Maybe you'd like to come right in and use one of the guest rooms," I offered.

"Really! Sammy's too fine for anything like that. I almost wish he weren't."

"It's one of the fastest ways I know for a girl to get married—even beneath her clawss, if you know what I mean."

"Leeee-ew-sha!" Mrs. Cantwell whinnied from the door. "Mother wants yew!"

Auntie Mame . . .

"Well," I said brightly, "see you tonight, Lucia! We'll really cut a rug. Heh-heh-heh!"

"Oh, the dahnce? How nice!" Mrs. Cantwell smirked.

"WELL, I'LL BE DOUBLE DAMNED," AUNTIE MAME said when we had finally torn ourselves loose from Mrs. Cantwell's clutches and got back to our own house next door. "What more do you suppose this place has in store for us? From the Kosher Côte d'Azur last night to the Lowell Ladies' Long-fellow League this afternoon!" she said trudging up the stairway. "Have you *ever* seen such a bevy of bovines in your life? After looking so, well, *undressed* for the Maharani of Miami, I thought the least I could do would be to have a little pizazz today, but then when I saw that gang of Ground Gripper girls I simply . . . Say, by the way, I didn't see the Mont d'Ors among the revelers at La Cantwell's."

"Not likely that you would," I said. "They're the local Montagues and Capulets." Then, reminded of these lovers of Verona, I slipped off to tell Seymour Mont d'Or of the tryst I had arranged for him in Auntie Mame's garden that night.

I WAS GETTING INTO MY DINNER JACKET WHEN Auntie Mame poked her head in at the door and said, "Where do you think *you're* going, my little love? Or is it the custom to dine at home in black tie in this provincial backwater?"

"I—I promised to take Lucia Cantwell to the club dance," I said with complete honesty.

"Oh. That's nice. She's a sweet thing, in spite of her old beast of a mother. Well, have fun. *I* plan on a tray in my room. Then I shall dip into the new books from the club library. So up to date! I don't know whether to begin with *The Green Hat* or *Three Weeks*. Try to be home at a reasonable hour, darling."

. . . and the Middle Eastern Powder Keg 259

THE HOUR OF MY RETURN COULDN'T HAVE BEEN more reasonable. Twenty minutes later, pumps in hand, I was tiptoeing up the stairs, having deposited Lucia with her lover in the leafy gazebo behind Auntie Mame's house. I was just congratulating myself on how suavely I'd handled the whole thing when the lights went on and there stood Auntie Mame in her peignoir, a pearl-handled revolver pointed in the general direction of my crotch. "Hands up or I'll . . . Patrick!"

"Put that thing down," I said. "You could hurt someone."

"What are you doing home so soon?"

"Oh," I said, "Lucia got sick and couldn't go. Confined to her bed with a temperature of . . ."

"Patrick," Auntie Mame said calmly, "you're lying in your teeth, for I was brushing *mine* when I saw you and Lucia leave the Cantwells' house. She was wearing white organdy with a gathered fichu—very pretty. I don't know where the girl gets her taste. *Now* tell me the truth."

I had little choice. So I told her.

"Ah, Patrick," she said, when I was finished, "my fond and foolish boy. How often have I told you *never ever* to meddle in other people's lives. Where do you suppose *I* would be today if I hadn't made it my business not to make my business of other people's business, if you follow me."

"I think you'd be married to Basil Fitz-Hugh and several other things that you're not. For God's sake, they're nice kids. Just go back to your reading and let them neck in your garden. They're not hurting anybody."

"That was both rude and insulting, Patrick. They are both under age and, as a woman with a difficult problem in child-rearing myself, I feel it my duty . . ."

"Oh, come off it, Mrs. Siddons," I said angrily.

"I feel it my duty to telephone their mothers and tell

them. . . . On the *other* hand, that would necessitate talking to *both* Mrs. Cantwell and Mrs. Mont d'Or and I'm not quite up to that. However, I *cannot* countenance their doing whatever it is they're doing in my garden. You will please to fetch them forthwith, Patrick."

"No," I said.

"Very well. You give me no other choice. I shall do it myself." With that she was skittering down the stairs. "Go to your room!"

"Talking about meddling!" I yelled after her.

THE MOONLIGHT WAS SO BRIGHT THAT I COULD plainly see Auntie Mame drifting across the lawn toward the gazebo. I also realized that she had seen me just as plainly a few minutes earlier. Then I saw the surprised lovers being shepherded back into the house. It seemed to me that a woman as broad-minded as Auntie Mame, who was always pushing people to the very verge of unvirtue, was acting mighty peculiarly. I waited for a few minutes after the sinners were driven from the garden. Nothing happened. An hour passed; then another. Then I went to bed. It was after two when I awoke to find Auntie Mame shaking me. "What is it now, Mrs. Grundy?"

"Get up, Patrick! Get up. Put your evening clothes on again and take Lucia home from the dance. I didn't raise you to be the sort of cad who takes a girl out and doesn't bring her back. If you're going to Live a Lie, you've got to go through with it. 'O what a tangled web we weave/When first we practise to deceive.' That's Shakespeare and it's true!"

"That's Scott and it stinks. And so do you, you old busy-body."

"Enough, Patrick. Dress immediately and then return Lucia to her loved ones."

I'D EXPECTED LUCIA TO BE DISTRAUGHT, TEARY, suicidal, and a lot of other things that might be hard to take. Instead, she was absolutely radiant—and just a little drunk— as I steered her homeward. "Oh, Patrick," she said, looking at me with starry eyes, "your aunt is the most amazing woman I ever met. Absolutely remarkable."

"She certainly is," I said, glumly, pushing open the Cantwell door.

"Have a good time, Lee-ew-sha?" I heard the old battle-ax call. "Why don't you bring that nice young man in for some orange squash?"

"Good night," I said, and hotfooted it back home.

WHEN I GOT UPSTAIRS, ALL THE LIGHTS WERE ON and Auntie Mame was waiting in the hall. "Ah, Patrick," she said, "just in time for a cozy little chat."

"I'm just in time to go back to bed. It's almost daybreak."

"Come, my little love," she said, clutching my sleeve and dragging me into her room. "You know there was such an odd play on Broadway years ago. It was *Abie's Irish Rose*. Dreadful, of course, but it ran for thousands of performances."

"Well, I didn't see a one of them, thank God. Now good night."

"Sit down, damn you! *You* started this thing and now *I'm* going to finish it."

"If you'd only finish talking and . . . *Finish what?*"

"Why, Sammy and Lucia, darling. Of course. I mean they're such sweet, levelheaded, attractive youngsters—although with those ghastly mothers I don't know how they can be. And, oh Patrick, they're *so* in love. So in love and so young and so helpless with no one older and wiser to guide them to their ultimate goal—marriage."

Auntie Mame . . .

"*Marriage?* My God, Auntie Mame, what do you think you're . . ."

"Well, *you* started it all, my little love, aiding and abetting those romantic young . . ."

"I didn't start *anything*. I took Lucia to your mosquito-ridden old summerhouse so she could see her boy friend. Now *you're* trying to tuck them into bed. Talk about not meddling and minding your own business . . ."

"There are times, Patrick, when one's heart dictates and one must obey."

"Your heart isn't dictating a damned thing. You're bored silly in this place. At least you *were* until you found a couple of lives to tamper with tonight. And so now you're going to set the whole town on its ear by . . ."

Although she tried gamely, Auntie Mame was unable to suppress a maddening little smile. "Perhaps Shufti is *not* the most stimulating of communities. But it may become so. Besides, *I* think that Sammy and Lucia deserve to be . . ."

"*I* think *you* deserve to be drowned in sheep-dip. I won't lift a finger to . . ."

"Very well, my little love, then I shall have to plan without you. You may go now."

"Good *night!*" I roared and slammed out of her room.

I OVERSLEPT THE NEXT MORNING AND AWOKE JUST in time to see what I thought, at first sleepy glance, was Auntie Mame trudging across the garden toward the Cantwell house. Of course I realized that it couldn't be Auntie Mame because this apparition was wearing a shapeless sack of a dress that seemed to be made of an old chintz bedspread. She carried a Roman-striped shawl over one arm, a basket of woebegone flowers over the other, and her feet were slapping along in what looked like my old saddle shoes. Then in a terrible flash

. . . and the Middle Eastern Powder Keg   263

of recognition, I dashed to the closet. My saddle shoes were gone. So, too, was the spread from my bed.

In a rage, I bathed and shaved and threw on some clothes. "I won't be home for lunch," I yelled at Ito. "I'll eat at the club. Anything to be out of this madhouse." Ito giggled helplessly.

I had a perfectly foul meal in the club dining room and then went down to the dressing room to get into my bathing things. A swim should at least cool me off. The first person I saw was Seymour Mont d'Or, struggling feverishly with his shirt buttons.

"Just going in for a dip?" I asked, almost too embarrassed to look at him.

"Just coming *out*! Boy, let me tell you, that aunt of yours! There's nobody else like her."

"And that's all to the good. But listen to me, Sammy; *don't* listen to her. Don't . . ." By that time, only half buttoned up, he was gone.

I put on my briefest pair of trunks, hoisting them well up the thighs and rolling the top down, so that if Auntie Mame was trying to play the Watch and Ward Society for Mrs. Cantwell, I'd at least be a disgrace to her.

The sun was blinding when I got out to the pool. I made a visor of my hand and squinted at the Cantwell cabana. It was vacant. Then I heard an unmistakable voice trilling, "*Hélas! Mais Sari, ma chère*, if you think the Schiaparelli bathing suits are brief you should try the ones designed by Pamplemouse," Auntie Mame shrilled.

"Pamplemouse, Mame, *chérie*?" Mrs. Mont d'Or asked, fascinated.

"*Mais oui, bébé*, he has *un atelier divin* on the *rue Blondell*. Of course he won't design for just anyone, *naturellement*, but my dear friend the Duchess du Pont-Eveque—*née* Miss Patty du Clam—introduced me there. He calls this little *numéro* Banana Bandanna."

Auntie Mame . . .

I looked and gasped. Auntie Mame had taken a long yellow muffler of mine and divided it, like Gaul, in three parts. One was wrapped about her loins—just; the second served as the most inadequate of brassières; the third—and by far the largest—section served as a turban, even more towering than Mrs. Mont d'Or's. In addition she was hung with gold, with amber, with topazes and canary diamonds. Mrs. Mont d'Or, in violet and aquamarines, looked conservative beside Auntie Mame. Conservative, but eager.

"Do go on, Mame *chérie*," Mrs. Mont d'Or said. "One feels so, um, *passé*, so *fin de siècle* way out here and not *au courant* with . . ."

"Yoo hoo, Patrick, *mon petit trésor, j'attend*," Auntie Mame screamed.

"Well, you can damned well *attend* until *enfer* freezes over if you think I'm going to be seen with you in that indecent . . ."

She drowned me out. "*Zut! Regardez*, Sari, *le pauvre petit* in that union suit he's wearing. *Droll, hein?* How I wish I could get him into something *chic et moderne*—a kind of, uh, how-you-say *cache de sexe.*"

Enraged, I stretched my bathing trunks to cover as much of me as possible. "I have a message for you, Auntie Mame," I called sweetly.

"From whom, *mon petit trésor*?"

"It's very urgent *and* confidential," I said. That brought her on the run, although I feared for her hastily improvised bathing suit.

"How do I look?" she asked.

"Like midnight at Minsky's. What the hell do you think you're got up as, anyhow? If Mrs. Cantwell ever saw you in that rig she'd have you run in, and I wouldn't blame her. It's the most disgusting . . ."

"Oh, don't worry about that old spoilsport. I've sent her to Beirut in the Rolls to buy binoculars and our bird logs. And since you weren't here to fetch and carry for me, I *had* to send Sammy Mont d'Or on the most important errand. That errand is Lucia and they should be in each other's arms at this very moment. Meanwhile, I'm having a perfectly marvelous time wowing Maman Mont d'Or with all the latest fashion tidbits. Of course I just make them up, but she believes every word. Do you think I might go in for designing beach wear?" she asked as she posed elegantly at the rim of the pool.

"Not if you want to keep on this side of the law," I said.

"Well, you're holding up my entire campaign. What's this important message?"

"It's this," I said, noticing that Mrs. Mont d'Or was engrossed with her lipstick, trying to duplicate the Ubangi mouth Auntie Mame had effected. "Go soak your head!" I gave Auntie Mame a slight shove and was rewarded by a resounding splash. Then I stomped off toward the dressing room.

"Patrick!" Auntie Mame cried. "Patrick! For God's sake throw me a towel!" I turned around to look and found the three parts of Auntie Mame's bathing costume floating, independent of Auntie Mame and one another, toward the shallow end of the pool.

THE NEXT MORNING AUNTIE MAME WAS UP WITH the birds—literally. I heard a lot of yoo-hooing and hallooing about sunrise and saw Auntie Mame loping toward Mrs. Cantwell in an outfit that only I could describe—because every stitch of it belonged to me—burdened with binoculars, sandwiches, and a guide to our feathered friends. The mainstay of her costume was an old turtle-neck sweater of mine, which reached almost mid-thigh. Beneath it was a dowdy pleated skirt made of the dust ruffle from my bed. She was wear-

Auntie Mame . . .

ing my best English knee-length hose, my brogues—with tongues—and my pork-pie hat, pulled down to the level of my sunglasses.

"How radiant yew look, dear Mrs. Burnside—*may* I call you Mame?" Mrs. Cantwell bawled. "Now, off to gaze at our birdies."

"What fun, Lucy!" Auntie Mame called.

As they stalked up the hillside, I saw Lucia dash out of her house and Sammy dash out of his to embrace in Auntie Mame's garden.

"Oh, my poor feet," Auntie Mame groaned at high noon when she had bade a ladylike farewell to Mrs. Cantwell. She sagged up to her room and kicked my brogues and quite a lot of sand across the carpet. "I'm simply sweltering under this sweater of yours. I . . ."

Just then Mrs. Mont d'Or's cockatoo voice cried up from the lawn. "Mame! Mame, *chérie! Bon jour!* I've come to kidnap you. We're driving to Aley for *petit déjeuner!* I want you to meet my friends."

"Oh God!" Auntie Mame groaned. Then she threw off my hat, fluffed her hair, and leaned out of the window. "*Magnifique*, Sari, *chérie!* I'll be right down."

"What are you going to wear this time, adhesive tape?"

"I'll think of something. Even if it's terrible, I can always tell her it's next year's."

It was terrible all right. She took off all of my clothes except the turtle-neck sweater. She pushed the sleeves up above her elbows, put on all her bracelets and all her pearls, painted on her Ubangi mouth, and stepped into a pair of high-heeled sandals. "How do I look?"

"What pretty kneecaps," I said. "Hey, don't stretch that sweater down any farther, it's all out of shape as it . . ." She was gone before I could say more. Below I could hear Mrs.

Mont d'Or and her two overdressed friends groaning in ecstasy. "How *chic*! How divine. *Très jolie!* Where did you get it, Chanel? *Combien?*"

THAT NIGHT AUNTIE MAME, MORE DEAD THAN alive, entertained the Cantwells and Lucia at a New England boiled dinner. She looked a bit like Marie Dressler in a smart shroud made from my best blue dressing gown adorned with a strand of coral beads. She wore no make-up. The turtle-neck sweater was again called into play, this time ripped to shreds and stabbed through with two meat skewers. From time to time Auntie Mame pretended to be knitting.

Grape juice was served, and Auntie Mame's conversation was just about as intoxicating. "Ah, when I was a girl at the convent, the dear sisters—Episcopalian, of course, Lucy, dear," she added hastily, allaying Mrs. Cantwell's dark suspicions of popery—"were ever so particular about our work with the needle. Ouch!" Her lips formed a short and most unholy word. "In my debutante year I wore the loveliest lace bertha. Daddy would have died if my, um, bosom—excuse me, Mr. Cantwell—had been uncovered." Over the tapioca she went into a long discourse about the old families being the best families. Ours, it appeared, was the *very* oldest. Sanka was served.

Mrs. Cantwell was purring with contentment when Auntie Mame said, "And now, Patrick, you and Lucia may be excused to go to the movies. It's *Little Women*, Lucy—so sweet, *if* a trifle dikey. And we old people will just sit here and reminisce about the good old days—the cotillions, the horse-cars, the hobble skirts."

"Such a pity your nice nephew is a few months younger than Lucia," Mrs. Cantwell was saying as we left.

"Nonsense, dear Lucy," Auntie Mame said, "age means nothing in marriage. Why Mrs. Mont d'Or tells me that you're *years* older than Humphrey. Don't be too late, children. No need to worry, Lucy; the Roxy's just a short way from here."

As soon as we got outside, Sammy materialized. Mrs. Mont d'Or had been told that he, too, was going to the Roxy with me—a stag evening.

"Gee, thanks, pal," he said. "Pick us up after the movies." They went off to the garden.

I went to *Little Women*—with Arabic subtitles.

When I got home to tell the lovers that *Little Women* had *finally* ended, Auntie Mame's house and the Cantwell house were dark, while the Mont d'Or house was ablaze with lights. There was no sign of Auntie Mame, but as I was getting into bed she appeared, looking like Sadie Thompson in a naked, scarlet satin rag that was slit to the thigh. It was pretty outlandish, but at least it had never been mine.

"My God, what have you done," I said, "decided to take the Cantwells on a tour of the brothels?"

"Oh, no, darling. They've been gone for ages. I had Ito put sleeping pills in their Sanka and they were nodding by nine. So I just slipped into something cool—*and* the ice—and trotted over to Sari's for some late revels with the local Fast Set."

"How were they?"

"Deadly. Lots of minor French Colonials, some Belgians, some Greeks, a ve-ry few wealthy Lebanese, some of those Silly Ass professional English, and some shrill international pansies. All rich, naturally, and *most* of them with eligible daughters!"

"Was it frightfully gay?"

"Both. Gay *and* frightful. I mean they all try so hard. They're stuck out here a million miles from nowhere with nobody to impress but one another and so that's what they do all day every day. It's almost incestuous. And the *pretense*! Some of them haven't been back home for ten years, but they'd die before they'd admit it. All they talk about are European resorts and restaurants and night clubs and dressmakers and playwrights that have been forgotten ages ago. They all scream with laughter at the dreariest old saws. They're not very hard to fool. And their gaiety is so *desperate*! Actually, they're just as dreary as Lucy Cantwell's crowd, but noisier and showier about it."

"Is it the Golden Ghetto sort of thing?"

"No, Patrick, not at all. And that's what I think is so very sad about Sari Mont d'Or. If she'd simply admit that she's just a Bronx housewife whose husband struck it rich and forget all this *haut monde* crap, she wouldn't be half bad. But no. She's going to be the Madame Pompadour of this silly little place. Swanking about, tucking in her bits and pieces of fashion magazine French, changing her nice old husband's name—it's actually Hyman Julius Goldberg and he asked me to call him Julius—and driving poor Sammy into what *she* considers a desirable life. There's nothing of the warm Jewish mother about her at all. She's as hard as her diamonds and every bit as cold."

"But maybe her objections to Lucia as a daughter-in-law are based on some sort of religious feeling that . . ."

"Not a bit of it, darling. It's money and chichi. If Sari were one of those Jewish mothers who didn't want her children to marry out of the faith that would be perfectly understandable. But she isn't. She'd died if Sammy *did* marry a Jewess. Actually, she's more anti-Semitic than Mrs. Cantwell, but in a different way. Probably because she's trying so hard to run away from it. I don't know exactly what it is, but I do know one thing. . . ."

"What's that?"

"She adores *me*. She thinks that I'm high life on the hoof, just as Lucy Cantwell thinks I'm the head of the ladies' aid society. They both trust me."

"*I* wouldn't trust you around a glass corner, you big ham."

"Who cares about *you*? They're the ones who matter and I've almost got them eating out of the palm of my hand."

"Just be careful they don't bite," I said.

FOR THE NEXT FEW DAYS, REVOLTED BUT FASCI-nated, I watched Auntie Mame seducing the two rival leaders of Shufti, keeping one occupied and the other out of sight while their children courted. Done up like something from a Mack Sennett comedy, she splashed in the club pool with Mrs. Cantwell while Mrs. Mont d'Or was safely off in Beirut being fitted into a turtle-neck tube. Dressed in my track pants, pleated evening shirt, tie, and her emeralds, she impressed Mrs. Mont d'Or and her fast friends at a picnic of absinthe and raw hamburger in the hills. In a grim middy blouse made of my pajama tops, she turned over her drawing room to a commotion which I discovered was a hymn sing for the Cantwell contingent. She was able to convince the Sari Mont d'Or set that jockey shorts and a T shirt, smartly wound with velvet and studded with star sapphires, were *de rigueur* for luncheon. Even though my wardrobe was going fast, Auntie Mame was making a terrific hit in both of Shufti's warring circles. Whenever I ran into either Mrs. Cantwell or Mrs. Mont d'Or, they were loud in their praises.

"Sew nice to have a real *lady* in our community," Mrs. Cantwell bellowed. "I had no idea that dear Mrs. Burnside was a direct descendant of George *and* Martha Washington."

Sammy's mother was even more effusive and just as hard to take in a burlap shift and a glittering tiara as she squealed, "*Oo-la-la! Quel chic! La divine tante!* A true Continental!"

Auntie Mame was feeling pretty tuckered out from all the

quick changes and the constant social whirl, which kept her hopping twenty hours a day, but she was the toast of Shufti and no doubt about it. After a week of the steady society of Mrs. Cantwell and Mrs. Mont d'Or, she came to my room one morning dressed just about like anyone else. "Good morning, my little love. Do you happen to know what day this is?"

"Certainly. It's Friday. Good morning."

"Of course it's Friday, but it's more than that. It's also Sammy Mont d'Or's twenty-first birthday."

"Isn't that nice. What are you giving him, some more of your brilliant advice?"

"No, darling. I'm giving him three things: a party, the car, and Ito."

"The car? *Ito*? Why would a boy of twenty-one want a big Rolls-Royce and what do you think Ito is, a slave?"

"Those are just temporary gifts, Patrick. A loan, so to speak. And as for the party, it's going to be so big that I'm having it at the club and . . ."

"Exactly who's coming to this brawl?"

"Oh, everybody—the Mont d'Ors and their friends, the Cantwells and *their* friends . . ."

"Is this to be a party or a free-for-all?"

"Well, Patrick," Auntie Mame said blushingly, "it's actually going to be *three* parties. For the sake of the Mont d'Ors, it's to be a surprise birthday party for Sammy. As far as the Cantwells are concerned, it's a debut for Lucia. *And*, my little love, for you and me, it is a farewell party. A sort of house cooling."

"Are we going someplace?"

"Yes, dear, I think it's going to be time for us to move on. So I suggest that you devote your day to packing. Who knows when we . . ."

"That should take me about two minutes. Thanks to you, I have almost no clothes left to pack."

"Poor darling. Any time you want to borrow something of mine . . ."

"Gee, thanks."

OWING TO AN UNFORESEEN COMPLICATION, MY packing took *three* minutes. After that I had a long day, the club, and practically the whole town of Shufti to myself. There was no one at the club except the usual army of servants, who were stringing up the Japanese lanterns and fairy lamps, indispensable to galas at the European Union, and waxing the ballroom floor. Otherwise the gentry were at home preparing for Auntie Mame's big surprise party. Servants were the only people to be seen abroad. The Packards and Hispano-Suizas of the Fast Set kept a perpetual pall of dust over the main street racing down to the high-fashion-type dressmaker in Beirut, while the *Dix Mille Articles* in the village reported a serious run on rice powder and *Quelques Fleurs* toilet water brought on by the Conservative Group's desire for utter glamour.

On my lonely way back home, I did see Mrs. Cantwell picking a corsage for herself in her garden. "Good afternoon," I said. "Where's Lucia?"

"Ah, dear Patrick," she said with the old shark face, "absence *does* make the heart grow fonder. Hahaha! Well, you won't see Lee-ew-sha today. Your sweet aunt has sent her into Beirut in her car for all those things sew important to a debutante. You know—hair, nails, a lovely white dress with a lace bertha. And dear Mame has arranged everything so that she won't be back until after the party has begun. It's going to be a real surprise." She was hinting broadly at Auntie Mame's giving Lucia a season in New York when I took leave of the old witch.

At dusk, "Achmed Maloof *et son Orchestre* 'Swing' *du le Kit Kat Club*" arrived in a chartered bus and announced that

Auntie Mame's party was about to commence. All packed, dressed, and waiting, I wondered just what sort of outfit Auntie Mame would wear that would satisfy both contingents of the European Union Club. But when she appeared, she looked very nice and just like her old self again. "Come, Patrick," she said, "we've got to get there first and keep the guests separated as much as possible. I thought the Fast Set in the smoking room and the pokes in the lounge."

From then on I felt a little like an usher at Radio City Music Hall, directing the Cantwell contingent to the right and the Mont d'Or crowd to the left. Even though I didn't know all the guests, it was easy to spot who belonged where just by looking at the outfits. Tatty to start with, Mrs. Cantwell's chums had done everything possible to tone down their toilettes to what they imagined the ultraconservative Mrs. Burnside would expect. Almost every woman had affected a lace bertha, and one or two elderly yellow fur tippets crackled into evidence. The Mont d'Or crowd, on the other hand, were bent on outdoing one another. Bodices could barely be said to exist, and there were some daring—and disastrous—experiments with straps and boning. None, however, was able to outdo the mother of the birthday boy. Mrs. Mont d'Or arrived encased in solid rhinestones so tight that she could hardly breathe, let alone sit down.

"Where's Sammy—I mean Seymour?" I asked her.

"Ah, *chère* Mame! So clever. *Diabolique!* She sent him into Beirut early this morning in her car on some ridiculous errand that will keep him until the party begins. Ah, *la belle* Mame! *Une ange!*" She went glistering off to the dressing room saying, "I don't know what magic Mame has with Seymour. I can never get him to do anything."

The Cantwells were the last to arrive. Mrs. C. was a dream in purple, a bertha, a boa, and the lovely, lovely opals. "Dear

Mame, can you forgive us for being so tardy? We waited and waited for Lee-ew-sha—didn't we, Humphrey?—and she's not back yet! I left instructions for her to come here directly. Good evening, dear boy. Are you going to have the first dance with Our Debutante?"

"Good evening, Mrs. Cantwell. The others are in the lounge."

"I'll just slip into the cloakroom to leave my boa." It was too late to stop her.

One of the club's servants handed Auntie Mame a sheaf of telegrams—three in all. She opened one, read it, and tucked the others into her bosom.

In a flash Mrs. Cantwell was out of the dressing room and breathing flames in front of us. "Mame. There must be some mistake. I went in to take off my boa and the first person I saw was that common Mrs. Mont d'Or."

"And wasn't that a striking outfit, Lucy? You should try something like that," Auntie Mame said calmly.

"But Mame, why is she here—at Lee-ew-sha's Coming Out?"

"Because I invited her, I suppose," Auntie Mame said.

"Mame, I realize that you're a newcomer in our little community, but Mrs. Mont d'Or—that's not her name a-tall—is not the sort of person One Knows."

"I think you'll get to know her quite well quite soon, Lucy. And the experience will undoubtedly do wonders for both of you. Now, why don't you go into the lounge and tell everyone to gather in the ballroom for the big surprise."

"Well!" Mrs. Cantwell snorted as she stomped off, kicking her train.

"*Zut, Mame! Quel horreur! Dieu me protège!* Uh, uh. *Dans le vestiaire . . .*" Mrs. Mont d'Or squealed as she rushed up to Auntie Mame.

"It's all right, Sadie. I speak English like a native. Probably better than you do. What's on your mind?"

"Well, I was in the dressing room and who should I see but that *awful* Mrs. Cantwell. So . . . so *mal fagotée* . . . like someone's charwoman. I mean she gives me one swift pain—her and that crowd of hers acting so superior to everybody else and absolutely *no* sense of style."

"Cheer up," Auntie Mame said calmly. "Goys will be goys. She hasn't got much else to feel superior about. Besides, I think she dresses quite sensibly for her age. Which is just about the same as yours."

"But, Mame! She's impossible. We have nothing in common."

"I think you're going to have. Now why don't you get your friends together and go into the ballroom? It's time now for the big surprise. Oh, and Sadie. Just one thing. Do try to be a little nicer to poor Julius."

"Zhuuuuul?"

"Yes, dear, Julius. He's a darling and for some reason he still loves you. I'd try to hang onto him. You wouldn't have all those furs and diamonds if it weren't for Hyman Julius Goldberg."

The noises that came from the ballroom were rather ominous. More murmurs than any definite sounds of shock or anger—well, I can't quite put my finger on it, but I've heard parties that sounded better integrated.

"Well, now that you've spread sweetness and light all over the European Union Club, when does the big surprise take place?" I asked.

"Just as soon as we get out of here, my little love," Auntie Mame said. "Oh, boy! Would you please give *this* telegram to Mrs. Cantwell and *this* one to Mrs. Mont d'Or? Thank you."

"What in the hell are you up to?" I growled.

"Read this," she said, handing me the third telegram.

Auntie Mame . . .

MARRIED AT SIMPLE REFORM CEREMONY THIS
MORNING. LOVE AND THANKS.

        LUCIA AND SAMUEL GOLDBERG.

"Jesus!" I said.

"A friend of both families, Patrick, and don't you forget it. Come! We've already overstayed our welcome in Shufti." As we reached the door I heard a shrill scream from the ballroom and then another.

TRUDGING DOWN THE MOUNTAIN ROAD HALF AN hour later, Auntie Mame was still talking about the triumph of True Love and Mrs. Burnside over all obstacles. "And to think, darling, that even now those handsome youngsters are spending their wedding night just because of a few sacrifices on my part. I do hope those bags aren't too much for you. I sent the heavy things on ahead, but . . ."

"Not at all. I *love* being out in the mountains wearing pumps and toting three suitcases."

"Don't worry, my little love, it won't be long. Ito's going to meet us with the car now that dear Lucia and Sammy are as one."

"Why didn't you say so? We could just sit down and wait."

"Oh, not up here in the hills, Patrick. At the Hotel Normandie in Beirut."

"In Beirut?" My God, Auntie Mame, that's twenty *miles* from here!"

"Perhaps, Patrick. But you mustn't mind. It's downhill—all the way."

Auntie Mame and the Long Voyage Home

"AND SO AFTER YOUR AUNT SOLVED ALL THE PROBlems of the Middle East what did you do?"

"Why, we came home."

"Which way?"

"Many ways."

"I mean which direction?"

"Well, we'd gone so far that Auntie Mame thought we might just as well keep on going. You know, go around the whole world instead of retracing our steps. So we went from the Far East to San Francisco."

"Oh, I can just see it now—Chinese war lords, opium dens, junks on the Yangtze, real *Terry and the Pirates* stuff."

"Not a bit of it," I said stuffily. "We had a very calm crossing. And one in which religion played an important part."

"In that case maybe you'd better not tell me."

I sighed with relief.

. . .

WELL, IF THIS ISN'T the bitter end," Auntie Mame growled, storming into her hotel room. "Not one single ship headed for New York until the middle of next week. So now we're stuck in a hole like Port Said for eleven endless days."

"It's not much of a town, is it?" I asked, looking at the street below. "Port Said always sounded so kind of sinister and romantic. You know, one of the Seven Cities of Sin."

"Well, it takes a dump like this to show you how utterly boring sin can be."

"Maybe," I said, "but it's kind of intriguing, too. Look at that fortuneteller in the cafe last night telling me that I'd soon meet a beautiful woman who would play an important part in my life."

"Oh, Patrick, poor naïve child. Those mitt artists tell that to everyone. I hope you're not going to be so stupid as to be taken in by some Bulgarian cow in brass curtain rings and *Djer Kiss* perfume."

"But she said that you were going to meet a romantic adventurer."

"I've met more than my share, thank you. Now I have all these divine Tauchnitz editions, I think I'll just lie down and have a fresh go at Proust. Eleven days in this hole and I could polish off Gibbon and the complete works of Shakespeare as well. What are you planning to do, darling?"

"Oh, I don't know. Snoop around the bazaar I guess. Want to come?"

"Thank you, no. You wouldn't catch me in that stinking

Auntie Mame ...

souk. But give me a call when you come back and we'll go downstairs for tea."

AS AUNTIE MAME HAD SAID, THE BAZAAR WAS NOT attractive. It smelled like a cesspool and had nothing for sale that anyone would conceivably want. Bored by the displays of plushy prayer rugs and hand-chased cuspidors, I was about to turn away and go back to the hotel when my eye was caught by a beautiful girl examining some silks. She had put her purse down on the counter and was holding up a length of material the color of moonstones, trying to visualize the effect in the speckled mirror. I could have told her that with her golden hair she looked even lovelier than Madeleine Carroll when I noticed that a street urchin had swept her purse off the pile of silks and was heading my way hell for leather.

"Hey!" I yelled.

The girl turned just in time to see me doing my stuff. "My stuff" was a magnificent flying tackle just like the one I had executed in the annual St. Boniface-Hotchkiss football game. It was the first and last time I'd ever been allowed off the bench, and my athletic feat had prevented Hotchkiss from winning 55-0. (Instead, they only won 49-0). The Arab kid went down like a ton of bricks. I grabbed the purse with one hand and the thief with the other. "Madame," I said suavely, "your purse. *And* the wretch who stole it."

"Oh, oh, thank you," she said. She was even lovelier close up, with translucent alabaster skin and eyes like violets. "Everything I own was . . ."

"And now, if you'll just come with me, we'll turn this thief over to the police."

"The *police*? Oh, no. Please! I *couldn't*. I don't know what Daddy would ever say."

"I think he'd say that I had done the only . . ."

"Oh, no. Never! My father is a man of God. He could never turn this poor sinner over to the law. No more could I. Please, please let him go and—and just forget the whole unfortunate incident." Her big blue eyes looked beseechingly into mine; her dark lashes fluttered exquisitely.

The purse-snatcher was struggling so fiercely that it seemed to me he'd be likely to get away anyhow. "Very well," I said, deepening my voice somewhat. "On one condition."

"Oh, *anything*," she said in her lilting English accent.

"You must allow me to see you safely back to—to wherever it is you're staying."

"Oh, gladly. I should be most grateful."

With that, I let the Arab go. He gave me a kick on the shins and disappeared into the crowd. "You dirty son of a . . ." Then I checked my language and added gravely, "Poor misguided, Godless heathen. And now," I said, offering my arm.

To my delight, the girl and her father were staying in the same hotel where Auntie Mame and I would be quartered for the next eleven days. "But how ripping," I said, allowing my voice to become just a bit deeper, a bit more British. "Do please have tea with me."

"Oh, thanks most awfully. I should adore to. But Daddy— my father, that is—is so frightfully strait-laced. I mean he just wouldn't understand my taking tea with a young man I hadn't been properly introduced to."

"That's right. We haven't been introduced. Let me do the honors. I am Patrick Dennis of New York City. Traveling with my widowed aunt, Mrs. Beauregard Burnside." Oh, was I worldly! "We are doing a cultural tour before I return to my university to finish off my studies of archaeology."

"Oh, you're in college then?"

"Well, uh, practically out of it." That certainly was true enough. At the rate we were getting back home, it looked as though I'd never get to any school. "I'm in my last year, of course. After all, I'm going on twenty-one. Now do just sit down here and I'll call for some tea. Ask your father to join us, if you like." Clapping my hands like a pasha, I ordered tea.

She sat, ankles demurely crossed, prim but provocative, if you know what I mean. "Very well," she said, "but I can't stay longer than a moment. My name is Rosemary Shumway. My father is a poor but dedicated missionary and we are on our way back to the remote little Chinese settlement—oh, I'm sure you would never have heard of it—where Daddy does his humble bit in the service of Our Lord."

"Say, Miss Shumway, that must be a very fascinating life. I'll bet you speak several dialects of Chinese."

"No, alas. Poor Daddy has been out there all these years without even me to lean on in his loneliness, while I have been at school in England. You see, I'm only eighteen."

"Gee. Same as I . . ." Then I said patronizingly, "How wonderful to be eighteen again."

"All these years Daddy and I have been separated it has been my fondest hope to be at his side spreading God's word among the luckless infidels. And now, with this ghastly war raging between China and Japan, I'm so happy at last to be able to help Daddy."

"Well, that's just fine," I said. It didn't sound like much of a life to me. "And I'm awfully glad you're staying here at this hotel. My aunt and I have to wait eleven days before we can get a ship bound for New York. But it won't seem nearly as long now that I've met you. Port Said isn't exactly Paris, but there's an orchestra here in the hotel and . . . Well, I mean we could have some very stimulating . . ."

"Oh, but I'm afraid we can't," Rosemary said, her lashes sweeping her cheeks. "Daddy and I just haven't the means to sit in expensive hotels waiting for luxury liners. We leave at dawn on a Greek freighter as soon as Daddy's shipment is put aboard."

"Shipment?"

"Oh, yes," Rosemary said, an ethereal light coming to her face. "It's always been Daddy's fondest wish to have enough Chinese Bibles for his whole parish and a lovely big pipe organ. And now he has them! I'm so happy for him! And so we set sail at dawn aboard the *Lesbos* for who knows what exciting adventure—two Christian Soldiers spreading His word."

"Gosh," I said, "that's too bad—for me, I mean. I've got to get back to America, but the idea of sitting around this dreary . . ."

"But the *Lesbos* is going to America. San Francisco. Actually, it's quite an interesting trip. Through the Suez Canal and the Red Sea to Aden—I'll be so eager to see the Red Sea. . . ."

"Do you think it'll part?"

"Then, possibly, Bombay, Columbo in Ceylon, Singapore, Saigon, Shanghai . . ."

"*Shanghai?* Hey, don't you know there's a war going on there? From what I see in the newspapers, Shanghai's in ruins."

"Well, as close to Shanghai as possible for the Bibles and Daddy's organ. And then . . ."

"Rosemary!" a man's voice called. "Rosemary, dearest, Daddy's been looking everywhere for you." I glanced up, and there, standing at our table, was the Reverend Dr. Shumway in his tropical-weight clericals. But, thank God, Rosemary resembled her father in no way. Dr. Shumway was a middle-aged, middle-sized man, florid, egg bald, and glossy with sweat. He had a rather large moon face, gooseberry eyes, a great, long, meandering sort of nose, and a prissy little drain hole of a mouth. "Rosemary, dear, you know that Daddy doesn't like you to talk to . . ."

"Oh, please, Daddy," Rosemary said, jumping up in girlish confusion. "This young American gentleman is Mr. Dennis. He's staying here at the hotel and, had it not been for his

Auntie Mame . . .

quick wit and chivalry, everything I own—my money, my traveler's checks, my passport—would have been hopelessly lost. Mr. Dennis, this is my father, Dr. Shumway. I've been telling him of our *missionary work in China*, Daddy."

"How do you do, sir," I said, taking his clammy hand. "Won't you join us?"

"Ah, indeed I shall," he said sitting down. "What a fearful blow it would be for a poor servant of the Dear Lord to be left destitute in this soulless city. As the Bible says, 'Who steals my purse steals trash. . . .' But even losing our, harumph, 'trash' would be a brutal blow for my daughter and I. Harumph. Lemon, please, no milk. Would you hand me a serviette, daughter dear?"

"And, Daddy dearest," Rosemary said, "Mr. Dennis tells me that he and his sweet old widowed aunt will be forced to stay in this dreadful place for nearly a fortnight before they can book passage back to America. Isn't that frightful?"

"Shocking. Those little *gâteau* cakes look monstrously good, Rosemary. Would you hand me one, dear girl?"

"From what Rosemary—I mean, from what your daughter tells me, sir, your trip sounds most interesting. I've never been to the Far East. But I'm sure that trying to buy a passage would be impossible. Everything seems to be pretty tight just now. So I guess that all my aunt and I can do is . . ."

"Mightn't there be something on our . . ." Rosemary began.

"How very strange that you should ask me that, dear girl," Dr. Shumway said, wiping his lips. "As the Bible tells us, 'God moves in a mysterious way His wonders to perform.' But only today did I learn that Dr. and Mrs. Partridge—a dear couple doing the Dear Lord's work—have had to cancel their passage at the last moment. A death in the family," he added in that confidential tone one usually employs to discuss criminal abortion. "So there just happen to be two extra berths on our ship. One of those éclairs, please, Rosemary dearest."

. . . and the Long Voyage Home 285

"Gee, that would be wonderful! But we actually need three places."

"Three?"

"The other is for Ito. He is my aunt's . . . he is a Japanese boy whom my aunt has instructed in the Christian way of life, Dr. Shumway. The car's already been sent home, but I don't think Auntie Mame would trust Ito in a town like . . . I mean she wouldn't want to leave him here under so much Moslem influence."

"Japanese?" Dr. Shumway said, furrowing his brow, his mouth puckering.

"Well, yes." Then I said hastily, "But thoroughly Americanized—and Christianized. My aunt is a very churchly woman. I mean Ito isn't even really Japanese. He was born in California. Well, I mean, Ito's what you'd call a neutral."

"Splendid! Splendid, dear boy!" Dr. Shumway said. "And it is again the hand of the Dear Lord, for I had quite forgotten that Dr. Partridge's manly little son, John Wesley, has had to give up his booking as well, owing to this unforseen tragedy. So, indeed, there is space enough on board for all of you. But remember, it's not one of them—er, one of those—de lukes Cunard boats. It is a simple, informal little craft—oh, neat as a pin—captained by an Athenian gentleman who I had the happy fortune to save from Greek Orthodoxy."

"Oh, my aunt has very simple tastes. I could go upstairs and speak to her right now and let you know immediately. Oh, and I wondered if you would object, sir, to my inviting your daughter to dinner tonight."

"Oh, Mr. Dennis, I just couldn't," Rosemary said, blushing entrancingly.

"Why, I should not mind at all, young man," Dr. Shumway said. "As a matter of fact, I have some last-minute business to attend to and I should do my labors for the Dear Lord with lighter heart knowing that my dear daughter was in good hands. Now we shall wait right here for your reply. Oh, and would you just signal to that waiter for more tea and perhaps some sandwiches and another platter of those delicious *petit-four* biscuits."

I BURST INTO OUR ROOMS CALLING AUNTIE MAME.

"Who was that lady I seen you with?" she said. "I was just going down to tea when I spied you through the potted palms. Rather attractive. I wonder *what* she uses on her hair. So I went to the bar, instead. And when I came back, my God, you were with the whole Epworth League. What has come over you, Patrick?"

"Her name is Rosemary Shumway," I said stuffily. "She and her father are missionaries in China. They're English and she's just eighteen."

"Patrick! I'd hate to be hanging since *she* was eighteen. Anyhow, where shall we dine? Certainly not that hovel with the fortuneteller."

"Well, gee, Auntie Mame, I sort of made this date for dinner—thinking of course, that you'd be holed up with Proust."

"I see," she said, giving me a quizzical glance.

"But, Auntie Mame, this is what I came to tell you. Dr. Shumway and Rosemary are leaving tomorrow morning on this very nice Greek ship—a sort of yacht, actually. And they say that they can get us three tickets. And it sounds like a very interesting trip—educational. We go to all sorts of interesting places like Aden and Columbo and Bombay and China and . . . Well, I mean since we've come so far around the world, we might as well keep on going. It lands in San Francisco eventually, and I've never seen California, either. It would be much faster than waiting for the *Rex* to get here and . . ."

"Patrick! *I* have all the time in the world, but I'd always thought that *you* were the one who was so eager to hustle back to college. This Rosalie girl hasn't . . ."

"Rosemary, Auntie Mame. Rosemary Shumway. Oh, Auntie Mame, she's a lovely girl. So beautiful and well bred and with such a spiritual quality. And her father is a truly dedicated man of God. I mean here they've gone out of their way to befriend us and offer us berths on this really cultural pleasure cruise and . . ."

"All right, darling," Auntie Mame sighed. "I may not recognize spiritual qualities and truly dedicated men at first glance, but I do know sex when I see it. You can have your shipboard romance. Besides, I like to visit places with a hot climate and political unrest. Go down and tell this Rosalind creature that we'll join her. A Greek yacht does sound sort of fun. How much are the tickets and what time do we sail?"

ROSEMARY AND I DINED TOGETHER IN THE DINING room of the hotel that evening. Having told her that I was twenty-one, practically out of college, and quite the man of the world, I really put on the dog—white tie, tails, bottle of champagne cooling next to the table. Rosemary looked ravishingly English in tulle and, while she seemed shocked that I had ordered champagne, she managed to finish off quite a lot of it and then—bless her heart—suggest another bottle. We danced to the strains of such new imported song hits as "Too Much Mustard" and "Dardenella." At first Rosemary was very reserved and standoffish, but later I was able to hold her quite closely on the dance floor and even to manage a little cheek-to-cheek.

It was two o'clock when I took her up to her room. She looked at me with dewy eyes and said, "I never knew that going about with men could be such fun. I've led so sheltered a life, you know." She squeezed my hand fiercely and I took it as a sign that she might be ready for at least a good-night kiss.

"Ah, but just wait for all those nights at sea. The ports of call—smart supper clubs and . . . Oh, Rosemary, I've never met a girl as beautiful as you." With that, I threw my arms around her—and none too aptly. The door opened and Dr. Shumway appeared in a dirty old flannel dressing gown.

"Rosemary, child," he said, "it's ever so late. You must come right in. Good night, dear boy. Until we sail!" That was the end of my big clinch.

I HAD JUST ABOUT TIME TO GET OUT OF MY EVENING clothes and into something more suitable for ocean travel when I heard Auntie Mame's traveling alarm clock go off. She got up spitting tacks. "My God! It's still as black as your hat outside! Ito!" Her mood was not much improved in the flea-bitten old taxi that took us to the harbor, and I was worried for fear she might see that the *Lesbos* was not sailing from one of the more fashionable piers, if, indeed, Port Said could be said to have a fashionable pier. But it was so dark that nobody could see where we were. From its indistinct outlines in the mole-gray dawn, the *Lesbos* looked small enough to be a yacht, but its dimly illuminated interior didn't boast of any of the niceties—shiny brass, glossy paneling—that one usually associated with the *Corsair*. Its pungent companionway was dirty and noisy with odd, murky puddles. There was a constant hissing and clanking of pipes, interspersed with loud and untranslatable curses in what I supposed was Greek.

A wiry little Greek steward—he was wearing a raveled old maroon sweater instead of a natty white jacket, but I *guess* he was a steward—shambled forward with a sneer and took a look at our baggage. Auntie Mame was never one to travel lightly.

«Ποῦ στὸ διάολο νομίζεις θὰ τὰ βάλω,» he said.

"Good evening!" Auntie Mame said, forcing a bright, false smile. "Or should I say good morning?"

«Τὸ Χριστό σου,» the steward said.

"Naturally I won't want all this luggage on the voyage," Auntie Mame said. "And I've done it all very efficiently. I've put my sports clothes and a few simple dinner dresses in those alligator bags. Those other bags and the trunks in the canvas covers can go right down to the hold. Is that clear?" She squandered a bewitching smile on the steward.

«'Ορίστ;»

"Uh, perhaps he doesn't understand. *Parlez-vous français?*"

«'Ορίστ;»

"Uh, *sprechen Sie Deutsch?*"

«'Ορίστ;»

"*Habla usted español?*"

The steward said, «'Ορίστ» again and then he mumbled something like, «'Η βρωμο-'Αμερικανίδα!» and spat. With that he called to some sort of side-kick, a tall, morose-looking sailor from Samos. «"Ε, ἐσύ, βοήθα με!»

The tall sailor picked up seven or eight of Auntie Mame's bags and said in English, "You come dis way."

For a ship as small as the *Lesbos*, it was a surprisingly long trip to our staterooms—not that those seagoing telephone booths should be dignified by so grandiose a term. We went down to what seemed almost the very hold of the old tub. It was awash with bilge and everywhere there was an odor as sour as an old dishrag. I thought at the time that the Reverend must have been transporting enough Bibles for everyone in China, because the ship sat so low in the water that it was sheer madness to open any of the portholes on our deck.

«'Εδῶ» the steward said, indicating three tiny cabins situated just over the screw.

«Ἐδῶ, θὰ πέσουνε στὴ θάλασσα!» the sailor roared, with a fine show of gold teeth.

"Just the alligator bags in my stateroom, please," Auntie Mame said. Then, with a few expressive gestures, she said, "*Seulement les portemanteaux*—I mean to say *le baggage d'alligateur*. . . . How in the hell do you say 'alligator,' darling? . . . *Seulement le baggage crocodile dans ma cabine.* Oh, no!" The steward and his chum, not even understanding her, piled the bags in.

Auntie Mame's cabin was a filthy affair about six by seven. It contained a bunk, a chest complete with pitcher and bowl, a straight chair, a life jacket, some complicated instructions in Greek about what to do in case of shipwreck, and eighteen pieces of luggage.

"*Dove il stanza di bagno?*" she tried in Italian.

«Σάσε,» the steward said and slammed Auntie Mame's door on the rest of her language lesson.

Ito's cabin and mine were even smaller than Auntie Mame's, but then we hadn't quite so much stuff to cram into them. The steward had just disappeared when Auntie Mame came banging into my room. "Greek *yacht*? This wretched boat is so old I'm sure it's one Homer was talking about."

"Oh, it's not so bad, Auntie Mame," I lied weakly.

"Not so bad? It's perfectly . . ." There was a blast of the whistle, and the engines directly beneath us started churning with a vibration that set the furniture to dancing.

"Hey, Auntie Mame! Let's go above and watch ourselves set sail."

"Now see here, young man, you're not going anywhere except where *I'm* going and that is back to bed for a few hours' sleep. You're not eighteen and I won't have you ruining your . . ."

"Please," I said. "Not so loud. Rosemary thinks I'm twenty-one and a senior at college. You won't say anything will you?"

"Oh?" Auntie Mame said. "Well, I don't care how old you say you are. Get to bed. I know *I'm* not old enough to stand much of this. You'll have plenty of time to see her tomorrow. And really, Patrick, this despicable ship isn't actually so terrible, darling. I mean if it's what you want. It's *different*." She kissed me good night and went back to her cubbyhole. I stretched out on my bunk for just a second. The next thing I knew it was nearly noon.

I awoke in a pool of sweat, the air in my tiny cabin flat and still. Wanting to look my best for Rosemary, I got into a robe and groped my way down the dark, filthy companionway looking for a bathroom. All the doors were labeled in Greek so I had to try all of them. The first three doors I approached were locked. The fourth led to a man who was snoring in a bunk. A rat ran out of the fifth. The sixth, marked μπάνιο turned out to be the right place—a hot, stinking chamber containing a filthy toilet, two scummy washbasins, and a big, old-fashioned tub with a velvety ring around it and a nest of hairs clogging the drain.

Only slightly refreshed, I dressed and made my way up to the open deck. I'd never seen the *Lesbos* except in the pitch dark. It was better that way. The ship Rosemary's father had described as "simple, informal," and "neat as a pin" was unbelievably filthy—its decks thick with rust, its paint peeling and untouched for years. Great flecks of soot fell from its single funnel directly onto its crew and passengers, the canvas awnings having long ago deteriorated to tatters. Mentioning crew and passengers reminds me that there were hardly any of either. If I had ever wondered why three vacancies suddenly came up at a time when space was at a premium, I didn't now. And as for a crew, what little work was done on the *Lesbos* was done by a miserable handful of sullen Turks, all of whom must have been shanghaied.

We were creeping down the Suez Canal by this time. It was

hideously hot on deck and there wasn't a breath of air stirring. I found a biggish but sordid-looking room designated as σαλόνι which I took to be the ship's lounge. Picking my way through the auction-room clutter of old wicker furniture, I sat down to wait for the radiant appearance of Rosemary. A fan in the dirty ceiling whirred away in a slow dispirited fashion. There were some dog-eared Greek magazines called *H Σοκράτικη Φιλοσφία* and *τῆς θιᾶς σου* and some copies of *The Modern Priscilla*, which had obviously been left out for the entertainment of the passengers at around 1907 and did nothing to tempt me. Hot and hungry and thirsty, I waited.

Nearly an hour went by. Not only was there no sign of Rosemary; nobody appeared. At one, Auntie Mame traipsed in.

"Oh, Patrick, my little love," she said. "There you are! Could you close an eye? I've never been so shaken up since Vera bought that reducing belt."

"It's not much of a Greek yacht, is it?" I asked glumly.

"Oh, don't worry about that, darling. No sacrifice is too great for your shipboard romance. La, will I ever forget the first time my father took *me* abroad. It was on the old *Lusitania* and it couldn't have been more divine. I had three Rhodes scholars, the whole Yale Glee Club, the younger officers, and Wally Reid all to myself. Well, of course, I wasn't the *only* girl aboard, but the others were this dreary trio from some utterly unheard-of denominational school out in—hell, I can't remember—Migraine, Missouri or some place like that. Anyhow—oh, this is too mad—I happened to be spooning in a lifeboat with this dashing young . . ."

"Um, excuse me, Auntie Mame, but there's just one thing I would like to take up with you before you meet Rosemary and Dr. Shumway. Uh, well, they're not like us—like *you*. They're missionaries and very strict. So if you wouldn't talk too much about drinking and if you'd kind of watch your language . . ."

"Oh, darling, don't give it a *thought*! As for drinking, I've searched high and low for a bar. There *isn't* one. And when it comes to language, my dear, I promise you that even if I stepped in a pile of it, I wouldn't say so much as . . . Heavens, Patrick! Can *this* be the Miss Shumway you've been telling me about. She's lovely!"

I looked up, and there was Rosemary, the picture of British reserve in virginal white. I made the introductions and then watched Auntie Mame and Rosemary sizing up one another as only two females can. Somehow, though, they made me think of two prize fighters in opposing corners.

"*Well!*" Auntie Mame said after a rather long silence. "This *is* going to be fun—a long, long voyage on this utterly unspoiled little ship. We'll all get to know one another *ever* so well, won't we? Now tell me, Rosamund de-ar, Patrick says you've been at boarding school in England. Which one? I want to hear all about it."

Rosemary seemed even more reticent with Auntie Mame than she had been with me, all lowered eyes and whispered responses. For once in my life, I wished that her windy old father would show up to carry the conversational ball.

I hadn't long to wait. With a loud "Harrrumph," Dr. Shumway was upon us, his strawberry mousse face glistening. Again I was all suave worldliness with the introductions.

"Ah, dear lady," Dr. Shumway said, puckering his sewery little mouth into a citric smile, "I have so looked forward to having the honor of making the acquaintance of, har-rrrumph, this splendid young man's aunt."

"Thank you, Father," Auntie Mame said, all but kissing his ring. I couldn't help noticing that her nostrils quivered. "The study of comparative religions has always fascinated me so that I know we'll have splendid chats aboard this sweet little ship."

Dr. Shumway looked rather startled and backed away a

pace or two, launching into a ferocious attack of catarrh. Even Rosemary looked aghast, her pale hands fluttering to the front of her dress. Having seen Joan Crawford in a remake of *Rain*, I wondered if Auntie Mame had struck the Reverend as a second Sadie Thompson. But a surreptitious glance at her reassured me. She was wearing natty navy blue with white piping, sensible shoes, and one strand of pearls. While Auntie Mame didn't look exactly like a churchmouse, she did have about her an air of Episcopalian *chicté* that could have offended only the most masochistic of sects.

Undaunted, she continued. "Ah yes, Dr. Shumway, the Bible as literature is a subject that has always interested me. Some of it a little farfetched in this day of the realistic novel, but withal . . ."

"Harrrrrumph!" Dr. Shumway said.

I gave Auntie Mame a beseeching glance and said, "Lunch seems to be a little late."

"Ah, which reminds me," Dr. Shumway said, "the captain has invited us all to sit at his table."

"Oh, isn't that lovely," Auntie Mame said. "I always say I don't mind how squalid—I mean, how simple—a ship is as long as the food and the company are good. And do let me tell you that authentic Greek cooking is sheer heaven. If that doesn't offend you, Father."

"Harrumph, not at all."

"My dear Greek friend Madame Adam is a superb cook. Ah, for her divine Greek caviar. It's made with pike roe and . . ."

Auntie Mame's dissertation was interrupted by an unshaven little monkey of a man in a spotted mess jacket. He poked his head in the door and said, «*Φαή.*» Then he gestured toward the dining saloon.

Of course we sat at the captain's table, because there wasn't any other. Its tablecloth was covered with wine spots, encrusted with old bits of gravy, ketchup, and rancid olive oil. There was a smart centerpiece of salt, pepper, oil, vinegar, ketchup, A-1 Sauce, and toothpicks. Everything jiggled and jingled to the vibrations of the engine. A vase of dusty artificial carnations and a large, tinted photograph of Pola Negri completed the *décor* of the officers' mess.

The captain was fat and furry. He wore an undershirt, trousers, the first two or three buttons open to accommodate his belly, carpet slippers, and—peering out shyly through the thick undergrowth of hair on his arms and chest—some tattoos of scantily clad ladies. All of his teeth were bright gold and he managed to eat, talk, smoke, and drink with a toothpick in his mouth.

The first mate, the chief engineer, and the second mate were the only officers who ever graced the captain's table—for all I know, the only other officers there were. They came and went, glum and never speaking except to quarrel loudly among themselves in Greek until the captain, slamming his ham of a hand down on the table violently said, *«Σκάστ, κερατάδες.»* Otherwise, the conversational ball was carried pretty much by Auntie Mame.

At that first meal Auntie Mame said, "Ooooh! Doesn't all this look fascinating." But when the mess steward handed her a grubby menu, she said, "Oy, it's the Rosetta Stone!" Since no one who could read Greek could—or would—speak English, Auntie Mame said, *"This* looks good." I watched her point a long red nail to an item called *καπαμά.*

"I'll have that, too," I said.

It was a sinewy stew. I left mine untouched.

I don't know what Lucullan goodies Auntie Mame's dear old friend Madame Adam had cooked up, but nothing even edible was being served aboard the *Lesbos* that day. The dining room was stifling and smelled of stale grease. Flies settled on everything and then disdainfully stalked away. The food didn't even tempt *them*.

"Strange," Auntie Mame said, "but I just don't feel very hungry this noon. All the Greek cooking I've ever had was delicious, but this . . ."

"Ah, dear lady, don't worry," Dr. Shumway said piously. "I expect that the cooking arrangements are not all they will be. This is, after all, the first meal out of port. Harrrumph!"

"Perhaps," Auntie Mame said. "Well, I'll just sample some of that table wine—*if* no one objects."

"Well, dear lady, my daughter and I do not partake of the grape or the grain. However . . ."

"Oh, come now, Dr. Shumway, as the Bible says, '. . . drink thy wine with a merry heart; for God now accepteth thy works.' Ecclesiastes Seven."

Auntie Mame poured out a glass of wine for herself. I prudently refused. "Ugh!" she said, putting down the glass. "That's not wine, it's *vinegar*! And now, Dr. Shumway, perhaps you'll tell us something about your interesting missionary work."

"Well, ah, dear lady, harrrumph . . . I, um, scarcely know where to begin." Perspiration poured off Alfred Shumway.

"Begin at the beginning. This is going to be a long journey and so there'll be plenty of time for you to tell me all. I should like to brush up on my Latin and what better opportunity to learn Greek—especially with a mentor such as you, carefully coached in the classical languages. Now which school of divinity did you attend?"

"Why, ur, harrrrumph, I . . ." Before Dr. Shumway could commence his liturgical reminiscences, the *Lesbos's* engines came to a grinding, screeching stop. "Ah," Dr. Shumway said, going to the prothole, "here we are at the end of the Suez and already at the mouth of the fabled Red Sea. Why don't we all go out on deck and watch?"

"Why don't we indeed!" Auntie Mame said.

We all went to the rear of the deck and sat on some splintery old chairs, watching a very proper British officer in white shorts come aboard. "Excuse me, madam, padre," he said, "but can you tell me where to find the captain. Um, let's see. This is the *Lesbos*, a Greek-owned ship under Nicaraguan registry. Odd."

"The, uh, captain, harrrrumph, is somewhere about, sir," Dr. Shumway said, "but unfortunately for you, he speaks no English."

"I have orders to inquire about the cargo. It's irregular, I know, but with the Chinese-Japanese dust-up . . ."

"Ah," Auntie Mame said, "you have come to the right person, sir. This gentleman owns the cargo, and precious cargo it is, for it consists entirely of Chinese Bibles through which Dr. Shumway, here, plans to spread His word to the heathens of the Orient. Is that not correct, Father?"

"Harrrrumphh. Well, um, yes."

"And there is also a mighty Wurlitzer pipe organ so that our yellow brethren may lift their voices in worshipful song," Auntie Mame continued. "La, Dr. Shumway, perhaps some evening we may all gather round the piano in the lounge and sing some of those grand, old-time hymns together. Ah, yes. It is cargo precious beyond pearls to Dr. Shumway and I am certain that he will display it to you with pride."

"Harrrrrumph. Well, um, this *is* unregular and, ah, harrrrumph . . ."

"Well, actually it does seem a waste of time. In this case I shan't bother to detain you," the officer said.

"Ah," Auntie Mame went on, holding up a pious hand, "but I should like to detain *you*. Let us all kneel down on this burning deck—if you don't mind the filth—and have Dr. Shumway lead us in a prayer for a safe journey and a peaceful settlement of this cruel war. Come, Patrick, Mary Rose, down on your knees . . ."

"Oh, but . . ." Dr. Shumway began, wiping his dripping brow.

"Forgive me," the officer said, looking most undone, "but with so many ships to check I simply . . . Good afternoon." With that he hotfooted it off the ship before the Diety could be consulted by Dr. Shumway.

"Ah, now," Dr. Shumway said, wiping his crimson brow, "Rosemary, dear girl, why don't you entertain this charming young man while we complete the formalities of getting out of the canal? It's so terribly warm that, for myself, I believe I shall go to my simple cell and, harrumph, *meditate*. If you all will excuse me."

"And I might just go down to *my* simple cell and try to sleep," Auntie Mame said.

That left Rosemary and me just the way I'd wanted to be since I first met her twenty-four hours earlier—alone together. I'll never forget that afternoon. Rosemary was too perfect for words; sweet and shy, yet yielding and warm. Well, warm is hardly the word. With the *Lesbos* standing stark still, waiting to get out of the Suez Canal, the temperature soared to well over a hundred. But I didn't notice. We sat on the squeaking wicker sofa in the lounge in the vapid, stagnant breeze of the fan. Trying to make inane social chitchat with Rosemary, I inched closer and closer to her. While I'd done a little heavy necking at Junior Holiday dances, my amorous experiments had always been conducted with rather fast young New York girls—oh, that one brunette from Miss Walker's! Love had always been a quick kiss in the cloakroom, a tussel in the taxi. Never before had I been all alone with a beautiful, carefully reared English clergyman's daughter. I was nervous. But Rosemary was poise personified, speaking softly and tenderly in her lovely English accent—an accent far more cultivated than her father's. And then she lunged. The next thing I knew, I was flat on my back, with Rosemary crawling over me and smothering me with kisses. I was just barely conscious of two canal officials standing in the doorway and totally unaware of their tiptoeing away.

When they were gone, however, Rosemary got to her feet, blushing furiously and straightening her frock. "Do forgive me, Patrick. I don't know what can have come over me," she said.

"That's all right," I panted. "I just hope it comes over you again."

And it did. Rosemary was talking about her mission work when I heard footsteps out on the deck. Again she threw herself upon me and again some startled English port-authority men slunk away. I wondered if there wasn't a touch of the exhibitionist in Rosemary. However, it was the most stimulating two hours I'd ever spent in female company.

I was just about to plan a frontal attack of my own when there was a great lurching and roaring. The ship's motors started up once again, and Rosemary dashed to the porthole.

"Look," she said. "We're underweigh again. We've finally got through the canal and now we're out in the Red Sea!" Sure enough, we were, and the *Lesbos*, its rusty throttle open, was puffing away at all seven or eight knots top speed.

"That's just fine. And now let's have another kiss. Oh, Rosemary! Your eyes, your lips, your hair!" Closing my eyes I moved forward to embrace her again. When I opened my eyes again Rosemary was halfway out of the door.

"Do forgive me," she said, "but it's so impossibly warm that I believe I'll go to my cabin. It's time for *my* meditations."

"Hey. Wait a . . ."

She blew a kiss in my direction and departed.

OVERCOME, I WAS JUST ABLE TO MAKE MY WAY DOWN to my hot little cabin, bathe again, and get into my white dinner jacket. Auntie Mame had also made some attempt at dressing for dinner, but the *Lesbos* had none of the affectations of the *Normandie*. Dr. Shumway was still in his tropical clericals, wet black stains deep beneath the arms. The captain and his officers, somewhat dirtier and sweatier than they had been at noon, were otherwise unchanged. Rosemary did not appear at all. When I asked about her, Dr. Shumway said, "Ah, dear boy, my poor daughter has found the heat too oppressive. She will most likely come up in the cool of the evening."

At dinner Auntie Mame pointed to a succulent item called Γαχνί saying, "This looks good. It'll be such fun to learn Greek here with Dr. Shumway to help me. I do know Sigma Chi and Phi Beta Kappa and the Omega watch but..." She was interrupted by a greasy plate slapped down in front of her. It was the same stew we had been served for lunch.

It took us no time to finish the meal. Dr. Shumway escorted Auntie Mame to the lounge and, excusing myself, I dashed off an impassioned note to Rosemary telling her that I would be waiting on the aft deck. I slipped it under her door and went back to join Auntie Mame and the Reverend Alfred Shumway. But when I returned to the lounge, Auntie Mame was alone. "I can't understand it, darling," she said. "Just to make a little shop talk for him I got onto Deuteronomy and he was out of here like a shot. Well, no matter. I'm going to get out of this suffocating dress and back into *Sodom and Gomorrah*. Don't be up too late, Lochinvar." She kissed me and was gone.

Even out on the sea with the sun down, it was no cooler. Making sure that every hair was in place, I went out to the rear deck to wait for Rosemary. It was some wait. Midnight came and there was still no sign of my inamorata. Then I must have fallen asleep because it was dawn when I awoke—still quite alone—but with a stiff neck and my white dinner jacket black with soot.

THE NEXT DAY WAS STILL HOTTER. ROSEMARY DID not appear for breakfast or for lunch. I slid another note under her door and waited all afternoon in the sweltering lounge. Auntie Mame read all day, and by dinnertime I had read all the copies of *The Modern Priscilla*. Dinner came and went. I ate it—or, rather, didn't eat it—alone with Auntie Mame. Dr. Shumway claimed to be too overheated to dine. "If that's the case," Auntie Mame said, "it's just as well, probably. I'm not sure I could stand it. I mean wouldn't you think that with all those efficacious deodorants and antiperspirants on the market even a man of God would do something about his everlasting..."

"Now, Auntie Mame," I said, "just don't bring up anything like that with him."

"Oh, certainly not, darling. I can never bring *anything* up with him without his running like a rabbit. They both seem to treat me like a she-devil. Especially the girl. But I thought that as another man, dear, you could just give poor Dr. Shumway a few pointers about masculine daintiness. I mean the idea is to win converts, not repel them and..."

"Have you gone crazy with the heat?" I demanded.

"Practically. I think I'll go below, have a cool bath, and read a bit. Don't be up too late with your lady friend. Good night."

There was no need to worry. Rosemary never came out. Ito was cooking for Auntie Mame and taking trays to her cabin. Her palate was such that no amount of money could have lured her to the officers' mess. And it was so hot that the captain took his meals clad only in a bath towel—a sight that would have put you off your feed at Laperouse, not to mention the dining saloon of the *Lesbos*. Another note under Rosemary's door still brought no results.

On the fourth day—hotter still—I was down to bathing trunks, like the rest of the ship's crew. None of the passengers appeared at all. A homemade "Do Not Disturb" sign hung on Auntie Mame's door. In desperation, I went up to the hurricane deck, hoping for a breath of wind. There was none, but, passing the radio shack, I was attracted by the fulsome strains of Carroll Gibbons and His Boyfriends coming—with a lot of static—over the BBC. I looked in at the open door and there was a young Greek swilling wine. He was seated at some outmoded radio equipment and had made his quarters quite homey in a hideous sort of way with a terrible Turkish rug on the floor, pink curtains at the windows, souvenir pillows on his bunk, a lead reproduction of the Statue of Liberty, and pictures pinned up everywhere. There must have been two hundred of them in the tiny cabin—"toots" shots of Jean Harlow, Toby Wing, Mary Carlisle, Ginger Rogers, Mae West, Anita Louise, Alice Faye; almost any blonde you care to mention.

The radioman saw me and smiled. "Hhhell-oh," he said in heavily accented English. "Come in. You spik Eenglees?"

"A little," I said. "I'm an American."

"Oh!" he said, effusively offering me a chair. "Verry guud, Amerrrica. Nize. Then you know my cozins in Edie."

"Who?"

"In Edie, Pencil-vonya, near Bofa-lo, New Yorrrk. Is nize Edie, Pencil-vonya. I have uncle in Edie, also cozins. Wait." He fled to a closet almost the size of my cabin and returned with sheaths of photographs and also a fresh bottle. "Hhhhere is Rrrretsina. Grik wine. Verrry guud." He poured me out a large tumbler of Retsina, a wine so resinous that it was more like licking a violin bow than drinking. "Is guuuud?"

"Very tasty," I lied.

"Hhhere is my cozins of Edie, Pencil-vonya. Eleni, Caliope, Achilles, Pythagoras, Socrates, Plato, Terpsichore, Ophelia, Athena, Hermaphrodite, Miltiades, Medusa, Pachysandra, and George. Nize?"

"Very nice," I said, gazing at a series of beetle-browed faces with eyes like plums.

"This is my last trip. I go to Amerrrica; to Edie, Pencil-vonya. I lairn rrrradio here on ship. In Amerrrica I will be deesk jockey on rrradio station WLEW in Edie. I spik Eenglees guud, no?"

"No," I said. "I mean you speak very well. I guess you're the only person on the ship who speaks English."

Turning up the BBC broadcast to an earsplitting volume, El Greco launched into an endless monologue about himself, about his cousins in Erie, about jazz, about being a disc jockey. After I'd bravely got down the first dose of Retsina, I was given an even larger glassful. I was staggering when I finally left. El Greco was worse.

I went down to the little kiln I called my cabin. There was a note there from Auntie Mame. It read:

> *Darling Boy—*
>
> *Don't worry about my protracted absence. I sense that Rosemarie is shy in my presence. For that reason I'm remaining in my cabin to give you every chance to carry on your first affaire. No sacrifice, as I said, is too great. And missing meals with the captain is no sacrifice whatsoever. If you'd like some decent food, come to my cabin. But I suppose you'd rather be with her. Do, however, be cautious. I'm not ready to manage another generation yet.*
>
> *Love, love, love,*
> *Auntie Mame*

Auntie Mame ...

Glad that Auntie Mame didn't know how badly my romance was going, I stripped and bathed again. It was so hot that just wallowing in that tepid salt water seemed refreshing. When I came out, I found Dr. Shumway in a most unclerical dressing gown—scarlet sateen—heading for the can. I was still so lovelorn for the sight of Rosemary that even Dr. Shumway seemed an adequate substitute. "Dr. Shumway!" I said, grasping him. I could sense what Auntie Mame meant. "It's so good to see you again. I've been worried. You haven't been to a meal since . . . Well, a long time. And Rosemary . . ."

"Harrumph, uh, she's, uh, fasting, dear boy. Fasting," he said. Then he brushed past me, went into the bathroom, and locked the door.

I went to my cabin and wrote Rosemary yet another note. It read:

> *My darling—*
>
> *Why haven't you seen me or at least answered my notes?*
> *I shall be waiting for you tonight as always.*
>
> > *Your devoted,*
> > *Patrick*

Then I got into my lightest-weight shirt and trousers and went up to the mess for stew. As I went along our companionway, I saw Ito carrying a tray to Auntie Mame's room. Not far behind him was the Greek steward, now clad in a suit of old B.V.D.'s, taking a much larger tray to Rosemary's room. In the dim light I could hardly see what was on it, but I thought I recognized a roast chicken.

Sick with love and boredom, I stayed out on deck that night waiting for Rosemary. Around eleven I knew it was useless. I was just about to turn in when El Greco came down the rickety ladder leading to the hurricane deck. "Guud eveneeng. You like Ben-nee Guudman? Come up. We have some Rrrretsina."

Even my cabin seemed better than El Greco's accounts of Sparta, Erie, and his cousins. I begged off and went to bed. When I awoke, the ship was pitching terribly, and great sprays of water were leaking through my porthole. It was also cold. Shivering, I gathered up my shaving things and headed for the bathroom. I got there just in time to see Auntie Mame sway out, pale and shaken.

"Auntie Mame," I said, "what's the matter. Where have you . . ."

"Oh, Patrick, my little love," she moaned, "don't even ask me to *speak*. I couldn't be more miserable. Thrown from my bed at four this morning and then buried alive under suitcases. Ohhhhhh."

The ship gave another heave and we toppled against the bulkhead. "Ohhhhh," Auntie Mame moaned again, and looked as though she might be terribly sick.

"You should get some air. You haven't stuck your nose out of your cabin for days."

Again the ship rolled violently, and she clung to me for support. "I was only trying to keep out of your way, my little love. I had my books and Ito to prepare my meals. Oh! Food! How could I even *mention* such a filthy four-letter word. Find out when we're docking at Aden, darling. You can stay aboard if you like, but I'll have to get off." With that she tottered back to her room.

No one—not even the officers—showed up for breakfast. The sea around us was gray and fierce. There were winds of gale velocity and waves that towered over the deck. Luckily I'm a good sailor, and, since I couldn't eat any of the food anyhow, there was nothing in me to disgorge.

Concerned about Auntie Mame, I went down to her cabin. On the way I passed Rosemary, looking pale and disheveled. "Rosemary," I cried. "Darling, how . . ."

"Please," she wailed and staggered into the bathroom. Dr. Shumway was not far behind.

"Gee, Auntie Mame," I said, tiptoeing into the tiny room where she was tossing and pitching in her bunk. "What can I do for you?" Then I dodged as two or three trunks came sliding across the bare floor toward me.

"Nothing, darling. Nothing but euthanasia. I've always tried to be a good guardian to you, remember that. Ohhhh-hhh."

"It'll be over soon," I said, trying to stack up her luggage in one corner. It was a hopeless task.

"Don't bother with the bags, Patrick. Just find out when we get to Aden. Dry land and a drink will be enough. You can get off with Ito and me—he's even sicker than I am, if such a thing is possible—or you can stay on this miserable tub if your love affair seems worth it. I've made all the sacrifices to Eros possible. But *do* find out about Aden."

The only person I could communicate with was El Greco up in the radio shack. Taking my life in my hands, I made it to the hurricane deck. El Greco was lying on his bunk singing along with Tommy Dorsey as his band came crackling over the short wave. He seemed awfully bleary-eyed, and I noticed two empty bottles of Retsina at his side.

"Guud morning," he said sloppily.

"Good morning," I said, not bothering much with formalities. "Tell me. Is the Red Sea always this rough?"

"Ssiss not Rrred Sea."

Realizing that he was drunk, I tried another tack. "But when are we going to land at Aden?"

"Odden? We arrrre not going to Odden. Pass Odden two, ssree days. Boat stop fairrst at Singapore in pairrheps two weeks."

"Two *weeks*? But what about Aden, Bombay, Columbo?"

"Oh, no. Never. Always go from Piraeus to Port Said to Singapore." With that the wireless started sending all sorts of messages, and El Greco passed out.

I put off telling Auntie Mame the news for several hours. The scene that took place when she learned that she had two more weeks aboard the *Lesbos* is too painful to relate.

The next day was worse and the day after that still worse. I saw no one save Auntie Mame on her numerous trips across the corridor. But she hadn't spoken one word to me since I told her that Singapore would be the first stop. Ito, the color of chartreuse, only pitched in his bunk babbling prayers that I was sure Dr. Shumway would never approve. I realized that we were in the midst of the equinoctial storms and, bored as I was with El Greco, I took to spending all my waking hours in the radio shack. I did this for three reasons: First, El Greco was the only person who could speak English and who had any contact with the world beyond the rickety railings of the *Lesbos*; second, because the radio shack was more comfortable than any place else; and third, because storms made El Greco so nervous that he always got drunk and stayed drunk until they were over. Considering the condition of the *Lesbos* and El Greco, I felt that it would be nice if *someone* else knew how to send an SOS. So I made El Greco teach me and even looked it up in one of his books to make certain—three dots, three dashes, three dots. And I don't think that on the fourth and worst day of the storm I wasn't sorely tempted to send out that very message when the *Lesbos* was pitched entirely out of the water and El Greco opened his sixth bottle of Retsina.

And then, as suddenly as it had begun, the storm stopped. I had slept in my life jacket after deciding that a night spent lashed to the mast would be just *too* uncomfortable and awoke to find the sea as calm as a lagoon, the sun shining, and cool breezes flapping the shredded tarpaulins of the *Lesbos*. Looking out of my porthole, I half expected to see a dove flying

Auntie Mame . . .

overhead with an olive branch in its beak. What I did see, however, was an American naval ship, the U.S.S. *Hoboken*, bobbing on the calm water, its personnel in hastily improvised bathing suits diving cheerfully into the water, laughing and splashing.

The sight of the U.S. Navy at play did a lot to bolster my spirits. It meant not only that the storms were over, that we were in calm water, free from shark and shipwreck, but that I was getting closer and closer to home. I dressed and went above with a song in my heart.

The captain and his men were bickering amiably, and even El Greco, fearfully hungover, offered me a wan smile and announced that Ambrose and his orchestra could be heard over the BBC.

Just before noon, Auntie Mame came up on deck in a fetching sun dress. Having been told most definitely that I was never to speak to her again, I tried to get out of her sight, but she was sunshine itself. "Good morning, my little love! Isn't it a lovely, lovely day!"

"Auntie Mame," I said. "Are you all right? Did you suffer much?"

"Hideously, my little love. Ah, the sacrifices we make for our young! But *look* at me. I'm a size ten again. This little Vionnet model simply *hangs* on me! No diet would ever do this. Yes, I forgive you, Patrick. Now tell me, how's the *grand amour* coming? I hope you haven't gone too far."

I was saved from telling Auntie Mame the shameful truth by the appearance of Dr. Shumway. He, too, was thinner, but sweating just as much, even in the cool weather.

"Dr. Shumway. Good morning! Just the man I wanted most to see," Auntie Mame said. "I've spent days in my cabin just reading my Bible so that I can discuss things intelligently with you. And I have another bit of good news: My man, Ito, also speaks Chinese, so that you can help him with his Bible study. But first there is a great favor I want to ask of you."

"Uh, what is that? Harrrumph."

"A prayer of thanks for our deliverance from this ghastly storm that might have finished us both off. I think it would be fun to call Ito and the whole ship's crew and your daughter, then you could do it in Chinese, Greek, and English. Please. Just for me."

"Well, dear lady, harrumph, I don't know if there *is* such a . . ."

"Nonsense, dear Dr. Shumway, I know that if you'd simply browse through your Book of Common Prayer, you'd find something most appropriate."

"My what?" With that Dr. Shumway went into such a barrage of throat clearing that no voice could be heard. Perspiration poured off him again.

"Excuse me, Dr. Shumway," I said, "but isn't Rosemary coming out now that it's cool and calm?"

"Uh, harrumph, um, no. No, Rosie—my daughter is unwell. She is still, harrrumph, fasting."

"With all those trays I see carried to her room?" Auntie Mame said. "For all her religious fervor she certainly seems to eat better than . . ."

"Excuse me," Dr. Shumway said and he went harrrumphing below.

"Auntie Mame!" I said. "You shouldn't have said that."

"Why not? It was true. 'Great is Truth, and mighty above all things.' Apochrypha Four, Forty-one. Oh, Patrick, I've been boning up on all this down in my cabin just hoping for a cosy little chat with our spiritual guide, Alfred Shumway—once the weather got cooler and he stopped oozing like a pig on a spit."

"Auntie Mame!"

"Well, that's true, too, and I'll also tell you something else that's the plain truth. Dr. Shumway doesn't know as much about religion as I do, which is precious little. He's a shabby,

Auntie Mame . . .

shoddy little fraud and so is his daughter; *if* she's his daughter, which I sincerely doubt. My cabin is next to hers and the things I've overheard from those two weren't the Lord's Prayer. I don't know what that bogus old skunk is up to, but whatever it is he's using us as a front for those embarrassing moments when officials . . ."

"Damn it," I said hotly, "that's a lie. Rosemary is a fine, upstanding girl. I love her and she loves me and . . ."

"Then go to her, Patrick. Go to her this instant. I insist."

"I will!" With that I stamped down the stinking stairs. My emotions are difficult to describe. I was furious with Auntie Mame; not so much for what she had said, but because, deep down, I was afraid that she was right. Dr. Shumway was a vulgar, stinking old grease ball who didn't know the Begats from the Beguine. I also knew that I wasn't having any love affair with Rosemary. But what really hurt was knowing that Auntie Mame knew it, too. It's one thing to be a sucker, but it's even worse to have other people find out about it. I decided to go straight to Rosemary for an explanation, and I was about to pound on the door when I heard the two of them quarreling inside.

"A fine pair you picked, Rosie, my girl," Shumway was saying in the least churchly of tones. "Here you go an' tell me you've got the ideal couple—rich Yanks an' her without a brain in her head. An' wotta yuh turn up with but a blasted Christer an' her kid."

"Oh, bugger off, Alf," Rosemary said, her voice thick and slurred. Gone was the delicate speech; if it wasn't quite Cockney, neither was it exactly Mount Street. "I seen her in the hotel, the travel agent's, the bar—her an' the kid an' the servant an' that big posh car—she didn't look like she knew her arse from . . ."

"Well, she does, Rosie. She knows a lot more than you do, my girl. An' small wonder, you sittin' down here on your bloody bum with your nose in a gin bottle till it looks like a cork . . ."

"Oh, come off it, Alfie."

"No, I won't come off of it. Just eighteen," Shumway mimicked shrilly. "My little daughter. Well your years for pullin' that are over, Rosie. Eighteen! There's a laugh. You look forty."

"Shut your bloody mouth. I'm not yet thirty and Christ knows I oughta look old. A fine life you lead me, Alf—a bloomin' bed of roses. Sellin' guns to whoever'll pay for 'em. Mixed up with the Spanish, the Eyetalians, and now a pack of bloody Chinks. Oh, a fine life. Who'd blame me for takin' a drop now and again? Floatin' from place to place in some bloody bucket of a boat like this here one. Lookin' like Shirley Temple. No decent hair treatments. Lovin' it up with any greasy gangster you say to—an' now this kid not dry behind the . . ."

"Since when did you ever mind a little tussle, Rosie? I recall . . ."

"Well, I liked it better with the kid than with you. At least he's clean . . ."

I grasped the doorknob just as a loud report was heard. I ran up to the open deck in time to see a large, Japanese destroyer sending a second shot across the bow of the *Lesbos*.

"My God, *now* what?" Auntie Mame said, grasping my hand.

"Auntie Mame, the Reverend isn't holy at all. He's a gunrunner and that organ and all those Chinese Bibles . . . they're contraband."

"But, darling, it's a neutral ship."

"It's still contraband. The Chinese-Japanese war."

The *Lesbos* came to a halt, and the Japanese destroyer, not a hundred feet away, prepared to send over a boarding party.

Auntie Mame . . .

"What can we do, darling? They'll probably draft Ito."

"Stall them," I said. "Stall them as long as you can."

Then I dashed up to the radio shack. El Greco was lying on his bunk listening to Hal Kemp and easing his hangover with the dregs of a bottle of Retsina.

"Hhhhello," he said furrily.

"Hi!" I said. "How about cracking out another bottle of that delicious resin wine?"

"Ah, guud," he said getting unsteadily to his feet.

I followed him to his closet, waited until he opened the door, then shoved him in and locked it. Then I sat down and started sending out the SOS message El Greco had taught me.

I sent and sent and sent until I thought my arm would fall off. Then I picked up El Greco's empty wine bottle and went down on deck, prepared to defend Auntie Mame against the gunrunners of the world and the Imperial Japanese Fleet.

I'd halfway expected to find Auntie Mame walking the plank, but when I got down from the radio shack, I found Auntie Mame seated on the deck surrounded by admiring Japanese officers. She was going through the somewhat formal ritual of the tea ceremony and—with Ito interpreting—seemed to have them all in stitches.

"Do kick off your shoes, Patrick, and join us," she said. "This attractive gentleman with all those stripes on his sleeve has been *so* understanding of a poor widow's plight. He also seems to be suffering under the delusion that Ito is some sort of cousin of his and I see no reason to contradict. One lump or two?"

I was about to answer when I saw my dream girl, Rosemary. She had been brought up on deck just as she was, a sorry sight. Not having been out of her cabin for more than a week, she blinked blindly into the sun, the limpid blue eyes veined with red, puffy, and swollen. Her unkempt hair, now decidedly dark at the roots, flew in every direction. She wore a sluttish, molting dressing gown that had once been white marabou, and filthy mules, one feathery pompom of which had long been lost. Alf was right; she may have been under thirty, but she certainly looked better than forty. At any rate, she was no eighteen. I felt my heartstrings give one last tug and then I looked away.

Then an American light cruiser, the U.S.S. *Hoboken* came splashing into sight and, with it, another boarding party.

"More cups, Ito," Auntie Mame called as the U.S. Navy hit the deck, "and you might just crack out some of our liquor. I know that, through some tiresome regulation, our valiant seafaring men never get a drop to drink when they're off shore. Now do slip out of your shoes, gentlemen, while I do all the introductions."

Half an hour later Auntie Mame managed to take the American lieutenant commander into the lounge and explain our plight—or some plight—because after a lot of waving of flags and blinking of signal lights and bawling back and forth through megaphones, yet another boat was rowed over to the rusty starboard side of the *Lesbos*. It was for Auntie Mame's luggage.

After slipping into a smart traveling suit, Auntie Mame was perfectly able to supervise the loading herself. "Careful, boys," she said to two strapping sailors. "Those alligator bags go into my stateroom. None of the rest of the things will be wanted on the voyage unless you give a costume ball or something the last night out."

"But, Mrs. Burnside," the lieutenant commander said, "we're on maneuvers."

"Then you can just maneuver a party. I can't *tell* you how bored I've been on this tatty little scow. Besides, I have gallons of refreshments in the trunk marked 'Fragile.' My, but aren't

Auntie Mame . . .

you American boys strong! Good-by, captain," she said. "I shall expect a refund for the unused portions of our tickets. Come, Patrick! Ito! Next stop San Francisco!"

JUST WHAT AUNTIE MAME TOLD THE AMERICAN naval officer I will never know, and she herself has always been maddeningly vague about it. The official report in the log read: "Evacuated three American nationals from imminent danger in connection with provocative incident in the Sino-Japanese War. A gunrunning vessel . . ." Well, it doesn't get any more informative from there. Whatever became of Rosemary, Alf, or the jolly crew of the *Lesbos* I neither know nor care.

WE WERE SEATED IN THE LAUNCH ON OUR WAY TO the U.S.S. *Hoboken* with Auntie Mame regaling the young officers with her plans for a party. "La, will I ever forget those jolly hops at Annapolis when I was a girl. And now it'll be my turn to repay the Navy for all it's done for me!"

"Auntie Mame," I said softly, "there's something I've got to confess. It's about Rosemary and me."

"No, my little love, not a word. I may have raised you to be a devil with the ladies, but I also raised you to be a gentleman. No kiss and tell, Patrick, *if* you please."

Auntie Mame and Home-coming

"AND THEN?" PEGEEN SAID.

"Well, and then I got home and went to college and met you and lived happily ever after."

"Is that all?"

"That's all. Why?" I said, avoiding her direct gaze.

"Well, it seems to me that for a man who earns his livelihood by writing scintillating advertising copy for products that no one would buy otherwise, you can make a voyage around the world sound less eventful than a trip on the commuters' local."

"But that's what I've been telling you all along, Pegeen. There's nothing to worry about. Auntie Mame may have been a whole lot of hot-cha back in the twenties, but you must remember that time isn't standing still with any of us. I don't know exactly how old Auntie Mame is by now . . ."

"She's still claiming thirty-nine."

"Well, it's more like sixty. She's a sweet, white-haired little old lady. Even now she's probably sitting up in some hotel suite with a jug of Ovaltine and the patience pack, after having heard Michael's prayers and tucked him into . . ."

Our doorbell interrupted me with the first bar of the "Doxology"—an annoying feature of all the houses in Verdant Greens.

"My God, who can that be?" I said.

"If it's Mrs. Merkin from the Current Events Club, tell her . . ."

The "Doxology" peeled out again.

"You don't suppose it could be Christmas carolers," Pegeen asked, peering out through the blinds.

"If it is, get out the hose," I said. "That's the trouble with this community; community spirit. Who is it?"

"Well, I don't know," Pegeen said. "All I can see are two people in the damnedest-looking outfits I've ever . . ."

"Treat or a Trick, maybe?"

Again the bell chimed "Praise God from Whom all blessings flow."

"Well, whoever they are," I said, striding to the door, "they'll get short shrift from me." I opened the door and said, "Yes?" There were two people in Eskimo parkas looking exactly like the Cliquot Kids.

"Patrick, darling," a silvery voice cried.

"Daddy!"

"My God!" I said. Anything else I had planned to say was muffled in wolverine furs. "Pegeen," I called, "they're back—Michael and Auntie Mame!"

"My baby!" Pegeen cried and made a dive at him from the living room. There was a scene of some ardor with a great deal of kissing and embracing and weeping. When things calmed down, Pegeen said, "Aren't you going to kiss Daddy, Michael?"

"I'm ten years old now and five feet tall," Michael said. "Auntie Mame says that men who go around kissing each other . . ."

"I think you might make an exception in this case, my little love," Auntie Mame said hastily. "Now I have just time for one drink and then I must be off. My Volvo's out in front, where I'm sure it shouldn't be."

"Your what?" I said.

Auntie Mame . . .

"My Volvo. It's this divine little Swedish car I picked up. The Rolls is just too big for hacking about. In fact, Ito's driving it down from Fairbanks, if he isn't lost. Ah, Patrick darling, a few fingers of Scotch will be just splendid." She removed her wolverine parka, displaying a figure as slim as always and a head of pewter curls.

"Well," I said, still stunned. "The return of Mrs. Burnside! Now that you're back, of course we're delighted, but there hasn't been a peep out of the two of you for four blessed months. Couldn't you at least have sent a post card?"

"We wrote lots of them, Daddy," Michael said, "but nobody in the nudist colony had a stamp."

"In the where?" Pegeen said.

"Now don't bore your parents with inconsequentials, Michael darling," Auntie Mame said quickly. "It was just a Swedish health resort—a tiny island in the Baltic Sea. Marvelous for toning up the system."

"And I had a terrible sore throat and . . ."

"Oh, Michael, did you?" Pegeen said. "I've been so worried about your health and . . ."

"It was nothing," Auntie Mame said airily. "I got permission for him to wear a muffler for a few days and he was just as good as new. You must admit that the child is the picture of health. And—just fancy—he knows seven languages; three fluently."

"But four livelong months," I persisted, "without a word. Pegeen and I have been worried sick. I've cabled everyone abroad I know; I've had the State Department, a detective agency . . ."

"Ah, but Patrick darling," Auntie Mame said, sipping her drink elegantly, "we've been to such remote places. I felt that instead of taking this dear child to such commonplace, touristy spots as Tibet and Afghanistan and Ethiopia, we should try something off the beaten track. So, after we polished off the Scandanavian Peninsula, we did Iceland, Greenland, and Alaska. Oh, I tell you there's a great future in the frozen . . ."

"Excuse me," I said, "but don't you hear an odd noise?"

"Oh, that's Muscatel, Daddy," Michael said.

"It's *what*?"

"Michael's musk ox. We picked it up at a trading post outside Godthaab when we were in Greenland. This dear old Danish man raises them, and we just couldn't resist him. Of course, Muscatel was only a baby then. Isn't full grown even now. But he's gentle as a lamb and I know that *everybody* will be wanting one once they see him."

"Wh-what do musk oxen eat?" Pegeen said.

"Shrubs, flowers. Things like that," Michael said. "Can he stay in my room tonight?"

"Certainly not," I said. "You don't know what kind of disease you might pick up. Besides, I believe they shed."

"Oh, I wouldn't pick up any disease from Muscatel, Daddy. In fact, when Auntie Mame and I visited the lepers in . . ."

"The *what*?" Pegeen said, stricken.

"Michael, darling," Auntie Mame said meaningfully, "your mother and father will think I haven't taught you *any* manners at all. You mustn't monopolize the conversation. Remember, that mature as you may be, you're still barely ten. He was speaking of some *leopards*, my dear. Passing through Somaliland we saw lots of them. *Didn't we, Michael?*"

"Oh, yes, Auntie Mame," Michael said, not quite at ease. "And then there was that time in the place where the man raised pythons and Auntie Mame let me go right in and . . ."

"She *what*?" Pegeen said.

"Michael, my little love," Auntie Mame said getting to her feet, "there are some things out in the car—just a few remembrances for your mother and father—which you can help me bring in. Besides, there's something I forgot to tell you."

Auntie Mame . . .

"I'll get them," I said.

"Oh, no, Patrick. I want one last word or so with Michael anyhow. Come, pet. Then Auntie Mame must fly. I'm to lecture at the Explorers' Club tonight. And I've promised Cris Alexander to sit for my portrait. Just little me and tons and tons of heavenly furs." With that they were gone.

"WELL, I CAN'T BELIEVE IT," PEGEEN SAID. "SHE'S brought back our child—and certainly in better condition than he was in when she spirited him away. But what do you suppose he meant about a leper colony and that . . ."

"Oh, nothing," I said hastily. "You know the vivid imaginations all children have."

"No. But I do know that we have to get ready for a good old-fashioned Christmas at jet speed. I mean here's our chance to have a tree again, to give Michael the electric train, the bicycle, the chemistry set, the microscope—all the things he wasn't here to get for the past two Christmases."

"We might also think about giving him some dinner and getting his room ready for him and Muscatel."

"Oh, look at that filthy thing!" Pegeen said, staring out of the open door. "He's eaten all the rhododendron! Shooo! Scat! And here they come, empty-handed back from the car. I don't see any sign of those 'little remembrances.' "

Going to the door, I said, "She probably left them somewhere. She's inclined to be . . ."

But I stopped short as I heard Auntie Mame saying, "Remember, my little love, there are *some* things that parents simply don't have to know about. It'll be our secret." Then she saw us and cried loudly, "La! How absent-minded I'm becoming! All of the presents are stacked up in the lobby at the St. Regis, along with my totem poles. Where I'm going to put those totem poles I *can't* imagine."

"I have a suggestion," I said, knowing from experience just what my son had been through with his great aunt.

"Alas, darling, I can't stop to hear it now. I shall be late for my lecture as it is." She kissed Pegeen and me briskly. "I'm sorry it's been so short a visit, but everyone wants to hear about every minute of our trip."

"No one more than I," I said.

"Good-by, Michael, my little love," Auntie Mame said, gathering him into her arms. "I don't know when I've had a more delightful traveling companion. Not since your father. Maybe next summer we can do it all over again."

"All two-and-a-half years of it?" Pegeen said.

"Oh no. Just a short trip—up or down the Amazon; possibly both. Well, *à bientôt*, darlings. And have a merry Christmas. I'm off to the Indies! And remember, Michael, what Auntie Mame just told you."

"You mean about not saying anything to . . ." Michael began.

"Good-by, darlings! Good-by, good-by, good-by!" Auntie Mame said loudly. She almost ran down the walk.

"Michael," Pegeen said, watching Auntie Mame get into her little Swedish car, "just where *did* you go?"

"Around the world, Mother."

"And what did you do?"

"Nothing."

"Good-by, my little love," Auntie Mame called over the roar of her motor. "It's been a lovely trip."

Auntie Mame . . .

© CRIS ALEXANDER

Edward Everett Tanner III (1921–1976), a.k.a. PATRICK
DENNIS, was one of the most widely read authors of
the 1950s and 1960s. The majority of his sixteen nov-
els, including *Auntie Mame, Around the World with
Auntie Mame,* and *Little Me,* were national bestsellers.
A celebrity in bohemian New York culture, he led a
double life as a bisexual man and a conventional husband and father of two children. Faced with financial
ruin in the 1970s, he spent the last chapter of his life
as a butler.

Back to charm a whole new generation, the classic *New York Times* bestselling novel

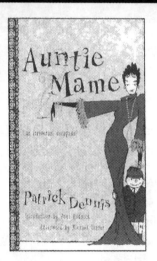

Fall in love with Auntie Mame in this new edition of Patrick Dennis's smash comic masterpiece.

"Hilarious, glamorous…among other wise lessons, one learns that true sophistication and innocence are two halves of the same glittering coin." —Charles Busch, author of *The Tale of the Allergist's Wife*

"Mame Dennis is the *grande dame* of grande dames and I, for one, am thrilled that she's back among us. She is still hilarious, sparkling, and utterly indestructible despite the best efforts of time, neglect, and Lucille Ball." —Joe Keenan, Emmy-Winning Writer/Producer for *Frasier*, author of *Blue Heaven* and *Putting on the Ritz*

"*Auntie Mame* is a unique literary achievement…Every page sparkles with wit, style, and—though Mame would cringe at the thought—high moral purpose." —Robert Plunket, author of *Love Junkie*

Printed in the United States
by Baker & Taylor Publisher Services